William Starbuck Mayo

Kaloolah

The Adventures of Jonathan Romer

William Starbuck Mayo

Kaloolah
The Adventures of Jonathan Romer

ISBN/EAN: 9783744780681

Printed in Europe, USA, Canada, Australia, Japan

Cover: Foto ©Andreas Hilbeck / pixelio.de

More available books at **www.hansebooks.com**

THE ADVENTURES OF JONATHAN ROMER

BY

W. S. MAYO, M.D.
AUTHOR OF "THE BERBER," "NEVER AGAIN," ETC.

THIRTIETH THOUSAND

THE FRAMAZUGDA EDITION

ILLUSTRATED BY FREDERICKS

NEW YORK AND LONDON
G. P. PUTNAM'S SONS
The Knickerbocker Press
1888

TO

MRS. MARIA MAYO SCOTT.

MADAM:

There are, I presume, a few " good-natured " people in the world who will be ready to attribute this dedication to a desire merely of connecting my name, however remotely or indirectly, with that of your illustrious husband—the Hero of Niagara and Mexico. There are some, also, who, deceived by the identity of our family names, may kindly give me credit, unless I put in this disclaimer, for a disposition to parade a relationship that does not exist. All, however, who have the honor of your friendship, will do my motives justice, inasmuch as they can readily comprehend the inducements to pay a compliment, where the highest terms of compliment are but the words of soberness and truth. They, at least, will find no difficulty in believing that I avail myself of your permission to inscribe to you the following pages, solely because it affords me an opportunity of expressing my appreciation of your many high qualities— your literary taste, cultivated conversational talent, happy grace of manner, and kindness of heart.

Your obedient servant,

THE EDITOR.

PREFACE.

The following letter will best explain the way in which these pages came into the editor's hands, and the degree of credit that may be fairly given to them as an authentic record of the travels and adventures of a young American :

DEAR DOCTOR :

You must know that I have recently come into the possession of a manuscript, purporting to be the travels and adventures of a young American, in various parts of the world, but mainly in the deserts of Africa, and in the unknown, and hitherto unvisited countries south of the Soudan. The manuscript strikes me as being curious, interesting, and apparently authentic ; but I have so little confidence in my own judgment, in such matters, that after a deal of patient and painful cogitation upon the subject, I find myself utterly unable to decide two questions that present themselves, to wit : Is it worth publishing ? and if so, what will be the best manner of giving it to the world ?

But first let me explain how the manuscript came into my possession. You have heard of Salee, I suppose ; or rather, of the Salee Rovers, who not many years since swept the Atlantic from Tercera to Teneriffe, and (with a degree of boldness that made them the bug-a-boos of crying babies for miles inland) carried their bloody swallow-tail pendants up the English Channel, and even through the intricate passages of the Skagerrack and Cattegat. You have heard of these rascals, and of their town ; but perhaps you would have to refer to your geography or to a gazetteer ; for the fact that it is situated at the mouth of the Buregreb, exactly opposite the flourishing town of Rabat, and precisely one hundred and twenty miles from the Straits of Hercules, down the Atlantic coast of the dominions of Muley Abderrahman. Now in this particular, to wit, the aspect and topography of Salee and its environs, I have the advantage of you ; for it so happens that, once upon a time, I was under its walls, and in momentary expectation of entering its gates, when I was advised that, owing to the fanaticism and ferocity of the inhabitants of the dilapidated town, it would be unsafe to enter, and that we must make a detour by the walls to reach the ferry and cross to Rabat. Passing the lofty arches of an ancient aqueduct, my guides hurried me along a road at the bottom of the ditch, with the crumbling walls on one hand, and the crest of the cactus-covered glacis on the other, until we debouched upon a broad reach of sand, which has filled up the port of the once famous town, and diverted the channel of the river to its rival Rabat.

The liberalizing influences of commerce are nowhere better to be seen than in its effect upon the character and manners of the people of Rabat. In the one—a flourishing town, where reside many Moorish and Jewish merchants who have intimate relations with the Rock of Gibraltar, Marseilles, and Leghorn,—a Christian can pass through the streets under the protection of a Moorish guide, without any great danger of violence from the manifestations of holy hatred with which the pious people look upon the dog of an unbeliever; in the other—a dilapidated town, whose inhabitants have nothing (spinning haicks and tanning goat-skins excepted) to do but to nurse their prejudices and dream of the glorious days when a hundred plunder-laden feluccas and polaccas crowded the now sand-choked harbor, and the groans of ten thousand cursed Kaffir captives resounded through the capacious vaults of the water wall and bastions,— any thing in cravat, coat, and pantaloons runs an imminent risk of life. In the one, the booted and beavered stranger has thrown at him dark scowls and sinister grins; in the other, he is sure to be pelted with stones; in the one he is spit at, in the other he is spit upon; in the one he gets merely curses, in the other he is sure to get kicks; in the one a single guard protects him from personal violence; in the other it may be questioned whether the Sultan's crack regiment, said to be composed wholly of his own sons, would be able to preserve an inch of Christian skin intact. Strange that there should be such a difference between the inhabitants of two places, situated not more than five or six hundred yards apart.

Arriving at Rabat, I found an order from the court requiring me to stop until I could explain more satisfactorily the object of my journey. As I afterwards found, commercial jealousy had been aroused, and representations made to the emperor that under the pretence of travelling for amusement, I in reality concealed some deep political designs. The suspicion of the most suspicious, ignorant, and bigoted court in the world once excited, there was an end to my visions of a gilt-edged, Morocco-bound volume, entitled, " Itineratings in the Atlas," or some other fanciful and taking title. The recollection of the Spanish impostor, who, about forty years since, under the name of Ali Bey, and disguised (Christian dog that he was) in the garb of the faithful, made his way to the capital, and afterwards perpetrated a book of travels, is still fresh in the minds of the Moors; and next to a spy of the French government, the last person they would like to see perambulating the country would be a gentleman suspected of paper-spoiling propensities, in search of the novel and the picturesque. At an audience with the governor of the town, I found that my return was equally impossible—not that I was positively prohibited from going back, but it was respectfully intimated that could I persuade my guards and muleteers to accompany me, they would have every particle of skin cut from their backs with thongs of bull's hide. There was no resource but to send a courier to the court and quietly await an answer, which I did with somewhat of the feeling of the worthy nephew of Gil Perez, when he found himself caught in the cave, like a rat in a trap.

A walk through the town, and a visit to the towers and battlements of the Kassbah, sufficed to pass the first day. A ride in the environs, and an examination of Sma Hassan, a superb square tower, said to have been built by the architect of the Giralda of Seville, answered for the second. The third day I amused myself mainly with an examination of the town of Salee, through my pocket telescope; the distance was so small that I could see every stone of the towers, matchicolated with stork's nests, and every crevice of the dilapidated curtains connecting them. Was it fancy, or did the breeze really waft to my ears a faint echo of the million sighs and groans that years past were borne upon every blast of the sea-breeze around those cruel walls? I could hardly tell, but one thing, at least, I made sure of, and that was that on the beach, between the river and the water gate, there was any quantity of long-legged biped, of the snipe genus—tall fellows, standing a foot high, at least, without counting the depth of their tracks. So on the fourth day I shouldered my gun, hired a boat, and had myself rowed across to a retired spot some distance below the ferry. I expected sport, but I must say that I was wholly unprepared for such kind of sport. It was almost impossible to get a shot at them, they were so tame. No sooner would I succeed in raising a fellow by poking him up with the muzzle of my gun, than, before I could draw trigger, down he would pop right at my feet, with an air as much as to say, wring my neck, if you please, but don't fire. At the first shot all Salee was alive, and a hundred vagabonds poked their dirty noses from the arches of the water gate. Before they could reach me,

I picked up my birds, stepped into the boat, and paddled back to Rabat.
When all was quiet I ventured across again, took another shot, stirred up
the old pirates' nest, bagged my bird, and made a similar retreat. This
interesting operation I repeated half a dozen times in the course of the
day, the game improving each time in shyness, and promising great sport
in a day or two, when its caution, so long in abeyance, should have become thoroughly aroused. But an end was put to my sporting calculations when, upon displaying my spoils at night, I found that my
worthy Jewish host, who was a strict constructionist of the law, would
have nothing to do with them, and that he would not even permit the
desecration of his only stew-pan by the blood of birds that had not been
slaughtered, *per formam theologicam.*

The resources of the place thus completely exhausted, the fifth day
hung heavy. I could do nothing but pace up and down the narrow pre-
cincts of the paved court-yard ; the Bashaw having sent me, with a present
of grapes and figs, an intimation that I had better not expose myself so
much on the roof and in the streets, lest some kief-smoking, hasheesh-
eating believer should, in his delirium, take it into his head to make of my
person a target for ball practice, and thus win heaven for himself by sending me to the devil.

"Have n't you a book of any kind ?" I inquired of my host, Isaac
Benshemole.

"Not one ; Rabbi Yacob Benolile, however, has several ; I will go
down to the Millah, or Jews' Quarter, and borrow them for you."

"Do so. If he has n't any Spanish or Latin books, bring any thing
that he has : Syriac, Coptic, any thing. I feel as if I could read an
Egyptian papyrus or a Runic tombstone."

The worthy representative of the two great commercial powers, England and America, started off on his errand ; but in a moment he returned,
and putting his head in at the door, exclaimed, " *Manuscritos, señor !*"

"Certainly, manuscripts or printed books ; any thing to read," I
replied.

"Well, then, señor, I now bethink me that I have two manuscripts" ;
and drawing aside a curtain from a dark recess, Isaac produced from a
dusty shelf a large bundle, enveloped in a fragment of an old Moorish haick.
Upon examination it was found to contain two stout rolls of paper : one of
these, with a very ancient appearance and fish-like smell, proved to be the
log-book of a Portuguese mistico, and besides the usual notices of courses
and winds, contained several accounts current with the crew for oil, garlic, salt fish, and Jew brandy, with frequent memorandums of cargo,

custom-house payments, and port charges. The other was a much cleaner and newer piece of writing, in a character that I at once concluded to be beyond my skill to decipher. I could not even conjecture, with confidence, the language. It clearly was not Arabic or Hebrew, and, therefore, it might be Tuaric or Shellock, and if so, I could pore over it a week, and be none the wiser: but still my eyes were rivetted on the pages; there was a familiar look in the turn of some of the letters that quite fascinated me. The writing was in a very fine and compact hand; it was divided into chapters, and what was the most curious thing about it, each chapter was numbered in Roman numerals. Upon questioning Isaac, he informed me that the manuscript had been in his possession about a year; that it had been brought to him by a Moor from Tafilet, who said that it had been left in his charge by a sick man who had arrived with the last caravan from the desert, and who had requested him to bring it with him, and give it to any of the commercial agents of Christian countries he should meet on the coast. At first Isaac had felt some curiosity in relation to it, and had shown it to a French wool-dealer, and to several learned rabbins, all of whom could make nothing of it. He then thought of sending it to the English consul-general, but business interfering, he had put it aside, and thus it had remained undisturbed ever since.

I was about closing the book in despair, when, upon the margin of one of the pages I saw, in parallel columns, the English alphabet, and the corresponding characters of the manuscript, which it was easy to perceive, when thus in juxtaposition, were nothing more or less than Roman letters, with the consonants trimmed down and condensed, and the vowels expressed by a single dot. Imagine my astonishment and delight, to find upon applying this key, and deciphering a few words, that the manuscript was written in English. After a few hours' practice I found that I could read this cypher quite easily, so that, at the end of five days I had read and re-read the whole of it. Permission now arriving from the court to resume my journey, I bade adieu to Rabat, and to the worthy Benshemole, who readily consented to my taking the manuscript with me.

It is a transcription of this manuscript that I now send you for your opinion. Is it worth publishing? as for me, I have sometimes had my doubts about it, although I have been, and am now, deeply interested in it; but then I am fond of any thing in the shape of travels and adventures, and my judgment may not be sufficiently discriminating. Should your opinion coincide with mine, I have to request that you will take the editorial charge of the matter, and prepare it for the press, with such corrections and emendations as may seem to you proper. I have the utmost confidence in your literary judgment, and besides, the work, written as it is by a medical student, and containing frequent allusions to medical matters, should have a medical editor. I entrust the affair, therefore, wholly to you.

There is still another point, in relation to which I must beg your opinion. It is now, according to the best estimate that I can make, about five years since the manuscript was written. Mr. Romer has been all this time in the interior of Central Africa, and if he is alive, and has at all prospered in his plans, he must have extended the boundaries of the kingdom of Framazugda far down towards the coast of the Gulf of Guinea. Don't you think that it would be well that all consular agents, and commanders of national vessels should be apprised of the fact, and officially required to keep a sharp look-out for any intimations of his advent, and especially for any letters or manuscripts he will most probably send to the coast in the hopes of their falling into civilized hands.

Hoping that you may find the manuscript worthy of the labor of preparing it for the press,

I am

Your obedient servant, etc., etc.

CONTENTS

CHAPTER VII.

CHAPTER VIII.

CHAPTER IX.

CHAPTER X.

CHAPTER XI.

CHAPTER XII.

CHAPTER XIII.

CHAPTER XIV.

CHAPTER XV.

CHAPTER XVI.

CHAPTER XVII.

CHAPTER XVIII.

CHAPTER XIX.

CHAPTER XX.

CHAPTER XXI.

CHAPTER XXIX.

CHAPTER XXX.

CHAPTER XXXI.

CHAPTER XXXII.

CHAPTER XXXIII.

CHAPTER XXXIV.

CHAPTER XXXV.

CHAPTER XXXVI.

CHAPTER XLV.

CHAPTER XLVI.

LIST OF ILLUSTRATIONS

KALOOLAH.

CHAPTER I.

 LIFE of adventure may be justly considered my birthright. Descended, on both sides of the house, from some of the earliest settlers of Nantucket, and more or less intimately related to the Coffins, the Folgers, the Macys, and the Starbucks of that adventurous population, it would seem that I have had a natural right to a roving disposition, and to a life of peril, privation, and vicissitude. Nearly all the male members of my family, for several generations, have been "followers of the sea": some of them in the calm and peaceful employment of the merchant-service; others, and by far the greater number, in the more dangerous pursuit of the ocean monster.

Whaling, it is well known, has been, almost from the first settlement of this country, the chief employment of the inhabitants of "the Island." All were directly or indirectly interested in it. By it were bounded the hopes of the young and the memories of the old. In it alone could the highest honors be won, and good blows and true with harpoon and lance were not of less effect in winning the regard of the fair and the respect of the men, than the most trenchant sword-cuts of gallant knights in the best days of chivalry. It was, consequently, pursued with an ardor and an enthusiasm that penetrated the remotest, wildest, ice-bound retreats of the flying *cetacea*, and which has served to associate with the character of a Nantucket whaler the idea of dauntless bravery, enduring fortitude, determined energy, industry, and skill.

In such a pursuit, the most thrilling adventures are the common incidents of life; and the traditions of my family abound with stories of shipwreck and death, and of "hair-breadth 'scapes" from the imminent dangers of the sea. One relative was wrecked upon a desert island of the Pacific, and supported life for months upon the eggs of the penguin. Another—a Macy—was found floating upon a spar three days after his ship had foundered with all her crew. Still another was an officer of a ship which was struck and destroyed by an infuriated *cachelot*, whether by accident or design remains a disputed point amongst whalers.

The boats of the ship were out in pursuit of a "school" of whales, when the officer in charge of the deck perceived an enormous animal coming down, in the direction on which the vessel was standing, with fearful rapidity. It was apparent that, unless the ship's course was changed, in an instant more a collision would take place; and the steersman was directed to put the helm up, in order to give her a sheer out of the way,—but it was too late. Her bows had fallen off but a point or two when the whale struck her, "head on," with tremendous force. Recovering from their astonishment, the crew proceeded to examine into the injury which the ship had suffered. It was soon ascertained that no very serious damage had been sustained, when one of the look-outs appalled them with the shout "Here she comes again!" and down came the whale with renewed fury,—a broad-sheet of white foam attesting the rapidity of her progress. Again she struck the ill-fated vessel in nearly the same place—just forward of the fore.chains. It was now evident that the ship was materially injured. Signals were made for the boats to return; they came alongside, and as the vessel was beginning to settle rapidly by the head, provisions and instruments were put into them. In a few hours she went down, and her crew in three boats were left in the middle of the vast Pacific. Only one of the three, after tossing months upon the ocean, and enduring the extremes of hunger and thirst, succeeded in reaching land.

Another member of my family was the identical boat-steerer of whom an anecdote has been often told, illustrative of the characteristic coolness of the Yankee whaler. The boat to which he belonged was once knocked several feet into the air by a blow from the tail of a fish to which it was fast. Upon coming down he fell into the whale's mouth, and the teeth of the animal closed upon his leg. After being in this terrible position for some time, he was released, picked up by another boat and carried on board, where, while preparations were making to amputate his crushed limb, he was asked "what he thought of while in the whale's mouth." With the utmost *sang froid* and simplicity, he replied: "Why, I thought she would yield about sixty barrels!"

But it is not my intention to detain the reader with anecdotes, of which I could relate enough to fill a volume. I mention a few here, only to illustrate my hereditary claims to a life of adventure.

It is a curious fact—one which I believe to be well established—that not only are physical and intellectual qualities communicated from parents to children, but also many of those mental habitudes and modes of thought which are stamped upon our minds by the circumstances in which we live. We are impressed from our earliest existence, with the spirit of the age or the community, and our mental and moral constitutions are modified by the influence of that spirit upon the generations immediately preceding us. In the days of chivalry, for instance, youths

"He fell into the whale's mouth, and the teeth of the animal closed upon his leg."

were not only educated into gallant and courteous knights, but they were also born with a natural predisposition to what were then esteemed knightly qualities, accomplishments, and vices. They were born with the chivalric idiosyncrasy.

My parents, both natives of this famous little sandy sea-girt isle, were induced, by considerations I need not detail, to take up their residence very early in the present century, on the then wilderness of the banks of the St. Lawrence.

The village of O—— is beautifully situated at the confluence of a small stream with the St. Lawrence, and, unlike most of the towns of our new country, it is not wholly destitute of romantic associations and historical remains. Upon a point of land across the affluent of the St. Lawrence, and opposite the village, stood the ruins of an old French trading house and fort; one of the chain of posts which the first masters of Canada undertook to establish from Montreal to Fort Duquesne. It consisted of four square buildings, erected upon the angles of a parallelogram, and connected by a curtain or wall of twelve or fourteen feet in height. Slightly constructed as a defence merely against musketry, or the arrows of the Indians, it was illy calculated to resist the ravages of time. Its crumbling walls, however, were the scenes of authentic tradition and romantic story. To me they furnished the richest food for the imagination, and more than one glorious castle in the air was raised while seated upon the fallen stones of that dilapidated pile. To me they supplied the place of the broken arches and moss-covered relics of the ancient abbey, or the ivy-crowned towers of the feudal castle. They were the birthplace and school of my ardent and excited fancy; and as such I shall always recollect them with more reverence and respect than I could feel now in looking upon the proudest monuments of the long-since-mighty dead.

The death of my father, when I was but eight years old, freeing me from a good deal of that salutary parental restraint which a father only can exercise, my adventurous disposition rapidly developed itself, and with it the physical capacities and energies best adapted to that constitution of mind. Even when quite a boy I had achieved no inconsiderable fame as a wrestler, jumper, swimmer, and marksman. At school, although far from industrious or attentive, I acquired a respectable standing, with the reputation of being "smart enough, if I would only apply myself," but out of school my supremacy was universally acknowledged. No one could run faster, swim farther, send a rifle or pistol bullet with surer aim, or was more expert at boyish mechanical contrivances. Even at some exercises which are not generally practised by boys in the country, such as fencing, I became quite a proficient. A deserter from the Canadian garrison, on the other side of the river, who had at one time of his life acted as a kind of *maitre d'armes* of a ship of war, gave me my first lessons.

But, although enjoying the practice of all gymnastic sports, and priding myself not a little upon my victories and successes, they were far from being my only amusement or occupation; an insatiable thirst for reading soon exhausted the scanty libraries of the village, and could only be gratified by reperusal, until many books were gotten almost by heart. Buried in the depths of the sombre forest, or floating upon the broad St. Lawrence on a raft of my own construction, or seated amid the ruins of the old trading house I have mentioned; tales, travels, plays, poetry, and history, were swallowed indiscriminately with the most comprehensive avidity. All came alike to me, and were believed alike. I knew that many people looked upon certain books as fictions. I could only wonder at such scepticism. Were there not kings and princes and beautiful ladies in the world? Then there must be dragons, griffons, and enchanted castles. The evidence was the same for both. I knew that the Seven Champions once flourished, each one in *propria persona*, and that some of their relations were still left in the world. I knew that Robinson Crusoe was a veritable personage; no imaginary amplification of a commonplace Scotchman, but a true *bona-fide* fellow, who had no more to do with Alexander Selkirk than I had. Even Jack the Giant Killer—if any boy had dared to doubt, in my presence, his bodily existence, that boy would have been flogged. At length this mania, for it amounted to that, reached its crisis. A copy of Don Quixote fell in my way. The pleasure—the excitement, as I read, amounted to agony. There was nothing ludicrous in any of the Don's adventures. Taking windmills for giants, was a mistake, no doubt, but then the windmills themselves were worthy opponents. I longed to attack a windmill. I had a perfectly clear conviction, that, if I could once fairly charge a windmill, I should overthrow it and compel it to resume its true shape, that of some gigantic magician. Unfortunately the only windmill in the neighborhood was one with wings that moved horizontally, and at some distance from the ground. The tallest knight that ever bestrode a charger of sixteen hands could not have touched the lower edge of them with the point of his lance. The windmill was safe, but I could not help feeling something like contempt for the great cowardly whirligig, that, confiding in its secure elevation, seemed to mock my ambition. The excitement of my mind continued to increase. My brain became as full of absurd conceits as the old Don's. I could not sleep, lost my appetite, grew pale and emaciated, and in fact was on the verge of settled insanity.

My mother, justly alarmed, resolved upon change of scene for me, and it was decided that I should be sent to the principal academy of the county, situated in a pleasant village, about thirty miles from my birthplace.

The day after my fourteenth birthday I started upon the journey. I have since wandered amid the most dreary wilds of the African continent, I have crossed the Sahara, have encountered its arid sands and its poisonous simoon, its desolate rocks and its remorseless robbers; but all can never efface the remembrance of that first going forth from home. Never as yet had I been a day from beneath my mother's eye. Never for a day had I lacked the consciousness of her watchful anxiety, or the efficacy of her blessing. Wild, wayward, self-willed, and often utterly reckless of her wishes or commands, I yet loved her with the intensest affection. The parting was hard, although the crotchets of Don Quixote running through my head very much blunted my sense of its pangs.

"Jonathan," said my mother, at the conclusion of a long conference, "I have packed your trunk with every thing that I can think necessary. If any thing is wanting, why the distance is really short, although it seems so long, and I can easily send it to you. You will find in one corner your Bible. Don't forget it, Jonathan. You say you like the Old Testament best, with its battles and sieges. Well, that 's a boy's taste. Read the Old Testament then, and perhaps some day you will learn to prefer the New. And by the Bible, Jonathan, you will find a small purse; I made it many years ago. It contains a gold coin, the first which your father earned, and sent to his mother as a testimony of his success and his filial remembrance. He was then, you know, several years younger than you are. Keep it carefully, it is a true talisman of more efficacy than ever fairy bestowed upon any of your favorite knights, and—and—Jonathan——"

My mother's voice faltered, and the tears again filled her eyes.

"What? dearest mother," I exclaimed, throwing my arms around her neck.

"You will find," she continued, composing herself with an effort, "you will find at the bottom of your trunk a garment different from your other linen, which might puzzle you to understand the use of. You are going far from me, Jonathan, among strangers. If you are sick I shall come to you—but then—many accidents may happen, you are so venturous, Jonathan, you may get thrown from a horse, or drowned——"

"Oh, no, mother, that 's impossible: did n't I break Jem Smith's colt after he had killed the circus-rider, and nobody else would mount him; and can't I swim four times across the O——, and that 's more than a mile."

"Yes, I know, every one says that you are the best rider and swimmer in the village, but you are also the boldest, and you run great risks. You have promised me to be cautious for my sake, but accidents, as I have said, may happen to any one, and I have thought proper to make you a—a——"

"Shroud, mother!"

"Why, no, not exactly a shroud, but something that will answer as a grave dress. God save you, my son, from requiring the use of it!"

Was ever maternal consideration carried farther? I might die among strangers, and be buried carelessly, without proper grave-clothes! Cotton, even tow cloth, might have answered for the living body, but nothing but the finest linen comported with the sanctity of the dead! For years I carried that garment at the bottom of my trunk. Somehow, it became known to my schoolmates, and at first was a source of considerable ridicule, but I soon contrived to flog them all into a proper appreciation of my mother's forethought and care. As the reader may perhaps

"Drawing down my head, I was completely concealed."

think with them, and as I have neither the inclination nor opportunity to correct his or her opinion in the same way, I can only say that my mother was from Nantucket, and they are all queer people there.

It was in the depth of winter that I left home, under the particular charge of a careful and respectable teamster, who was going to P——— with a sleigh-load of salt. It was just after a heavy fall of snow, and the narrow track, imperfectly broken, was bounded by immense banks of snow, almost as high as our heads, as we were seated on the front and only seat of the long, low, open sleigh. On either side stretched the interminable forest, its leafless branches loaded with icy crystals, and glittering in the struggling sunbeams as brilliantly as the gemmed trees in the cavern of Aladdin. Here and there, at the distance apart, sometimes of several miles, would be seen the small clearing surrounding the solitary log-house of some enterprising settler. Covered by unvarying carpet of white, through which peeped the unpicturesque stumps, they were far from presenting a very cheerful appearance,—they served, like the slight breaks sometimes in a firmament of storm clouds, to reveal—not relieve —the surrounding sternness and gloom.

For several miles after leaving the village we rode along in perfect silence, my companion occasionally eying me with a curious look, and evidently making preparations for opening a conversation. To several remarks upon the state of the weather. the road, etc., I made no answer; my mind was filled with too many contending emotions for speech.

" I say, sonny," he at length exclaimed, evidently determined to come to the point at once with the moody boy at his side, " I say, sonny, you don't seem to like leaving home for the first time. Well, well, nobody does. I did n't. I was the homesickest fellow once, you ever did see, and I was a good deal older than you are too." And then he went on to give me a long account of his first journey, to all of which I made no reply. I was indignant at being called sonny. I was indignant at being addressed at all—at having my confused meditations interrupted,—and each moment I grew more and more provoked.

"Come, come, why don't you talk a little? it will do you good. Well," after a pause, " they say that you are a queer fellow, and I really believe they 're right. I 've heard tell some curious stories about you. They say that you knocked old Clark, the schoolmaster, off his chair, with the broomstick, because you thought that you was St. George, and that he was a dragon going to eat up a little boy. How was that, was that so? Come, tell us the story. Some thinks you was cracked, but I guess old Clark's head was the most cracked in that affair." And then followed a long and hearty laugh at his own wit.

I could stand it no longer,—so, putting my foot upon the edge of the sleigh, and exerting that agility which, a little later, has often enabled me, with one running-jump, to clear nearly twenty-two feet of ground, I gave a spring entirely over the perpendicular snow-bank, and landed nearly up to my neck in the roadside ditch. By drawing down my head I was completely concealed for a while from the astonished teamster. He checked his horses, stretched himself up in his sleigh, and looked around with a countenance irresistibly ludicrous, from amazement and fear.

" Soh! whow!" to his restive horses. "Whow! I tell you.—Where has he gone to? Good Lord! what shall I do? Dear me! where on airth is he? Whoa! I tell you. Darnation! Whoa! darn your skins!—Jonathan!" I looked up and saw his comical phiz above the snowbank. The spirit of fun revived. After some little parley I made my way through the snow and took my seat in the sleigh, heartily enjoying both his fright and his satisfaction in recovering part of his load, for the safe arrival of which he knew that he should be held responsible. I could not retain ill feelings against the honest man any longer, and we chatted and laughed, at first with some little reserve on his part, but on overturning in getting out of the road for the mail, I assisted him in righting his sleigh, and restoring its load with so much activity, strength, and good-will, that I quite won his heart. "Good-bye, sonny," he exclaimed, as he landed me at the door of the house to which I had been consigned, "Good-bye; if I can do any thing for you, just let me know, for—a—for you 're not such a darned fool as they say you are."

CHAPTER II.

School Life—Boyish Adventures—A Revival—School Broken Up—Wanderings and Reflections in the Woods—Joe Downs, the Trapper—An Indian Killed with a Ramrod—Arrangements for an Expedition into the Wilderness—A Letter From the Writer's Mother.

T would be a waste of time and space to give all the little adventures and incidents of my academic course of four years. With but little exertion I continued to maintain a respectable standing in my classes, at the same time that I acquired, by a desultory and extensive course of reading, a great deal of knowledge which frequently gave me many advantages over my more industrious and regular schoolmates. It was often a wonder how I knew so much upon the most recondite and out-of-the-way subjects, when I was seldom seen to study, and devoted so much of my time to fishing, gunning, and gymnastic sports.

As in all small towns where academic institutions are situated, there was a good deal of jealousy, rivalry, and sometimes downright ill-feeling between the students and the youths of the village, occasionally displaying itself in serious and even dangerous battles, but most generally in the more harmless, but not less exciting trials of activity and skill. On fourths of July, training days, and other occasions, young men from the country around, at a distance of ten or fifteen miles, would come for the purpose of competing for the championship in these contests, in which, as the leader of the school, I soon became conspicuous. Was there a game at cricket or base-ball to be played, my name headed the list of the athletæ. Was some foot-race or leaping-match to be contested, I was the academic champion. Did some burly wrestler from a neighboring village want the "conceit" taken out of him, either at back-hold, side-hold, or arms-end, I was the one to do it; or if I could not do it, it was pretty clear that no one else could. With my pistol, at fifteen paces, I could drill a mark the size of a half dollar at every shot, and with the rifle it was universally concluded by all the getters-up of turkey-shooting matches, that it would never do to put the birds up for me at twenty rods, for a shilling a shot. I dwell upon these qualities, not so much from the pride that I took in them, as from the service that they have since rendered me, in situations where nothing but a quick eye, practised hand, and agile foot could have saved me. I say not so much from the pride that I took in them, but why pride, and a pretty good share of it too, is not allowable, I cannot understand. Formerly, merely animal strength was held in the greatest repute; but since, in modern days, the intellectual, as a source of power, has been gaining so much upon the physical, that the latter seems to me to have been unnecessarily and unjustly decried, and its proper cultivation neglected. The physical powers are as much the gift of God—in all situations their highest development is serviceable, and in some cases essential, and even by a happy relation the health and strength of the intellectual qualities are dependent upon it. Fortunately, our boys, particularly those who have the advantage of a country life, educate, to some extent, their *physique* for themselves. Future generations will undoubtedly enjoy the advantage of having gymnastics taught as a science, and the highest development given to the body as well as to the mind.

I am far from wishing to convey the idea that I was free from the faults incident to youth. A perfect character may read very well in fictions, but would at once appear improbable and out of place in a plain and simple autobiography of a real personage. Rousseau, I recollect, in his confessions, draws rather a dark picture of his early character, and honestly allows that he was a liar, a thief, and given to a variety of boyish evil practices. I can hardly admit that I was as bad as the sentimental Frenchman. Although I had in the abstract no very great regard for the truth, yet a certain boldness and recklessness of character saved me from being much of a liar; a good share of generosity kept me from those vices which result from selfishness; but if robbing hens' nests, cornfields, orchards, and melon grounds, be stealing, we were all thieves, and I was one of the greatest and most inveterate.

Upon my first arrival at the school this kind of robbery was carried on in a small way; there was nothing dignified and grand enough about it to suit my notions. I soon reformed the system, made it much more comprehensive, and organized a band, which became a perfect nuisance to the whole country round, particularly to those who had a reputation for stinginess, or who, too incautiously boasted of their watch and ward. If a farmer was heard to threaten the unknown depredators with his gun or dogs if they dared to visit his grounds, he was sure to be the subject of a desolating nocturnal foray, or if too strict a watch was kept up at night, the day-time would be selected, when the men were away from home. Upon a signal given, a dozen boys disguised, who had been lying perdu perhaps for two or three hours, would jump his fences, each one with a large bag, and rapidly collecting the fruit, make off amid the screams of the women and the barking of dogs, and vanish with the plunder in the most mysterious manner in the neighboring wood. In a short time some of the gang would perhaps saunter back to the same house, and with the most innocent air ask the enraged women for a cup of buttermilk, or a draught from the well.

A revival of religion, as it was called, at last put an end to my academic course ; in fact it came pretty near putting an end to the academy itself. It was simultaneously manifest in each of the three churches into which the town was divided, the Baptists, Methodists, and Presbyterians, and gradually included the members of our own school, as well as the inhabitants of the village. It spread itself like an epidemic, and seemed to be governed by similar laws. Rapidly increasing in violence as it advanced, it attacked all classes, but evinced particular power over the very young, the very aged, and the very vicious. No revival in that section of country had ever been more complete, or had been more stronly characterized by enthusiastic zeal and intense, wild, passionate excitement ; and none, I may say, supposing it to have been at first the true spirit of God stirring up the apathetic consciences of men, was ever more thoroughly perverted from its proper ends, or marked by more disgusting scenes of intemperance or fanaticism, or followed by a more complete and striking reaction.

In a short time, out of one hundred and eighty scholars, male and female, but five remained " unconverted." The school was entirely broken up, all recitations and studies were neglected. Every one went and came as he pleased ; teachers and pupils were all too busy with the concerns of the soul to heed the duties of the school, with the exception of our venerable president, who was also the pastor of the Presbyterian church. He had set himself sternly and strongly against what his good-sense led him to pronounce an unhealthy if not an unholy excitement. He predicted that much evil would come of it, and endeavored to moderate the inflammatory zeal of his flock ; but in vain. He could not withstand the overwhelming and impetuous tide of public opinion. A highly cultivated mind, refined taste, gentle manners, and undoubted piety served not to save him from contumely and insult. Excited zealots prayed for him even in his own church as a blind leader, a weak brother, an agent of the Devil, while he, finding that he could not repress or divert the storm, calmly awaited its subsidence, knowing that with the return of reason would return the influence of his character and his counsels.

At this time most of my hours were spent in the woods, either fishing, reading, or perchance dreaming. Often stretched at length upon the sunny bank of the most beautiful trout stream in the world, or seated upon some prostrate giant of the forest, I have turned with shuddering and loathing from the sight and sounds of the distant village, and have felt borne to my innermost soul the conviction that cant and rant are utterly inconsistent with the true worship of God. How soft, and low, and calm, yet deep and full of meaning and power are the hymns sung to His praise in the great temple of nature. How varied too! How infinitely expressive! Listen to the hot sunbeams striking upon the thick pendent foliage, to the soft sighing of the million leaves, as, disturbed by the fitful breeze, they twist and wriggle themselves back to stillness and rest. Listen to the low hum of the lazy insects; the hesitating twitter of the sleepy birds, or to the occasional sullen sluggish plash of some trout, who has been lured from his siesta by the temptation of a careless fly. The blended whole makes music—it speaks of life, health, vigor; but of life, health, vigor, doomed to decay. It is prophetic in its tones; the deepest well-springs of the soul are stirred, gently, sadly, but not unpleasantly, as the foreboding notes rise, and swell, and fall. Anon, the tempest comes, the majestic clouds speak to each other and to earth in the deep voices of the pealing thunder; the sturdy woods re-echo, and prolong the crashing sounds; the wind sweeps through the foliage with a hollow rushing, as if a myriad viewless spirits were flapping their pinions and careering before it; the big drops fall with leaden sound upon the leaves. Does not the whole make the wildest, sublimest harmony? There is nothing dismal or gloomy in it; it is sternly joyous; it speaks of power—of might; but it speaks too in solemn and majestic tones—no ranting or canting—of a power above and beyond mere drooping and decaying nature. Stand forth, and enjoy it! Quail not! Bare your brow to the storm—look with a steady eye upon the lightning's flash—listen to the awful chorus and feel alike the infinity of God and the greatness of the soul.

The storm has passed—the moistened foliage rustles in the breeze, but with a different tone—a tone of pure gladness; the insects beat the air with their tiny wings to a more joyful measure; the birds sing freely, blithely; the trout spring actively from the placid lake, and dash the sparkling circles with a sound of merriment and glee. The harmony is of nature revived, restored. It speaks of hope and confidence—it presages immortality. But how easy, natural, and quiet! How deep and strong, and heart-pervading in that very naturalness and quiet! Ah! in all that infinite variety of praise, and prayer, and thanksgiving, you can discover nothing like rant or cant.

It was with such thoughts in my head that, early one beautiful morning, I was ranging the woods, gun in hand, occasionally stopping to listen for the drumming of the partridge, or the cooing of the wild pigeon. The peculiar sound of the former struck upon my ear; I took aim—fired, and was reloading my rifle, when a loud and hearty salutation rang through the trees.

"Hallo! Mr. Jonathan, good morning. How are you?" exclaimed the stranger, picking up the partridge as he advanced towards me. "That's a capital shot of yours—a first-rate shot; ten rods at least, and head taken off as clean as a whistle."

The speaker was old Joe Downs, well known as an expert trapper and hunter; and as generally liked as he was known. There was nothing rough or outré in his appearance or style of conversation; none of the half-horse and half-alligator characteristics generally attributed to the woodsman of the south and west. Nothing could be more simple or respectable than his air and looks; so much so that more than once Joe had been taken for a country parson. His ostensible home was in the village, but his real home was in the woods, the greater part of his time being spent in expeditions up to the sources of the Rackett and Grass Rivers, in the dense and perfectly uninhabited wilderness in the northern part of the State of New York, known as John Brown's tract. A few beaver yet lingered round their old favorite haunts on the numerous beautiful little lakes, which, like dimples here and there, lighted up the face of nature with smiles, and relieved the stern solitude of the woods. They were, however, not in sufficient numbers to attract the hunter, who found more profitable enjoyment in trapping the muskrat, or in killing deer for their skins. Even in these pursuits but very few whites were engaged, the most of the hunters being Indians, of the St. Regis nation, or from some Canadian tribes, who, once a year, made an excursion up the Rackett for two or three months, and then returned with their spoils to their home on the St. Lawrence.

Joe had frequently proposed to me to accompany him on one of his expeditions; and circumstances now seemed to favor the plan.

"I'll tell you what it is now," he exclaimed, as we took our seats upon the trunk of a fallen tree. " I 'll tell you what it is, you can't do nothing here. There 's no decent game within ten miles of us. The psalm-singing and praising the Lord has knocked all business in the head, and broke up the Academy; so you haint no school to go to; well, you wont pray, you can't study, and you can't hunt; so what 's the use of staying here. No, go along with me for three or four weeks, and I 'll show you some sport that would even make that tarnal old scoundrel, Deacon Zeb, stop his snuffle, and haw-haw right out like a decent white man. What do you say to a wolf! Pooh! they are not worth the powder and shot, unless you can shoot two at a time. But what do you say to a bear or two; real old fellows, that will take half a dozen balls in the body and still make a respectable fight! Why, I 'll do still better by you than that; if I don't put you right alongside of the biggest catamount you ever heard tell of, my name aint Joe. I will, 'pon my word. You shall stand right under the tree, and take him in the eye just as he is about to spring upon you. There 's nothing better for the nerves. It kind of braces them up, and you feel always afterwards just as though you could shoot the Devil."

" But, Joe!——"

" Oh, there 's no but about it. If you don't kill him dead, I 'll just stand one side and wont say a word, and you can take it out—fair play—with hatchet and knife. 'Pon my word you shall have a chance to kill a catamount, if you can't stir for three weeks afterwards."

Joe's promises were too tempting to be resisted. There were no studies, or recitations; and vacation, when I was to return home, would take place in about a month; giving me just time enough for the excursion.

" When shall we start?" I demanded.

" Oh, to-morrow or next day if you 're a mind to. I 've got my old bark-canoe all nicely patched up, and my rat-traps all fixed. You just get a couple of blankets and your shooting and fishing fixings all in order, and mind and bring along a strong pickerel line. I 'll show you a pond up there where the youngest infants of a genteel pickerel's family weigh at least three pounds."

" Shall we have any company?" I inquired.

" No, not a white face within forty miles of us. There 'll be plenty of red-skins—half a dozen canoes went up the river yesterday, but they aint of no account. They are a poor, lying, cheating, stealing set of vagabonds. There is n't one of them that I 'd trust within a mile of my camp."

" But don't you ever have any difficulty with them ? "

" Why, no, not what you may call real downright difficulty. We used to a good many years ago, but now, although they 'll murder you if they get a chance for a pack of skins, they don't vally a scalp. No— since I finished off one of the biggest scoundrels in the whole St. Regis nation, I haint been troubled."

" How was that ? "

" Why, I 'll tell you : you see it was way towards Tupper's Lake. There had been a light fall of snow, and I was scouting round, when I happened to make a circumbendibus, and came across my own tract, and there I saw the marks of an Indian's foot right on my trail. Thinks I, that is kind of queer ; the fellow must have been following me ; howsomever, I 'll try him and make sure ; so I made another large circle, and again struck my own track, and there was the tarnal Indian's foot again. Says I, this wont do ; I must find out what this customer wants, and how he 'll have it. So I stopped short, and soon got sight of him ; he knew that I saw him, so he came along up in the most friendly manner you can think. But I did n't like his looks, he was altogether too darned glad to see me. He had no gun, but he had an almighty long-handled tomahawk, and a lot of skins and rat-traps. Thinks I, may be, old fellow your gun has burst or you 've pawned it for rum, and you can't raise skins enough to redeem it, and you want mine, and perhaps you 'll get it.

" At last I grew kind of nervous : I knew the fellow would hatchet me if I gave him a chance, and yet I did n't want to shoot him right down just on suspicion. But I thought, if I let him cut my throat first, it would be too late to shoot him afterwards. So I concluded that the best way would be to give him a chance to play his hand ; and, if it so be, he 'd lead the wrong card, why I should have a right to take the trick. Just then at the right time a partridge flew into a clump that stood five or six rods off. So I kind of 'neuvred round a little. I drew out my ramrod as if to feel whether the ball in my rifle was well down, but instead of returning it again, I kept it in my hand, and without letting the vagabond see me, I got out a handful of powder. I then sauntered off to the bush, shot the partridge, and in an instant passed my hand over the muzzle of my rifle, and dropped the powder in. I picked up the bird, and then just took and run my ramrod right down upon the powder. Now he thought was his chance before I loaded my gun again. He came towards me with his hatchet in his hand. I saw that he was determined to act wicked, and began to back off ; he still came on. I lowered my rifle and told him to keep away. He raised his tomahawk, gave one yell, and bounded right at me. When he was just about three or four feet from the muzzle, I fired. You never see a fellow jump so. He kicked his heels up in the air and came down plump on his head."

" Dead ? "

" Dead as Juliar Cæsar. He never winked ; the ramrod—a good hard, tough piece of hickory—had gone clean through him, and stuck out about two feet from his back. Sarved him right, did n't it ? "

" Certainly. I don't see what else you could have done."

" Nor I, nother. But I am sorry I took his traps. Howsomever, I

" Dead as Julius Cæsar."

did n't keep them long. I gave them away to a half-drowned redskin, who had lost his in trying to cross the river, right at the head of the big wolf chute. There 's a story about that too ; but we 'll put it off till we get up to our camp. So, what do you say ? shall we go ? "

" Agreed," said I. And in a few words our plans were all laid, and we returned to town to make arrangements for carrying them out.

Arrived at my room, I found a long letter from my mother. How well I recollect its contents, although years have elapsed since I have read it. There was nothing in it that struck me at the moment as very important, but it afterwards acquired a peculiar interest—it was her last.

* * * * * * * *

It is now one month," she wrote, "to your vacation, but I have just heard some reports which make me somewhat curious to know what you are doing. You have alluded to the revival, in one of your letters, but I had no idea that it had gone so far as they say it has, or that there was any thing strikingly or strongly opposed to a proper cultivated Christian taste. You know how deeply and ardently I have wished to impress you with a proper sense of religion, but I have no sympathy with the passionate enthusiasm—the mere animal excitement which has recently been so common in this neighborhood. I think that I can trust your taste and good sense; however, you might better come home without waiting for your vacation. Upon the whole, I think that you might better come immediately."

* * * * * * * *

I wrote a hasty answer to my mother's letter, expressing my assent to her proposition, and informing her that the remainder of the term I had determined to devote to an expedition into the woods, which I thought would have a very beneficial effect upon my health, and enable me to commence the study of medicine with much greater vigor. The letter was dispatched, and in a few hours all my arrangements were made to join the old trapper upon my first grand hunt.

CHAPTER III.

UR outfit was simple enough. I took with me a rifle and a double-barrelled fowling-piece, with plenty of powder, ball, and shot, etc., together with an ample assortment of fishing tackle, a pocket telescope, two blankets, a pouch of pepper and salt, and a bag of crackers. Joe brought with him his rifle, axe, blanket, and traps, an iron jack to hold a light of pine knots in the bow of our boat, and a bag of wheat and Indian meal.

Thus supplied we launched our light birchen canoe upon the river at daybreak, and were soon gliding rapidly along the winding and narrow channel formed by the numerous little islands which intervene between the village and the foot of the first rapid or falls.

Arrived at the rapids, we were compelled to unload our canoe and carry it and our baggage around some distance to reach the smooth water above—a performance which we found occasion to repeat not unfrequently in the course of our voyage. The labor, however, though rather arduous, was far from distressing ; our baggage being divided into parcels of light weight, with the exception of our canoe. This, however, though rather large and heavy for its kind, was not too much for Joe alone, who would " catch " his shoulder under the " gunnel " and trot off with it for a mile or so without stopping. Of course I could not allow myself to feel unequal to any exertion which the old man (who was also my inferior in size and weight) was capable of making. Working " with a will," the portages seemed short, and when launched again, paddling the canoe was merely an agreeable exercise.

It was on the second morning of our voyage that I was aroused from the sweetest and most profound sleep that I had ever enjoyed, by the voice of Joe : " Come, come, Mr. Jonathan, it 's time to start. Don't you hear the black-birds. and they aint very early risers. Come let 's bundle our traps into the canoe and you shall crack two or three of the darkies over, as we go by the willow islands. They are as fat as butter, and will make a first-rate breakfast when we get up to ' Blue Ledge Point.' "

I awoke and gazed around ; I could at first scarcely comprehend my position. Our canoe had been hauled up on land and turned over our baggage to protect it from the rain or dew. At my feet, as I lay wrapped in my blanket, were the smouldering embers of our evening fire ; the dark overshadowing masses of trees on one side, and the bluish sheen of the rippling river on the other, were just veiled by the purple light which began to appear in the east. I started up—opened my eyes—rubbed them —stared at Joe, the woods, the stream, the clouds, and felt the exciting conviction rush upon my mind, that at last I was engaged in a veritable adventure.

In ten minutes our canoe was launched and loaded, and we were again afloat. It grew momentarily lighter, until at last the lagging sun popped up suddenly his full-orbed face above the horizon, shedding a flood of glory upon forest, glade, and stream.

" Take your gun now," said Joe, " while I 'll paddle along close by the willows of that island—just see how thick they are—you can get three or four at a shot."

" Not at them ! not at them ! " exclaimed Joe, as I was taking aim, " they are too far in—we shall have to wade in the mud for them. Wait till you can catch 'em on the edge of the water. But—hush ! I hear voices."

We listened, and could distinctly hear some low guttural sounds, and the occasional plash of the water on the other side of the long narrow mud island. Resuming my paddle, we soon shot ahead, so as to command a view of the opposite channel. At the instant that we reached the head of the island, a canoe, manned by three Indians, came in sight close alongside of us, and followed by several others a little farther down.

" *Sago—sago neechie*," shouted Joe. " Good morning—how do you do?"

The savage wielding the stern paddle of the foremost canoe turned upon us a countenance, the natural diabolical expression of which was not diminished by a few patches of black paint. A scowl of intense hatred and malice was his only reply to our salutation, as with a sweep of his paddle he turned the bow of his boat from us, and with a few vigorous strokes shot it ahead.

" Oh ! I know you, you sneaking scoundrel ! " growled Joe, between his clenched teeth; "I know you, and I'll make you know me if you don't look out. But here comes Captain Pete, he's almost the only decent chap in the whole tribe."

The other boats now came up to us. Their crews returned our salutations with apparent good-will. We even rested upon our oars, and had quite a long chat about the weather, the game, and the prices of powder, shot, and muskrat skins.

"Who was that polite fellow in the first canoe?" I demanded, as we turned off and resumed our course.

"His name," replied Joe, "is Blacksnake, and a darned good name it is for him. He's black enough as you see, and he's a regular snake at heart. I'm afraid I shall have to put stones on his tail one of these days, as the boys do when they catch his namesake."

"But what's the difficulty?" I inquired. "He did n't seem to look at you in the most loving temper."

"Why, no; and I must allow he has n't any very great reason. You see he's the brother of that fellow I was telling you about—the one that I pinned with the ramrod; and there's a whole lot of relations. They don't know exactly that I did it, but they kind of conceit that I did, and that's just about as bad."

"And have they never sought to revenge his death?"

"Certainly! I was leaning out of the second-story door-way of Jone's shop one day, looking across the river, when, whiz, a rifle bullet came and buried itself in the door post. I haint the least doubt that that very identical Blacksnake sent it. Thank God, his aim was not as good as his will! He's a bad chap. Why, I really believe it was he who murdered my old friend Dan White, the trapper. If I only knew it was the fact, I wish I may be stuck forked end uppermost in a coon hole, if I would n't send a ball through his painted old brain-case this ere very identical minute. Darn your skin!" energetically growled Joe, shaking his fist at the distant canoe.

"But how is it that you have escaped until this time?" I inquired. "Blacksnake and his friends must have had opportunities enough of settling your business for you, if they had sought them. How long is it since you killed that fellow?"

"Why, about three years," replied Joe; "but then you see they are such thundering cowards. They would like to fix me, but they dares n't. They know it is n't so easy to catch me asleep; and besides that, they are kind o' fraid of the law ever since the Indian was hung for killing a white man up in Brown's settlement. They don't like hanging, and they'll take pretty good care how they do any thing to bring their necks into the noose. No, the fellows know the law just as well as white men. Why, I once cleared away the ground in a little open piece of woods, about a mile out of town, and thought I 'd make a melon-patch. Well, I planted some, and they came on to grow very nice, and I calculated that being as how they were all open, and no fence around them, that nobody would be so mean as to steal them. But one day I found that somebody had been at 'em, and had picked all the ripe ones, and had trod down the vines, and done a monstrous sight of damage. I saw that there had been a good many fellows at work, and they had left a pretty broad trail; so I just started off upon it, and about a quarter of a mile I found six great red devils squatted down, and a grunting, and a giggling, and a sucking my water melons, just as though they had bought and paid for them. I tell you I was almighty mad, and there happened to be lying just right, a broken hoop that had been pretty well straightened by the rain. I seized that, and jumped right into the midst of them, and the way I did lather them fellows was really ridiculous. The hoop was tough and limber, and every time I 'd strike it would double clear round their bodies. Such a dancing and screaming and capering you never did see! They soon scattered themselves, I tell you—the fat lazy old war chief last. He made a spring at a rail fence, and I believe would have gone over it at the first jump, although he carried weight with his two pounds of pewter and brass rings in his ears, but just as he cleared the ground I wollopped the hoop around him and snaked him back, head over heels; he gathered himself like a frightened deer, and cleared the fence next jump easy. And what do you think these fellows did?

" What on 'arth do you think they did?" demanded Joe.

" I can't imagine, I 'm sure." I replied.

" No! I know you can't! You could n't guess if you should try a week. They went and took the law of me—'pon my word they did! The justice said they deserved the licking, but he must fine me five dollars. I told him I thought that was very reasonable, and if I caught them at my melon-patch again, I 'd take ten dollars worth at the same rate."

Our conversation did not interrupt the continued and vigorous strokes of our paddles, which forced our light canoe along the surface of the water with a rapidity which gave one hardly time to observe the striking natural features of the scenery by which we were surrounded. In some places the river contracted its banks until it was almost overshadowed by the densely wooded height; at others, expanded itself into little silvery lakes, dotted with islands, crowded with ducks of several species, and alive with fish. The shores varied at each instant in their colors and forms, verdant flats, low marshes, overhanging with willows; rolling hillocks, and lofty ledges of red freestone succeeded each other with a perfect prodigality of picturesqueness; while at every few miles, some tributary creek would open up such a vista of inviting beauty, that at times I could with difficulty resist an inclination to arrest the progress of the canoe and propose an exploration. My companion, however, would hardly have consented to such a waste of time; and I was therefore compelled to suffer the painful sentiment of a sense of beauty lost forever, as we glided so rapidly by.

"Here 's something that I want to show you," said Joe, as he turned our canoe into a narrow channel not more than ten feet wide, that ran between a little islet and the lofty bank of rock, which rose almost perpendicularly directly from the water to a height of some seventy feet. "You would n't think," continued Joe, "that five hundred men might be stowed within ten feet of us, and without the least danger that the most thorough search could discover them?"

I looked all around—at the little island, which barely concealed our canoe from the main channel, and at the solid wall of smooth rock that towered overhead.

"You don't believe it!" said Joe.

I shook my head.

"Well, I 'll show you. Do you see that little ledge jutting out from the face of the rock, about ten feet above there? Well, you 'd think that it was no more than two feet broad, and that it was close to the bank, but you 'd make a great mistake; it stands out clear three feet at least, and right behind it is a large hole that leads to one of the nicest caves you ever did see. It 's as dry as a bone, and I don't believe that anybody without wings ever looked into it except myself."

"You see I was coming along here one day, three or four years ago, when all of a sudden I heard a noise on the top of the cliff; I looked up, and there I saw a young catamount, scrambling up that little old oak; he stretched himself out on that branch and looked down upon me so kind of impudent, I thought I 'd take a crack at him. I raised my rifle and fired; and down he came—ker-chunk—right on the edge of the precipice. He gave a jump or two, but it was the wrong way, and down he came right along the face of the wall, and right on that ledge. I thought he 'd bound off, and perhaps tumble aboard of me; but he did n't; he stopped short, and went right out of sight. Thinks I, that 's queer. I must see about that. So I pushed right in here, between these two stones, and fastened my canoe to this bush."

Suiting the action to the word, Joe stopped and fastened our boat, and we both commenced climbing the face of the rock, by means of two or three jutting points, that could hardly have been observed from the river, until we had reached the ledge.

" Here ! " said Joe, " I found the critter, right behind this. I pulled him out, and then I thought I 'd see where this opening went to.—Come in, come in ! "

We entered and found ourselves in an irregular but roomy apartment. The dim light, as we had no torches with us, enabled me to form but a very indefinite idea of its size, but I could not but think what a palace it would have been thought by the Troglodytes, of whom I had just been reading in Herodotus. Several large cracks and orifices led off to other parts of the cavern ; but as we had no light, and Joe was anxious to get to the camping ground, which he had selected some six or eight miles above, I had no opportunity of examining it very closely at the time, although afterwards I had good cause to know it better.

" I 've shown this to you," said Joe, " but I would n't have it known to any one else for a good deal of money. It has served me often to hide my traps or a bundle of skins in. There 's no danger of a skulking Indian finding them there. It can't be seen from above, and no one would begin to think of it from below unless they happen to tumble a panther into it as I did."

Two or three miles farther brought us to the largest lake, or expansion of the river, that we had yet seen. It burst upon us as we rounded the rocky promontory, which had hidden it from our view, like some scene of enchantment, and I thought at the time that were I the master of all the genii of the Arabian Nights I could not have commanded for my own especial admiration and enjoyment a more delicious and picturesque scene. But neither space nor time will permit me to undertake a description.

" Beautiful ! beautiful ! " I exclaimed, dropping my paddle, and gazing with delight.

" Yes, it 's first rate," replied my companion. " There 's lots of deer all along here for ten miles, up to the head of the lake, and muskrats are as plenty as blackberries on them islands, and around them flats. But do you see them pine woods yonder ? that 's our place. It 's just about half way up the lake, and a capital spot for a camp—dry as a bone—plenty of wood, and no mosquitoes." And Joe industriously plied his paddle in the direction he pointed.

We soon reached the spot indicated—the edge of an extensive pine barren; no underwood obstructed the view through the gigantic trees, which towered their lofty heads to the clouds; and in some places not even the scantiest vegetation held the movable sand, that whirled in the gusts of wind around the sturdy trees with the uncontrolled freedom of the desert.

Our baggage was soon landed, a place selected, and preparations made for erecting our hut. A few saplings and bushes from the edge of the river were all that were required, and in a few hours we had a comfortable wigwam—completely sheltered from the weather on three sides, and a huge log fire blazing in front. An hour more, and a couple of black squirrels hung dangling from the ends of sticks implanted in the ground, and inclined at an angle towards the fire, while a magnificent trout was broiling upon the glowing embers, and diffusing a most savory odor, which soon brought numerous lupine and vulpine visitors, who, by their howling, snuffing, and scampering around our camp, seemed to envy us our luxurious repast. A thin cake of Indian meal, skilfully mixed by the old trapper, and baked upon a heated stone, completed the materials for our supper.—And such a supper! I thought of the *petits soupers* of Aspasia, and of Alcibiades, and of Lucullus and the purple chamber, with feelings of the most perfect contempt.

"Yes, as you say," exclaimed the old man, "this fish is first rate, but it aint a circumstance to what can be done in the cooking way. I'll tell you how you can cook a fish to make it taste just as you please. We'll try it some day. You take some nice clean clay and work it up a little, then catch your trout—or any other kind of fish,—and don't scale or dress him, but just plaster him all over with the clay about an inch thick, and put him right into the hot ashes. When he's done, the clay and scales will all peel off, and you'll have a dish that would bring to life any starved man, if he had n't been dead more nor a week. That's the natural way"—*au naturel*, Joe would have said, had he been acquainted with the technicalities of the *cuisine*,—"but if you want an extra touch, cut a hole in him, and stick in a piece of salt pork or bear's feet, and a few beechnuts, or the meat of walnuts or butternuts, and, Lord, bless you, you'd think you was eating a water angel."

"But come!" continued Joe, "we've got through supper, let's stir round and do something. It's too late to set the traps, but we can take a shot at the deer."

Our boat was soon prepared. The jack, or light iron grate, was erected upon a stake in the bow, at the height of six or seven feet. Soon from it flamed a blazing fire of pine knots, throwing its light far around and beneath the surface of the calm clear water, and illuminating the giant trees and wild rocks of the shores with the most curious effects of light and shade. The trapper stationed himself directly beneath the light, rifle in hand, while I cautiously and silently plied the paddle. A plashing in the water along the bank of the lake, where the deer had come down to drink and refresh themselves with a standing bath in the cool water, betrayed the game to Joe's practised ear. Our canoe slowly approached them. The simple animals, startled, but fascinated by the mysterious light, stood stupidly gazing at the flaming jack, and allowed us to approach within two or three rods. The spell that held them was broken by the crack of the rifle, and one of their number fell instantly dead with a ball through the brain.

We obtained five the first night. The next day was spent in looking up muskrat tracks, and setting our traps, and in the evening the deer-shooting was resumed with equal success. In this way several days glided by, with nothing to disturb the perfect enjoyment of the scene, except an occasional doubt as to how my mother would like my escapade.

CHAPTER IV.

WEEK had passed—a week that, tested by the home associations which would once in a while intrude themselves, seemed long, but which, measured by the current feelings of the moment, seemed but as an hour. It is thus the flight of time is ever noted: brooding over the reminiscences of the past, or the hopes of the future, time seems a laggard, and we are tempted to direct all the offensive weapons we can muster, against the lazy fellow as he floats on sluggish pinions by; absorbed in the engagements, the thoughts, or the duties of the present, with what fearful and relentless velocity he passes; we no longer think of "killing" him any more than we should think of killing the eagle as he stoops in the very majesty of speed with a wild startling rush and whir from his lofty perch upon the finny prey that his appearance has frightened from the clutches of some straggling hawk.

A week had passed, and as yet we had met with no very extraordinary or thrilling adventure. I had not even seen a panther or a bear. The ordinary routine of deer-shooting and muskrat-catching employed us so fully, that we had not had time to look for them, but the interest and excitement of that occupation was beginning to flag. I began to long for something more piquant.

It was just at the close of a laborious day that I took the canoe and pushed out into the lake for the purpose of procuring the piscatory portion of our evening meal; no difficult job, as may be supposed, where the fish were so plentiful and so unsophisticated—so utterly unaccustomed to the specious illusions of the baited hook. I had captured enough for the appetites of any two ordinary ichthyophagi, and was debating with myself the exceeding impropriety of continuing the sport merely as sport, when a gruff, guttural salutation struck my ear, and a canoe with a single Indian, who I immediately recognized as Captain Pete, glided alongside.

"The general—where is him?" demanded the captain.

27

The general was a title in which I knew that Joe sometimes luxuriated, especially with his Indian friends, although I was ignorant of the source, or the manner in which it had been acquired. I replied that the general was ashore at the camp, and would be glad to see a friend that he thought so much of, as I knew that he did of Captain Pete.

" No," said the captain, " no stay—you tell him look out—Blacksnake bad man—he mean bad—I know him—tell general to sleep with one eye—take plenty care. You tell him ? "

"Certainly, I 'll tell him———"

" Good ! " and the captain dropped his paddle into the water and urged his light birchen bark towards the opposite side of the lake.

There was something in the captain's voice and manner that conveyed far more meaning than his words. I saw that he was in earnest, and that he, at least, entertained the conviction that Joe was in some danger. My suspicions, and I must confess to some little extent my fears, were thoroughly aroused. I had heard so much of Indian revenge, that notwithstanding Joe's contempt for the semi-civilized and wholly demoralized red-skins that were about us, I was disposed to believe them still equal to those daring and bloody deeds that authentic history, as well as doubtful tradition, has so often described. I was sorry I had not questioned Captain Pete a little, but he had started away so abruptly, having evidently wished to convey his warning without being seen lingering in the neighborhood of our camp, that I had not time to fairly recover myself before he was out of hearing. However, Joe will be able to form some judgment of the extent and character of the danger that threatens us, thought I, as I pulled up my anchor and made all haste to the shore.

" Pooh ! pooh ! " said Joe, as I finished my story, " 't aint nothing worth thinking of. Captain Pete is a good old fellow, and he 's always been a warm friend, as he ought to be, since I have done him some good turns in my time ; but he don't know over much. He 's afraid of Blacksnake himself, and he thinks he 's doing a service by trying to frighten me."

Joe's assurances were far from satisfying me. I could easily perceive that Captain Pete's message had made a much greater impression upon him than he was willing to allow. While I was telling my story he had looked around for his rifle, had taken it up, examined the flint and priming, and passed the ramrod down to be sure that it was loaded, all the time listening with evident interest, and asking questions that betrayed not quite so much recklessness as he endeavored to assume.

" Pooh ! pooh ! " said Joe, as he turned off and rested his rifle against the corner of our hut; but I was far from being assured either by his tone or his words.

"You seem," said I, at the conclusion of quite a long and hot argument, in which I defended the received notions of Indian character,— "you seem, Mr. Downs, to have a poor opinion of red-skin courage."

"That I have, and with good reason too. I don't know what they might have been once, but I know that rum and civilization have made them a poor, sneaking, cowardly set. Now off to the west they are a little better; but even there, they 're no great shakes. Why, I was out there with Harrison, in Tecumseh's time, and I know that a deuced sight of nonsense has been written and talked about the 'lords of the forest'

" A Canoe with a single Indian glided alongside "

as you call 'em. There was not a scout in the army that valued a single Indian more nor the snap of his thumb. They can't shoot—can't run — can't row—can't swim—can't do any thing with a white man, unless it is to starve longer, and that they have been brought up to. You see I 'm a small man, and an old man, but if I can't lick, in fair fight, any single Indian you can pick up between here and the Rocky Mountains, my name aint Downs, and I aint given to bragging much neither. They are just like them wolves," and Joe pointed to a lot of lupine attendants, that, as usual, were howling about at a respectful distance from our camp. "They are just like them wolves; they 'll hang around just as though they would eat you, and if you move a step towards them, they 'll run like so many sheep."

" Well, well," said I, " it may be as you say; we won't argue the subject any further—but I must say that if Blacksnake feels towards you as you think he does, he has got no Indian blood in him if, sooner or later, he does not contrive to get a shot at you. Why, I should n't wonder if he was prowling round here this very night."

Joe laughed.

" You laugh," said I, " but, tell me, what is there to prevent him ? "

" Nothing on earth," replied Joe, " excepting that he 's afraid. I tell you he no more dares to come within speaking distance of this old tool," touching his rifle, " than one of them wolves dares to come in here and help himself to fat out of that stewpan."

" Well," said I, " if there is no more danger than that, we 're safe enough. There 's no wolf yonder fool enough to give us a fair sight of his countenance ; so as I want a wolf-skin badly, I 'll just step out and try once more if I can't get a shot at these noisy cowards that you liken the ' lords of the forest ' so contemptuously to." Taking up my double-barrelled gun, I carefully loaded it with a full charge of heavy buck-shot.

" Go round by the right," replied Joe, " and you 'll hem 'em in between the lake and our fire ; and perhaps you 'll get a chance to take one of the fellows as they rush by you."

Following his directions I started off, making a small detour, and leaving the trapper seated before the fire industriously platting a deer-skin rope. Long after I had passed out of sight of the camp into the shade of the tall woods I could see his figure fully revealed in the flashing light of the pine-log fire.

The night was an impressive one ; there was something heavy and threatening in the air, although there were no decided indications of a storm. The wind came sluggishly across the bosom of the lake, slightly wrinkling its surface, and sighing with gentle but exceedingly mournful tones among the tops of the lofty trees. It is curious what different sounds are produced by winds of equal force at different times in the same place. It is true the phenomenon can be explained by reference to the comparative temperature, moisture, and density of the atmosphere ; but the difference of those tones has a meaning to many ears that cannot be explained away with the explanation of the physical cause. In this instance the wind had perhaps additional significance from its harmony with my feelings—it was a foreboding wind. The moon, too, seemed triste as she worked her way through the masses of fleecy clouds, occasionally darting upon the surface of the ruffled lake a beam that was instantly broken into a thousand sparkling gems of light, and anon hiding behind some jealous cloud, as if glad for a moment to fly the sight of a bad earth. It was altogether such an evening as the Huntsman of the Hartz would have selected for a pleasant moonlight ride.

But although as sensible to the spiritual influences of the weather as I have ever been impassive to its physical effects, I had but a short time to indulge in the mere sentiment of the time and scene. The wolves are much the most interesting objects of the moment, and fully occupied my attention. I had succeeded in approaching a party of them without being perceived. I could not see them; but I could distinguish the spot, from their noises, at which they were congregated, and was slowly and cautiously closing in upon them. I had arrived within about fifty yards of the lake, and some three or four hundred yards below our camp, the light of which I could clearly see, when a sudden rush took place, and the gaunt forms of·half a dozen of the famished wretches flitted by me. I raised my gun, and with finger on the trigger fairly covered one of them as he bounded by at a distance of not more than three or four rods; but I did not fire. Why or for what reason it is impossible to say. It seemed as though there was something providential in it, although it was probably nothing but one of those moments of indecision which the keenest sportsman will recollect to have felt. It was but an instant; but that instant was enough. The next, or to speak more correctly, the very same moment a tall shadowy figure glided from behind the trunk of a mighty pine. I dropped my gun from its level, and stared with pure unthinking and unreflective wonder at the strange apparition. In a moment another figure glided out, and again another, and there were clearly revealed the forms of three stalwart Indians, creeping along from tree to tree in the direction of our fire. Without a moment's thought I turned in nearly upon their rear, and followed them with a step as noiseless as ever trod an Indian warpath. I was not afraid—in fact, I never was more perfectly cool; but I had that intense concentration of feeling which, while it leaves the physical powers in full play, prevents thought; or perhaps the mind in such cases is so lightning-like in its action that we do not perceive its processes. At any rate, it seemed to me as if I only felt. I acted by a kind of instinct; my mind appeared to be diffused through my whole body, and my legs and arms to know as much as my head.

Slowly and cautiously the Indians drew towards our camp, and slowly and cautiously I followed them. I have since frequently thought of a dozen plans that I might have adopted. I might, by firing my gun, have

frightened the Indians from their purpose, and perhaps put Joe on his
guard, or I might, by swiftly making a detour, have reached the camp,
when by taking to the trees we could have had a fair fight, and had there
been six Indians, instead of three, we should undoubtedly have had the
best of it. But I did not know what objects the Indians had in view,
and these are thoughts that came afterwards, or that can only be made
advantageous at the moment by great natural courage, thoroughly educated in the school of danger. I had a fair share of the first, but the
education was wanting, and, as I have said, I felt rather than thought.

The Indians had arrived within ten or fifteen rods of our hut when
they stopped, and appeared to me to be holding a consultation, while
grouped for a moment in the deep shadow of the trees. They had evidently not the slightest suspicion that any one was in their rear. They
were altogether too much occupied with the sight in front of them to
think of suspecting danger from any other quarter. Cautiously closing
up, I had advanced to within twenty or thirty paces of them, and could
distinctly see their figures well defined in all their outlines, especially as I
now had got them nearly in a line with our fire, which was blazing away
right merrily, and throwing a prodigious volume of light to the tops of
the loftiest trees. Joe was seated in precisely the same position in which
I had left him. His face was turned nearly towards us, and his body
slightly bent downwards, as he held on to the thongs of deer-skin attached to a peg driven into the ground. The firelight shone full upon
his person, making a fair and easy target.

A slight movement was made by the group. I had hardly time to
see and comprehend it, when two rifles flashed almost simultaneously,
and the echoes of their sharp reports rolled through the woods. I saw
the trapper jump to his feet, raise his hand above his head and totter
backwards, and at the same instant the third Indian levelled his rifle at
him, but the skulking murderer was too slow in his motions; with a kind
of sigh and a grunt he jumped a step or two forwards, his gun going
off at random, and fell dead with a charge of buck-shot through his body.
In the thousandth part of a second, and with an aim as calm and as sure
as ever pointed gun against whirring partridge or flitting quail, I gave
one of the other two the contents of my remaining barrel— he never
knew what killed him. Without pausing for a moment, I dashed forward
at the third fellow. He turned, jumped back a few feet, and clubbed his
unloaded rifle to receive me. Without making at first a downright blow,
against which, perhaps, he would have been upon his guard, and which,
from the imperfect light, might have exposed myself, had he too been

making a blow at the same time, I made a straight forward thrust, and struck him a severe blow in the face. He staggered back, and before he could recover himself, with an overhand slashing cut, I brought the heavy barrels down upon his bare skull. He fell like a log. There was no need of any questions. I knew that he was dead. I felt the bones crack and crumble beneath the force of my blow. Without stopping a moment I bounded on to our hut, there I saw a sight that for a moment completely stupefied me. Joe had fallen backwards, his head resting, slightly raised, against the upright of our hut, where leaned his rifle, and, to first appearance, dead. A large portion of the left eyebrow was cut away and hung down over the eye, and from the dangerous-looking wound the dark blood slowly dribbled down over his face. A slight movement showed that there was still some life left in him. I raised his head, and placed it in an easy position, and felt his pulse, which was beating with wonderful rapidity, but so faintly as to be almost imperceptible. In a moment he opened his eyes, or rather eye, which gradually lightened with returning consciousness. His lips moved—I put my ear close to his mouth—"Water," he murmured.

In an instant I was myself again. I felt that it was no time for doubt and indecision. The little medical knowledge that I had picked up by stray reading, and visiting "doctor shops," was instantly available, and I thought of all the curious cases that I had heard of, where people had been shot all to pieces and survived. "Never say die," thought I, and with that vulgar but encouraging maxim almost on my lips, I jumped to the lake and returned with a can of the fresh water. Joe took a draught which revived him a little, while I set to and washed his face. Upon cleaning the wound, I found it did not present so formidable an appearance. By passing my finger along through it, I found that the ball had glanced obliquely above and through the eyebrow, but that the bone was not injured, although the concussion had at first stunned him. I was preparing to restore the flap and bind it up, when I became sensible that the old man, who had again become unconscious, was lying in a pool of blood, which had completely staturated his clothes on one side, and the ground around him. The true cause of his exhaustion was revealed. The wound in the head, as I had thought, was of no great consequence. He was dying from loss of blood. There was no time to lose—I threw a few pine-knots on the fire, turned Joe over on one side, and cut and tore the bloody part of his clothes from him, in less time than it takes to tell of it. A small wound, corresponding nearly to the intercostal space of the fifth and sixth ribs, was slowly pouring forth the tide of life, already reduced to its lowest ebb. I had no means of probing it, but I could feel, upon pressure, the crepitation of the broken rib. Some indefinite ideas of internal bleeding flashed through my mind, but, thought I, he may as well die from internal as external bleeding—the only thing that I can do is to plug the wound. Tearing off a square piece of linen, I placed it over the wound and forced the centre of it into the surface between the two ribs with the point of my ramrod, making a kind of pouch, into which I continued to cram small pieces of linen until I had distended it into a good and efficient plug. This finished, I commenced clearing away the coagulated clots, when, as I was passing my hand over his side, imagine my joy at feeling a hard round substance, directly beneath the skin, and in a line some six or eight inches backwards from the wound. I felt it again; it was clearly and decidedly a rifle ball. The case was now clear; it needed no surgeon to make a correct *diagnosis*. The ball had not entered the body, it had touched the lower end of the rib, fracturing it and rupturing the intercostal artery, and glancing a little upwards, had slipped round upon the bone, directly beneath the skin. "He 'll live! I know he 'll live!" I exclaimed, and as if in confirmation of my opinion, the old trapper opened his eyes and exhibited signs of returning consciousness.

But much remained to be done. There, at a little distance, lay three savages dead!—killed by my own hand! It seemed like a dream. I could hardly believe it possible, and yet there was no room to doubt. There were too many proofs of a fact, which, if I had read it in any of my favorite romances, I should have thought improbable and exaggerated. One, or at most two Indians would have been enough for any ordinary hero of a novel. But three! What a complete verification of the old adage, that "truth is strange, stranger than fiction." I took a torch and went to where they lay. Their contorted and stiffening forms, and convulsed features, were far more fearful to look upon than they could have been when alive and armed with the powers and energies of determined malice. They looked as though they yet meditated revenge, and revenged they assuredly would be as soon as their fate became known to their friends in the neighborhood, unless something was done to baffle detection or pursuit. Without Joe's assistance I could hardly expect to make much resistance; without his advice, I knew not what to do. I thought of changing our camp; but where could we go? I thought of putting my companion into the canoe and starting for home—but could he stand so long a voyage; and how could I get him round the rapids? It would kill him to carry him on my shoulders in his present state. I tried to talk with him and get his opinion of the probable danger of attack from other Indians, and as to the course we should pursue, but he was too exhausted with loss of blood to comprehend even what I said, much less reply. I was in a perfect quandary. It seemed as if every moment lost was as much as our lives were worth, and I could not but look around upon the tall shadowy trees, and fancy that I could almost hear the yells of a dozen savages, leaping with brandished tomahawks from behind them. In such a case I might perhaps escape by taking to the bush, but poor Joe! his little spark of life would be readily extinguished.

At this moment of my greatest perplexity, a thought of the cave Joe had pointed out to me flashed upon my mind. It came like an inspiration from Deity. I did not wait to think twice, and in less than twenty minutes I had all our essential goods and chattels in the canoe. A few leaves in the bottom of the boat, and our blankets folded on them, made as comfortable a bed as any invalid could wish, and taking up Joe in my arms, who really seemed light from loss of blood, I laid him so gently upon it as hardly to extort a sigh.

Not a little relieved in my mind did I feel when I had pushed out fairly into the lake.' Steering as direct a course as I could, two hours' paddling brought us to where the expanded water again contracted itself to the narrow boundaries of the river. The range of tall black cliffs in which I knew the cave to be, here commenced, but as it ran a distance of several miles, I began to be afraid that I might have some difficulty in finding the exact spot. Fortune, however, favored me, and I had not gone much farther when my canoe ran almost bow-on the little island lying before the cave. Gliding into the narrow and shallow channel between the two, I soon succeeded in fastening the canoe to a small bush directly beneath the ledge that concealed the entrance. Taking a pine-knot and a tinder-box, I commenced climbing up to it, which, as the moon was exceedingly fitful in her light, and as I could not recollect precisely the steps we had taken in the daytime, was more difficult than I expected. Once up, I crept inside and struck a light. A few small bats were at first a little startled by the intrusion, but besides these all was quiet. The aspect of the place was eminently comfortable; it was so dry and clean, while the windings of the long, nearly level, and lofty saloon put at rest all fear of the possibility of a light being seen from the entrance.

But the next question was how to get Joe into it. However, I felt so inspired by my success so far, that I considered that a minor difficulty, which I was determined should not trouble me. I knew I could haul him in easy enough, but my great care was to do it so as not to give him pain, or again start the hemorrhage of his wound. This I contrived to accomplish by pulling the corners of the blanket from beneath him, leaving him in the middle of it, and bringing them up over him and tying them in a firm knot. To this knot I attached a cord of deer-skin, and taking the other end up to the ledge, with a good strong steady pull I brought the blanket, with Joe in it, up to the ledge. A few low groans, which I heard with almost positive pleasure, inasmuch as they showed there was still life in him, a fact which I had more than once doubted as we were coming down, were the only evidences of suffering in his rough ascent. Stretching him temporarily upon the softest-looking stone I could find, in a few minutes I had a bed rigged for him, which, as Joe afterwards acknowledged, was "good enough for the president or the queen of England." A few moments more I had all our goods hauled up, our canoe stowed away in the bushes of the little island, and a good fire throwing around its mellow light and sending up its smoke among the arches and crevices of the cavern, disturbing no one but the bats, who soon found themselves compelled to evacuate the premises.

CHAPTER V.

FOR three weeks we lived in these comfortable and secure quarters, the old man gradually gaining strength, but still incapable of any exertion. He had been so nearly exsanguinated that his recovery was necessarily slow, although it isprobable that but for the loss of blood inflammatory symptoms might have developed themselves, that would have severely taxed my little stock of medical science to treat. For three weeks we thus lived, and yet time did not pass tardily. I had so much responsibility, so much to do, and so much to think of, that the hours glided by with the greatest rapidity.

In the daytime I mostly stayed at home, except during two or three cautious excursions for partridges and other small game, amusing myself as I best might, preparing our meals, talking with Joe, or rather to him, for I would not allow him to say much for fear of the wound in his side, and walking up and down, building castles in the air, in every one of which there was precisely such a nice, cozy, comfortable and secret cavern as ours. In the night I sallied out for fuel and fish: on the other side of the little island, in the main channel, there were plenty of rock-bass, perch, and sunfish; and towards some marshy ground on the opposite side of the river, with an hour's bobbing I could half fill the canoe with eels.

The cooking afforded much occupation and amusement, and exercised my ingenuity not a little. I took it into my head that Joe must have soups of some kind, and boiled meats instead of roast; but unfortunately our tin can had become leaky, and our only other vessel was a small wooden pail; but by unstocking my rifle-barrel, closing up the vent, and inserting the muzzle into an orifice cut into the side of the pail a little above the level of the bottom, I contrived to make a machine that answered every purpose. By inserting the gun-barrel, and putting the other end in the fire, I had a capital soup pot: on plugging up the orifice, I had a water pail or a live-bait bucket. The best materials for soup I

37

found, after several trials, were thin pieces of fish dried in the sun and pounded up with a cracker. "How do you like that?" said I, as I fed the first mess of it to Joe, with a piece of birch bark folded up for a spoon.

"Good!" whispered Joe, "it goes right into my veins."

And then such a variety of soups as we had! There was bass-soup—pickerel-soup—mullet-soup—and eel-soup, with partridge and blackbird broths, and I even attempted a number of experiments at flavoring them with wintergreen, birch-bark, and sassafrass, some of which, I could not but think were tolerably successful, although Joe allowed that he "rather liked the plain soup the best."

It was the last evening of our third week that I was seated before the fire busily engaged stringing worms for an eel-bob : Joe was stretched upon his bed on the opposite side, and, as I supposed, in a sound sleep, but upon looking up from my work I found his eyes fixed upon me with the greatest intentness, and with a peculiar expression that induced me to ask him if he wanted any thing.

"My God! Mr. Jonathan," exclaimed Joe, "how can I ever repay you?"

"Repay me! what for? what do you mean?"

"For all that you have done for me. Here, you have saved my life, and have nursed and tended me just like a mother, and have fed me, and what 's more have stayed here shut up in this old den, without a single impatient look or gesture. I 've watched you all the time. But if I can't repay you perhaps God will, and that 's some comfort."

"Pshaw! Joe, don't talk foolish."

"There 's no foolishness about it. It must be tiresome. This aint no place for a fellow as young and strong as you are, and 't is n't what I bargained you should have, and I 'm not going to stand it any longer. I 've been thinking of something. We may have to stay here three weeks more before I shall be strong enough to walk round the long portage, and you see my ribs want a little tinkering up by the doctors, and that ball cut out of my back ; and besides that, our meal is all out, and our crackers must be nearly gone, for I have noticed that you have not eaten one for several days. Now, I can move about a little here and help myself, and I think that the best plan is for you to lay in a pretty good stock of wood and fish, and then take the canoe and start for the village. We 've got a good moon now, and if you start just at sundown, and paddle all night, you 'll be in the morning at the first rapids, and from there you can easily get in town by three or four o'clock in the afternoon, and then you go right to Dan Wright who keeps the red wooden grocery store, and tell him all about it, and he 'll get somebody with him and start in ten minutes. He 'll be up here in two days, and then I can be carried round the falls and reach home before the week is out."

Joe's proposition was debated *pro* and *con*, but, as it really appeared the only feasible plan, and as he was perfectly confident of being able to do his part, I at last, although with some reluctance, consented to it. Fortunately, however, we were not compelled to put it into execution, as the very next morning the means of escape from our confinement were presented to us.

I had risen rather late, having been employed according to Joe's suggestion during most of the night in laying in a good stock of wood and eels, when, stepping to the mouth of the cave to take a look out, I saw a canoe with two persons in it coming up the stream. I ran for my pocket spy-glass, and soon ascertained that they were white men.

"Then they must be old Simmons and his son," said Joe, "there 's no one else that would be coming up this way."

Satisfied that the old man was right, I got our canoe out from its hiding-place, and paddled out into the main channel to meet them. They were somewhat surprised at seeing me, and listened with not a little interest and even uneasiness to my story.

"Well, I declare now, that 's monstrous bad," exclaimed old Simmons, "why, the ugly critters might take a notion to have a shot at us."

"I should n't wonder," said I. "It would be far the safest plan for you to turn round, and help me to get Mr. Downs down the river."

"Well, perhaps so, but where is he? let 's see him, and see what he says."

We ascended to the cave, when, after a little conversation with Joe, the matter was arranged. A slight touch of anxiety as to the notions of revenge the "ugly critters" might take into their heads quickening the really kind and benevolent feelings of the new-comers, all was soon ready. Joe was lowered into the canoe, and we started off. Arrived at the rapids, we easily made a litter of two poles and a blanket, and carried him round. In the afternoon of the third day we reached the village. Joe was at once put in the doctor's hands, who assured him that he could n't have been better treated, and that a few weeks more would make him as sound and strong as ever. I, however, could not look after him any further, as I found an urgent letter, which had been awaiting me for three or four days, requiring me to come home immediately. "My mother," it stated, "had suddenly been taken quite ill, very ill, indeed dangerously ill"; and I "must lose no time."

Early the next morning I had taken my seat on the mail-stage, and was hurrying home as fast as the nature of the roads would admit, but at a pace that seemed to me the very antithesis of speed. Going over the ground as often as I had at the commencement and end of our quarterly vacations, I had formed quite an intimate acquaintance with the coach-man ; so, seating myself on the box, I plied him with all manner of per-suasives, not forgetting the brandy and water at the stopping-places, and thus made out to get a mile or two an hour more out of his straining team.

Notwithstanding our haste we did not arrive at my native village until quite late in the afternoon. As the coach had a number of passengers to set down, I knew that I could reach home sooner on foot : so jumping from the box, I rushed onward with the speed of fear and hope. As I came within sight of the house, a good many strange and unusual circum-stances attracted my attention. The windows were all open, and I could perceive that a number of people were moving about within. At the door and in the long low porch, where in early infancy I had so often played bo-peep with my mother, through the foliage of the thick wood-bine, and where later she so often sat and listened, with half a smile and half a tear, to the legends I was so fond of reading to her, were several persons silent and motionless, or if moving at all, with evidently cautious steps. In the broad esplanade of green in front of the dwelling, or lean-ing on the white paling, lined with the lilac, the rose, and the honey-suckle, were several quiet groups gazing at the house with a subdued and serious air that sent an icy chill through my beating heart. Some of these were miserably clad—in rags—and had the wo-begone look that poverty, superadded to ill-health, cannot fail to produce, but they were the only natural or cheering part of the sight, for my mother I had been accustomed to see surrounded, more than half her time, by the sick and the poor.

I strode on across the green, and ascended the porch. An old friend of my mother advanced and took my hand. I could not speak, but must have looked the question, for he instantly replied, " She is living yet."

I passed on, and entered the sick room ; the doctor, nurse, and attend-ing friends made way for me, and I stood by her side. My mother must have heard and recognized my footstep, for her glazed eyes had been already dimmed by the touch of death. Her hand extended itself to greet me. I took it, and felt the feeble pressure of her small fingers upon mine. A faint but happy smile played upon her lips ; they parted, and gently, but distinctly, she murmured, " My son ! " The next moment her features were fixed in the cold, hard rigidity of death.

Dead! impossible! It could not be! It could not be that the pleasant and beautiful world had been thus instantaneously palsied at a single stroke—that the sun was for ever darkened, and that the moon would no longer give her cheerful light—that the trees were withered, and the grass faded, and all nature tinged with a black funereal hue of grief and death!

It could not be that life, to me so full of happiness and joy, had, at one blow, been converted into a dismal and dreary blank—a voyage without a haven—a pilgrimage without a shrine! It could not be! and yet it was. There lay the remains of all that made the world a pleasure, life an object, and even heaven a hope.

Oh! the agony of that first night! The darkness of my chamber was comparative light to the intense thick blackness that seemed to fill my brain, and to clog the pulses of my heart. I buried my head in the folds of the pillow, compressed my beating temples with my hands, and struggled, as if with a mighty and fearful demon, who, with a grasp upon my throat, was crushing me to the ground.

The long night had nearly passed, when I was startled by a slight noise in my apartment. It sounded like the passage of some light body through the air, or like the gentle rustling of a leaf. I raised my head from the bed on which I had thrown myself without undressing, and listened. It came again. There was a low, slight murmur, and then my mother's voice distinctly pronounced the words:

"My son! my son!"

The words seemed for a time to float upon the air, and then die away with a cadence so reproachful, yet so sweet and mild, as to pierce the deepest recesses of my heart. They ceased! I raised myself from the bed, and stretching forth my arms, exclaimed, "Mother! mother! speak to me!" But no answer was returned. All was silent, save the occasional foot-fall of the watchers of the dead.

I know that all this can be easily and naturally explained as the effect of imagination—as the mere fancy of a distempered and excited brain. But, if dubious about accepting such an explanation even now, I should have scorned it at the time. The words—the tones, were too distinct—too real. They fell upon my soul like oil upon the troubled waters; or like the voice of Him upon the billows of Gennesareth.

I rose and stood by the side of my mother's remains. I could gaze upon them without feeling longer that utter prostration of soul, that intense and desperate anguish. I knew that that lifeless clay was not my mother; it was something that once appertained to her, and therefore

sacred—something that she had used and had discarded, while she herself was still with me and around me. I felt perfectly calm—almost
happy in the thought, and I acted as I felt; so much so as to excite
remark. On the day of the funeral I overheard one of the spectators say,
      " Well, he seems to take it mighty easy."

      What answer, if I had wished to answer it, could I have made to such
an observation? Have told them, as I then firmly believed, that that was
not my mother they were bearing to the tomb, that she still remained in
the old home, had visited me in my chamber, had spoken to me; I should
have been met with an almost universal smile of derision and contempt.
Fools! fools who thus dare to dogmatize upon the awful and mysterious
possibilities of the spiritual world.

CHAPTER VI.

HOW aptly has time been termed " The Consoler." " The Destroyer " is hardly more appropriate, for surely he relieves as much distress as he causes ; cures as many wounds as he inflicts.

I could not but continue to mourn my mother's death, but time, in his rapid flight, had brought so many new scenes, and thoughts, and feelings, that in a few short weeks I found, much to my surprise, that the keen edge of grief had become materially blunted. I was not only surprised, but ashamed—ashamed that I could not keep up the strong sense of woe—ashamed that I could allow any of the objects or interests of life to drive her image, for a moment, from my mind. I thought there must be something wrong in my moral constitution, and that I deserved to be looked upon by all with that contempt that I felt for myself.

She was so much more than a mere mother to me—a friend and companion: one who took, or with the most delicate tact affected to take, an interest in all my boyish sports and occupations—seldom directly opposing my wishes and inclinations, but adroitly curbing and directing them. How well I could recollect numberless instances of that kind of gentle leading and guiding, which, at the time, I did not perceive or understand ! How many instances, too, of the sacrifice of her feelings and taste to a jealous anxiety for my safety and welfare.

Alas for my sensibility and feeling ! it was but a very few weeks after her decease that I began, as I have said, to take a renewed interest in the affairs of life. In this, however, respect for her expressed wishes actuated me, and, when joined to the solicitations of my guardian and friends, and the desire for some kind of agreeable and useful occupation, induced me to enter upon a course of medical study. I had but little idea that I should ever carry my professional knowledge into practice, but the study itself was sufficiently enticing, and soon it absorbed every faculty of my mind.

There is so much in the science of medicine and its collateral branches

43

to gratify the noblest, as well as the meanest and most prurient curiosity, that it is no wonder that young men take to it with an avidity and enthusiasm that the students of other professions seldom feel. There is none of the aridity complained of in the law—none of the dulness and formality of theology. Every thing is new, fresh, and interesting. The most fertile portion of the broad field of nature is thrown open, wherein lie hidden the most recondite secrets—the most curious mysteries. Anatomy reveals the structure of that wonderful machine, which, in point of complexity, yet perfect adjustment and adaptation of parts, so infinitely surpasses the most ingenious products of the mechanician's skill; Physiology, the vital functions and the intricate laws of life; and Pathology, the organic lesions—the changes of structure—the wear and tear of the animal machine. Chemistry and Materia Medica are broad paths to the very arcana of nature; a little rough, perhaps, at first, but paved with the gems of science and strewn with the flowers of truth. As the student advances, the path grows more and more pleasant and picturesque, disclosing, at each step, new scenes to stimulate curiosity or reward toil. The Institutes and History of Medicine furnish themes for the profoundest reflections, subjects for the most refined philosophic analysis, and incitements to the most engrossing application. The student, as he advances, ascends: his views grow more and more comprehensive; his mental vision takes in the vast materials of a long-continued and copious induction. He finds that there is much truth mingled with much error, but he learns to distinguish between the two; he learns to separate the logical deductions from the vagaries of theory, the prejudices of ignorance, or the perversions of craft. He learns to estimate at their proper value the pretensions of charlatans and the crudities of professional humbugs, who take advantage of that quality of the human mind that disposes it to believe any thing, if it is sufficiently improbable, to foist upon the world some miserable but fortunately short-lived delusion. He sees that there always have been, and probably always will be, such pretenders, and that they always have had, and always will have their dupes, who greedily swallow as new and important discoveries what are oftentimes nothing more than the exploded quackeries of ignorant antiquity. But amid all, he sees the pure stream of science welling from its fountain in Cos—for centuries after the time of Hippocrates, receiving scarce an addition,—now gradually and slowly enlarging its current, steadily winding its way in despite of all obstacles, and mirroring in its waters the very image of truth—truth often indemonstrable from the nature of its essence, and often incommunicable to the vulgar from its form, but still truth. He feels a pride in his profession, the ground of which the uninitiated cannot appreciate or understand. He feels a confidence, too, that, although the credulity of a portion of the public, like the stomach of the ostrich, rejects nothing, however crude, the majority of the intelligent classes will ever believe, that a man of clear head and thorough education, who practises the received principles of his profession, and combines with his personal observation the experience of ages, is full as likely to form correct opinions and give correct advice, as any seventh son of a seventh son, however ignorant ; or any crotchety German enthusiast, however wild.

The time for the commencement of the winter course of lectures approaching, I repaired to the medical college, at New York, where I at first found that every thing did not appear invested with the rose-tints in which my imagination had luxuriated—that there was much in the study of medicine that was disagreeable, much that was downright disgusting. This however was, in the main, but a transient impression. It soon vanished after a little familiarity with the *subject*. It could not long co-exist with that intense professional curiosity which induces men, intended by nature for physicians, to fight with the worms of the charnel-house, their way to knowledge, through the most disgusting masses of putrefying humanity. It could not withstand the contagious recklessness of a medical class.

At the close of the lectures I returned to the village, bringing with me some little experience in metropolitan life, and an increased enthusiasm for professional study.

" How is Smith's child ? " inquired Doctor H——, the younger partner of Doctor S——, as the latter entered the office.

" Dead. He died about half an hour since."

" I thought so," was the reply. " I knew last night that he could n't live twenty-four hours."

The child spoken of was a boy of ten or twelve years of age, and the son of quite an influential, but ignorant and bigoted man, who was noted for his illiberal opposition to any and every one whom he suspected of having pretensions to more knowledge or influence than himself. The boy had been sick some time with a curious and novel form of disease, which had sorely taxed the skill and science of our preceptors. The indications had been investigated and the pathognomic circumstances watched and compared, with a degree of care and anxiety common enough in medical practice, but for which the profession seldom receive any credit, but from the peculiar difficulties of the case, no positive conclusion, as to the exact seat and nature of the complaint, had been arrived at. The symptoms were almost wholly referable to an anomalous lesion of the brain, but the physicians were strongly of opinion that the original cause was some irritation of the digestive organs, which had contrived to mask itself and simulate an affection of the head.

" I suppose they will let us examine him " said Dr. H——.

" That they will not," replied Doctor S——" I have had a talk with them about it, and strongly urged the necessity of an autopsy. The mother is quite willing, in fact she wishes it, but the stupid old fool of a father politely informed me that he 'd see me and all the profession further first."

" That 's very unfortunate."

" Provoking is n't it ? "

" Too bad! too bad ! Can't something be done ? " and the two doctors looked each other full in the eyes for some time with a peculiar wistful inquiring expression, which struck me as rather comical.

" No, no," said Doctor S——, as he turned off with a sigh and a shake of the head. " I 've done every thing I could—the father won't give his consent—if I was thirty years younger that would n't make much differ- ence—but now—I 'm too old. I wish I was a medical student ! "

" I 'd give a hundred dollars for a chance at a post-mortem of that case," said Doctor H—— . " When is the child to be buried ? "

" To-morrow afternoon."

" A hundred dollars," muttered Dr. H—— again, unconsciously.

" And I 'd give twice the sum," replied Doctor S——.

" You need n't give yourselves any trouble about it," said I to myself. " I 'll see what I can do for you," and beckoning to the only one of the students in whose energy and courage I had any confidence, I left the room.

" What do you think ? " said I, as soon as we were outside of the office.

" We can't have a better chance."

" You 're right, and we must improve it ; but we can't trust any of our fellow-students till after it is over. If we should say any thing to them about it, the whole town would know what an astonishing feat was con- templated ; if they did not tell it, they would look so frightened that every one would see there was something in the wind."

Punctual to the hour, we took up our line of march for the graveyard, which was almost a mile distant, and completely buried in the woods. The moon had gone down, leaving a somewhat cloudy sky ; but still there was sufficient starlight to reveal the masses of thick foliage, with black, giant-looking trunks, and the uncouth shadowy branches of the trees. But why enter into a minute account of an adventure which, with many, will excite disagreeable associations, and which I should not allude to at all were it not for the lasting influence it has had upon my destiny. Suffice it to say, that in silence, save a few whispered sentences, we made our way to the grave, which had been previously examined and marked, so that we could readily find it in the dark, when we should come to restore the little one to his resting-place.

Arrived at the office, of which we had taken the precaution to secure a key, we stealthily entered, and secreted our prize in a little unoccupied attic. This done, the door carefully secured, we betook ourselves each to his home and to bed.

To bed, but not to sleep. I was altogether too inexperienced in the art of body-snatching for that. I tossed and tumbled about as wakeful and as restless as if I had been dining with a party of ghouls, and the charnel-house viands had produced a fit of indigestion. I felt not so much remorse, but the dread of detection came strong upon me. I had an overwhelming presentiment that the result of the affair would be exceedingly disagreeable.

The morning came; but it brought no relief. It seemed as though the night's exploit must be already publicly known; and as I sneaked along to the office I fancied that every one whom I encountered looked at me with a peculiarly inquisitive and suspicious glance. I would have given worlds that the deed had been left undone, especially as the worst of it was still to come, and that was to make it known to the principals of the office. How would they receive the news? What would they say? What would they do? I began to have strong doubts of the meaning that I had attributed to their remark of the day before; and my fellow-student I found in an equal degree of perplexity. Several times I attempted to broach the subject to Dr. H——, as the one least likely to find fault with our performance, but as often the slightest word or circumstance would be sufficient to turn me from the point, and the day passed in doubt and indecision. The next day came, and with it a firm determination to know the worst; but before I could get a chance to talk about it with either of our preceptors, circumstances transpired which saved me the trouble, and put an end for ever to my professional career.

It was just as Dr. S—— was getting into his gig to visit a distant patient, whose case I knew to be urgent, that I saw Squire D——, one of the justices of the peace, come up to him and speak a few words, which seemed strongly to excite the doctor's attention. A feeling of apprehension came over me, which was still further increased, when after a short conversation, the doctor refastened his horse, and the two entered the office, retiring to a private room, and carefully shutting the door. At any other time the circumstance would have excited no remark; but just then it had a most portentous aspect, and I awaited the result of the conference with the profoundest conviction that the subject of it was the cold and silent tenant that we had introduced to the attic room.

In a few minutes I had confirmation strong—the door opened, and the doctor called me in.

"Do you know any thing about these articles?" said he, pointing to a splinter of mahogany and a small piece of linen that were lying on the table.

I shook my head.

"Come, come!— be quick! A nice scrape you 've got yourself into, and, if you want to get out of it, there 's no time to lose. John told me that you came into the office night before last with a bundle in your arms, and old Jackson, coming through the graveyard, picked up these things alongside of the grave of Smith's child. He handed them to our friend here; but several other persons know of it, and a good deal of suspicion is excited. As soon as it comes to Smith's ears the grave will be examined, a formal complaint made, and a search-warrant issued, and then we shall be in a devilish pretty mess."

I saw that the game was all up, and that I might as well tell the whole story. Doctor H—— was called in, my guardian and the friends of my companion sent for, and a consultation held as to the best means of escaping the consequences of our ill-advised and ill-conducted performance. It was decided that, to exonerate themselves, the doctors should lay a regular information before the justice of the peace, who would be in no hurry to act upon it, and that towards evening, two young men, carefully disguised, should be rowed with an appearance of mystery to the Canada side of the St. Lawrence, while my fellow-student should be despatched to some distant relatives, and I should start for New York. This would lead to the belief that we had gone to Canada, and, in a short time, it was expected, some compromise could be made, and the affair entirely blow over.

Acting upon this plan, I made my way, by a circuitous route to the high road, at a point some distance from the town, and awaited the arrival of Dr. H——, who came along in his gig, and taking me up, carried me on to the next village, where I was to take a seat in the mail-stage as it past through.

I took my seat in the coach in no pleasant frame of mind; but the *nil desperandum* principle, which was constitutionally a favorite with me, soon regained its influence, and I began to think that a trip to the great city, under any circumstances, could hardly fail to be agreeable. In four days' staging, canalling, and steaming, during which I had ample time to reflect upon the prominent events of my life, which in less than a year had followed each other with so much rapidity, I arrived in New York; but until I had fairly set foot upon Cortlandt Street quay, I could hardly believe that I had not been all the time in a dream. I found the utmost difficulty in impressing myself with a " realizing sense" of my position and prospects. Events so important, and apparently so improbable, had happened so easily and so naturally, that I was almost inclined to think that they had not happened at all. I pondered over my adventure with Joe

from whom, by-the-by, I had received a letter, informing me that he had recovered from his wound, and that the Indians having returned to their homes in Canada without saying any thing about our adventure, it had ceased to be talked of, and would in a short time be forgotten ; and I thought of the death of my mother, of my medical course and of my body-snatching performance, until I had almost thought myself into quite a distressing state of dubitation as to my personal identity.

The first two days after my arrival were passed in calling upon a few friends, looking up some college acquaintances who resided in the city, and visiting my former haunts, the infirmaries, hospitals, and museums. On the third, at an early hour, I repaired to the post-office, and received, as I expected, several letters—one from Dr. H——, one from my guardian, and one from my fellow-students. But what was my disappointment and consternation at their contents ! They were all of the same tenor and to the effect that the affair had become public, and had produced infinitely more excitement than had been anticipated ; that the father and family were perfectly implacable ; that old Smith, enraged at what he considered a gross insult to his standing and position in society, was determined to pursue the case to the utmost ; that he had, somehow, got information that I had not gone to Canada, and that he was about to offer a large reward for my apprehension ; that this would stimulate the activity of the city police, and I would certainly be arrested unless I got out of the country immediately. For this purpose a draft was enclosed by my guardian, which I was directed to get turned into a bill upon Liverpool, London, or Havre, or any place to which the first packet should sail. It was particularly and repeatedly urged that I should be quick in my movements, as my enemies were in earnest, and their operations would be pushed with vigor and decision.

I had turned into the large and splendid refectory in the neighborhood of the post-office, and seated myself in a corner to read my letters. The room began gradually to fill with hungry and thirsty customers, and to resound with a confused babble of sounds, many of which would have puzzled any one but an American, however well acquainted with the English language, to understand. From one side came loud and frequent calls for certain familiar eatables, such as sandwiches, buckwheat cakes, mince pie, and cranberry tarts; while from the other proceeded certain cabalistic exclamations, quite unintelligible to me, such as "dodger," "smasher," "whiskey-skin," and "gin-doodle," with an occasional stentorian invitation "to take something," and the kind inquiry "what 'll you have?" The confusion, however, disturbed me but little, as I sat abstracted, pondering upon the contents of my letters and the course of conduct marked out for me.

My revery was interrupted by a heavy hand upon my shoulder. I started and turned, expecting to meet nothing less than the visage of that renowned impersonation of prehensile acuteness—the Vidocq of New York—old Hays. But I was agreeably surprised to find only the rough, but good-natured face of an old acquaintance, Captain Coffin, who had formerly commanded, in my father's service, a schooner upon Lake Ontario, and who had several times visited the St. Lawrence, since his death. The captain was a short, thick-set man, with a dark sunburnt countenance, but with a heart big enough for a giant, and as pure and as soft as a child's. A thorough seaman, with a good deal of general information, and as generous as that often-quoted model of generosity, "a prince," he was one of the class of men who have done so much honor to our mercantile marine; having elevated the character of the merchant-captain to a level with that of the officers of our national service.

"Jonathan Romer, as I 'm alive!" he exclaimed. "How do you do? How long have you been in town? What is the news? Here, Captain Folger," speaking to his companion, "I 'll make you acquainted with Jonathan Romer, son of your old master, Seth Romer. Captain Folger, Jonathan."

"Chip of the old block, aint he, captain? My stars, how he has grown! When I first knew him he was n't more than so high, and now just see what a tall fellow, full six feet in the clear, and as tough and as withy as a young hickory. Do you recollect, Jonathan, your ride upon the main-gaff? I 'll tell you how it was, Captain Folger. The schooner that I commanded had just got in from her trip up the lake, when Captain Romer, my owner, came on board, bringing this youngster, then not much over three years old, with him. The fore- and main-sails had been hauled up; the crew had most of them strolled ashore, and the captain and I went down into the cabin to look over some papers. In a few minutes his father missed Jonathan, and we ran up on deck but could n't see any thing of him. ' Jonathan ! ' sung out the captain, as if he was hailing to windward in a hurricane. ' Here I am, father,' squeaked a voice right overhead. We looked up, and there was the young monkey astride of the main-gaff, and holding on to the peak halliards. The vangs had n't been hauled taut, and the gaff was swinging about, and every now and then bringing up with a jerk that would have sent a cat with ten claws flying. I 'll tell you what, if no one ever saw Seth Romer turn pale or tremble before, they might have seen him then. He could n't speak, and I was glad of it, for I did n't want to startle or frighten the boy. I jumped and took in the slack of the vangs. ' Hold on tight,' said I, ' until I come up and help you down.' ' No,' said he, ' I 'll come down myself,' and before I could say a word he slewed himself under the gaff, got hold of the vang, and came down by the run as neatly as ever you saw a fellow slide down a backstay. ' How on earth did you get up there? ' said I, for I was puzzled. We had n't missed him more than five minutes. There were no ratlines to our main rigging, and there was an uncommon hoist to the main-sail ; besides, the throat halliards had been slackened a little, and the gaff peaked up considerably more than half-way between nothing at all and a church steeple. ' How on earth did you get up there? ' ' Oh, I creeped up them ropes, and then I creeped down them ropes, and I creeped out on that big stick —'

" ' Yes, and I 'll teach you how to creep out of my sight next time,' said his father, untwisting a nice nettle from a piece of inch-and-half.

" ' No, no,' said I, ' you must pardon him this time ; he won't do so again. Why, captain,' said I to him aside, ' you might flog him for a week, you could n't flog it out of him— it 's in his blood ; he 'll know the ropes yet.' ' God forbid,' said the captain ; ' but was n't it beautiful? '

" But come, Jonathan. What 's the news? "

Captain Folger taking his leave, we drew our chairs to one side, and entered into a long and circumstantial conversation, in the course of which I explained to Captain Coffin the business that had brought me to New York, and showed him the letters which I had just received.

" Well, I declare now," said he, as he finished reading them, " it 's the luckiest thing in the world."

" What is the luckiest thing? " I demanded, somewhat surprised at his tone and words.

"Why, that I happened to meet you," he replied. "I've got one of the finest foretopsail schooners you ever saw, and she's all ready loaded with staves and a few boards for the Western Islands. I did not intend to sail until day after to-morrow; but I guess I can make my arrangements to get off to-morrow morning. You shall go along with me. It will be just fifty chances to one that we shall have to go on to Malaga to dispose of our cargo and take in a load of dried fruit and wine. You'll have a first-rate chance to practise your Spanish with the Malaga señoras."

Nothing of course could have been more agreeable or better timed than the captain's proposition, and I at once addressed myself with activity to the required preparations. The rest of the day was just sufficient to finish several letters, and make the necessary purchases of clothing, nautical charts, quadrant, spy-glass, etc., with some fifty volumes of miscellaneous books, consisting principally of old voyages and travels from the shelves of the street book-stands. Early the next morning I boarded the *Lively Anne*, just as she had commenced pulling out from the dock. The sails were soon hoisted and shifted well aft, and we commenced working down the bay against a wind that compelled us to make several tacks. Upon rounding fairly into the offing the wind became more free, and the *Lively Anne* bounded off at a rate that soon sank the highlands of Jersey below the edge of the distant horizon, leaving me for the first time shut in by the blue concave, upon the foam flecked expanse of the restless, heaving sea. Who that has ever ventured forth upon the great deep but will recollect, if he cannot describe, the whirl of contending emotions with which for the first time he has seen the blue vault of ether resting in uninterrupted union upon that

> "Glorious mirror, where th' Almighty's form
> Glasses itself in tempests,"

or listened to the deep tones of

> "The strongest of creation's sons,
> That rolls the wild, profound, eternal bass
> In nature's anthem."

CHAPTER VII.

MY emotions were cut short by certain queer feelings in the epigastric region, which warned me of a very common circumstance in a first voyage, that I had left out entirely in all my calculations of the pleasures of the sea. Although I had inherited a taste for the bounding billows, I had by no means inherited an immunity

" Much shattered and contained no one."

from their nauseating influence. Disappointed and indignant, I had to take to my berth with such a distressing gyration of the brain, such a combination of disgusting tastes in my mouth, and such a complete prostration of all mental and physical power, that I would have given worlds for the use of the smallest possible portion of terra firma for an hour.

Early in the morning of the sixth day out, it was announced that there was something like a boat in sight. We altered our course a little and, when near enough, discovered, as it inclined upon the side of a wave, that it was much shattered and that it contained no one. We stood on, however, and picked it up for firewood. When hauled out of the water a "school" of little rudder fish, which had been playing in and about the boat, took up their quarters directly beneath the stern of the schooner, whence I amused myself in transferring them to the "doctor's" frying-pan. Conjecture was of course busy in my brain, as to how and why this boat was abroad in the middle of the Atlantic, and I persisted in boring Captain Coffin with all manner of supposable cases.

"Oh, no, there is no *ground* for your conclusions," said the captain, quite unconscious of the fact that he had perpetrated a very tolerable pun.

But I would n't give it up so. In fancy, I saw a distressing shipwreck, with all the attending circumstances; and, returning to my berth, I composed some verses, in which largely figured a young husband—who, from having forgotten the name I then chose, I will now call John Smith—and his interesting wife and children. John was hastening home after a long absence, with feelings of unabated affection, and Mrs. Smith was expecting his return with tears of hope and fear. But Smith is dead, "dead ere his prime! young John Smith!" Oh, Smith!

> "It was that fated and perfidious bark,
> Built in the eclipse, and rigged with curses dark,
> That sunk so low that sacred head of thine."

"There," said I to the captain, "what do you think of that?" showing him my elegiac attempt.

"Why, I think," he replied, carefully conning over the lines, "think that Mrs. Smith's tears are all in my eye, and that her children, like beggars' babies, are borrowed for the occasion. That boat shipped a little water, and broke from her davits; and that's all about it. Such things happen every day. But what is the meaning of this motto you 've got here at the head—' rigged with curses dark'? I don't understand that. If it was 'loaded with curses dark' there would be some sense in it. I recollect a case in point. It was said that old Commodore Ben Swain never required any ballast, because he could curse his ship's hold full of oaths, and bring her down to her heavy-load line in less than five minutes; but *rigging* a ship with curses is a different matter. To be sure, you can rattle 'em *out* fast enough; but how can you rattle 'em *down?*"

"Land ho!" cut short the captain's criticism upon Milton's famous elegy. It proved to be the islands of Corvo and Flores, the most westerly of the Azores, or Western Islands. Corvo, a small rocky island, so named from its resemblance to a crow, and on which it is said was found by the first visitors, some time before the discovery of America, an equestrian statue, with a hand pointing to the west, was too far to the north of us for a distinct view. Flores we saw more distinctly. Passing within a few miles of it we could plainly perceive the masses of volcanic rock of which it is composed. As far inland as the eye could reach along the verdant ravines and gorges the land appeared to be in the highest state of cultivation. Every foot of the meagre soil seemed to have been wrested by the hand of industry from the dominion of nature, and made to subserve the interests of a poor, ignorant, superstitious, but honest and hard-working, population. We all concluded from the distant, but tolerably distinct view that we had of it, that Flores must be worthy of its name—the island of flowers.

Passing by Flores we saw the next morning in the distance the island of Fayal, and about four in the afternoon we rounded the high point which juts out on one side of the harbor or roadstead of Orta, and came all at once in full view of the town. Orta, with its white-washed stone buildings, and, interspersed, the towers and steeples of churches and convents, presents a brilliant and interesting aspect from the sea; but upon landing the illusion is soon dissipated, as is generally the case with all Spanish, Portuguese, or African towns. Dilapidated buildings, narrow, dirty streets, and a forlorn-looking population give token of ignorance, superstition, and misgovernment. The situation of the town is exceedingly beautiful, lying along the base of a steep range of volcanic hills, which rise from the shore to the height of a thousand feet, and enclose it on three sides; it has spread before it the roadstead, in which are frequently displayed the flags of our American whalers, who visit it for vegetable supplies; and across the harbor, at the distance of five or six miles, the island of Pico, from which shoots up, to the height of seven or eight thousand feet, one of the most beautiful natural objects in the world. It is a perfectly symmetrical, conical mountain, called the "Peak," occupying nearly the whole of the small island to which it gives its name; and rising, as it were, directly from the sea, the eye commands every foot of the acclivity, and takes in at one glance the whole of its beautiful proportions. Frequently a great part of the scenic effect of a lofty mountain is lost from the irregularity of the base and the difficulty of determining at what point the mountain commences. In this case there is no uncertainty, and the whole elevation is at once attributed to the magnificent cone, which rears its lofty apex far into the region of the clouds, which in a thousand fantastic and ever-varying shapes wreath their vapory forms around it.

Upon landing we were politely welcomed by the American consul, and conducted to his house, where I was received with unexpected kindness and attention, and invited to take up my quarters while I remained, an invitation which I was unfortunately able to avail myself of for only one night, as Captain Coffin soon ascertained that his staves, which were intended for the Pico wine—large quantities of which are obtained from the vineyards on the slopes of the Peak, and exported from Fayal to the United States,—were not in demand, and that he must seek a market in some other port.

Sound and sweet was the first night's sleep in a foreign land. Once in the night the loud bray of a donkey directly beneath my window broke in on my slumbers, but the interruption was far from being unpleasant. I had never heard a donkey's voice before, and I was somewhat startled and astonished, and quite delighted. It was really spirit-stirring. It spoke in deep and, as I thought, melodious tones of a thousand things new, strange, foreign, and exciting. I longed to hear it again, but the stupid beast, with the perversity of his nature, refused to gratify me. Perhaps, however, in this I do him, as the world has ever done his kind, injustice. Could he have known how much I wished to hear his tuneful voice once more, it may be that he would have pitched his pipes to their most sonorous key. But he was ignorant of my feelings, and, vainly waiting and wishing, I sunk again to sleep.

Taking a hint from the sun, I arose, and in company with some members of the consular family descended to the gardens and extensive orangeries, devoted to the supply of a good portion of the fruit of the English market. Coming from the cold latitudes of the St. Lawrence, where nature's feeble hortulan efforts had received but little assistance from the ingenuity of man, I enjoyed to ecstasy the colors, perfumes, and motions of the affluent vegetation. The garden of what was the old American consulate I was prepared to admire, from the descriptions of several travellers, who had particularly noticed it in their accounts of the Western Islands. I found it small, consisting of several terraces upon the side of a hill, but well laid out and beautifully cultivated. There, in friendly contiguity, were growing the fruits and flowers of almost every clime—the camphor, coffee, ginger, cinnamon; the orange, lime, lemon, banana, and dragon tree, with the aloe, peach, plum, fig, and the passion-flower, with its delicious pendulous fruit; and a hundred others were all grouped in this delightful spot. Of flowers there was a great variety of the most magnificent kinds—roses, dahlias, hydrangias, heliotropes, honeysuckles, japonicas, and some splendid specimens of the cactus. I have since seen many of those trees and flowers in their native climes, and under skies more congenial ·to their habits and constitutions, but never in the profusest luxuriance of their favorite abodes have they seemed to me as beautiful as then. For a blissful hour I revelled in their morning sweets, forgetful of the past, and happily unconscious of the dreary doom impending over my head.

" Hurrah for Malaga!" exclaimed Captain Coffin, jumping upon the deck of the *Lively Anne.* "Up with the anchor. Mr. Sims—we'll get under weigh immediately!"

"Aye! aye, sir!" responded the mate. "Is the cargo of fruit coming on board?" pointing to a boat-load of apricots, figs, plums, and melons that I had brought off with me. "Very well, sir," he continued, receiving an affirmative reply. "If it will only keep till it is all eaten, there would be no fear of scurvy for one six months, but I should n't like to insure the ship against cholera morbus. Come! bustle about, men. Hitch on the boat falls, and rouse her in. Do you hear? stir, your d——d lazy stumps. Ship the windlass bars—heave away—heave with a will! What, in the devil's name are you at there you d——d lubberly monkey, with a blue skin stuck in your mouth as big as a frigate's dead-eye? can't you work first and eat afterwards?"

This polite inquiry was addressed to a youngster, who, loath to lose a fine blue fig, had seized it with his teeth, while with both hands he took a pull at the topping lift.

"Softly! softly! Mr. Sims," interposed the captain. "You know I don't like to have the men damned, unless it is absolutely necessary. There never was a crew that needed it less than ours."

"You'd a sworn too, I guess," retorted Mr. Sims, "if you'd seen the fellow. Apples of gold in pictures of silver are said to be beautiful, but blue figs in such a d——d mahogany frame as that, aint the thing at sea, when work is to be done."

"A good fellow is Sims," said the captain to me, as the mate turned off to his duty, "and a capital officer, if he would only give up his habit of grumbling and cursing. He's got a notion that it is necessary to find fault, and swear freely, in order to command the attention and respect of the crew, and I can't convince him how wonderfully he is mistaken. Your regular tartar is often respected by sailors; but it is generally for other qualities than tartness and severity, and, least of all, for injustice and inhumanity. Sailors never liked to be cursed and hectored about, however much they be used to it. Why, I 'll bet, with a right kind of a first officer, I can take an American crew and go around the world, without a high word spoken after the first three days."

Captain Coffin paused in his discourse, and we both turned to take a parting look of the Peak, which was rapidly growing bluer and smaller, with the wind abeam, we gradually sunk it over our starboard quarter.

The breeze veered two or three points by the stern. "You may, Mr. Sims, set the fore-topmast studding-sails, this wind is too good to last long, and we 'd better make the most of it," saying which, the captain descended to the cabin, leaving me to promenade the deck, and watch the stars emerging from the last beams of the purple twilight, that with unwonted pertinacity, of such a low latitude, continued to struggle against advancing night for the mastery of the water and the heavens.

In conformance to our wishes, rather than our expectations, the wind continued all night full and free, and we bowled along before it at a rate which, by morning, left nothing of the isles behind us in sight. As the day advanced the wind gradually decreased, until about noon it nearly ceased, coming only in gentle cat's paws, with hardly strength enough to wrinkle the surface of the water, or steady the flapping sails, and followed by intervals of dead calm. The intense heat of the sun, despite of my broad-brimmed Panama hat, had driven me below, where I found the captain quietly seated at his desk, and busy with a voluminous manuscript, which he intended as a letter to his wife, to be sent by the first homeward-bound vessel we should encounter. Ten chances to one we should have no such opportunity, but then it was a labor of love which, even if the captain had to deliver the letter himself, would not be entirely thrown away. The example had its influence, and I also got out my writing materials, and was soon absorbed in the labor of turning sentences and rounding periods, which, although addressed to one, my vanity intended for the admiration of all of my friends in the village of O——. Scratch, scratch went our pens over the paper, interrupted by no sound except an occasional flap of the huge main-sail, or the creaking, now and then, of a block or a bulkhead, as the schooner lazily rolled, and rose and fell upon the long smooth seas.

Suddenly the loud, stern voice of Mr. Sims, in tones of the highest excitement, burst upon us like a clap of thunder in a cloudless sky.

" Luff ! luff ! " he exclaimed with startling energy. " Down with your helm ! hard down ! Let go the head sheets ! Let go every thing ! "

At the first order Captain Coffin sprang up the companion-way, and I followed directly behind him. As my head fairly emerged above deck I heard the captain shriek out the order to let go the halliards. At this instant the schooner was knocked clear over, and a portion of spray, driven with a rapidity that gave it a force almost as great as that of grape-shot, struck me on the side of the head and dashed me against the side of the hatchway, when I must have rolled back down the cabin stairs perfectly senseless.

CHAPTER VIII.

HOW long I remained in that condition I know not, but I suppose it could not have been more than ten or fifteen minutes. Upon recovering I found myself stretched out alongside the starboard lockers beneath a pile of chairs, tables, writing-desks, books, etc., and the cabin floor standing up almost perpendicularly, like a wall, down which every thing movable had rolled to leeward. The schooner was on her beam ends. A good deal bruised, I contrived to extricate myself with some difficulty, and clamber by the inclined stairway to the deck. There a scene of destruction and desolation broke upon me, to which I feel myself perfectly incapable of doing full justice; still less can I expect to convey any thing like a true impression of the emotions which it excited. The short time that I had been insensible had sufficed for the furious squall to do its worst; and sailing off, perhaps in search of other objects, on which to vent its mighty wrath, it had left its shattered prey a wreck upon the bosom of the quiet, gently undulating sea. Not the slightest commotion indicated the recent passage of the storm-fiend, and hardly a breath of air ruffled the surface of the sluggish swell that slowly rolled its slumbering length beneath the fierce brightness of the unclouded sky. Yet there lay the *Lively Anne*, a few minutes before so trim and buoyant, now capsized and hampered with the wreck of spars and sails, and shorn of the graceful gear, wherein had lain the greater portion of her beauty and her speed. The jib-boom and fore-mast were gone by the board; the main-mast, however, remained, and that, with the heavy sail and gaff top-sail, which had got loaded with water, held the schooner down and prevented her from righting herself. Portions of the weather bulwarks were shattered, and the whole of the starboard bulwarks stove fore and aft, leaving only three or four stanchions standing. The long boat, cook's galley, water casks, harness casks, tool chest, and all the fixtures of the deck, except the windlass, were gone. Not a vestige of any thing movable remained, save the axe, which hung in a becket by the main-mast, and a few splinters of the shattered wheel binnacle and booby hatch.

But the most distressing part of the affair was that not the slightest indication of a living being presented itself. I crept forward and shouted down the forecastle. No voice answered. I was alone upon the waste of waters, "sole monarch" not, alas! of a "peopled deck," but of a solitary and dismantled wreck. Of all our company, consisting of captain, mate, cook, and five seamen, not one remained to explain the how and wherefore of our sad mishap. Whether it was a white squall or a water-

" The first thing was to give the schooner a chance to right itself."

spout ; whether the destruction had been principally effected by the wind or water, and whether proper care might not have saved us, are questions which must forever remain unanswered. I would have asked them, but alas! there was no one to reply. The conviction of the sad fate of my companions, and of the awful solitariness of my situation, which for some time I was loath to admit, completely unmanned me. Seating myself upon the stump of the broken mast, I freely paid the tribute of my bitter tears to the cruel and deceitful sea. But mine, as I have said, was not a temperament given to weeping ; in fact, it needed but a little more age, and a little more seasoning in the rough school of active life, to dry up the fountains of grief for ever. I soon had my "cry out," and, drying my eyes, took a long look around the horizon for sails. Not one was in sight.   Satisfied that it was in vain to hope for assistance from any quarter, at least for the present, my regards naturally returned to the wreck. Something must be done, and, as I was the only living thing, it was pretty evident that, if it was done at all, it must be done by myself.

The first thing was to give the schooner a chance to right itself, which I saw she would readily do if relieved of the mainmast and heavy sails. I thought that perhaps it might be useful to leave a portion of the mast standing for the purpose of hoisting a signal if I should be so fortunate as to fall in with any vessels.   So, taking the axe, I crept out upon the inclined spar about ten or twelve feet, and made a deep cut, where I proposed the fracture should take place.   Returning on board, a few blows upon the lanyards of the tautened rigging released from its supports the mast, which instantly, with a loud crack, broke off short at the point which I had scored.   The schooner, relieved from the powerful leverage of the heavy water-logged top hamper, righted herself at once, with a violent surge, and as none of the cargo had shifted, resumed a perfectly upright and stable position.   I was not much of a practical seaman, as the reader may judge from the little experience I had had; but I was tolerably familar with many of the expedients resorted to in various cases, and as I knew not how long I might have to remain on the wreck, I concluded that the safest way would be to make at once the best disposition I could against a storm.   With this view I got up the end of a small hawser from the fore-hatch, passed it out the hawse-hole, and made it fast to the rigging of the main-mast, fore-mast, and jib-boom, which were still alongside, and attached to the hull by portions of the lee-shrouds and running rigging.   I then cut away every thing, and veered out the hawser, making the inner end fast to the windlass and the splinters of the fore-mast.   A light breeze had now sprung up, and, as I expected, the comparatively high hull of the schooner floated before it faster than the mass of spars, which, lagging behind, dragged upon the hawser, and kept the schooner head to the wind.   In a hard blow the force exerted by the spars would be very great; they would also serve to break the force of the sea, and if, in addition to them, I could contrive to rig a tarpaulin or some rag of canvas upon the remnant of the mainmast, I had no doubt of being able to keep my vessel in a very comfortable and weatherly position.   The correctness of these calculations I afterwards found repeatedly verified.

My next movement, after clearing the wreck, was to examine the pumps.   To my great delight, I found upon sounding, but two feet of water in the hold, which I concluded must have come in, the greater portion of it, at least, through the strained seams of her upper works while the schooner was on her beam ends. Not that there was much immediate danger, the nature of her cargo considered, even if she leaked freely, but it would be so much more agreeable to have a dry, tight, and buoyant vessel, although shorn of her fair proportions and left an unmanageable float upon the surface of the ocean. A few vigorous strokes by lessening the depth of water confirmed my conclusion. Satisfied that there was no dangerous or permanent leak, I continued under the excitement of hope the exertion of pumping until I had nearly exhausted both the water and my own strength. I paused, wiped away the perspiration rolling in torrents down my face, and took another long, steady look around the horizon. A flock of Mother Carey's chickens and a few fleecy clouds in the sky were the only moving objects in sight.

It was now nearly four o'clock in the afternoon, and certain cravings of the stomach reminded me that my usual dinner hour had long since passed. It may seem strange that under the circumstances I could think of eating : but in a hearty youth of twenty, the physical appetites do not give place so readily to mental emotions, however strong the latter may be. I felt thirsty too, and I looked around for some means of satisfying the desire. At this moment the awful truth burst upon me, that not a drop of fresh water remained. I knew that our whole stock was upon deck, in casks, lashed to the booms and the stanchions of the bulwarks. The whole had been swept away. I ran up and down the deck, and looked under and over the remaining bulwarks in perfect dismay. I thought that there must be a small cask left somewhere, although there was no place on the open and clear deck where could have been concealed an ordinary drinking can. I no longer thought of eating, but my thirst increased with wonderful rapidity. A few minutes before, a glass of water would have sufficed, now I felt as though I could drain a hogshead. "Good Lord !" I exclaimed, with that curious mingling of the ridiculous and the serious, common to some minds : "if I were only the highlands of the Hudson, with the North River running right through me !"

I rushed down into the cabin, with the poor hope of finding a little water in the pitcher, that might serve to avert, at least for a few hours, the approach of death in his most horrible form ; it had been overturned and broken ! The steward's pantry hardly better repaid my anxious search. About half a glass of cold coffee, the remains of our last comfortable and social breakfast, was all the fluid that I could find. My thirst increased, my mouth grew parched and feverish, my pulses throbbed, and my whole frame trembled with excitement, as the conviction of the ultimate certainty of death, by the pangs of thirst, came stronger and stronger upon me. All that I had ever heard or read of suffering from thirst, by sea or land, rushed, thronging to my recollection. Brissot, Adams, Paddoc, Riley, with his horrible expedient of double and treble refiltrations, and a dozen more, whose records of hardships, endured upon the Sahara and other desert coasts, had been my favorite reading, started up all at once, in high relief upon the surface of memory. Could it be that I had been saved from the comparatively mild fate of my companions, only to suffer the lingering agonies which these voyagers had so strongly depicted? Amid the vast ocean of water, was there not one drop of hope—one sweet draught, with which to dilute the cup of despair? "O God! save me!" I ejaculated, as I fell, rather than seated myself, upon the transom. I bowed my head to my knees, and prayed with that fervor resulting from an aroused and all-pervading sense of dependence upon the Supreme Being for the simplest and most common elements of life. Let him who looks upon the choicest gifts of Providence, the air, the water, or the light, as his natural and indefeasable right, as something valueless, from the profusion with which they have been bestowed, and as demanding no thankful acknowledgments like the more immediate personal and particular evidences of God's merciful care—let such a one be placed in my situation, and he will feel, what is often enough admitted in general terms, that gratitude is due as much, or more, for the gifts which administer to the necessities of our physical being, than for the luxuries of appetite, the gratification of intellect, or the pleasures of taste.

I arose, calm, collected, and confiding. My prayers had been heard, and, somehow, I felt confident would be answered. A ship would heave in sight, or genial showers would be sent to my relief! something! any thing! I knew not what or how, but at any rate, I was not to be abandoned to perish. At this moment, my eye happened to be directed to the captain's state-room, in one corner of which were standing, fastened to a rack, a couple of old muskets, with a long leather shot pouch dangling between them. The means and mode of my salvation were revealed. With these and the coffee-pot, I felt confident of making an apparatus with which sea water might be distilled in sufficient quantities. The reaction of mind and body, upon this discovery, was astonishing. I no longer felt thirsty or fatigued; relieved from the apprehension of the greater evil, all that had passed seemed light in comparison. The sad fate of my companions, cut off, as they had been, so suddenly, in the bloom of health and happiness, was almost forgotten. Even the dreary solitude and uncertainty of my situation gave me no further trouble. Every thing was for the best! God was above me, and around me, and I should not die of thirst!

Some cold Indian cake, a biscuit, with a slice of pork, and the dregs of the coffee-pot, made a capital meal; after which I set myself actively to work upon my proposed distilling apparatus. The two muskets were soon unstocked and unbreeched and cleaned; the two ends of the barrels were notched with a file, approximated to each other, and inserted into a short tube of leather, cut from the shot pouch, which was afterwards sewed all around, and firmly secured, with tarred twine. A long pipe, conveniently flexible at the leather joint, was thus formed, and the whole of it afterwards wrapped from end to end with strips of blanket, for the purpose of keeping it wet with the cool sea water. A small block of pine, hewn from the stump of the fore-mast, was bored through by means of the file and jack-knife, to a size that on one side would tightly fit the end of my musket barrel worm, and on the other, closely cap the spout of the coffee-pot. By turning and grinding it upon the ends of the pipe and the spout, and carefully working it with a round file, the joints were made sufficiently close and accurate. The lid of the vessel not fitting very perfectly, it took some time to adapt a cover of wood, which, upon trial, was found to answer the purpose exactly, as the slight swelling of the wood, from the effects of the steam, made the joint completely airtight.

It remained now to rig some kind of a furnace, by which heat could be applied to my rude apparatus. It had become quite dark, but I had no disposition to give over work until the experiment had been tried, and my sanguine hopes either dissipated or realized. The cook's galley, with the other fixtures of the deck had been swept away, and not a fragment of stove, stew-pans, or any articles of kitchen furniture remained, but, in the cabin pantry I found a large earthen baking dish, from which the unfortunate " Doctor " had not unfrequently regaled us with divers pleasing compounds of pastry, with rice, apples, eggs, chickens, and pork. He little dreamed to what last uses his pudding dish would come to be applied! An empty flour barrel, firmly fastened down to the deck with a number of spikes driven into the upper head, served as a stand for the dish, across which a few pieces of wire were arranged as a grate. Upon this I placed the coffee-pot filled up to the spout with sea water, and joined to it the pipe, which led down to a tin can placed upon the deck. A fire of splinters of dry staves was soon kindled, and I had nothing left to do but to feed it occasionally and anxiously await the result. Never did alchemist watch his crucible for the moment of projection with a more curious eye than did I for the ebullition of my still. At last the water boiled, and the strong firelight streaming up in the calmness of the dark night, and illuminating the deck of the desolate wreck, showed the big drops slowly falling into the vessel below. I continued to feed the fire, and to apply cold water to the tube, and soon had the satisfaction of seeing the condensed fluid trickle down in an almost continuous stream. By nine o'clock I had collected nearly a pint : it was warm, flat, and bitter, and had a taste of the wood, the iron, and the leather, but a cup of nectar from the hand of Ganymede himself was never more delicious.

The success of the experiment established, and the excitement of conflicting hope and anxiety abated, my body began to be sensible of its bruises and its fatigue. Another slice of pork and a biscuit, with the result of my distillation, satisfied all the cravings of appetite, and carefully securing my still below, for fear of accidents during the night, I retired to my berth with the profoundest feelings of gratitude to Him, in whose hands are the issues of life and death, for my happy preservation.

CHAPTER IX.

SINGULARLY enough, the most pleasant and profound repose soothed my bodily ailings and rewarded my toils. Not a dream of past or future calamity disturbed the serene and pleasant reveries of the night ; the which I attribute solely to the relief of my mind from the stronger and overwhelming apprehensions of a lingering death. As, when on the sea-shore, the largest wave effaces the ripple marks of its smaller predecessors, and retiring, leaves the beach level and smooth ; so the last tide of threatened affliction, in rolling back, had carried with it the otherwise strong and permanent impressions of inferior grief.

The morning was calm and beautiful. One distant sail showed itself, like a dark spot, upon the farthest verge of the horizon, and suggested the idea of preparing some signals, to be used in case of a nearer approach. The distilling machine put in operation, with some little improvements in its mounting and fixtures, which daylight enabled me better to make, I descended to the cabin, and commenced overhauling the lockers and drawers. In one of these I found the schooner's flag ; attaching a loop to one end of a gunstock, I climbed to the top of the broken main-mast, and firmly lashed the other end of the stock to the head of the stump. This gave a hoist of about fifteen feet, and by reeving the halliards through the loop, the flag was ready to be run up, union down, at a moment, when required. I also got ready a quantity of oakum and chopped staves, for the purpose of making a smoke, as being calculated to attract attention from a distance at which the flag might not be seen. By the time these preparations were completed, the vessel, at the instigation of whose top-gallant sails they had been undertaken, was no longer in sight. But happy are they who expect nothing, for they are seldom disappointed ; and as I had not calculated upon her coming near enough to notice me, I saw the last speck of her royals disappear without any regret.

My next operation, was an examination into the state of the bread pantry, and the provision-room, in the run of the schooner, beneath the cabin floor. In the first was a bag of rice, half a bag of coffee, a large canister of tea, about half a barrel of brown sugar, and a large cheese ; in the latter, among other articles, were three barrels of pork and beef, as many more of ship-bread, two barrels of potatoes, four hams, and a keg of molasses. As may be supposed, I was somewhat interested in the account of stock much more so, perhaps, it may be thought, than the reader can possibly be and the inventory made a permanent impression on my memory. Satisfied that the schooner was provisioned for at least a year's cruise, reduced as she was in hands, or rather mouths, I grew quite contented with my lot, which, in reality presented a disagreeable aspect only when I thought of the friends and companions I had lost. It would be, I thought, impossible to float about the ocean for many weeks, in the track of so many ships, without being picked up ; and in the meantime, I had a strong and safe vessel beneath me ; plenty of room for exercise ; plenty of books ; plenty to eat and drink, and plenty of occupation in preparing my meals, feeding my distillery, catching fish, and looking out for sails. My only apprehension was that the current might set me down toward the African coast, and land me upon the inhospitable shores of the Sahara. There was no means of accurately determining longitude that I was familiar with, but my observations for latitude, which I took regularly every day, showed that a strong current was setting the schooner to the south.

A week of unclouded weather imperceptibly glided by, when upon coming upon deck shortly before sunrise, I found upon different points of the horizon five sail of vessels in sight, one of which appeared to be standing on a course which would bring her quite close to me. My signals were immediately prepared ; the flag was run up to the gun-stock, and a tall column of smoke arose from the forecastle, and sailed off to leeward before the light northerly breeze. On came the stately ship, until, with the glass, I could just see her quarter rails, but not the slightest notice did she appear disposed to take of me ; so far from it, she availed herself of a slight change in the direction of the wind, to hold up and pass me some distance to the north. Her stupid crew could hardly have failed to see the smoke, and most probably when arrived in port, had a wondrous story to tell of a volcanic eruption, or some curious meteoric phenomenon, which, with the uninquiring, unenterprising, money-getting stolidity too common in the merchant service, they could not afford time to investigate. My heart somewhat failed me, when I found the ill-success of my effort to attract attention, but with the consoling motto " better luck next time," and a continued reliance upon the mercy of an immediate superintending Providence, I made out to resign myself to my fate, and resume with cheerfulness my usual avocations.

The distillery worked to perfection—a good day's run yielding me fully a pint more of the water than I consumed. The surplus was carefully bottled and put away against bad weather, when it might not be quite so easy to keep the steam a-going. The earthen pan had given way, but in the meantime, while it lasted, a large quantity of ashes had been accumulated, and by wetting these with sea water, and pressing them down upon a bed of boards, a kind of hearth, impervious to the heat, was formed, which supported the fire.

Nor was the luxury of fresh provisions wanting. In rummaging the unfortunate mate's stock of sail, needles, palms, fish-hooks, etc., a small pair of grains, for spearing fish, were discovered. This instrument, consisting of a bunch of barbed points on a socket of iron, when attached to a staff, formed by splicing together pieces of staves, proved an invaluable instrument. By means of it, any quantity of the rudder fish that thronged round the schooner, and now and then a dolphin or bonito, were transferred from the water to the broiling coals of my distillery fire. It also served to fish up the bunches of sea-weed that floated by. From these, when thrown upon deck, would creep out hundreds of small crabs, not one larger than the end of my little finger ; lively, active, healthy fellows, with the shells perfectly formed, and of various colors. Whether they were a distinct species by themselves, or the young of a larger kind, I could not decide ; from the uniformity, however, in size, of those that came under my observation, I should think it probable that the first was the case. They were so numerous, that when the sea-weed was plenty I could collect a pint of them in a couple of hours. If upon them was poured some boiling vinegar, or a handful of them distributed into the pork fat that hissed and bubbled over the fire in the bent and battered up bottom of an old tin canister, they made a dish, that, swallowed shell and all, more than rivalled in delicacy and piquant crispness the delicious shedders and soft shells of the New York restaurants.

Neither was the range of my appetite necessarily confined to such small game. It was one calm afternoon, that a large turtle, weighing at least sixty pounds, made his appearance at the distance of a few yards from the schooner. His shellship had come to the surface for a siesta, and was quietly floating, unconscious of impending danger, in a sound sleep. A longing to appropriate the delicate steaks and green fat of the lethargic monster, who seemed to have been expressly sent for my use, took possession of me ; but how to accomplish it was a question.　There was no harpoon with which to pierce his defensive armor, and even if there had been, there was no boat with which to get at him—the stern boat, with my load of fruit, having followed the way of the long boat, and all the other furniture of the deck.　The only means of reaching him that presented itself, was by swimming.　Fortunately, a piece of whale line, of sufficient length, had been stowed away in the run of the vessel, with a large shark hook attached to it.　Fastening, at intervals of ten or twelve feet, some pieces of staves to act as floats, and securing the other end to a stanchion, I slipped off my clothes, dropped into the water, and taking the hook in my teeth, carefully stretched out towards my prey. By taking him a little in the rear, the slumbering animal was undisturbed by my noiseless approach, and he suffered me to gently take his extended flipper, and with a sudden thrust pass the large hook through it.　For an instant the astonished sleeper lashed the water with head, tail, and paws, and the next disappeared with a rapidity which I had not supposed him capable of, while I swam back to the schooner.　When within a few yards of the main chains, a large black moving object appeared above the water, at about the same distance from the vessel's side towards the bow.　It was plainly a shark's fin, and, from the size of it, belonged to no small fellow.　How, or by what means I reached the deck I could not recollect precisely in five minutes afterwards, but I knew that the process had not taken much time.　Upon trying the tautened whale line, the prize, for which I had run the risk of being dined upon, instead of dining, was found secure, and a good deal of hard tugging brought him alongside.　A combination of slip nooses were now passed round him, and he was soon flat on his back upon the deck.

The poor fellow lay so quiet and looked so resigned that my heart misgave me as to the propriety of his capture.　I did not much like the idea that one in my situation—one who was living only by the special mercy of the Almighty, and who could not offer the plea of necessity, should, for the gratification of the mere caprice of appetite, sacrifice the life of a breathing, sentient, warm-blooded animal.　As to the fish, they were in a different category ; their cold blood and want of lungs and limbs put them too far beyond the pale of humanity ; their natural destiny was, to be caught, cooked, and eaten ; and, besides, I destroyed no more of them than I actually required and consumed.　With the turtle, the case was different ; four fifths, at least, of his flesh would spoil before I could use it.　This last consideration prevailed, so filing off the barb and extracting

the hook, the fellow was bundled overboard, when he instantly made
off, heedless, probably, of his slight wound, in the joy of his recovered
freedom.

" Go," said I, thinking of Uncle Toby and his fly, " go ! the ocean is
wide enough for us both, and if I am destined to test its depth also, I
hope that you, at least, will have gratitude enough to refrain from nibbling my bones ! "

I felt better, as any one always does after a humane and kindly act to
any of God's creatures ; although the deed was, perhaps, much less merito-
rious as an act of self-denial on my part, than it would have been in an
aldermanic disciple of Apicius, whose taste had been formed in the festal
schools of Guildhall or Bellevue. I felt better, but I am afraid that had
a harpoon been at hand, my overstrained humanity would have reacted
with cruel violence upon the body of " Johnny Shark," who, with the
impudence of his tribe, when feeling secure from attack, continued for
several days to rub his huge carcass against the sides of the schooner, and
to interfere in the comfort of my daily bath.

For several days now in succession, numerous ships appeared in sight,
but none came near enough to notice my signals. They were, most of
them, standing east, and, as I supposed, bound up the Straits of Gibraltar.
It was about a week after the capture and liberation of the turtle, making
four weeks from the time of the capsize, that a small dark bank appeared
in the east, which presented very much the aspect of land. As my latitude, by observation, was nearly that of Madeira, and as the light winds
had been blowing most of the time from the northwest, I concluded that
it was that island that was in sight. But if my course was so much east
of south, when and what would be the end of my cruise ? The answer to
the question involved some alarming conclusions. The chart was atten-
tively studied, and presented, in every view of it, confirmation of the fact,
that if my present course should be persisted in for any length of time, the
shores of the African desert would bring me up. Africa had ever been to
me the land in which, more than any other, my imagination had delighted
to wander. I had even conceived the design of attempting, in emulation
of my gallant countryman, Ledyard, the exploration of the unknown interior ; but I had no idea of making my entrance into the country by way
of the coasts of the Sahara. Yet such clearly threatened to be the termination of my voyage.

Time passed on ; the moon again poured, in bountiful effulgence, her
silver light upon the bosom of the deep, which, with the exception of
two days out of the six weeks, had been as placid as a lake. The nights

were delicious, and the greater portion of each was spent in walking the
deck, gazing into the clear blue sky, or down into the dark unfathomable
sea. Emotions, which to coldly analyze, would be to deprive of half
their beauty and sublimity, would, at such times, rush upon the mind
and overwhelm it in the vain attempt to grasp the great mysteries of
nature. Drunk with the glory of the scene, the soul, not unfrequently,
felt an almost irresistible longing to plunge into the deep, and seek in its
profundity the Infinite, the Eternal. Shuddering like him who looks
from tower or precipice, I was often compelled to draw back and rush below to escape from the delirious whirl of feelings, common enough, perhaps, to all, but felt in their full intensity and force, only in solitude upon
the calm and moonlight sea. At other times, again, the mind could
study the same scenes in a more quiet spirit—perhaps a better—in

> " That serene and blessed mood,
> In which the affections gently led us on,
> Until the breath of this corporeal frame,
> And even the motion of our human blood,
> Almost suspended, we are laid asleep,
> In body, and become a living soul ;
> While with a heart made quiet by the power
> Of harmony, and the deep sense of joy,
> We see into the life of things."

Then it was that with the eye of fancy I could see each one of the
myriad, silver-tipped ripples between me and the Jersey shore, the long
reach of the noble Hudson, and the rough roads and rocky hills that
stretched to the St. Lawrence, without a repining or impatient thought
—with hardly a sigh for the comforts of home, or the companionship of
friends.

It was one night, when the moon was just at the full, that I was upon
deck, later than usual, enjoying the flood of rich and mellow light. The
day had been exceedingly hazy, and the boundary of vision much contracted ; but shortly after sunset the mists had dispersed, and the full orb
looked down through an unclouded sky. The surface of the long, slow
swell ever agitating the bosom of the ocean—a token of the resistless
energies slumbering within—was slightly furrowed by the wind, and each
beam, as it fell, paved with fragments of gems the broad pathway of
light. All at once a lofty and somewhat indistinct object upon the water,
apparently at but a short distance off, attracted my attention. " Sail,
ho ! " I shouted in ecstasy of delight ; although what appeared to be the
gleaming canvas of a large ship was evidently a mile beyond the reach

of my voice. A signal, by fire, might, perhaps, serve the purpose, and soon a bright flame sent forth its imploring light. No answer followed, and what was much more mysterious, the relative position of the schooner and the object had hardly altered in the course of an hour's attentive watching, or, at least, had altered so slightly as to be utterly inconsistent with the idea of the latter being a ship under full sail. At length my ear caught the sound of water dashing against some solid body. The idea of the Salvages, a group of naked rocks, which rear their tall forms, in solitary dignity, from the middle of the ocean, about half-way between Madeira and the Canaries, occurred to me. More than one mariner, it is asserted, has been deceived in the same way, from their resemblance to the sails of a ship, and, perhaps too, more than one ship has been lost upon them, while ploughing her way heedless of danger in the darkness of the night. Uninhabited and uninhabitable, they are visited only at certain seasons by a few Portuguese from Madeira, for the purpose of collecting the feathers of the sea fowl, who, in great numbers, have made them their home. An examination of the chart and a comparison of my latitude, and the probable influence of the winds which had prevailed for several days, confirmed the conjecture which was fully established the next day, during the whole of which, their ragged points continued plainly in sight.

Thus again, for nearly the twentieth time, had my hopes of succor been excited only to be depressed. But I had got pretty well inured to that kind of disappointment, and my confidence in my ultimate preservation, through the mercy of Providence, continued unabated. Satisfied by a close watch of a couple of hours, that the schooner was increasing her distance from the rocks, I retired to rest, after praying, as usual, for the merciful protection of the Almighty, and especially for the continued influence of my mother's spiritual presence and affection. "O Lord!" prayed the great Doctor Johnson, "if Thou hast ordained the souls of the dead to minister to the living, grant that I may enjoy the good effects of my departed wife's attention and ministration, whether exercised by appearances, impulses, dreams, or in any other manner agreeable to Thy government!" If Doctor Johnson could so pray, why might not I?

CHAPTER X.

Land Ho!—A Weatherly Craft—The Peak of Teneriffe—Oratavo—A Dark Night—Shore
Lights—Hailing a Fisherman—Beauties of Quarantine—A Disappointment—A Storm—
Dining Like a Gentleman—A Ship in Sight—Visit from Her Captain—Leaving the *Lively
Anne.*

LAND ho!" The famous Peak of Teneriffe was in sight. This
was on the tenth of September, or a little more than eight
weeks since my visit to the Azores. It really seemed, that
in my solitary floatings I was destined to have a glimpse,
in succession, of the principal insular curiosities of the Atlantic, and I began to speculate upon the prospect of the Cape de Verde, St. Helena,
and Ascension; or, with greater probability, of getting into the trade
winds, and turning up, along the great western current, among the West
Indies.

After leaving the Salvages, a succession of gales and squalls from almost every point of the compass, for nearly a week, completely upset all
calculations of longitude; and it was no little satisfaction to have a fresh
landmark, even if it was but to prove, in common as well as technical
meaning, a "point of departure." It was in these gales that the schooner
demonstrated her possession of very excellent weatherly qualities for a
dismasted wreck. Unsteadied by any top hamper, her rolling was rather
sharp and uncomfortable, but her pitching was beautiful. The float of
spars kept her pretty well "head on," and she craned and ducked to the
heavy sea as gracefully as a boarding-school miss in the preparatory backing and filling of her first public quadrille—each time slowly bowing her
nose to it, and then lifting herself as buoyant as a cork, and "as dry as a
bone."

For nearly three days the schooner remained in full view of the port
of Oratavo, on the northern side of the island, at a distance of not more
than ten or fifteen miles. Palma was in view in the northwest, and with
the glass large objects could be distinctly seen on the shore of Teneriffe.
I amused myself for some time in trying to pick out, but without the
most remote idea of being able to do so, the big dragon tree of Oratavo,

celebrated by Humboldt and other travellers. The distance was of course too great. A more satisfactory subject of examination was the cinder-covered summit of the famous Peak, from which arose from time to time light puffs of vapor, apparently smoke. I kept my glass upon it by the hour, but no one seemed disposed to return the compliment, or even so much as glance seaward long enough to fix in their eye the black speck that bore me and my hopes. Certain it is, at least, that they made no demonstration of aid in answer to all my signals, and it is perhaps more charitable to attribute the fact to their blindness than to their laziness or inhumanity. Had the schooner been within the same distance of the shores of Cape Cod, Nantucket, or Long Island, the case would have been different. Some sharp-eyed, wide-awake Yankee would have been sure to make the discovery, and half a dozen whale-boats would have run a race for the prize.

Slowly the schooner drew towards the east end of the island, until, at sunset of the third day, she was not more than three miles from the perpendicular wall of basaltic rock. The current evidently set round the point, and along the southern side of the island, which was now just beginning to open. The schooner might perhaps go ashore in the night, which, considering the abrupt and rocky nature of the coast, against which I could hear the surf dashing, was not particularly desirable, or what was much better, she might be swept along into, or off, the roadstead of Santa Cruz, whence, as being the chief town and seaport of Teneriffe, she would stand a greater chance of being seen. I prepared myself for either event. The night set in exceedingly dark, but I could perceive that the schooner slowly followed the line of the coast, and that she kept gradually edging in nearer to it. On the shore, close to the water's edge, were numerous large lights, as from fires, which it was evident were kindled for the purpose of fishing. The sight was cheering. How pleasant it would be to plump right ashore at a fishing station, amid a set of honest, generous *pescadores!* The idea of it was so absorbing that I most unaccountably forgot to make my own signal fire. Some of the lights were stationary, and by them I could compare the changes in the schooner's position. Other lights appeared to move, as if carried in boats along beneath the base of the cliffs. Up to twelve o'clock they continued to increase in number. New ones were lighted, and others were brought into view as the schooner fully opened the whole reach of the southern side of the island, until at least fifty or sixty were in sight at once.

About three o'clock in the morning dense masses of black clouds, which had been gradually accumulating, spread themselves over the whole face of the heavens, leaving no loop-hole from which a solitary star could look out upon the surface of the benighted deep. A few flashes of lightning in the north, dimly lighting at considerable intervals the black line of the coast, betokened a collection of electric materials on the opposite side of the island. One by one the lights on land began to disappear, and those in the boats to steal along homeward between the schooner and the shore. I tried my voice, but without effect—the surf perhaps prevented it from being heard. Several times the idea occurred to me of trusting myself to the water, and swimming to the land; but, although the distance was not more than a mile, the intense darkness, and my utter ignorance of the character of the beach, together with a desire to save if possible my money, papers, etc., prevented the attempt.

Suddenly there was a sound of oars—it grew louder and louder. The boat, from which it proceeded, was evidently moving in a direction that would bring her past the schooner at no great distance—some fisherman, perhaps, who was returning with his load to the market of Santa Cruz. I strained both eyes and ears—a few low sounds, as if of voices, occasionally floated upon the water, but not a glimpse of any object could be had in the thick, pitchy darkness. Waiting until the boat, to judge from the sound of the oars in the rowlocks, had got nearly abreast of me, and as close, as from the indications of her course, she would be likely to come, I nerved myself for a tremendous vocal effort. " *El Bote! Bote de pescar*, ahoy!" I shouted at the top of as stout a pair of lungs as ever served a boatswain's mate in a storm. " *Hola! Señores Tente! Venga V. por aquí!* "

The noise of the oars ceased, and, after apparently a moment's consultation, an answer was returned to my hail, " *No tengo ningun pescado*," was all that could be distinguished.

"No, no, señor. I don't want any fish. I want to get ashore. Come, come, *venga, venga, aed!* "

" *No, es imposible!* " and then followed something, of which I could only catch the words *práctico* and *hacer cuarentena*. The oars again commenced moving in the rowlocks.

" *Maldita sea vuestra cuarentena!* " I ejaculated, "and all the quarantines that were ever invented for no earthly good, except to hamper commerce and fatten a few prejudiced officials!" But it was no time to stand anathematizing a system of humbug, from which my own enlightened country is not yet wholly free.

" *Por el amor de Dios, señores*, come to me. I 'm alone, upon a wreck —*un naufragio!* " and I shrieked the last word with redoubled energy.

" *No, no, es imposible.* Your ship must get practique first, and besides it 's coming on to blow, we must hurry ashore."

" *Oh, señor, pare V. el barco! Estese quieto por un momento!* Stop the boat! Stop for one moment! I 'll come to you! I 'll swim to you! Wait for me, for God's sake!" But the vigorous and continued strokes of the oar showed that my hospitable and generous *pescadores* were fully determined not to risk a scrape with the practique office, or custom-house, by having any thing to do with me.

And thus again did a chance of escape vanish from my excited vision. My hopes at once fell below zero. It was not despair, but a kind of dogged indifference to the frowns of fate, that took possession of me. It was the contentment of contempt for any and all of the ills of my destiny, and a determination never again to humbug myself with the delusions of hope. With a blow-away-and-do-your-worst kind of feeling, I listened to the roar of the wind, as it swept down the steep cliffs and deep gorges of the mountains, and striking the schooner, bore her away from the land to the southwest. Such a mood of mind, however, cannot long withstand the influence of prayer. The direct appeal to Deity necessarily induces a mental state utterly incompatible with either the rebellious promptings of the haughty and self-relying spirit, the indifference of mere stoicism, or the self-abandonment of despair. I prayed and slept.

As the wind came off the land in a direction about northeast by north, there could be no danger of running foul of the Grand Canary, or any other of the islands, so, without hesitation or concern, I surrendered myself to the somniferous influences of the tempest's tones until eight o'clock the next morning. Upon getting upon deck at that hour, no land could be seen—a regular northeast storm, with a driving rain, shut out every thing from view except a narrow circle of the tossing and hissing sea. All day and most of the next night the wind continued to blow a gale—veering occasionally a point or two to the east, but always puffing away with unflinching vigor. It was cheerless and comfortless enough, but there was consolation in the thought that it was slanting me off from the African shore. Had it been from the northwest, it would have puzzled the most inveterate optimist to have extracted from it a particle of comfort. Towards morning it began gradually to abate, but still continued to blow a pretty stiff breeze until about three o'clock in the afternoon, when it suddenly moderated; the sea subsided, the clouds dispersed, and the sun shone out with unwonted brilliancy, chasing the lingering mists, and pouring his serene and soothing light upon the fretted sea.

I set about my employments with something like my usual spirit and vigor. The schooner had made a good deal of water, and it took a hard hour's "spell" at the pump to relieve her of it. The cabin floor, too, was all afloat with what had rained in, or been dashed in, from the tops of the sea, which had, once in awhile, tumbled aboard, and it was necessary to swab it up. The culinary department had been much neglected, having contented myself during the storm with a piece of salt pork and a biscuit. Now it was necessary to have something "good." But what should it be ? After much consultation and debate, it was decided *nem. con.* that it should be hot johnny-cake and molasses, with a few raisins in it. There was a good deal of philosophy in the choice. First, there were the pleasant home associations hanging around a hot johnny-cake ; second, its intrinsic palatableness, especially with molasses, which none but some recreant to the true principles of taste can deny ; third, the raisins were my own invention—a gratifying exercise of ingenuity— a hopeful attempt to combine the merits of a johnny-cake and an Indian plum-pudding ; fourth, the making and baking would take some trouble and time, and afford an interesting and diverting employment—a "something to do." Ay, there 's wonderful virtue in that same "something to do" in this world. Fortunately, most people have enough of it, and have therefore never been made to feel, in its full force, the admitted truth, that without it time would prove no better than a curse, and life a cheat.

Acting upon this principle, I resolved to reform my mode of eating altogether. Before, I had taken my meals as I could get them—at all times—without any regularity—sitting or standing—with or without plates—in the cabin or on the deck. Henceforth, I should set out a table with the remnants of crockery, cook my dinners after a more elaborate fashion, serve them in proper style, and then dine like a gentleman. Thus, in the threefold capacity of cook, waiter, and master, I should occupy more of my superabundant time, which, as I had pretty much read up my books, began to drag rather heavily. I could, at least, pelt away at the old gentleman of the scythe with some of the proprieties of society, if I could not kill him with its luxuries and its pleasures.

My solitary dreams were, however, destined to have an end. As the third I sat longer at the table than usual, in the enjoyment of imaginary hob-nobbings, with divers dignitaries of the earth. I had ever the faculty of surrendering myself, body and soul, to the fancy of the moment, however ridiculous or improbable. In fact, the impossible was no let or hindrance. I fought, when a boy, as readily upon the banks of the

Scamander, or the plains of Arbela, as at Warsaw or Missolonghi: built castles in the air as easily in the moon as upon earth. Coming upon deck with my guests, Wellington, General Jackson, and Mehemet Ali, three of the greatest men, as I thought, that the world had produced, I was too much absorbed in them to notice, at first, a ship on the starboard tack, close-hauled to the wind—which was changed to the south,—and heading up in a direct line for the schooner. If she kept on without tacking she could not fail to notice me. The duke, general, and pacha taking their leave, I hoisted my flag and awaited the event.

As she came on I had full time to note all her beautiful proportions.

"' You have had rough work here!' *he continued, stepping upon deck.*"

She was small, apparently not above three hundred tons, and had a peculiarly trim and clipper-like look. Her bright copper, flashing occasionally in the sunlight, showed that she was in light sailing trim; while from the cut of her sails, the symmetrical arrangement of her spars and rigging, and her quarter boats, I concluded that she must be a man-of-war. Passing me about half a mile astern, she stood on for a little distance, then hoisting the bilious-looking flag of Spain, she tacked and ran for me, backing her main top-sail within twenty rods of my larboard beam. Her quarter-boat was immediately lowered, and half a dozen fellows, in red caps and flannel shirts, jumped into it, followed by an officer in a blue velvet jacket, with a strip of gold lace upon his shoulders, and a broad-brimmed straw hat upon his head. I ran below, stuffed all the money that I had in gold—about a thousand dollars—into my pockets, and got upon deck again just as the boat touched the side.

"Welcome, señor," I exclaimed in Spanish, "I am exceedingly glad to see you."

"I should think so," returned the stranger in very good English, but with a marked Spanish accent. "I should think so; you have had rough work here," he continued, stepping upon deck, and turning a glance upon the shattered bulwarks and splintered stanchions and masts. "Rough work! but where is your crew?"

By this time, the boat's crew were on deck, running about, asking questions all at once, and addressing their velvet-coated companion with a degree of familiarity that I was unaccustomed to see between an officer and his men. Some of them had made their way to the cabin; and I congratulated myself, not a little, upon my forethought in securing the gold upon my person, as I heard them rummaging about and overhauling every thing they could lay their hands on. Velvet Jacket himself seemed disposed to have a finger in the pie, and led the way below without any ceremony.

He was a large stout-looking man, with a face strongly marked with the small-pox, and deeply scarred, upon the chin and cheek, by a cut, which was only partially concealed amid a black forest of moustache and whisker. With a low projecting forehead, piercing black eyes, rendered peculiarly sinister by a whitish speck in one of them, and coarse grisly hair, it must be allowed that he was not much of a beauty, and his men, if possible, were still less prepossessing; they all had a kind of cut-throat expression, that suggested the idea of pirates. The chief reason for not thinking them so, was that their vessel was square-rigged, a long low rakish schooner seeming to be the only natural craft for a pirate. But why might they not have chosen the unusual rig of the ship, for the very purpose of better deceiving their prey or their foes? I must own that the idea gave me some little pleasure. I had no objection to a practical acquaintance with piratical life, if it was forced upon me. I might, perhaps, be the means of doing much good and preventing much evil—perhaps save some lovely damsel and her doting father, and be rewarded with a heart and a fortune; nothing more natural, and, if the novelists could be depended upon, nothing more common. Physically, I felt myself a match for any half-dozen pirates; and mentally, what youth, almost twenty-one, ever felt any doubt about his ingenuity, his courage, his resources, or his knowledge of men and the world? If I had had, however, a little more of the latter quality, I might have saved my speculations as to the chances and turn-ups of the piratical profession, and have made a shrewder guess at the character and employment of my new acquaintances. Not even when Velvet Jacket told me that she was bound from Cuba to the coast of Africa, did I begin to suspect that that beautiful craft was, if any thing, worse than a pirate—a slaver.

"What is the name of your vessel?" said I, after telling my story, as we were all huddled about a bottle of Pico wine, in the small cabin.

"*El Bonito*, and mine, Captain Pedro Garbez, at your service."

"And to what port in Africa are you going?"

"I don't know, exactly, yet," he replied, in a hesitating manner: "it will depend upon circumstances and the state of trade."

"You are going for dye-woods and palm oil, I suppose," said I.

"*Si, señor, por palo de tinte y aceite de senegal,*" he replied, repeating my words in Spanish, and looking round upon his men with an impressive glance.

In the course of conversation it came out that I was a *medico*, which fact seemed to give general satisfaction. The men, when they heard it, repeated it to each other with many expressions of pleasure, while the captain, taking my hand, warmly welcomed me to his ship.

"We are lucky in falling in with you," said he. "The doctor that was to have accompanied us was taken sick just before we sailed, and we could not get another. We have already three or four men on the sick list—one of them with a dislocation of the shoulder joint; we've nearly all of us taken a pull in turn at him, but we can't get the arm back again —so, you see, you're just the man we want; you will tinker up our short sick-list now, and in a few weeks we'll have plenty of other work for you; but I'll explain all about that another time. Come, now, let us get on board."

Securing my trunk, clothing, papers, and nautical and surgical instruments, while the men did the like service for the captain's and mate's personal property, we pushed off, and in a few strokes of the oar were alongside the ship. The captain and I mounted to the deck, while the boat was ordered back for another load of cabin furniture, bedding, and provisions. In about an hour she returned, when the ship immediately filled her main top-sail, and stretched off to the southeast.

I could not but part from the old wreck with feelings of regret—she had borne me in solitude so long and so gallantly—she seemed so much like home! I gazed at her until she dwindled to the smallest speck, and after she had disappeared from the deck, stepped into the mizzen-top to take one last lingering look.

CHAPTER XI.

DESERVING of her name was *El Bonito*—as much so as the well-known fish after which she had been baptized, and which have acquired their name in an adjectival expression for beauty and grace. Of great breadth of beam, but sharp forward and very lean aft, and heavily sparred, she gave indications of speed, which, one could not be long on board without perceiving, were abundantly realized. Six small pieces of ordnance piercing her high and comfortable bulwarks, and a long twenty-four pound pivot-gun constituted her armament. Her crew consisted of about thirty men, among whom were several Portuguese, most of them rather hard-looking fellows, and all of them dressed in the characteristic red cap, striped woollen shirt and worsted sash. Beside these there were several officers of various grades. *contramaestres, carpinteros, pilotos,* and *capitanes.* Between these and the men there was a degree of familiarity that in an American ship would have been destructive of all discipline. There seemed to be no idea of subordination, except in matters immediately pertaining to the duties of the ship, but still, the work was performed with a degree of regularity, the ship kept quite trim, and, for a Spanish ship, tolerably clean.

The second officer was, if possible, a more truculent-looking fellow than the captain. He had a peculiarly savage and morose expression—a kind of look that spoke of murdering, in all its tenses, past, present, and future. He spoke but little, except in occasional bursts of the most outrageous blasphemy, when any thing crossed his wishes. I never knew to what extent profanity could be carried, until one day he gave me an instance. We had been bothered for several days with a calm, common enough in those latitudes, and the sailors had placed an image of St.

Anthony against the main-mast, with a prayer to send them wind, and a threat that his saintship should remain in his uncomfortable position until he did. Either the saint was unable or unwilling to comply, and no wind came. *El segundo capitan* began to mutter and to curse. At last his rage broke all bounds ; his eyes glowed like the flues of a steam boiler, and his face became as bloated and speckled as a toad's back. He stamped upon the deck, tore his hair, and shrieked out volleys of curses upon the air, the sea, the sky, the God that made them, and the whole Holy Trinity. He anathematized the Virgin Mary, called her all manner of names, and cursed all the saints in the calendar, with an affluence of objurgatory pro-fanity, rivalled only by the denunciatory anathema-maranathas of Rome, and jumping forward to the main-mast, he gave St. Anthony a kick that almost sent him overboard. I was inexpressibly shocked, but I could not help laughing until my sides ached. With this worthy I had but little to do. We had conceived a dislike of each other from the moment that we first met.

I could easily spin out a chapter or two in the description of the ship and my companions, and in the recital of the interesting but comparatively trivial occurrences of our voyage, but the space I have already occupied warns me that I must hasten the more important incidents of my story.

The tenth day of baffling winds, squalls, and calms saw us floating motionless upon the quiet sea, directly beneath the frowning cliffs of Fuego, one of the Cape de Verdes. I had been gratified with the sight of the Peak of Pico, afterwards with the Peak of Teneriffe, and now with the Peak of Fuego. The first was the most beautiful, the second the loftiest ; indeed, struck with its majestic and imposing appearance, there have not been wanting visitors who have claimed for it the credit of being the far-famed Atlas of the ancients. The claim vanishes, however, before the better-founded pretensions of the Mauritanian giant, and the Peak of Teneriffe must content itself with its modern fame and the classic associ-ations of the Fortunate Isles, of which it is the pride.

Both Pico and Teneriffe are smouldering volcanoes—sleeping giants, who, as if tired out with their exertions in past ages, had composed them-selves to rest ; an occasional groan—a sighing sulphurous expiration—a deep but transient shivering alone giving evidence of the vitality—the raging life—the restless energies within. The Peak of Fuego, on the con-trary, has been almost always, since its discovery, in a state of active erup-tion. From the accounts of the earliest voyagers, however, it would seem that they were much more violent formerly, than in the present day. " It is most horrible to behold, especially in the night," says Beckman. "What prodigious flames and vast clouds of smoke it vomits up continually, which we could perceive afterwards in a clear day, though we were above sixty miles distant." Captain Roberts, who in 1721 was captured by pirates, and landed at the Cape de Verdes, says, in his account of his remarkable adventures : " It is almost incredible what huge rocks are cast out, and to what a great height, the noise of which, in falling again, breaking and rolling down, may very easily be heard eight or nine leagues off in a still air, and in the night be seen rolling down the Peak all in a flame."

It is a curious fact that at the time of the discovery of the islands the Peak of Fuego did not exist ; that is, if we may believe the traditions of the inhabitants. Certain it is, that Cada Mosto, an adventurous Genoese —in the service of the Portuguese—who discovered them, makes no mention of it ; and it was some time after his day that the name he gave it, St. Felipe, was superseded by that of Fuego, or island of fire. It seems that shortly after Cada Mosto's visit the whole island was enveloped in flames, and that, in consequence, no efforts were made to people it for many years. At length the fire having subsided, excepting at what is now the Peak, the king of Portugal issued an edict, granting the lands to whoever would settle upon them, and a scanty population was soon drawn from St. Jago, Mayo, and the other islands, partly allured by the hope of finding some of the gold, which, according to tradition, was the cause of the fire.

Among our crew, as I have said, were several Portuguese, two or three of whom were natives of the Cape de Verdes—black, curly-headed fellows, with marks of the strong infusion of negro blood, common to all the inhabitants of the islands. It was of these, and surrounded by a group of other sailors, that I was making some inquiries in relation to *Fonta de Villa* and the little town of *La Ghate,* off which we were becalmed. All at once a broad glare of light shot up from the dark mountain, illuminating its rugged sides, and streaming in the darkness of the night far out to seaward.

" El Pico! El Pico !" exclaimed a dozen voices.

Two tall columns flashed upwards from the mountain—at one moment steady and erect—the next, quivering and swaying to and fro in the currents of the wind : now seeming to repel each other, now bowing, crouching, and turning, like wary combatants preparing for a struggle for life or death, they would rush at each other, close, and writhe for an instant in the fierce embrace.

" *Los Padres !*" shouted one fellow. " *Los Mágicos !*" exclaimed a second. "*Los Alquimistas !*" bellowed a third.

" Priests, magicians, and alchemists! What do you mean?" I demanded.

"Oh, ask Pedro Vosalo," replied one of the crew, " he was born just round the point, where you see so many sea-weed fires in the little bay of *Nossa Señora*, and he knows all about it. Pedro, Pedro! come here, and tell *señor el médico* the story of the magicians."

Nothing loath, Master Pedro, a little, round-shouldered, bandy-legged mulatto, came forward, and throwing aside the stump of his paper segar, commenced his story, which, fortunately for the reader, I am not disposed to attempt giving in the execrable *patois*, half Spanish and half Portuguese, in which it was told.

For nearly a week we were struggling along in that part of the ocean, in the neighborhood of the Cape de Verdes, which seems to have been destined to an eternal alternation of squalls and calms. Since the days of the early Spanish voyagers, who frequently suffered terrible hardships in these latitudes, no piece of navigation has been found more trying to the temper and patience of mariners, and *el segundo capitan*, as might be supposed, profited not a little by the opportunity for the continued exercise of his peculiar gifts. His oaths, however, did not seem to do much good, though were it possible for a captain to take his ship through the horse-latitudes, as is frequently done through the custom-house, by dint of hard swearing, he was the man to do it.

The regular wind came mostly from the south, compelling us to stand east, toward the African continent, while that accompanying the squalls blew in all manner of ways, but not with sufficient force to raise much of a sea. Indeed, that would have been impossible, for any wind under the depressing influence of the torrents of water that poured from the sky. If a person will imagine all the thunder showers of a summer season in New York, concentrated into one thunder shower, and the whole poured upon him at once, in drops, somewhat less in size than common billiard balls; or, if anxious for a more particular illustration, he will put his head directly beneath the Catskill Falls, where an extra quantity of water has been turned on for the amusement of visitors, he will begin to have some idea of the way in which it rained. For my part, I almost questioned, several times, whether the story of the creation was intended to apply to this part of the world; whether the waters under the firmament ever had been separated from the waters above the firmament—they seemed to be all one. In the intervals of the squalls the sky was generally clear overhead, but loaded with dense black banks of vapor in the eastern horizon, through which continually played the most vivid lightning; while in the west invariably gathered groups of bashful clouds, which, when blushing beneath the kisses of the setting sun, glowed with far deeper and richer hues than I had ever seen among their more brazen-faced sisters of the north.

In twenty days after leaving Fuego we had reached the meridian of Cape Palmas, and standing close-hauled on the larboard tack, steered across the Gulf of Guinea. As we advanced, the sea became literally alive with fish. Myriads of albicore—a kind of tunny-fish, weighing from one to two hundred pounds, continually surrounded the ship; while all around us could be seen, almost at any moment, thousands of flying-fish upon the wing. The faculty of flying, however, seemed to avail them but little as a means of escape from their numerous enemies. What with the dolphins, bonitos, and albicores in the water, and the tropic and man-of-war birds in the air, their life appeared to be any thing but a charmed or a charming one. Rising with a few quick flaps of their wings or fins, if against the wind, they almost immediately dropped into the voracious jaws below; if before it, they sailed off some distance, exposed to the re-morseless claws and beaks above. The hunted fish were not safe from this latter danger, even when in their proper element. Flying low, and skimming the water like a gull, the tropic-bird picked them up from the surface; while hovering on the wing, the man-of-war taking aim, and de-scending like a hawk, seized them in the depths.

Numerous boobies, a bird well known to sailors, now visited us, skimming the surface of the water in pairs, with outstretched necks and expanded tails, and sometimes settling upon the spars in the dusk of the evening, when they allowed themselves to be easily caught.

On the twenty-fifth of October we crossed the line, with the thickly-wooded island of St. Thomas in sight. Through the open space that separates a rock called the *Mono Cacada*, from the north end of the island, we could see a large brig standing to the south. As *el capitan* had no disposition to come upon a British cruiser at the southern end, we hauled to the wind, as close as possible, and stood to the southwest.

I had, long before this, ascertained the character of our ship and the object of her voyage; and, as may be supposed, I would gladly have em-braced any opportunity of leaving her; but with her superior sailing qualities, and the indisposition of her officers to hold any communication with the ships that we occasionally saw, it appeared not at all likely that any such chance would offer. The prospect would have appeared infinite-ly more gloomy, had I had a more definite idea of all the horrors of such a voyage. True, I had been accustomed to hear the detestable traffic in human flesh spoken of in terms of the utmost abhorrence, and had something of a general notion of the cruelties of the " middle passage," but it was too vague and imperfect to excite much apprehension on the score of mere physical suffering, when I looked at the clean decks and roomy proportions of *El Bonito.* I had the utmost confidence in the capacity for any thing diabolical of both officers and crew ; but the ship herself was such a beauty, such nice between-decks—no mere temporary slave deck, with a space between it and a spar deck of only two or three feet in height, into which to cram hundreds of human beings, where half of them die from suffocation ; but a permanent berth-deck, with more than five feet in the clear. She might be an agent in great moral guilt, but certainly not in the production of death, disease, and physical pain. So I then thought. And it was not a little satisfaction to think, that if compelled to make the whole voyage, I should not be shocked by the usual horrors, and might perhaps do much towards relieving the ills to which, under the best of circumstances a cargo of human flesh must be exposed.

I had already acquired considerable influence with the captain. A violent bilious attack had readily yielded to my active treatment, and although he was not very profuse in his expressions of gratitude, I could see that he felt that I had been the means of saving his life. This feeling was evinced, most to my satisfaction, by turning the mulatto steward out of my state-room, or rather, perhaps, his state-room, as he had the right of priority, leaving me all the room to myself. I was also on pretty good terms with most of the other officers and crew, with the exception of *el segundo capitan,* who, for some reason that I could not comprehend, continually looked daggers at me, and had there been a good opportunity, would, ro doubt, have used them. His enmity, I afterwards found, was not wholly personal ; it comprehended within its limits my country and my countrymen, and with good reason too, if the story told me in confidence by the fellow whose dislocation I had reduced, was true. " *El segundo capitan,*" said he, " was formerly a pirate, and conducted a very flourishing business on the coast of Cuba, in a little brigantine which he owned ; but one day the boats of an American man-of-war chased him on shore, captured his vessel, and landing, destroyed his boat, stores, and a good many of his men, and completely broke up his establishment. *Pobre hombre !* he was ruined ! "

Holding in our southwest course long enough to clear the vessel that we had seen, we bore away again for the coast, in the direction of Cabenda, the port for which we were destined. A steady run of ten days brought us in sight of the reddish-gray cliffs which extend along from Loango Bay to between Cabenda and the mouth of the Congo.

In the course of the evening several canoes, paddled by naked blacks, came alongside. Their crews were invited on board to take a drink of brandy, and give us any information as to the state of the slave-market, and the probabilities of interference from the British cruisers. The invitation seemed to give them great pleasure, particularly that part of it respecting the brandy. Several of them spoke Spanish and French, and one or two a little English. To one of these, after some conversation in English, I gave a strong glass of New England rum. " I can speak English too," said one of his companions, addressing me in Spanish.

" Indeed! let us hear you speak it."

" *Dame un poco de aguardiente.* Den me speak."

Respect for his polyglot pretensions would not allow me to refuse. He took the glass, turned it off, and smacking his lips, exclaimed with marked emphasis:

"Good! d——n good! *c'est tout— Yo no savey mas ?* "

If the fellow had exhausted the English vocabulary, he could n't have marched off with a more dignified swagger.

They were all fine-looking men, tall, well made, and with features more nearly resembling the European than is usual in the negro. Of their forms, we had a good opportunity of judging, as they were quite naked, except two or three who had strips of palm-leaf matting around their waists, and red woollen caps upon their heads. Indurated ridges—the cicatrices of repeated scarifications adorned their breasts ; rings of copper encircled their wrists and arms ; and fetishes or charms, consisting of bunches of rags, feathers or fur, with oyster-shells, iron spikes, alligators' teeth, and snakes' tails, dangled from their necks, and protected their person from all evil influences.

From them we learned that there were no slaves at Cabenda, a statement which was confirmed the next morning by the Mafooka himself, who came off to visit the ship. This officer, who is the head of the custom-house, or rather the chief of the board of trade, for his master, the Chenoo, was attended with quite a retinue of persons of distinction, who had plainly much higher pretensions to the genteel, in dress, than our first visitors. Their picturesque variety of costume would have made them admirable subjects for a Broadway lounge. The Mafooka was habited in a red cloth cloak, and a round embroidered cap, the symbol of his office. The three next in rank had made a partnership affair of some European officer's uniform—one wore the coat and epaulets, another the vest buttoned up to the chin, but without a particle of other clothing, while the third indemnified himself for the nakedness of the upper-half of his person, by encasing his long muscular nether limbs in the short tight-fitting pantaloons. Two or three others had on sailors' jackets and red woollen shirts; but the most remarkable swell was cut by a huge fellow in an old cocked-hat; a flashy, but somewhat dilapidated silk gown, which looked as though it might once have belonged to the wardrobe of a dowager of quality, and a pair of jack boots without soles. The peculiar elegance of this distinguished-looking gentleman's equipments was still further enhanced by a monstrous *fetish* encircling his neck, consisting of the brim of an old hat, covered with grease and filth, and loaded with scraps of tin, copper, and iron, and pieces of twine and rope yarn, with bunches of rags and hair. It was, as the owner asserted, esteemed the most powerful fetish in the country—"a perfect life-preserver; no beast, however wild, dared look at it; if he did he became blind."

Upon ascertaining that there were no slaves at Cabenda, it was resolved, much to my regret, to run round into the mouth of the Congo or Zaire. I was anxious to visit Cabenda, which, from its fine port and fertile country, has been called the paradise of the coast, partly from curiosity, and partly in the hope that I might find it possible to leave the ship, and await the arrival of some trading vessel or man-of-war. Once in the Congo, the chances of escape, as far as I could judge from the slight information I obtained, would be but small. The strong current of the river, in the rainy season, and the peculiar unhealthiness of its banks, rendered it very unlikely that any ships engaged in an honest trade would be found, in which case the only alternative would be to remain among the negroes an indefinite time, or make the voyage with *El Bonito.* As the last would, perhaps, be inevitable, I felt the necessity of keeping on good terms with the captain, and of not exciting his suspicions beforehand by too minute inquiries. With Monté, the first mate, my relations had rapidly come to be those of avowed hostility; and it was evident that, through his representations, I had grown into great disfavor with the majority of the crew, who, however, seemed to consider it a settled thing, that I was to remain with them. I could not doubt that, to secure my services, they would have no hesitation in restraining my personal freedom.

Weighing anchor, with a light sea breeze from the west, we stood down the coast, which, a little below Cabenda Bay, becomes flat and marshy, and covered with a thick growth of mangroves. About noon, Cape Padron, on the further side of the river's mouth, was in sight. Instead of crossing the current and rounding Cape Padron and Shark's

Point from the southward, as is usually done, Captain Garbez determined to anchor on the edge of the Moena Moesa bank, just outside of Fathomless Point, on the north, and await a more favorable turn of tide. In three or four hours we got under weigh again, and by the aid of the tide and the strong sea breeze which had freshened considerably, made out to stem the current, which here ran at the rate of five or six miles in the hour, and at night we again dropped anchor some distance within Fathomless Point. Here the Mafooka of Boolembemda came off to the ship, and informed us that there were plenty of slaves at Embomma, the chief town, some forty miles up the *Moenza Enzadda*, or great river, as the natives call the Congo, and that there were no vessels of any kind to interfere in the trade.

We at length reached Lombee, and anchored off the town, which is the chief market or slave depôt for Embomma. It consists of about a hundred huts of palm leaves, with two or three block houses, where the slaves are confined. About two hundred slaves were already collected and more were on their way down the river, and from different towns in the interior. After presents for the king of Embomma, and to the Mafooka, and other officials had been made, and a deal of brandy drank, we landed, and in company with several Fukas, or native merchants, and two or three Portuguese, went to take a look at the slaves. Each dealer paraded his gang for inspection, and loudly dilated upon their respective qualities. They were all entirely naked, and of all ages, sexes, and conditions, and all had an air of stolid indifference, varied only in some of them by an expression of surprise and fear at the sight of the white men. I had the satisfaction of perceiving that my appearance produced a stronger sensation of dread, astonishment, and disgust, than that of either of my companions.

After looking at them for some time, and making some inquiries about the places they had been brought from, I was turning off, leaving Captain Garbez to finish his examination, when my attention was attracted to a shrinking figure that I had not before noticed. It was that of a young girl, apparently twelve or thirteen years old, which, as is well known, corresponds in warm countries to the sixteen of colder climes. Her features were not at all of the usual African stamp. Her forehead was moderately high, but very broad, clear, and perpendicular—the facial angle being as great as is ever seen in the finest European heads. Her eyebrows were arched, eyes large, dark and fringed with the longest and blackest lashes I had ever seen. Her nose was straight and well formed ; lips full, but not thick ; teeth as white as snow, and chin beautifully rounded and dimpled. Her complexion would not have been deemed at all too dark for a brunette. Her hair was curly, but not crisp, nor woolly, while her figure, slight and finely framed, contrasted curiously with the fat forms and ebony skins behind which she was trying to hide herself from sight. A sentiment of modesty was pleasingly evinced by a tattered waist cloth of palm leaves, the only attempt at clothing in the whole group.

It will be supposed from this description that she was beautiful, and so she was, but it was beauty under an eclipse. The sunken eye and hollow cheek, and attenuated frame, spoke of long weeks and months of mental anguish and physical pain. Her hair, that once curled gracefully as the tendrils of the vine, was matted into one dense and unsightly mass. Her skin, begrimed with dirt, was marked with the lash, which had urged on her weary steps in her long and dreadful journeyings. Several recent wounds, aggravated by exposure to the sun, disfigured her limbs, and her whole form and face had that expression of spirits crushed, hopes blighted, feelings outraged, and strength prostrated seen only in the slave. For some time I could not take my eyes from her. She was dreadfully interesting! disgustingly attractive!

I looked at her long and steadily: compassion must have beamed from my face, for I felt it like a mountain at my heart, and as she met my gaze, her eye lighted, and a mournful smile parted her lips, and showed her snowy teeth—the only feature that had not been affected by suffering and pain.

"Who is this?" said I, speaking through an interpreter to a slave-dealer, a great burly negro wielding a long thong of plaited buffalo hide.

"Who is this? Why, she is about as worthless a piece of goods as I have got in my stock. She is hardly worth the crack of my whip. I am sorry I bought her, for she has given me more trouble than all the rest put together."

"Where did she come from?" I inquired, arresting the fellow's arm, as he whirled his whip round the heads of the crouching and shrinking slaves.

"A great way off in that direction," he replied, pointing a little north of east. I bought her two moons from this, and she had then come a great journey. She comes from what the Youga Jagas call the Gerboo Blanda, or white nation. I've got another one of them—a young man: I believe her brother. He's at a Banza, about a quarter of a day from this."

"Do you often get people of her nation?"

"No, I never saw one before, and I never saw any one who had seen them; but I have heard the slaves that I have bought from the eastern Jagas talk about them."

"And what do the slaves you have seen say about this Gerboo Blanda?"

"Oh, they know but little about it, except that it is a great nation of white people—living in big stone houses, on a great plain on the top of a mountain."

"Can any one here speak this girl's language?"

"I believe not. There is a slave who can talk with her in his own language, of which she understands a little, and she has also picked up a few words of Congo, but not much."

Our conversation was here interrupted by preparations for a grand *palaver*, at which all hands were to assist, and where the price of slaves was to be settled, the dues of the Chenoo, Mafooka, and other officers arranged, and as much brandy drank as would serve to elucidate any points in dispute, and bind the bargains. Making an engagement with the slave-dealer to visit the Banza where the brother of the girl was confined, in the afternoon, I returned to the ship.

CHAPTER XII.

N board every one was busy in preparations for the reception of the slaves, which were to be all sent off the next day. Some were engaged in filling the water-casks, while others were taking in stores of Indian corn, plantains, and potatoes. Crowds of Fukas with their *linguistas*, or interpreters, were on board, or around the ship in their canoes; most of them half dressed and invariably with some piece of European clothing.

I tried to make some minutes in my journal, but the noise and confusion were too great, and, besides, the face of the Gerboo girl haunted me so as to preclude thought of any other subject. I felt the deepest compassion for her; but how could I lighten her hard fate? I longed to do something, but what? The question recurred again and again. Should I purchase her, and thus, however innocently, become a participant in a trade denounced by my government as piracy, and punished with death? Or, should I leave her to the mercies of her negro masters, and to all the horrors of African slavery? I was certain that in her present weak and exhausted state, she would not be purchased as a part of our regular cargo, and merely to give her her freedom, and leave her behind, would not at all better her condition.

Without being able to come to any settled resolution, I picked out from my store of money a few Spanish pillar dollars, the only current coin, and, stepping into a native canoe, returned to the shore. Making my way among the scattered and irregularly arranged huts, composed of stakes covered with a matting of palm leaves, I arrived at the stockade, or picketed enclosure, in which she was confined. Here I found a partner or assistant of the slave-dealer with whom I had spoken. He was a stout muscular man, with a peculiarly malignant expression of face. The skin of his breast and body was raised in the most frightful ridges by the process of repeated scarification ; his front teeth projected far from his mouth, and were filed down to sharp points—a custom which prevails extensively among different nations of Africa—and his thick bushy hair was shaved so as to leave it in tufts, like bunches of bog-grass, standing out from different parts of his head.

We entered and found within the enclosure an open area, without any shelter from the sun or rains. Here and there were pools of stagnant water, and, all around, the ground was covered with a thick black mud, into which, in the driest part, we sank ankle deep at every step. In this place, that was more than equalled in comfort by any ordinary pig-sty, were about thirty females, most of them sitting or lying, half-buried, in the abominable recking compost.

The Gerboo girl was not, at first, in sight. The slave-dealer called for her two or three times, in tones that gave indication of the treatment to which she must have been subjected. " Kaloolah! Kaloolah!" he shouted, and at last espying her crouching behind a picket that projected from the side of the entrance, he sprang towards her with every mark of fury in his face, and, before I could prevent him, struck her a heavy blow with his whip of raw hide. I saw the quivering flesh, where fell the lash, marked with a long streak of blood, and I saw the whip half raised, as if for a second blow. It was altogether too much for my share of human nature to bear. I have said that I had never yet met my match for muscular power, and twice my usual strength was in my arm as with my left hand I grasped his brawny throat, and dashed his head against the wall with a force that, if it had been a white man's, would have seriously endangered the continuity of its bones. I drew back my right hand to strike, and, had the blow been given under the energetic impulse of the moment, I verily believe it would have killed him. Fortunately, a thought of the consequences restrained me, and the blow was arrested in time. I loosened my grasp, and the big brute sank to the ground, apparently as lifeless as a log. What with the concussion of the brain, and the compression of the wind-pipe, he was decidedly in a bad way.

In an instant there was a tremendous hubbub and uproar. The countenances of the poor slaves expressed the height of astonishment and terror, while the spectators, who had accompanied us in, drew back, screaming and gesticulating, and loudly asserting that I must be *Caddee M'Pemba*, or the devil, to dare thus attack one of the stoutest and most desperate lion hunters and jaga killers in the country. Soon a large crowd collected, and among them the Mafooka and the principal slave-owner. I was, of

THE SLAVE-PEN.   AN ASSAULT AND BATTERY.

course, exceedingly anxious to settle matters, not at all on my own account, but for fear the slaves, and particularly the Gerboo girl, might have to suffer for my doings. The unbounded influence of money favored me, and a few dollars, judiciously distributed, soon brought about a most amicable understanding. Not that there was much ill-feeling evinced towards me, my opponent being pretty generally hated and feared, but a natural sense of justice told them that a man ought to be paid for maltreatment administered without the slightest (to them) provocation. So, after a deal of talk, it was settled that I should pay the plaintiff in the suit, who was beginning to recover his breath, the sum of four dollars, and also the costs of court, in the shape of a five-gallon keg of rum, to be shared by all hands, judges and jurors, witnesses and spectators.

Taking me aside with a very mysterious air, the principal slave-dealer informed me that he was confident that I must have in my possession a very powerful fetish, that had enabled me to handle so easily his assistant, who was notorious for his strength and courage, and who had killed with his one hand more than fifty men; that if I would sell him my fetish, he would give me any two slaves for it, and that he would guarantee me against injury from my late antagonist, who, notwithstanding the award of four dollars, would most assuredly seek revenge.

I replied that I could not think of selling my fetish, but that I would give him ten dollars for the girl, and as to his man, I was not afraid of him or any of his friends, and that he had better be careful how he meditated any evil to me, for if I had occasion to put hands on him again, he would not escape so easily.

Finding me inexorable in relation to the fetish, my offer was accepted after much chaffering, and Kaloolah was delivered over to me. Never did a poor creature's countenance brighten from the darkest shades of despair to the full light of hope more rapidly than hers, when she found, that she was to accompany me. Strength seemed almost instantly restored to her limbs, and even health and beauty to her face.

Taking her into one of the huts, I put her in charge of some Congo women, who, for the consideration of a small coin, readily undertook to obey my directions. I gave her to understand, as well as it was possible without a common language, that she should be well treated, have plenty to eat, and that after bathing in the river she must dress herself in a piece of cotton long cloth, which I had purchased of a fooka, or native merchant; that I was going to see her brother, and would perhaps purchase him; and that when I came back I would attend to dressing her wounds and excoriations. She listened with the greatest interest, apparently compre-

hending with intuitive rapidity every word and gesture, and expressing
her apprehension of my meaning by a few exclamations in Congo and in
her own language, which last struck me as being peculiarly mellifluous.
When the cotton was produced, her eyes sparkled with delight, and when
she understood that she would see her brother, the tears rolled down her
cheeks; she clasped her hands, and, overcome with joy and gratitude,
threw herself upon the ground and tried to embrace my feet. Her motions were so perfectly natural, graceful, and expressive, that I found it
difficult to keep from crying myself.

The road to Banza Embemda led directly back from the banks of the
river, through a fertile and tolerably well-cultivated country. Groups of
the wine palm and the gigantic baobab occurred at intervals, and between
them, fields of manioc, corn, beans, and cabbages, and groves of limes,
papaws, and plantains. Numerous huts, generally grouped in twos or
threes within a fence of canes, and invariably dignified by the name of
" town," sheltered the lazy husbandmen ; and several fields of tall grass,
as high as a man's head, performed the like office for immense quantities
of birds, reptiles, and wild beasts. When dry, these covers are frequently
set on fire by the natives, and their dangerous inhabitants either roasted
to death or expelled.

A three hours' walk brought us to Embemda, a small town of some
thirty or forty huts, situated upon the slope of a rocky hill, to which it appeared the town had been recently removed from the low ground for safety
and comfort during the season of the rains. Here we found about twenty
slaves secured, as at Lembee, in an enclosure of pickets, with the addition
of stout cords upon the legs and arms of several of them who were most
restive. Most of them were of the Modongo nation, and quite a number
had gun-shot wounds, inflicted by the slave hunters, who are in the habit
of waylaying their prey, shooting it down like wild game, and then securing their wounded captives with cords.

Among others, tied neck and heels, which the slave-merchant said was
as much to prevent them from killing themselves as to guard against
their running away, was the Gerboo. A single glance at him was sufficient
to put his relationship to Kaloolah beyond a doubt. He had the same
characteristics of form, face, and expression, except that his skin was a
little darker—a clear nut-brown, and his look, one of fierce dogged defiance, rather than hopeless despair. His body was much emaciated, and he,
too, bore the marks of the lash, and the deep ulcerations caused by the
tightened cords. But, although worn down with suffering and confinement, his eye quailed not, and the lines of his well-formed mouth seemed

curved to the concentrated expression of regal scorn and pride. He was tall, but rather delicately framed, and, as near as could be judged from his looks, about nineteen or twenty years of age.

The sum of twenty dollars, after the usual chaffering characteristic of Congo trade, even in the meanest trifles, made him my property; and drawing my knife I was proceeding to sever the bonds that confined his arms, when the slave-merchant arrested me.

"Don't do that," said he, "you can't think what a bad fellow he is. Leave the cords on his arms and loosen those on his legs a little, so that he can just walk. If you take them all off, he will certainly kill himself or run away. I 've had more difficulty with this fellow and the girl than

" And drawing my knife I was proceeding to sever the bonds that confined his arms."

I 've had with all the other slaves. They tried to drown themselves in every river we had to cross. One day we came to a ford and had got almost over, when an enormous lion came bounding out of the reeds upon the bank behind us. We all rushed on, but this fellow turned round and walked back towards the lion on purpose to be killed. The lion was so astonished that he ran away faster than he came. At last I found a way to manage him. I bought his sister from another gang who were going to Malemba, and kept her a little before him, and when he tried any of his tricks I made my men flog her. He did n't like that. But don't untie him, if you do you will lose him."

Paying no attention to his remonstrances, I put the slave-merchant aside and passed my knife through the cords. The young man started from the ground, stretched himself up, and held out his hands as if to assure himself that they were free. He seemed, for a few moments, to think himself in a dream—that compassion must be a mockery—freedom an illusion.

Taking off a white worsted sash, that in imitation of my Spanish companions, was wound round me, I signified to him that he should spread it open, and gird it about his loins. He readily complied, with a look of surprise, which was, however, more than equalled by the utter astonishment of the surrounding slaves and spectators. Their wonder was still further increased when an offer was made for a cap and a kind of capote of fine grass work, and the articles bought and presented to him.

I now put my hand upon the slave-merchant, pronouncing his name, then upon my breast, repeating my own, and pointing to the Gerboo, awaited his answer.

"Enphadde Ban Shounse," he instantly replied, or Enphadde the son of Shounse, the "Ban," having clearly the same force as "Ben" in the Arabic and Hebrew.

It was nearly sunset when we started upon our return to Lembee, with several blacks in company, who tried to act as interpreters between Enphadde and myself, but his knowledge of the Mandongo and Congo dialects was too limited to admit of much communication, and I had to content myself with taking a lesson in his own language, by pointing to the different objects that we passed, and making him repeat their names. This he did with evident marks of quickness and general intelligence, and with great apparent interest in the correctness of my pronunciation.

Upon arriving at Lembee, the sun had set, still enough of the short twilight remained to render objects upon the river distinctly visible, but, to my astonishment, *El Bonito* was nowhere to be seen. Hurrying on to ascertain the cause of her disappearance, we found the town in the utmost confusion, and so many anxious to make explanations all at once, that it was some time before the real truth could be arrived at, but, at last one of the most expert *linguistas* obtained the floor.

"King of English he come," said he, "catchee ship. Ship no like him —no stay. He pull em up anchor, an' run away. Man-of-war big- -plenty boats—plenty guns—plenty men—but no habee ship. When he gone, ship come back."

It appeared that about an hour before, news had arrived that an English cruiser had entered the river, and made her way up as high as Loobondi Island, where she had come to anchor. In ten minutes Captain Garbez got under way, preferring to slip by her at night, in another channel, and stand out to sea, rather than to run the chance of an attack. He left word that in a week he should return, when the merchants were to have slaves enough ready to complete his loading at once.

It would be hard to tell whether I was most pleased or displeased with the news. The former feeling would have undoubtedly predominated, could I have sent word to the captain of the man-of-war, but I observed that the bare mention of it excited surprise and distrust, and that the safest way would be to wait the turn of events. If the English should visit Embomma, communication could be had with them in person, if not, it was hardly possible that they would remain long enough at their unhealthy anchorage to receive my message, even should the Mafooka allow me to forward it.

This point satisfactorily settled in my mind, my attention naturally recurred to my interesting protegés, and to the means of disposing, in the meanwhile, of them and myself.

Kaloolah we found settled upon a mat in a corner of the hut where she had been left, but so metamorphized in appearance, that it was difficult to recognize in her the dispirited, dirty, and naked slave of the morning. The bath and a full meal had worked wonders for her, and the cotton, which with true feminine taste she had contrived to dispose about her person in the most graceful folds, something after the manner of the Moorish haik, concealed the marks of suffering, and the painful emaciation of her figure. As Enphadde entered the hut, she gazed at him a moment in the glare of the torch-light, uttered a shrill cry of delight, and bounded into his arms. Never was the intensity of fraternal affection more strongly evinced than by him as he pressed her to his bosom. Even the negroes of the hut had their sympathies aroused, and evinced quite a pleasurable interest in the scene.

The first exclamations of endearment past, Kaloolah, in the most animated and excited manner, poured forth a flood of melodious words, which, from her glances, evidently had reference to me. Enphadde listened for a moment, and then, without saying a word, stepped towards me, dropped upon his knees, and seizing my hand placed it upon the back of his bended neck. Raising him, I took each of them by the hand, looked at them as benignly as features not naturally very stern would permit, and putting their hands together left the hut to look up a house of my own.

" House hunting by torch-light in a negro Banza " would make a good title for a full chapter, but I must forbear; suffice it to say that after a good deal of trouble and a monstrous expenditure of words, I succeeded in purchasing a house in tolerably good repair. The owner, a Formio of distinction, was seated before his hut, a large fire burning in front, and "tum tumming" on a kind of gourd banjo an accompaniment to the monotonous and drawling cadences of a song. Several spectators soon assembled to assist in the bargain, and every possible advantage, except that of its being a "corner lot," was urged to enhance the price. At last it was settled that I should have the house for the sum of five dollars, cash down, and two jugs of brandy, to be paid when the ship returned. This was just double its fair value, but the terms were agreed to upon condition of immediate possession, and that a piece of palm matting, large enough for several partitions, should be thrown in. A few minutes sufficed to remove the noble owner's furniture and family to other quarters, when, with Kaloolah and Enphadde, I was duly installed as master, *in fee*, of the slight but not uncomfortable domicile.

CHAPTER XIII.

E were not destined to a long enjoyment, in quiet, of our new habitation. It was the second night of our possession that Enphadde and myself were startled by a scream from Kaloolah, as she rushed from the door of the hut. Jumping up on the instant, before we could get out we were covered with a swarm of small black ants. which, in countless myriads, had broken into our hut like a perfect torrent. The noise soon brought some of our neighbors, who commenced throwing fire-brands into the mass, that by this time covered the ground in the rooms to the depth of four or five inches. There had been no rain for two or three days, and the palm-leaf matting was quite dry, so that, one of the brands coming in contact with it, we had the satisfaction of seeing the ants well roasted, but at the expense of our house, which was utterly destroyed in about fifteen minutes. Fortunately my clothes. gun, etc., were saved. This accident involved the necessity of purchasing another hut, which, at last, with a great deal of trouble was obtained. It was situated a little out of the village. amid a grove of palms. and consequently more exposed to the attacks of wild beasts, particularly the lion, which is sometimes known to enter the centre of a town, but, as some compensation for its isolation, it was surrounded by a high fence of reeds.

But it was not so much the wild beasts that we had to dread, as it was our enemies in human form, who had already commenced their machinations. Seeing the interest I took in my companions, and instigated, no doubt, by his brutal assistant, the slave-merchant from whom I had purchased them, paid me a visit, and demanded that the bargain should be rescinded, upon the ground that a leaf or blade of grass had not been broken between us, and that without such ceremony no contract was valid. He had even the impudence to lay hands on Kaloolah, as if to drag her off with him. With every mark of horror and disgust she shrank from his grasp, and fled into the hut. Indignant at such an outrageous attempt at imposition, I saw that no deprecatory measures would answer, and that the only way to prevent further difficulty, was to meet the fellow half way, and frighten him out of his wits by a prompt and energetic resistance : so, giving way, all of a sudden, to an expression of the fiercest rage, I drew a pistol, fired it towards him, taking good care not to hit him. He bounded out of the gate-way with surprising agility, and, as I was close upon his heels, necessarily had to take a path that led away from the town. It would have been easy at any moment to have overtaken him, but such was not my object; so, following him just close enough to keep him up to his full speed, away we went through the mud, and over the jagged slate-beds, and around the trees at a perfectly killing pace for a distance of at least two miles. He had rather too much flesh for a long heat, and, before he had gone far, his wind began to fail him. His breath came short, hard, and wheezy, like the asthmatic puffings of a high-pressure steamboat. His eyes protruded from their sockets, his thick bloodless lips were flecked with foam, and the ebony of his complexion fairly terrified into a spotted and dirty drab. Whenever he turned his glances behind him at the "white devil" on his track, the loudest yells that my lungs were capable of, aroused his flagging energies, and urged him on in his supposed race for life.

Just as my own powers were nearly exhausted, we came to a slate bed, upon the edge of a narrow muddy bayou. Down this the fellow rushed with unabated speed, and, taking to the water, stretched out for the other side, while I stopped short, and employed myself in quickening his motions by the aid of several large stones, thrown into the water around him. Scrambling up the other bank, he had just strength enough left to throw himself prostrate at the edge of a thicket of tall grass, and creep on hands and knees into the friendly cover.

Upon returning to the town I sought the Mafooka, and slipping a dollar into his hand, to sharpen his eyesight, told him that he must clearly see that the demand of the slave-merchant was unjust, that the bargain had been fairly made, and that however imperative the custom of breaking a leaf might be, between natives, it was not at all necessary between a native and a white man, who could not be supposed to know any thing about it. The Mafooka allowed that my view of the case was the only one consistent with equity, good conscience, and his own interest, and that any degree of force in resisting such preposterous pretensions would be perfectly justifiable.

" Kill him ! kill him ! " continued the worthy official, in very intelligible English ; " you give me two five dollar you shall kill him by G—d. Knock him head—break him bones—cut him throat—so,—" and here the speaker gave a spirited pantomimic representation of the different processes he proposed.

Promising to give him the ten dollars, whenever I should conclude to do the deed, I took my leave, but not without repeated cautions from him to beware of the fetish. More than once the same warning was repeated by friendly natives, who either could not, or would not give me any precise information of the nature or extent of the danger. The most that I could learn was, that Bergamme, the Jaga killer, had employed some of the most renowned gangams, or priests, to make him a fetish of wonderful power, that was to be employed in some way against me. The earnestness of the natives, and the vagueness of the danger, produced a feeling of apprehension that was far from comfortable. I had no fears for myself, but I felt much solicitude for the safety of Kaloolah and Enphadde.

The more I had seen of this young couple, the more had my sympathies become interested in their favor, and the better satisfied did I feel with the relation I had assumed towards them. On their part, every look and action evinced the profoundest sense of gratitude and obligation ; and their whole deportment continually astonished me with evidences of delicacy, refinement, and mental cultivation far beyond what I had been prepared to expect. Kaloolah, in particular, evinced the most surprising quickness of comprehension—mastering a large number of English phrases with a readiness and tenacity of memory that very far surpassed my most strenuous efforts in the acquisition of her own tongue. My progress, however, was not slow, and I knew not which to admire most, her tact as a teacher, or her quickness as a pupil. Both she and her brother wrote their language with apparent ease, in characters somewhat resembling the Hebrew, but arranged after the style called *Boustrophedon*, or alternately from left to right and from right to left. I regretted exceedingly, that my knowledge of the Hebrew extended only to the letters of the language, and that I was unable to compare the words and grammatical forms.

With the aid of their language, the Congo, a few words of English, and Kaloolah's expressive pantomime, I was soon able to understand the main points of their interesting story.

The Gerboo Blanda, I found, was a name given to their country by the Jagas. that its true name was *Framazugda*, and that the people were called *Framazugs.* That it was situated at a great distance in the interior, in a direction west by north, and that it was surrounded by negro and savage nations, through whom a trade was carried on with people at the northwest and east, none of whom, however, were ever seen at Framazugda, as the trade had to pass through a number of hands. Enphadde represented the country to be of considerable extent, consisting mostly of a lofty plateau or elevated plain, and exceedingly populous, containing numerous large cities, surrounded by high walls, and filled with houses of stone. Several large streams and lakes watered the soil, which, according to his account, was closely cultivated, and produced in abundance the greatest variety of trees, fruits, flowers, and grain. Over this country ruled Selha Shounse, the father of Enphadde and Kaloolah, as king.

It was in going from the capital to one of the royal gardens that their escort was attacked by a party of blacks from the lowlands, the attendants killed or dispersed, and the young prince and princess carried off. The blacks belonging to a powerful nation that had, within a few years, conquered their way to the borders of Framazugda, and who had even made frequent inroads upon the Framazugs themselves, retreated in haste, dragging with them their victims, and depriving, at one audacious blow, the bereaved monarch of his only son and daughter. Enphadde and his sister were tied hand and foot, and thrown across horses, which, at full speed, soon carried them beyond reach of assistance. Once in the country of their captors, there was no chance of rescue, as the Framazugs had repeatedly found the impossibility of contending successfully against an enemy who had a numerous cavalry, and an immense superiority in the knowledge and possession of fire-arms.

At first the youthful captives were carried towards the northwest, for three or four days' journey, until they arrived at a small walled town, where they were sold for a piece of red cloth and some beads to a kaffila of slave-merchants, travelling in a southwesterly direction. On this course they continued about thirty days, crossing several rivers and steep ranges of hills, and passing numerous villages, until they came to a large town, composed of reed huts and tents of skins, which was situated upon the borders of a sandy desert. Here they were bought by a party of Jagas, and journeyed with them for ten days over a dreary, barren waste, where not a particle of vegetation was to be seen. In this journey they suffered the greatest hardships, having to walk barefoot over a surface of hard flints, with their arms tied behind them, in the hot, tropical sun, and with but a single sip of brackish water in the twenty-four hours. Twice they were separated and conducted off in different directions, but at last were reunited at a town of the Yonga Jagas, on a branch of the Congo. Here they were again sold, placed in boats, and carried down to the main stream, where they were bought by their Congo master. Leaving the banks of the stream, they journeyed for sixty days, including stoppages, through a country of lofty forests, prairies, and swamps, constantly exposed to the attacks of serpents, elephants, lions, and tigers. Several times the kaffila were compelled to take to the trees, or set fire to the tall, dry grass, to save themselves from the wild beasts, and several times they were attacked at night by the still wilder bushmen, who were said, by the slave-merchants, to be inveterate cannibals. Enphadde seemed to have a good idea of the course they had pursued, and made continual reference to the cardinal points of the compass, as indicated by the stars. He even explained the position of his country, by showing the difference in the length of his shadow, at times when the sun had the greatest northern and southern declination. He showed me that when the sun, at noon, was over the tropic of Capricorn, his shadow, falling towards the north, was about one thirteenth part longer than when the sun was in the opposite solstice, and the shadow was projected to the south. From this fact, I deduced the position of the capital of Framazugda, in about one degree of north latitude, and from Enphadde's courses and dead-reckoning it could not be far from about thirteen hundred miles in a direct line from the north of the Congo. I was gratified in being able to obtain so accurate an idea of its position, but it was still more gratifying to find in Enphadde such an evidence of education, and so much knowledge of the principles of astronomical science. No native of Congo would have dreamed of conveying an idea of the latitude of places by the comparative length of shadows, and I was so unprepared for such a thing, even in him, that I could not at first comprehend his meaning, which he illustrated in a variety of ways, by pointing to his own shadow, and to the sun's movements in declination along the meridian, and by setting up perpendicular sticks, and measuring on the ground their supposed northern and southern shadows. Of course it was only the comparative length of the shadows, and not the positive length, as indicated by any actual system of measure. This rendered the problem of the latitude rather complex. The solution required the finding of two angles, the sum of which should amount to 26° 56', whose tangents should be to each other as twelve to thirteen. I had no table of tangents, and my only resource was a series of rough projections and approximations, which served to pass the time, and to demonstrate that the capital of Framazugda was situated within a few miles of the line, and, of course, within a region wholly unknown to the civilized world.

Although so near the equator, Enphadde and Kaloolah represented the climate to be delightfully temperate, which it might well be, from the great elevation of the country, and from the influence of the snow eternally covering the lofty peaks of a mountainous chain, stretching off to the south and east. An abundance of delicious fruits, for many of which Enphadde could point out no parallel in Congo, were found growing wild in boundless profusion. A vast variety of flowers enamelled the fields, or were cultivated in regular gardens, which were also adorned with works of art, such as hot-houses, fountains, and statuary. Interminable fields of grain, pasturage, and orchards covered the plains and the valleys, except where groves of umbrageous trees afforded shelter to tribes of monkeys, and small quadrupeds of different species, and innumerable birds, with every possible variety of magnificent plumage. The architectural structures Enphadde represented to be on a scale commensurate with the splendid natural features of the country, and worthy of a nation which had reached a high point in civilization and refinement.

My imagination was so excited by Enphadde's accounts, that I conceived the design of starting with him, and endeavoring to reach his country by the same route by which he had come. Upon proposing it to them, Kaloolah clapped her hands with delight, and Enphadde's eyes sparkled for a moment with eager joy, but his glances soon fell, as the conviction of the utter impossibility of accomplishing such a journey came upon him. He explained, by a rough chart drawn upon the ground, that the nations to the north of Framazugda were much less savage, and that were we to approach his country in that direction it would be difficult, but still possible to reach it ; but in going east-by-north from the Congo there would be no hope. Even were we alone, there would not be the slightest probability of success—with Kaloolah it would be impossible. Leaving out the formidable difficulties and dangers of the route, the desert of *Srah*, would be an obstacle impassable, except by the consent and assistance of the cruel and ferocious beings who inhabit it.

Kaloolah was by no means disposed to submit to the reasoning of her brother. She persisted in asserting her willingness and ability to encounter and endure any hardships and dangers ; and to all his objections, made answer by pointing, sometimes to me, and sometimes to my gun, as if, with that in hand, I alone could ensure their safety against wild beasts, cannibals, and bushmen. Poor Kaloolah ! woman-like, she followed the dictates of her heart rather than her head ; and danger, suffering, even death itself, had no power to stay her in the route affection pointed out. Forgetting fear, in the excess of hope, she would joyfully, had we consented, have commenced the long and fearful pilgrimage, though a thousand deaths had stared her in the face.

We were debating the point, when our conversation was interrupted by the protrusion of a black shining face through the open wicket. Glancing carefully round, and making sundry grimaces, to indicate caution, our friendly visitor delivered himself of the same warning that had been so often repeated.

" *Prenez garde*," said he, " Bergamme make fetish, *muy grande*. *Prenez garde*," and before I had time to question him, the speaker had disappeared.

There was something exceedingly annoying in this threatening of an indefinite danger, the nature of which it was impossible to ascertain, and against which it was, of course, impossible to guard. Although there was nothing to apprehend, from the fetish itself, it was quite probable that, encouraged by the supposed power of the charm, Bergamme, and his partner the slave-merchant, might undertake something, which, from the wholesome fear I had instilled into them, they would not otherwise dare to attempt.

In company with Enphadde I made a thorough search of the neighborhood around our hut, but nothing of a suspicious character could be found. Not a single native was in sight, and no unusual sights or sounds indicated danger from the distant village.

It was quite dark when we re-entered the hut, where we found Kaloolah, who had taken upon herself, with true feminine spirit, the duties of house-keeping, busy in preparing supper. Within the court a small fire of mangrove branches was blazing brightly, upon which was cooking, in an earthen pot, a hodge-podge of chicken, rice, peppers, and potatoes. I threw myself upon a mat in one corner of the large room, or hall, while Enphadde seated himself in the other. The cheerful light streamed in at the open door-way, and occasionally a puff of savory steam diffused its exciting odor through the apartment. Kaloolah was seated upon the ground just without the door, but in full view from the outside, and in such a position that, by leaning back a little, she could listen to, and join in, our conversation. Nothing could be more admirable than the unstudied grace of her attitudes, or the good-humored archness of her face, as revealed in the flashes of the strong firelight. Her body was constantly in motion: sometimes bending forward to feed the fire with dry leaves, and singing, the while, snatches of a plaintive song, and then stretching

her gracefully turned head and neck into the hut, repeating English
words and phrases, and laughing at their oddness in those dulcet tones
that make the gushing, gurgling laugh of a pretty woman the most delicious sound in nature.

"Oh! Jon'than, now fire burn—make supper very quick. Sheeken
supper very good—supper, dinner, breakfast—one—two—three," and
then, as if there was something irresistibly comic in the sounds, she would
laugh heartily, while her bright black eyes danced, and her whole face
beamed with a matchless expression of mingled archness and *naïveté*.

"Sing a song, Kaloolah," I exclaimed.

She hesitated.   " I will sing," said I ; and I sang a verse of Inkle and
Yarico.   It was an old song of my mother's, but it struck me as singular
that, at that moment it should have occurred to me ; I took it as a
warning.

"Now, Kaloolah, you sing," said I, as I finished.

"Oh, yes—I sing—much—very good," she replied, and pausing for an
instant, commenced a love ditty.   The *Tul-tul*, I afterwards found was a
species of sweet-scented lily, growing upon the banks of the mountain
streams of Framazugda, and the following is a literal translation of the
words, which a better acquaintance with the language than I then had
has since enabled me to make.   There is not much in the words, but the
sentiment indicates a greater refinement in love, than would be found in
a savage and debased state of society, while the air was exceedingly
plaintive and sweet, reminding me very much of some of the simple but
touching melodies of the Irish school of composers.

THE TUL-TUL AND THE STREAM.

By Streamlet's brink a Tul-tul grew,
And from her leaflets, moist with dew,
Enchanting fragrance far she threw.
  Ah ! Tul, beware the fickle Stream !
  Love's life is but a giddy dream,
  Where shadows flit, and false lights gleam.

The Streamlet saw the blooming flower ;
" Ah, Tul," he cried, " 't is now love's hour,
Come, yield thee, sweet one, to his power."
  Ah ! Tul, beware ! if thy heart owns
  The melody of his low tones,
  Thou 'lt answer yet with sighs and moans.

By blushing Tul the strain is heard :
She smiles, and drinks the honeyed word ;

With half-formed hopes her breast is stirred.
    Ah! Tul, beware! His quiet mien,
    His gentle tones, his glittering sheen,
    Are naught but lures, I sadly ween.

Sweet Tul-tul's feet his ripples lave;
She sees her image in his wave;
Can naught be done poor Tul to save?
    Ah! Tul, beware! The fickle Tide
    Will well around thee deep and wide,
    But soon love's claims he will deride.

The dew has failed, the ground is dry,
The air is hot, the sun is high,
Sweet Tul now sees her lover fly.
    Ah! Tul, sweet Tul! She hangs her head;
    The blight of love is o'er her shed;
    The faithless stream afar has fled.

From noontide heats in shady dell,
The Streamlet seeks his rocky cell.
Ah! who poor Tul-tul's grief can tell?
    Poor Tul! Her fragrant breath has flown;
    Her withered leaves around are strown;
    Rustling with saddening sigh and moan.

As the last words of the song died upon the air, we were startled by the loud report of a musket, and the crashing of the bullet through the slight reed fence and the palm-leaf matting. It had evidently been aimed at Kaloolah, through the interstices of the canes, but, deviating slightly from its course in its passage, it just missed her person, and striking a brand, knocked the fire about in all directions, and passed in at the doorway and out through the matting at the farther side, a little above Enphadde's head. I seized my gun and rushed out of the wicket, followed by Enphadde, but it was so dark that it was impossible to see any object, not in motion, at ten paces distant. We listened intently, and fancied that we could hear retreating feet; it was useless, however, to pursue them, and we were compelled to return no wiser than we went. Kaloolah was very much frightened, and I must confess that my own fears were thoroughly aroused; but the only thing that could be done was to put out our fire and keep a good look-out for any further attack. In the morning I was determined to see Bergamme, and take such action in the case as the occasion might require. We passed a sleepless night, but nothing more occurred to excite particular attention or alarm.

CHAPTER XIV.

IT is the custom in Congo to suffer an interval of time to elapse between the decease and burial of members of the higher classes, proportioned to the rank of the subject and the wealth of surviving friends. In the meantime the body is enveloped in voluminous folds of cotton cloth, pieces of which are weekly and almost daily added, so as to conceal any signs of decomposition. This process goes on until the corpse attains an enormous size. When too large for the house in which it is contained, the building is taken down and a larger one erected in its place. In the case of very distinguished individuals, this is frequently done two or three times: and a fellow who, in his lifetime, never had clothing enough to cover his nakedness, is, after death, swathed into a capital illustration of the principle of compensation—clothing himself then (or rather his friends doing so for him) in all the cloth which he was formerly entitled to but did not have.

The day after the night which closes the last chapter was appointed for the burial of a distinguished personage who had been dead seven or eight years. During the whole of this long period, the body had been undergoing this epidemic accretion. Every rag of cotton that could be bought, begged, or stolen, had been added by mourning relatives, until a bulk sufficient to satisfy the pride of affection had been attained.

The grave was at some little distance from the village, and consisted of a large pit, ten feet wide and at least twenty feet deep. To it the corpse was borne on a bier of poles by a procession of all the inhabitants of the town, accompanied by bands of musicians, some of them blowing conch shells, others rattling strings of gourds, and others beating with the open hand large drums made of skins stretched across the mouths of hollow logs. A kind of guitar or banjo aided the harmony with its tinkling sounds, while tones, not unlike in quality to those of a small organ, were produced from a row of gourds fastened to a board, and across the open mouths of which were placed three slips of reeds. These were struck with small sticks, precisely in the same way as are the pieces of glass in a musical instrument common enough in Christian countries, but of which I do not now recollect the name.

Surrounding the corpse were bands of mourning females, who made the air additionally vocal with cries, groans, and ejaculations—keeping up a continuous torrent of questions addressed to the dead man, or shrieking his praises at the utmost pitch of their voices.

" Oh, why did you die ? Why did you go away ? Will you ever come back ? Are you happy ? Do you forget us all ? Oh ! hoo ! oh ! hoo ! He was such a good man ! He kept all his wives so fat ! He gave them so much to eat ! And he gave them so much rum to drink ! Oh ! hoo ! He was such a good man ! Oh ! hoo ! Oh ! hoo ! "

Numerous *gangams* (priests) added to the clamor of the women the most frantic and diabolical yells. They ran, leaped, and danced about the corpse with uncouth gestures and horrid grimaces, and practised various ceremonies of incantation which it would be tedious to particularize.

It was intimated that it would be considered a compliment to the family, and a favor to the whole town, if my gun was discharged a few times—a request with which I very readily complied. After the burial, a grand feast, open to all, finished the services of the day. All signs of grief were now thrown by. Those who could get it, inspirited themselves with rum and brandy, while those who could not continued to reach an equally glorious degree of elevation by means of old and strong palm wine. The festivity was kept up with music, obscene songs, and lascivious dances until a late hour in the night.

About sunset I walked down to the village to see the ceremonies of the feast, which had commenced an hour or two before I arrived. A large group of the principal men, surrounded by inferior parties, were squatted on the ground in an open space in front of the widow's house. I was quite warmly received, and invited to take a seat upon the leopard skins of the Mafooka and his officers, which invitation I was about to accept, when I spied Bergamme and his partner seated together, at a little distance off. I had been on the watch for him during the whole day, but, conscious of guilt, and dreading to meet me, the fellow had not thought proper to show himself. I determined, on the instant, not to let slip the opportunity of making a decided impression.

He was seated about twenty feet from the Mafooka, with half a dozen blacks immediately about him, and in such a position as to be in full view of all upon the ground. By his side lay an old Spanish musket, and around his neck hung his famous fetish. It consisted of an uncouth hollow figure of dried clay, the upper part of which was fashioned somewhat into the resemblance of the human face. The body of it was studded with parrot feathers of different colors, every one of which had been particularly blessed by the *gangam*, and inserted into the clay with magical ceremonies and incantations. For every feather a fowl had been sacrificed by the priests, and the point dipped into the blood. No expense had been spared by Bergamme to make it as perfect as possible, and the *gangams* had exerted their utmost skill. With the credulous faith of his superstitious countrymen in the power of these ignorant but exceedingly cunning impostors, he believed that he had got a charm that would preserve him from any danger; even a musket-ball would be diverted from his own person, and turned back against the breast of the sacrilegious wretch by whom it had been fired.

Declining the invitation to be seated, I strode up to Bergamme, and stopped directly in front of him. He quailed a little at my presence, but kept his position, while his companion scrambled backwards some yards in the greatest affright.

" Listen," said I, looking around and over the reclining audience, and directing a friendly *linguista*, who spoke excellent Spanish, to interpret my words.

" Listen ! Last night a musket was fired into my house. It came very near killing one of my slaves. I charge this man with the deed ! "

All eyes were now directed towards us, but not a word was spoken ; even Bergamme, although he looked utterly confounded, retained his position without stirring.

" This man," I continued, " fired that shot. I know it. He dare not deny it ; he wishes to take my life ! Will you allow such a crime ? Shall he not be punished ? I came among you as a friend. I have been received as a friend. How would the Chenoo, your master at Emboma, receive the news, that a friendly white man, who came to ' make trade,' had been killed or maltreated ? "

" He shall drink the kisha water," said the Mafooka. " If he is innocent it will do him no harm ; if he is guilty it will kill him."

" No, no," I replied, " I don't wish to compel him to drink the kisha. He knows that he is guilty, and that if it is a true test he would die."

The proposition by no means suited me, as I knew that if he was subjected to the ordeal, his friends, the *gangams*, who administer it, would give him some harmlesss potion, and the fellow would have all the advantage of an honorable acquittal.

" No I wont subject him to the test of guilt ; I want only to warn him against any further crime. If he attacks me again he must look out ; the consequences will be bad for him ; he can't hurt me, but he may hurt himself. He puts his trust in this thing," and here, with a sudden grasp, I seized the fetish, and tore it from his neck. My motions were so quick and unexpected, that he could offer no resistance, even had he been disposed, which he was not ; he fairly shivered with astonishment at the audacity of the act.

" He puts his trust in this thing," said I, holding it up. " It can't protect him if I resolve to punish him. It may be the most powerful

' And bringing up my gun to bear upon it, fired both barrels in immediate succession."

fetish in the country, but I care nothing for it. What can it do to me? Look ! "

Every eye was upon me as I spat contemptuously in the face of the grinning figure. A general groan of terror expressed the apprehensions of the audience. If the earth had yawned and swallowed me up, or the Evil One had caught me up bodily in his clutches, they would not have been at all surprised.

" Look ! " I continued, " you see it has no power to harm me. I am too strong for it. I fear it not ; I despise it—that for his fetish ! " and

I tossed the figure into the air, and bringing up my gun to bear upon it, fired both barrels in immediate succession. They were heavily loaded with duck-shot, and both charges took effect. The clay figure was broken into a thousand pieces, and the feathers cut and scattered in every direction.

" Do you see that ? " said I, addressing Bergamme. " Well, if ever you or that fellow there come around my house again, with evil intent, by the great and ever-living Zamba Em Pounga, I will serve you in the same way. The darkness of the darkest night won't save you."

Wonder, admiration, and fear were variously depicted upon the faces of my audience, and, as their tongues became loosened, were expressed in all kinds of curious exclamations. Never did actor on the stage feel better assured of having made a decided hit than did I, when I looked at the powerless and prostrate form of the killer, shivering as if with an ague fit. There was no further harm to be apprehended from him.

Stepping up to the Mafooka, I took a sup from his brandy jug.

" You did not get this from *El Bonito* ? " said I.

" No ! it is Portuguese," he replied.

" I thought so. It is very good ; but we have some much better on board. When she comes back I will send you a couple of bottles."

" And won't you give me one ? " demanded a Formio of distinction.

" With the greatest pleasure."

" And me ? " said another.

" Certainly."

" And me ? and me ? and me ? " shouted the crowd.

In a moment I had promised a dozen bottles, and, fearful of committing myself further, I made a rapid but dignified retreat.

Kaloolah was on the watch for me. I saw her intently peering from the entrance to the court in the direction of the village. As I came in sight she suddenly started, and withdrew within the gate-way. In a moment she re-appeared, and came bounding towards me with a handful of the sweet-scented wild flowers that grew in endless variety on the uncultivated land along the margin of the river. Upon entering the house I found a large bouquet of the same flowers arranged in an earthen jug at the side of my palm-leaf bed. This delicate and considerate attention delighted but did not surprise me. I was prepared to receive any evidence of refined sensibility and feminine taste in Kaloolah as a matter of course. Thanking her warmly for her kindness, I assured her that I was very fond of flowers, and that those she had selected were very beautiful and very sweet.

"Very sweet flowers," she replied, repeating my words. "Ah, yes, very sweet!"

She raised the flowers to inhale their fragrance, and as she did so her smile died away to a most touching sadness, and the tears started to her eyes.

"What is the matter, Kaloolah?" said I, taking her hand; "what makes you sad?"

She understood the import of my question, if not the exact meaning of each word.

"Ah!" she replied, "flowers very much sweet in Framazugda!"

The mysterious chain of association had been struck, and vibrated in every link, responsive to the blow. The delicate perfume had aroused the slumbering recollections of fair gardens and fragrant bowers, and with them the thoughts of home and friends—the sacred memories of the heart. Who could wonder at her tears?

In a moment her smiles returned, and aided by Enphadde she set about preparing for the evening meal. In these household affairs I carefully abstained from offering any assistance, feeling that it was best to leave to them the only means they had of showing their overflowing gratitude and respect. The supper over, the remainder of the evening was passed in conversation and song. Kaloolah sang several simple and pleasing melodies, accompanying herself with small pieces of reed of different lengths and sizes, that, twirled by the fingers with wonderful rapidity, gave a few low, buzzing notes that harmonized with her voice, and produced a very agreeable effect. Enphadde had also contrived an instrument, consisting of a sounding-board, into which were inserted slips of reed which were supported by a bridge. The instrument was held by the left hand, at an angle of inclination sufficient to bring the row of reeds into a horizontal position, which were then snapped by the fingers of the right hand with a degree of dexterity that must have required much practice to attain. The tones were pleasant, and the divisions of the musical scale perfectly accurate. Both Kaloolah and her brother evinced the possession of a very fine and accurate ear, and a quick and tenacious musical memory. Several English airs Kaloolah could repeat after hearing them once, without missing a note.

Our entertainment was kept up until a late hour in the evening, and, although I may not say that it would have fully satisfied the fastidious ears of a critical bravurist, it gave us as much pleasure as ever was derived from the loftiest harmonies of Beethoven, or the sprightliest melodies of Rossini. Time, place, and circumstance ever powerfully influence the effect that music produces upon the mind; and our music must have been indeed execrable, if in a negro hut, far from home, in the wilds of Congo, it had not power to excite agreeable associations, and gently, perhaps sadly, but withal not unpleasantly, arouse emotion, and stir the heart.

Upon retiring to rest I resigned myself to slumber, with a sense of security, as far as the former masters of Kaloolah were concerned, which for several previous nights it had been impossible to feel. Still my sleep was broken and disturbed. A vague impression of coming evil took possession of me. Shadowy, half-formed fancies—the gaunt, gloaming ghosts of horrible ideas stalked through my mind, and kept me tossing and tumbling on my bed of leaves until nearly daylight. A few hours' unquiet sleep, and I awoke with a slight headache, a feeling of general lassitude, and chillness and dull pains in my back and lower extremities. Then it was that I first suspected that I was ill. Kaloolah's expressive face was a mirror in which I could see that I looked fully as unwell as I felt, and, if further confirmation were wanted, it was present in the furred tongue and the yellow tinge with which all objects appeared invested.

The grasp of the malaria—that curse of the African coast—was upon me. Brooding in darkness and in damp over the low alluviums of the intertropical shores, that mysterious power, innocuous to the negro, but a deadly foe to the Caucasian constitution, presents a barrier which the white man has not yet been able to pass. I was to prove no exception, and I shuddered as well at the thought as beneath the direct chilling touch of this relentless agent of death.

My headache gradually increased, accompanied with nausea and a sensation of weight in the region of the stomach, and all my symptoms began to be aggravated, except perhaps the feeling of chilliness. The rapidity with which in many cases the African fever develops itself is well known. There was no time to lose, if any preparatory remedial measures were to be adapted. Fortunately, I had a small paper of medicines in the pocket of my instrument-case, and as there was not much doubt in my mind of the propriety of emetics in the forming stage of all fevers, it was not difficult to decide upon a full dose of the tartrate of antimony.

By night reaction had taken place, and the fever was fully developed. Strong cerebral symptoms convinced me that it would not answer much longer to confide in my medical judgment, even should my senses be preserved, and that the best way would be to make sure of one good dose of calomel and jalap, and then trusting to a good constitution, leave the disease to its course. The powder was prepared, and swallowing it, with somewhat of the feeling with which the mariner casts his last anchor to windward on a lee-shore, I resigned myself to my fate.

Delirium soon supervened; but amid the wanderings of reason and the vagaries of maddened fancy, I was still conscious of the soothing influences of woman's gentle attentions. The figure of Kaloolah, multiplied by diseased sensation into a dozen angelic forms, was ever around me. Flitting spirits, bearing her face and form, constantly hovered over me, fanning my hot cheek with their gentle wings, or, with light fingers, parting my hair, and bathing my throbbing temples—at each moment smoothing the rumpled palm leaves, chasing the buzzing insects, and refreshing my parched mouth with draughts of cool water or the pleasant juice of the sweet lemon. I knew not all the time that it was she; but still, even when most bewildered, there remained a distinct consciousness of some power without that kept down the raging demon, who roared and struggled for mastery within.

On the ninth day the fever reached its crisis, and, thanks to a good constitution and kind nursing, the crisis was safely passed. From that day recovery was no longer doubtful, and in three or four days more I was able to sit up, and indulge with a good appetite in the convalescent's luxury—a bowel of chicken broth. It would require weeks, however, to regain my full strength. Although the disease had manifested itself in a comparatively mild and simple form, and had not been complicated by any severe local congestions, and had in consequence lasted hardly a quarter of its usual time, it had nevertheless left marks of its power behind, which it would require time to remove.

I learned from Enphadde that during my illness the inhabitants of the village had in general evinced a great deal of good feeling; the women in particular frequently visiting the hut and offering assistance. The Mafooka had sent several times to inquire after my health, accompanying his messages with presents of fowls and eggs. A native physician had offered to perform the operation of cupping, but Enphadde did not dare give his consent.

The favorable change in the disease was soon known, and brought a succession of visits of congratulation from the principal citizens of the town. Each one, as is sometimes the case in more civilized countries, had something to suggest in aid of my speedy recovery. One recommended lion's-tail soup; another, a dish of alligator's eyes; and a third, a fricassee of monkeys' tongues, and each one offered to provide his remedy for a proper consideration. The terms were too high, and if for no other reason, I was compelled to respectfully decline their assistance, and rely upon chicken broth and the culinary skill of Kaloolah.

It was now more than three weeks since the departure of the slaver, and as yet nothing had been heard from her. It was known that she had succeeded in passing, without molestation, the English man-of-war, and that the latter, the next morning had also weighed her anchor and stood out of the river. Had she overtaken the *Bonito?* and if so, what was to become of me and my companions? It must be recollected that I was sick—worn down in body, and depressed in mind, and it will not appear strange that a supposition of the slaver's having been captured, which, under other circumstances would have given me pleasure, now excited nothing but dismay. I brooded over the thought with the most melancholy anticipations. My money was nearly gone. When all was spent how were we to obtain the commonest necessities of life? When, and how should we find means to escape from a country and climate that desponding imagination began to invest with all the horrors of purgatory?

Feeling thus, it may be supposed that I was overjoyed when, at near the close of the fourth week, the news came that the *Bonito* had arrived in the river, and was at anchor about twenty miles below. My spirits, however, were far from undergoing an elation corresponding to their previous depression. Doubts and fears intruded themselves, and very much qualified the anticipated pleasures of freedom and pure ocean air.

One great source of anxiety was the beauty of Kaloolah, which had been growing more and more striking as her face daily recovered some portion of its original fulness, and her figure its rounded and graceful proportions. I knew my own powerlessness on shipboard, especially in my then state of health; and I knew well the lawlessness of the *Bonito's* crew. Fortunately, among my other medicines there was a stick of nitrate of silver, or lunar caustic, and the idea occurred to me that by means of it her dangerous beauty might be deprived for a time of its power. I at once proposed it to her, and after explaining that we were going among bad men, who might be rude to her, and that it would be perhaps much easier for me to protect her from insult if we could get rid of her good looks, she at once consented to the application of the caustic. In a few minutes her face was covered with black spots and blotches which completely altered its expression. There was the same lustrous eye, the same finely turned features, but a stranger would have turned from them with pity for the horrible disease with which they were overcast. The change was so great that Enphadde, who better than Kaloolah had comprehended the object I had in view, looked quite shocked, and would hardly be satisfied with my repeated assurance that the spots would wear off, and his sister's skin resume its natural hue.

CHAPTER XV.

"QUIÉN ES V.?" exclaimed Captain Garbez, as I mounted the
side of the slaver just as her anchor struck the ground off
Lembee. "*Madre de Dios!* how you have altered! One
would hardly know you, you have changed so! Ah, the rascally
fever! I know it well, for I 've had it myself. But, what is the news?
what has happened during the last month?"

"Nothing," I replied, "but what you can see for yourself. The
fever has pulled me down, as you perceive. It was sharp, but short, and
I am recovering now as fast as I could reasonably expect. It is but five
days since I was confined to the bed. But what has kept you so long? I
had begun to think that perhaps you were figuring before your friends of
the mixed commission."

"No, they don't catch me so easy," replied the captain. "The
Bonito has broad wings, and you might as well send a turkey-cock after a
sea-gull as to chase her with any English craft that I know of. It is the
cursed calms that have kept us so long. See, I 've lost half the hair on
my head. *Caramba!* I would n't mind having my whole scalp blown
off in a gale of wind, but to be compelled to tear my hair out, in a stupid
calm, is too bad. We 've had but one capful of wind since we left, and
that was a regular buttender right in our teeth. You see, just as we left
the mouth of the river we came across the consort of the fellow we had
left behind. As soon as he saw us he loosened and sheeted home every
thing, and took after us, but it was of no use. We stretched off to the
west, and soon dropped him ; but when we began to think about turning
back, the wind came on to blow a perfect hurricane from the east. We
were compelled to lie-to for eight and forty hours, and although the
Bonito is a pretty weatherly craft, we drifted to leeward like the D——l

in Lent. Since then we had nothing but calms and light head-winds. I promised our Holy Mother the price of a young negro in wax lights, but she did n't do us any good, and burn my eyes if she may n't find her own candles, or sit in the dark for aught I care."

" How soon do you get under way again ? " said I, interrupting the captain, who was rapidly working himself into a passion about the weather.

" As soon as possible, but the Lord only knows when that will be. I shall try to be off in less than a week. It will depend upon the time it takes to bring all the slaves in. The negroes here are wretchedly slow in all their movements, and what is worse, there is not much use in trying to stir them up. Along the coast, from Cabenda up, they do business more promptly. When the barracoons are full, the shipping a cargo will not take more than an hour or two. The slaves suffer so much from their confinement and want of food in the barracoons, that when the gates are opened they frequently run and skip down to the canoes in their delight at being taken to ' the white man's country', where they will have plenty to eat.' But I must hurry ashore and see what can be done."

The captain's boat was ready, and he stepped into it and shoved off, while I turned into the cabin to look after my personal property, which, including my money, I was happy to find had been undisturbed.

Preparations were actively resumed for the reception of the slaves, and in a few hours after the captain's visit to the shore several boat-loads of unhappy wretches were sent on board. The first comers were taken below the berth-deck and arranged upon a temporary slave-deck placed over the water-casks, and at a distance of not more than three feet and a half from the deck overhead. Into the planks eye-bolts were inserted, and firmly secured at different intervals, in four rows, running fore and aft the ship. Through these bolts traversed iron shackle bars, which were prevented from slipping by a knob at one end and a padlock at the other. When the padlock was removed the bar could be shoved back, and the slaves strung upon it in gangs of five, six, or eight in number. The shackle was a stout piece of iron, curved like a horse-shoe, with holes in the ends for the bar to pass through. Each slave had one of these shackles placed over his ankle ; the long bar was drawn through the ends of it along the under side of his leg, and so on of each slave belonging to the gang ; the end of the bar was then passed through the eye-bolt and secured by the padlock. This arrangement made it very convenient to air the slaves on deck, when the weather would permit. All that was necessary was to remove the lock, slide the bar back, and slip the shackles off, when the limbs of the whole gang were at once unfettered. After their airing they could be strung along on the bar, and the end of it again secured with hardly more time or trouble. It was somewhat unusual, the captain informed me, to shackle slaves taken from the coast south of Cape Lopez, inasmuch as they are generally a mild and timid race, but for those obtained from any of the stations from Cape Lopez north to the Gambia shackles are essential.

The slaves, as I have said, were arranged in four ranks. When lying down, the heads of the two outer ranks touched the sides of the ship ; their feet pointing inboard or athwart the vessel. They, of course, occupied a space fore and aft the ship of about six feet on either side, or twelve feet of the whole breadth. At the feet of the outside rank come the heads of the inner row. They took up a space of six feet more on either side, or together twelve feet. There was still left a space running up and down the centre of the deck, two or three feet in breadth ; along this were stretched single slaves, between the feet of the two inner rows, so that when all were lying down almost every square foot of the deck was covered with a mass of human flesh. Not the slightest space was allowed between the individuals of the ranks, but the whole were packed as closely as they could be, each slave having just room enough to stretch himself out flat upon his back, and no more. In this way about two hundred and fifty were crowded upon the slave-deck, and as many more upon the berth-deck.

Horrible as this may seem, it was nothing compared to the "packing" generally practised by slavers. Captain Garbez boasted that he had tried both systems, tight packing and loose packing thoroughly, and that he had found the latter the best.

"If you call this loose packing," I replied, "have the goodness to explain what you mean by tight packing."

"Why, tight packing consists in making a row sit with their legs stretched apart, and then another row is placed between their legs, and so on, until the whole deck is filled. In the one case each slave has as much room as he can cover lying ; in the other, only as much room as he can occupy sitting. With tight packing this craft ought to stow fifteen hundred." About fifty of the whole number were females, who were left unshackled, but were closely confined in a small space at the stern, which was cut off from the apartment of the males by a stout bulkhead.

It was with a good deal of difficulty that I made arrangements for Kaloolah and Enphadde. The captain, at first, strongly objected to receiving them at all. He could not spare the room ; but that difficulty was obviated by my offering to indemnify him for any loss, in a sum equal to the clear profit his owners would receive for the two slaves, that, as he asserted, would be displaced.

"Besides," continued I, " they will not take up any of the room of the ship that could be otherwise occupied. I intend to take them both into my state-room."

"Impossible ! " he exclaimed.

"Not at all," said I, " it may be, perhaps, inconvenient for me, but they won't be in the way of any one else. Come, captain, you must consent. I assure you I will fully satisfy your owners. You can see for yourself that I have the means," and I showed to the captain a large purse of gold.

The captain eyed me for some time in silence.

"I 'll go still further than that," I continued ; " I 'll not only pay for their passage, but if you allow me to put them into the cabin, where they won't disturb any one but myself, there 's my chronometer—you have often admired it—it is yours."

"Well, doctor, do as you please—but what the d—l you see in those two slaves to like so much, I can't understand. They are not niggers, it is true, and that is the reason why they are not worth half so much as a pair of full-blooded blacks. We often get queer kinds of people, of all colors, shapes, and sizes, but they are good for nothing in the market. They can't stand heat or labor with the pure blacks. I once took a cargo to Brazil, of which about one half were real whites—some of them with blue eyes and light hair ; there was not as much negro blood in them as you see in the whitest slaves in New-Orleans or Havana. They went off at half prices, and when put down to work they all died in less than a year. So if you expect to make a speculation with these you will find yourself much mistaken. The girl, perhaps, would bring a good price, if you can cure those spots on her face, but the boy is good for nothing in the field, and for house-work people like only slaves that have been trained."

Most fortunately *el segundo capitan* was confined to his berth with a violent attack of inflammatory rheumatism, and incapable of making any opposition to my plans.

In five days the Bonito's compliment of slaves was on board, and all ready for departure. At the last moment I joined the ship, with Kaloolah and Enphadde ; the anchor was weighed, and with a fair and stiff breeze we ran down the rapid current on the top of an ebbing tide. In a few hours, we were dancing upon the lively swell of the open ocean, and inhaling with delight the breeze which, although coming from the land, seemed to have lost its malevolent and oppressive character. As we increased our distance from the shore, my breath came deeper, freer: each draught seemed to penetrate farther and farther among the clogged air cells of the lungs, stirring the sluggish blood, and chasing the lingering remnants of disease. What an inestimable blessing is plenty of pure fresh air! What exquisite pleasure in the free and easy performance of the respiratory function! Alas! five hundred unhappy wretches were beneath my feet, who had been cruelly cut off from that pleasure—deprived of that blessing! Despite the refreshing influences of the breeze I sickened at the thought.

As night set in the wind freshened, with a short, quick head-sea, through which the ship, under full sail, ploughed her uneasy way. As the motion increased, the most heart-rending sounds began to issue from between her decks. It grew stronger and stronger—blending with and almost overpowering the creaking of spars and bulkheads, and the melancholy wail of the breeze among the tautened cords of the weather-rigging. A deep, dull chorus of moans and sobs, and sighs, arose from the grated hatchways spread around upon the air, and enwrapped the cursed craft in all the harmonies of hell. It was the shrill cry of youth, and the sobbing voices of woman in the hour of fright and distress. It was the deep groans of manhood, wrung by pain from the panting breast. It was the choking sobs of oppressed respiration—the retchings of nausea the clanking of fetters, and the stertorous gaspings of wretches in the last agonies of death.

The next morning five corpses were picked out from among the men, and two from among the women, and thrown overboard.

"Only seven!" exclaimed the captain, "well, that's devilish good luck so far. I always calculate, with a full cargo, to lose from fifteen to twenty by the first touch of sea-sickness. Come, bear a-hand there, and give them an airing!"

From forty to fifty at a time were now brought upon deck. As they emerged from the hatchway they were manacled together in gangs of six or eight, as much to prevent individuals from jumping overboard as to guard against resistance. Each gang was then placed in turn on the forecastle, the brakes of a forcing pump manned, and a powerful stream of water directed through a hose upon them. After being thoroughly drenched, they were allowed to walk about and dry themselves for fifteen or twenty minutes, and were then passed down to their shackles, to be succeeded by another set.

Never but in a slaver were seen such groups of woe-begone wretches.

Many were ill with previous disease, and all of them laboring under the distressing effects of sea-sickness; their naked bodies, begrimed with filth, shivered and shrunk in the cool fresh air and their quivering lips and rolling eyes expressed the height of bodily suffering, mental agony, and hopeless despair. There was none of that stolid indifference which had characterized the expression of their faces on shore. There, cruelty and hardship had assumed familiar forms, and a dogged endurance opposed itself to the frowns of fate. Here they were upon a new and fearful element—new terrors aroused their jaded and sluggish fears—new pangs developed the secret sensations of their benumbed and hardened frames. Alas! they were only at the commencement of their fearful voyage—at the threshold merely of the horrors that were to multiply, in geometric ratio, the farther they advanced.

I attempted to visit the slave-decks. The sights, sounds, and smells were intolerable; and, with a death-like sickness at the heart, I was compelled to retire. "Good heavens!" I exclaimed, "I had no idea of this."

"Why, it is n't very pleasant," said the captain, "but what can you expect when they are all sea-sick? Wait till they get over that, and we shall be able to keep them in better order; and, besides, they 'll naturally thin out a little, and that will make them more comfortable."

"But if such is the state of things in fair weather," I demanded, "how will it be if it should come on to blow?"

"If it is a downright regular gale, we shall have the d——l's own time, of course," replied the captain. "When it comes to closing the hatches, it is all up with the voyage. You can hardly save enough to pay expenses. They die like leeches in a thunder-storm. I was once in a little schooner with three hundred on board, and we were compelled to lie-to for three days. It was the worst sea I ever saw, and came near swamping us several times. We lost two hundred and fifty slaves in that gale. We could n't get at the dead ones to throw them overboard very handily, and so those that did n't die from want of air were killed by the rolling and tumbling about of the corpses. Of the living ones, some had their limbs broken, and every one had the flesh of his leg worn to the bone by the shackle-irons."

"Good God! and you still puruse the horrible trade?"

"Certainly: why not? Despite of accidents the trade is profitable, and for the cruelty of it no one is to blame except the English. Were it not for them, large and roomy vessels would be employed, and it would be an object to bring the slaves over with every comfort, and in as good condition as possible. Now every consideration must be sacrificed to the one great object—escape from capture by the British cruisers."

I had no wish to reply to the captain's argument. One might as well reply to a defence of blasphemy or murder. Giddy, faint, and sick, I turned with loathing from the fiends in human guise, and sought the more genial companionship of the inmates of my state-room.

Kaloolah and Enphadde were suffering slightly from the effects of sea-sickness, but in every other respect they were as comfortable as could be wished. Enphadde was stretched upon the narrow floor, wrapped in a blanket, with a carpet-bag for a pillow. Kaloolah occupied the lower berth, while the upper berth was reserved for myself. We were thus rather closely stowed, but I had only to think of the miserable beings between decks and the sense of constraint and discomfort vanished.

In two or three days my interesting room-mates were so far recovered as to be able to take the air upon deck. Kaloolah, however, I kept closely confined in the daytime, and allowed her to come out only at night. I wished to prevent either her seeing or being seen; and even Enphadde, according to my instructions, exposed himself as little as possible to the notice of the crew. As soon as it grew dark we would all three creep over the taffrail into the stern-boat, and enjoy several hours' unmolested and interesting conversation. I had already made so much progress in the Framazug tongue that I could already comprehend the minutest descriptions of the wonderful scenes of their native country; and, in turn, astonish them with an account of the curious things that they were to see in mine. At such times it was impossible to resist the temptation to encourage their hopes of returning through the northern negro countries to their home.

" You will go with us, won't you, Jon'than ? " said Kaloolah, one evening, when I had been explaining how easy it would be to go from my country to some of the French or English ports south of the great desert, and that from thence it would be possible to reach the Niger or Quorah, of which river they had heard the name. Once upon the Quorah, Enphadde felt confident that he would be able to make his way to Framazugda.

" You will go with us, won't you, Jon'than ? "

" Perhaps so," I replied.

" Ah, yes, you must go. You will see so many pleasant things in Framazugda. Your country is very grand and beautiful, but it can't equal ours. The trees, the flowers, the birds ! Ah, I 'm sure no country in the world can equal Framazugda."

Poor girl! I could not bear to disturb with a doubt her happy dreams, the realization of which seemed to her so certain—to me, so distant and improbable.

It may, perhaps, be asked what were my plans respecting her and her brother. The subject was one that I did not, at the time, wish to think about. I had paid the price of their freedom, because I had become interested in their appearance and manners, and because my sympathies had been aroused by their sufferings. I was bringing them to the United States simply because it would have been the height of cruelty to leave them behind. There was no alternative. Mere freedom would have been but an idle gift in the wilds of Congo. I could not doubt but that my motives would be appreciated, and the force of my reasons allowed; but what was to be their ultimate fate was a question that I rather shrunk from entertaining. Certain crude ideas would occasionally intrude themselves, but I generally contrived to banish them without allowing them to assume full shape. Trusting that time would develop nothing but favorable circumstances, I rested satisfied with the resolution that my best exertions should never be wanting to mitigate the hardships of their fate and insure, in future, the comfort and, if possible, the happiness of their lives.

But however practicable were my resolutions for the future, my power was unequal to their protection from a good many present annoyances. Monte, the second captain, had got about again, and seemed more maliciously inclined than ever. Several times, when I was not by, he struck Enphadde with a rope's end, and one evening when I had left Kaloolah alone in the stern-boat for a few minutes she was roughly dragged out and pushed, or rather thrown, down from the poop-deck. My blood boiled at the outrage. I complained to Captain Garbez, but to no purpose; to speak to Monte would be to subject myself to useless insult. I was compelled to keep my wrath to itself, but it lost nothing by nursing.

CHAPTER XVI.

TWO weeks of fine weather, but with rather unfavorable winds, brought us to the line, which was crossed in about five or six degrees of longitude west.

The slaves had become by this time somewhat used to the motion of the ship, and the mortality had diminished from five or six to one or two in the twenty-four hours. They were regularly aired and washed every day, and had pretty good food, though rather a short allowance of it ; but although every care possible was taken to preserve their health, even to administering to them at regular intervals brimstone and molasses, and other slave-ship prescriptions of supposed efficacy, nothing could compensate for the injurious effects of confinement in a close and vitiated atmosphere. They grew weaker and weaker, and their bodies rapidly reached a state of distressing emaciation. Putrid sores and malignant eruptions broke out upon them : in some cases old wounds that had been healed for years reopened, asuming a peculiarly unhealthy aspect ; in others a virulent ophthalmia completely destroyed the tissues of the eye. Many became afflicted with scrofula, developing itself in tubercular phthisis, or in swellings and ulcerations of the glandular sys-tem, and many were attacked with pneumonia, terminating, in the case of one poor fellow, in that most loathsome form of disease, gangrene of the lungs. Nothing can equal the horrible odor of the expectorations in this disease ; and to get rid of the offensive smell which, with its kindred perfumes, seemed to permeate every pore of the ship, the sick man was brought up at night and coolly thrown overboard—alive. A happy re-lease ! the reader will think, for him.

When told of his fate the next morning, indignation mastered pru-

dence, and I freely expressed, in the most unqualified terms, my opinion
of the deed. I was met with scowling looks and muttered imprecations.

"Take care," exclaimed *el segundo capitan*, "or you'll go the same
way. *Por la madre de Dios!* I will have no one to meddle or make on
board this ship."

"Murderer! Coward!" I shouted, completely carried away by rising
passion. "Repeat that threat if you dare!"

His face grew purple with rage, and drawing a long Spanish bladed
sheath knife, he darted towards me, but when within almost arm's reach,
he was checked by the muzzle of a pistol, which, with a motion as quick
as his own, I had pulled from my pocket, and levelled at his head.

"Stir one step," I exclaimed, "and you die!"

He stopped motionless, but in the very attitude of springing upon me,
a horrible convulsion of the muscles of his mouth drew aside his lips,
and disclosed his jagged teeth. A grin, like that of an infuriated hyena,
overspread his face, and his whole body worked and quivered with passion; but he stirred not, and fortunately for him, or rather for both, he
did not. The least motion—and I should have scattered his brains, without the slightest regard to consequences.

We stood thus, both perfectly motionless, confronting each other for
quite a space of time. The sailors who happened to be by were also
taken by surprise, and offered no interference. Their feelings were
against me, but I do not know that they would have taken any decided
part: at any rate the scene was got up so quickly that it reached its *de-
nouement* before they had time to recover their thoughts.

The captain was the first to come to his senses, and wildly shouting
and gesticulating, he rushed between and motioned us apart. I dropped
my pistol, and Captain Garbez grasping my antagonist's arm, compelled
him to put up his knife. Slowly he returned it to its sheath, and drew
himself off among the crew. The scowl of determined malice was on
his face, and I felt that, from that moment, it was war to the knife between us.

The captain, seizing my arm, hurried me aft, beyond the hearing of
the crew.

"Good G-d, *señor el medico*," he exclaimed, "do you want your throat
cut, or your heart's blood let out, that you thus quarrel with Monte?
He'll have your life—he never forgets nor forgives. You must be careful, or I can't protect you."

"I am much obliged to you, Captain Garbez," said I, "but if you
cannot protect me, I can protect myself."

"You can't," replied he; "let me beg of you not to provoke him again—he'll surely have revenge. There is a bad feeling among some of the crew towards you. They overheard your foolish and improper remarks about the ship and the trade, and they say that you will make difficulty for us yet. If they take it into their heads, they would make nothing of throwing you overboard."

"Let them try it!" I exclaimed, although secretly I allowed it would not be very prudent to provoke them to the attempt. "Let them try it! but I have no fear that they will do so. I have not given, and shall not give, them any cause. But as to this Monte, he had better look to him-

"Stir one step," I exclaimed, "and you die!"

self. I've borne enough from him. He threatens to turn Enphadde and his sister out of my stateroom, and send them below upon the slave-deck. Now, mark you, he'll never live to see the sun set on the day that is done. I've paid for their passage, and a good price too, as you know, and you'd better see to it."

"Well, for heaven's sake be careful," replied the captain: "Monte and some of the crew are part owners of the ship, and he's about as much captain as I am. I shall be sorry to have any thing happen to you."

The day after this little fracas a violent gale sprang up from the south-west. The regular trades were compelled to succumb to the influence of the new-comer; and between them both a tremendous irregular cross-sea was knocked up, which made the situation of the ship full as dangerous as it was uncomfortable. Each moment heavy masses of water tumbled aboard of us, shaking the ship throughout every fibre of her frame, and flooding her decks, so that the fore and main-hatches had to be closed, cutting off the supply of air for more than four hundred breathing beings, except what could find its way down the after-hatch.

For nearly twenty-four hours we lay-to on the larboard tack, under the fore, main, and mizzen stay-sails; but the sea becoming more and more dangerous, and the motion of the ship more and more distressing to herself as well as to her cargo, it was resolved to bear away, and scud before the wind. We should thus lose a good deal of ground, and be running north and east towards the African coast, but there was no alternative.

All hands being ready, the closed-reefed main-top-sail was loosed and sheeted home. The fore-sail loosed, the larboard tack got down, and the starboard sheet aft. The main and mizzen stay-sails were then hauled down; the main and top-sail braces hauled in to shiver the top-sail, and the helm put hard-a-weather. The ship fell off rapidly, and, when before the wind, the yards were squared, the fore-sheets both hauled aft, and away we went under closed-reefed main-top-sail and reefed fore-sail.

The motion of the ship was now much easier; we flew before the sea in a way that prevented it from breaking on-board. Every few minutes a huge, hissing wave, with numerous little waves furrowing his surface, would come sweeping after us, apparently threatening inevitable destruction, and as the gallant ship eluded his grasp, dash a portion of spray with resistless force over the stern, and roll on indignantly beneath us. But no swell succeeded in boarding us bodily, as when we were lying-to.

The hatches were now opened, and more than thirty dead bodies picked out from among the mass of human flesh, and thrown overboard.

In ten or twelve hours after the ship was got before the wind, the gale abated; the wind shifted to the east, and the heavy sea gradually subsided. But, although without, the elements had ceased their strife for the dominion of nature, within, the effects of the contest were only beginning to develop themselves. Owing, undoubtedly, to their close confinement during the gale in the vitiated air between-decks, the eyes of nearly one half the slaves became affected simultaneously with acute and painful inflammation. It was purulent ophthalmia in its most virulent form. There had been a few cases previous to the storm, but the disease then was limited in its progress, and assumed a milder and less malignant character.

It was wonderful, the rapidity with which it ran its course. In some cases not three days would elapse from the first symptoms, until the eye-lids would be swelled to an enormous extent—the lower one so much so as, to rest—a huge mass of disease—upon the cheek. Ulcerations of the cornea, and the utter disorganization of the ball of the eye, was, in most cases, the result. Fever, violent pains in the head, and, in many cases, the most excruciating pains in the eye, from the motion of the upper eyelid over the ulcerated cornea, where the conjunctiva had been abraded or ab-sorbed, accompanied the disease. In three days one hundred slaves had lost an eye, and more than twenty, deprived of both eyes, were irrecover-ably blind.

I exerted myself to the utmost to alleviate their sufferings ; but my best efforts were of little avail. No form of medical treatment seemed adapted to the case, and the disease only ran a more rapid race when any attempts were made to arrest it. I had nothing, however, to reproach myself with on that score ; for I felt the conviction that under all the at-tending circumstances the most powerful medicines in the most skilful hands would have been administered in vain.

Emerging from the fore hatchway, after a useless visit to the unfortu-nates below, I observed some of the sailors engaged in slinging several twelve-pound shots to pieces of rope two or three feet in length. I stopped for a moment to inquire for what they were intended, when at the moment a shout of "Sail ho!" came from the look-out at the mast-head. Upon looking in the direction indicated a large brig was to be seen not more than five or six miles off, on our lee-beam. The weather, which had been thick and cloudy all day, had prevented her from being noticed sooner, and her sudden appearance now, about four o'clock in the afternoon, took us completely by surprise. Spy-glasses were produced and levelled at the stranger—the result of the examination was evidently far from satisfac-tory. The two vessels were standing on converging courses, which, if persisted in, would soon bring them within hailing distance. A hurried consultation between the captain and his officers took place in a low tone, at the conclusion of which Garbez and Monte, glass in hand, mounted into the main-rigging. A new hope sprang up in my breast at the evident anxiety of all hands. "God send that she prove a British cruiser!" In a minute this hope was strengthened by the voice of the captain as he descended from the top.

"All hands make sail"! he shouted. "Haul out the spanker--bonnet the jib, and set the flying jib. Ease off the weather-braces. Luff!"

These orders were executed with wonderful rapidity, and the ship, with all sail set, was hauled up close to the wind on the starboard tack.

I had a glass to my eye as the *Bonito* sprung to her luff. The brig was carrying single reefed top-sails, with top-gallant sails over them. What was my delight to see the reefs shaken out and the sails trimmed sharp on a wind.

"Captain," said I, "that fellow is an Englishman."

"To be sure he is," he replied, "but he 'll have to fly, *caramba!* to catch us."

For more than an hour I stood gazing at the pursuing vessel. I measured with my straining eye every foot of the intervening distance. One moment it seemed to diminish. She gains! She gains! No, no, 't is only fancy, flattering hope. Another look! She is as far from us as ever! For the love of Heaven and humanity, gentlemen, take another pull on your lee-braces, and steer small! Alas! 't is all in vain. The *Bonito* is both too fast and too weatherly. What an honor and a reproach to the perverted skill of her Yankee builders!

By nightfall we had gained three or four miles dead to windward, and the brig was left nearly hull down. At ten o'clock Captain Garbez gave orders to tack ship, expecting to stand on for two or three hours, and then bear away on his course with a free wind; but shortly after executing this manœuvre the wind lulled, and by three o'clock in the morning it was perfectly calm.

It was just at daybreak that while lying in my berth my attention was aroused by some sounds on the forward deck. I heard a confused noise —a number of voices speaking together in rather a low key, and then a shrill cry of pain and fright, followed by a plunge of some heavy body into the water. In a minute or two the sounds were repeated. Again and again they struck upon my ear. "What devil's work is going on now?" I exclaimed, jumping from my berth and stepping out upon deck.

A dense fog brooded upon the surface of the ocean, and closely enveloped the ship—standing up on either side, like huge perpendicular walls of granite, and leaving a comparatively clear space—the area of the deck and the height of the maintop-mast cross-trees. In-board the sight ranged nearly free fore-and-aft the ship; but seaward no eye could penetrate more than a yard or two the solid-looking barrier of vapor. A man standing at the taffrail might have seen the cat-heads the whole length of the deck, while at the same time behind him the end of the spanker-boom, projecting over the water, was lost in the mist. I looked up at the perpendicular walls, and the lofty arch overhead with feelings of awe, and, I may add, fear. Cursed indeed must be our craft, when the genius of the mist so carefully avoided the pollution of actual contact. His rolling legions were close around us; but vapory horse and misty foot shrunk back affrighted from the horrors of our blood-stained decks.

The cause of the phenomenon I concluded to be the hot air generated in the crowded space between decks, but I had not time for much speculation as to the precise manner of its action. The same shrill cry and heavy plunging sound was repeated, and turning in the direction from whence it came, I saw a sight that riveted every faculty. A slave was standing amid a group of sailors, one of whom was busy fastening to his leg one of the twelve-pound balls that I had noticed the day before. When this was done, four men standing upon a grating, raised a foot or two from the deck, seized him on either side, and elevating him with a dexterous jerk, pitched him head first over the bulwark. His wild shriek of fear, when he found himself going, was hardly commenced before it was stifled by the waters closing over his head. Another succeeded, and again another.

"Are you sure that there are no more?" demanded Monte, who superintended the operation.

"All at present," responded a sailor; "there is a dozen more that will have to go to-morrow; but we may as well let them have their chance out."

And this was the fate of the blind! Of what value is a slave who has lost his sight? None! He is worth less than nothing! He is an incumbrance—a useless expense—an unsalable article. Pitch him overboard! twenty-five to-day, and "a dozen more to-morrow!"

There are a good many elements of the sublime in a cold-blooded, deliberate murder. The rush and roar of Niagara, the awful voices of the tempest, the wild heaving of the ocean, the death-dealing charge of the battle-field, even the judicial killings called capital punishments, are nothing in comparison. A cool, unimpassioned murder is certainly one of the most wonderful, the most incomprehensible, the most awful, and the most horrible sights that can be witnessed in this world—it is nothing less than the immediate and astounding revelation of the full majesty of hell.

The sun was now some two hours and more above the horizon, and gathering power as he rose, began to make a sensible impression upon the gray banks of vapor. Gradually it resolved itself into detached masses, with deep caves and ravines between, into which the eye could penetrate for some distance, and slowly and gracefully the whole body of it lifted itself from the surface of the ocean, disclosing each instant some new expanse of the sheeny water, and some new effect of the struggling light.

Kaloolah and Enphadde were with me, upon the cabin deck, watching the evolution and dissolution of the myriad fantastic forms.

"Look, look, Enphadde!" exclaimed his sister; "there's the giant of the Diamond Rock, and see, there's his famous dog with the two heads, following after him."

"And who is the Giant of the Diamond Rock?" I demanded.

"Oh, there's a long story about him," replied Kaloolah; "too long to tell now. His home is in a high mountain peak in Framazugda, called the Diamond, but he wanders all about the world with his dog. When he is seen, and his dog makes no noise, it is considered a happy omen; but if his dog growls it bodes bad luck for some one. Are you not glad, Jon'than," continued Kaloolah, playfully, "that the two-headed monster marches on so silently?"

The question had hardly passed her lips when a low, rumbling sound came over the water in the direction of the misty figure, which an active fancy might as well have likened to any thing else as to a giant and a dog. Kaloolah started and turned pale. Enphadde's ear had also caught the sound.

We listened intently, and again heard the same sound, but more faintly than at first. It was evidently from a much farther distance than the column of mist, which had now almost melted into air.

"It must be from some vessel!" I exclaimed; "would to God that we were on board of her! Can you swim, Kaloolah?" Enphadde, I knew, was accomplished in the art.

"Like a fish," interrupted her brother; "she is a real water-witch. I've known her to sport for hours in the great lake of Wollo; she can swim almost as fast and as far as I can."

"Oh, yes, I can swim!" exclaimed Kaloolah, raising both hands, while an expression of delighted energy beamed from her large lustrous eyes. "I could swim miles, to escape from this horrible ship. Come, come, let us go!"

"Where to?" said I, pulling her back from the low rail, upon which she placed one foot, in the attitude for a plunge.

"To the vessel yonder; we surely can reach it."

"Ah! but we don't know that there is a vessel there; and if there was, how could we find it in this fog? A breeze might come before we could swim half the distance, and then we should be left in the middle of the Atlantic. No, if we can escape only by swimming, our chance is a poor one."

While speaking, a slight ripple ran along the surface of the water, and in a moment the coiling wreaths of vapor glided before it, and upwards, into the higher regions of the air. As they vanished, a flood of light poured upon the glassy slopes of the undulating water, and standing out clearly into view, was to be seen the hull and spars of a large, full-rigged brig. If it had suddenly popped up from the bosom of the deep, the effect could not have been more startling. It was the brig that had chased us the evening before. She must have tacked about the same time that we did, and by hugging the light wind, while we had been moving slowly with it on a free course, had brought herself into a position about a mile and a quarter to windward. At any rate, there she lay, and the sight of her was any thing but agreeable to the officers and crew of *El Bonito*, although they had too much confidence in the speed of their ship off the wind as well as on it to feel any very serious alarm.

At once, all was excitement and bustle—the wind freshened rapidly—the slaves, who had been brought up for their morning ablutions, were hurried below, and all hands called to make sail. The fore course was hauled down, royals loosened, and sheeted home, studding-sails got out, the yards braced square, and away we went, with the wind directly over the taffrail. In the meantime, the stranger had not been idle. We had got a little the start of him, but almost as soon as ourselves, he was moving through the water under every available rag of canvas.

A stern chase is said to be a long one, even when the pursuer is the fleetest : what hope then when the advantage of superior speed is on the side of the pursued. It was clearly so in this instance. In half an hour we had increased our distance almost half a mile.

Monte bustled about with a smile, and a malicious scowl, alternately, upon his ugly countenance—at one moment chuckling with fiendish glee, and the next pouring forth a volley of profane imprecations. Several times he passed me, and always with a muttering curse. In this there was not much harm, but it was exceedingly annoying to live in continual dread of some treacherous attack—perhaps a pistol-shot, or a stab in the back. Happily it had been ordered that this state of suspense and fear should not be of much longer duration.

Enphadde and myself were standing well aft upon the raised deck of the cabin, watching the progress of the chase, which had now lasted about an hour. Kaloolah was a little behind us, and Monte had just mounted the ladder, and was walking aft. Kaloolah made a step backwards, and slightly jostled against him. I heard a heavy blow—a groan of pain, and turning, saw her stretched upon the deck. With one bound I was upon him. He grasped the handle of his knife, but before he could draw it, my left hand reached his frontlet, followed by the right, strongly planted on his chin. The blows were given with an irresistible earnestness of purpose. Monte's body was projected before them, and thrown violently against the foot of the mizzen-mast, where he lay for a moment without sense or motion.

Enphadde raised Kaloolah—she was perfectly sensible, but her breath, at first, came with difficultly and pain—Monte had stricken her down with a heavy blow on the breast. There was, however, no time to inquire into particulars. Monte was upon his feet again—knife in hand—his face streaming with blood, and his eyes glaring with maniacal rage. Unfortunately my pistol was below, and I had nothing to oppose to the deadly weapon, in the use of which all Spaniards are so well skilled. Superior coolness, quickness, and strength, were the only advantages upon which I had to rely against such fearful odds.

Monte advanced swiftly, crouching low, and holding the point of his long knife slightly depressed. It was no time for hesitation ; my only hope was in the offensive. I rushed at him, and struck out with my left hand. He was on the point of making a thrust at the lower part of my body, but instinctively raising his hand in guard, the point of the knife entered my arm, inflicting a deep, but not a disabling wound. With the rapidity of light I seized his wrist with my right hand, and thrusting my left on the outside, grasped his face : applying, at the same moment, my left foot to the outside of his ankle, with a sudden and powerful effort I bore him backwards and sideways to the deck—falling upon him heavily with my whole weight. The point of the knife entered the deck, and the handle of it was wrenched from his grasp. He struggled to regain it, but I succeeded in rolling him over and beyond it. It was now within my reach, and my first impulse was to seize it, and drive it into his heart, but I had no wish to kill the fellow, although I knew that if he lived there was hardly a chance for my own life.

It must be understood, that there was no one upon the cabin-deck except ourselves and Kaloolah and Enphadde, and that the whole affair took place in much less time than it takes to describe it. From the beginning to the end was hardly half a minute.

By this time the noise had aroused the officers and crew, and they all came pouring aft, gesticulating and screaming as only Spaniards can gesticulate and scream. Two or three sprung upon the ladder, at once interfering with each other, and giving a practical illustration of the truth of the old saying, " the more haste the less speed." Already one or two had a footing upon the deck. Had I awaited the onset, ten chances to one my life would have been instantly sacrificed, or, at least, I should have been put in some way so completely *hors de combat*, that Monte would have been able to give me the finishing touch. The risk was too great!

"Overboard! overboard!" I shouted to Enphadde, who was supporting the fainting form of his sister. "Jump overboard. I'll follow you—quick!"

I made an effort to tear myself from Monte's grasp, but he was far from being deficient in personal strength, and with one hand in my long hair, and the other on my throat, he clung to me with the tenacious clutch of a tiger.

"Hands off! You won't?——go too, then!" and, clasping him with both arms, I raised him clear from the deck and dashed over the low quarter rail, head first into the water, just as half a dozen hands were extended to grasp my person.

Down, down into the depths of ocean, many feet, we sank ere our tense muscles relaxed, in the deadly fierceness of that close embrace. We talk of the dogged courage—the sullen persistence the unyielding game of the Anglo-Saxon character—there is as much of the same quality in the Celtiberian blood. If the Englishman typifies himself in his own bull-dog, the Spaniard's "totem" may, with equal justice, be found in the indomitable mastiff of the *Sierra de Cuenca*.

Upon coming to the surface, the first objects of interest were Kaloolah and Enphadde at a few feet distance, supporting themselves with ease amid the dancing foam of the ship's wake. The *Bonito* was twenty rods off, and flying from us at the rate of ten knots an hour. It was no time for her to heave to, with a fleet enemy not more than two miles astern. The brig was heading directly down upon us. She could hardly pass without seeing us, but it was an object to let her know our situation in good time. For this purpose I held Enphadde as high out of the water as possible, while he waved around his head a straw hat which luckily had accompanied him overboard. Satisfied that Monte could swim, I gave myself no further trouble about him.

Down came the stately brig, her broad wings stretching far on either side over the glancing water, and towering in graceful symmetry to the sky. Nearer and yet nearer, until the smallest rope could be distinguished, as well as the sparkling "bone in her teeth," as the sailors sometimes call the foam round a ship's bows. Nearer and yet nearer—still no sign of any preparation for picking us up. Can it be possible that she will pass us unnoticed? No! Hurrah! hurrah!—there go the studding-sails,

simultaneously alow and aloft ! the fore course rises. " Port ! port your
helm ! " cries a clear voice. " Royal and top-gallant halliards ! Starboard
fore-brace—larboard main-brace ! haul out the try-sail ! "

Gracefully she sweeps round to the wind, and heaves to with her fore-
top-sail aback. Men in the larboard chains stand ready as she sags down
upon us. A few strokes of the arm and we are alongside. The ropes
are thrown—grasped—and we mount the bulwarks ! We stand safe and
sound upon the snow-white decks of the British brig !

" Fill away, my hearties ! brail up the try-sail—shiver the main and
mizzen—brace round the fore-yard—down with your fore-course—right
your helm and away, away again, after yonder ' hell afloat.' If you can't
close with her, you can, at least, show your good will. So mind your
helm, my fine fellow, and keep your jib-boom end-on to her stern-post ! "

CHAPTER XVII.

RATHER an unceremonious way of boarding your ship, gentlemen," said I, bowing to a group of officers, " but I hope you 'll pardon us ; necessity can't always stop to ask leave."

" No excuses—you are heartily welcome," replied a short, portly middle-aged man with a rubicund but good-natured face. " But I should like to know who the d——l you are, where you come from, and what you come for."

" My name, sir, is Romer—passenger on board of an American vessel, I was wrecked at sea, and picked up by a slaver : These two are Africans, brother and sister, and that pleasant-looking chap yonder is first officer of the ship ahead. We left her about fifteen minutes since, and we have come on board you simply because we could n't help it."

Several questions were propounded by the officer, who proved to be the commander of the brig, to which I replied in a few words, succinctly detailing the most important circumstances of our adventure. As I proceeded, his quarter-deckish air and tone changed to a decided expression of frank and sailor-like affability. Putting out his hand, he exclaimed : " Well, sir, I 'm glad to see you. Come, walk below, we 'll see if we can't find some dry clothes for you and your protegés. I 've got an old dressing gown that will just fit Mademoiselle Kaloolah, especially about the waist." The other officers were equally liberal in their expressions of interest and offers of service, and it was no little satisfaction to find that getting on board of her majesty's brig *Fly-away*, we had got among as polite and gentlemanly a set of fellows as ever walked a quarter-deck.

" Mr. Crawford," said the captain, addressing the officer of the deck, " see that that Spanish rascal has a dry suit, and then clap him in irons. Put a sentry over him, for when the story of the twenty-five blind men gets forward the crew may not treat him very politely."

" Why not run him up to the yard-arm at once?" replied Mr. Craw-ford.

" I wish I could," said the captain : " if you 'll find law for it, I 'm sure I 'll find rope."

" Hanging is too good for him.   I should like to cut his liver out with the double cats," muttered Mr. Crawford, as he turned away to his duty.

Instinctively Monte had drawn himself forward and away from the quarter-deck.   He knew that his case was one that would excite for him but little sympathy ; in fact, that nothing but a want of jurisdiction saved him from instant and condign punishment. The only thing that could be done to him, was to put him in irons, which, as a kind of compromise to the public opinion of the forecastle, was essential to his comfort and per-haps to his safety.   He had no fear, therefore, as to the ultimate result ; but, in the meantime, he had to endure the pangs of baffled revenge. His countenance betrayed the emotions of his fiendish heart, the scowl of un-dying hate, the sullen glare of settled malice, the lines of desperate resolve for evil drove from his truculent visage the last remnant of a humanizing expression.

In the cabin we found the breakfast-table waiting for the captain to finish his meal ; and, on changing our clothes, we were politely invited to take a seat at it ; an invitation which our salt-water bath had disposed us with good appetites to accept.   Enphadde and myself did full justice to the good sea fare, but Kaloolah was still suffering from the blow ; and to the polite persuasions of the captain could only return a faint smile of denial.

" Poor thing!" said Captain Halsey; " you say she 's a princess. Well, I don't doubt it. She looks like one. My old velvet becomes her admira-bly.   What magnificent eyes!—pity she 's got those spots on her face. She does n't understand English?" he continued, observing a blush mant-ling her face.

" A little," I replied, " just enough to know that you are talking about her."

" Ah, clever too as well as handsome ; but I suppose you have taken particular pains in her instruction, notwithstanding her spotted skin."

" No, I have been rather anxious to learn her language than to teach her English ; and as to the spots that you regret so much, they are only temporary ; I made them myself with caustic.   As we were going among rather a lawless set, I thought it would be wise to counteract as far as possible the force of her personal attractions."

"Good! A capital idea! A kind of quarantine flag, ha! painted ports to frighten off the pirates! I took them for indications of the black blood; but, if these were made with caustic, she must be of a pure white breed. I have seen a number of Africans that were called white, but they always had some of the negro characteristics of form or feature. However, I have never had any doubts that there were white nations far in the interior. I have heard many negroes assert the fact, and the remove between some of the Fellatah tribes and a white race is not so great as between them and a full-blooded black."

"I agree with you," said the surgeon, who had just entered the cabin. "What can be more probable than that in the vast central regions of Africa, about which we know literally nothing, there should be tribes as purely white as the Tuaries of the Sahara, or the Shilloes and Berbers of the Atlas—descendants perhaps of the old Gætulians or Garimantes. I have always thought so, and I'm glad now to see it proved. There is no negro blood in these two."

"If there is," replied the captain, "it must have been pretty well diluted. By George! they are a good-looking couple. Give the young fellow a full-dress fit, and a small black mustache, and what a swell he could cut in a London drawing-room. He looks very much like some of those handsome Armenians you see up the Levant, but he's got more 'eye' than an Armenian ever had."

"What are their names?" demanded the doctor.

"Kaloolah and Enphadde—Enphadde ban Shounsi," I replied; "and their country they call Framazugda."

"Framazugda!" exclaimed the doctor, "that is curious—I should n't wonder!—it must be so—it is."

"What?" demanded Captain Halsey.

"Why, almost proof positive of the truth of my suggestion about the Garimantes and Gætulians. You see many of the tribes of Barbary and the Sahara, who are the undoubted aboriginal inhabitants, are known by the name of Amazergs. Now, what can be more clear than the derivation of Framazugda from the word Amazerg. The prefix *fr*, or *fra*, perhaps means from, and the affix *dah* perhaps means people or nation—nation derived from the Amazergs; or perhaps the *dah* may mean from, and the *fra* may mean people; or perhaps the *fra* and the *dah* may both mean——"

"Bravo, doctor!" interrupted the captain, "you extract an etymology as dexterously as if it were a cataract, or an old double tooth. Get hold of the roots! eh! By George, I had no idea that you were so expert at reducing compound philological dislocations."

A midshipman entered with a message from Mr. Crawford that the ship continued to gain upon the brig.

" I suppose so," said the captain, "she's too fast for us. Tell Mr. Crawford that we 'll hold on for an hour longer, to make assurance doubly sure, and then we 'll haul our wind, and stand on our old course."

' And where may that take us to ?" I inquired.

" To Sierra Leone ! back again to Africa. How do you like that, my princess ? "

I interpreted the question.

" Can we reach the Quorra from thence ? " demanded Enphadde.

" Why, yes, but it will be rather a long and hard journey ; especially for your sister."

" No matter," said Enphadde ; " there are no dangers or hardships that I will not dare."

" And none that I would not share with you," interposed Kaloolah ; " oh, how willingly I would die, for even a distant sight of the towers of Kiloam ! "

" And is there nothing, or nobody," inquired the captain, glancing at me, " that you care for out of Framazugda ? "

" Jon'than, he go wid us," said Kaloolah, in English, when I had explained the captain's question, the meaning of which she had already comprehended. " Jon'than hab no fadder, no modder, no brodder, no sister—he will get all—very much—in Framazugda."

" And a wife, too, I suppose, if he wants one ? " said the doctor, with a meaning look.

A deep blush crimsoned Kaloolah's cheek. " Come, come, doctor," interposed the captain, " you are probing the matter too closely. Recollect that a young, unsophisticated female heart is rather more tender than a tough *deltoid* or *gluteus.* There is some difference between a puncture from one of Cupid's darts and a gun-shot wound."

" You 're right," returned the doctor, " there is a difference ; one is always curable, the other is not."

" Ah, doctor, you 're getting to be perfectly incorrigible ! you talk treason, sir, rank treason. We shall have to arraign you before the judges of Cupidom, and have you bound over to *court.*"

" I 'm sure I should forfeit my bail."

" Well, then, you will be declared an outlaw, and be doomed to wander round the world, a confirmed old bachelor."

" Well, there are worse *batches* than a *bach*elor. What do you say to a *batch* of squalling children ? "

" Horrible ! " exclaimed the captain ; " the most horrible attempt at a pun I 've heard this long time. Doctor, you deserve a round dozen."

" Of children ? " said the doctor, opening the cabin door.

" No, of the cats ; or rather, you ought to be kept at the mast-head, on the look-out for *squalls.* You seem to have as good a scent for them as you have for the roots. Don't forget the *fra* and the *dah*," shouted the captain, as the doctor ascended the stairs.

This colloquial smartness was, of course, wholly lost upon my companions ; but the captain's good-natured face, jolly tones, and hearty laugh, had none the less an inspiriting effect. Kaloolah and Enphadde watched him with a pleased and confiding expression, which, to judge from physiognomical indications, was fully deserved.

" And now," said the captain, putting his hand familiarly on my shoulder, " we must see about your sleeping arrangements. I 've one spare state-room here, which will just do for the princess ; and a hammock for you can be swung in the open cabin ; it can be put up at night, and taken down in the morning, so as not to be at all in our way. As for his royal highness, we 'll find a hammock for him in the steerage. You 'll all three mess at my table."

I commenced expressing my sense of his kindness and politeness, but was cut short with a rough " Come, come, none of that—let us take a look on deck," and together we ascended to the open air.

The brig had been hauled by the wind, and was steering nearly northeast. The ship was almost out of sight—her snow-white top-sails dotting the horizon, and gleaming as gaily in the sunshine as if they were not wafting a freight of misery and sin. Press on, thou fearfully laden bark ! the ocean groaneth not beneath thy weight—the skies frown not on thy bloody decks—the breeze not ungently distends thy well-trimmed sails, but the eye of Almighty justice is upon thee ! Press on !

A week of pleasant weather and pleasant company ! Time flew—so rapidly, that seemingly without an interval his glittering pinions reflected the golden flood of morning, the deep azure of noon, the glory of sunset, and the sable of night !

Kaloolah had entirely recovered from the effects of the blow, and together we passed many pleasant hours, in walking the deck and discoursing of the wonders of the deep, or of the curious and magnificent social, natural, or artificial features of her distant home. In these conversations the officers of the brig often took part, making the minutest inquiries, and listening, with marks of the strongest interest to her artless descriptions of strange scenes, and to her and her brother's details of a novel and peculiar civilization. It was especially gratifying to perceive the respect which both she and her brother excited, exhibiting itself in a degree of kind and courteous deference, in which not even my jealous and watchful anxiety could find the slightest ground of reproach. Captain Halsey was uniformly affable and polite, and any one who knows any thing of a man-of-war, knows what influence the character of the commander has upon his subordinates. It might, perhaps, be expected that I should be more particular in my description of him; that I should attempt a portrait of his person, and draw more minutely the peculiarities of his manner and his mind; that I should undertake to individualize him, like a character in a novel, but delicacy forbids. He is probably still alive (at least I hope so, and a post-captain too), and I know not how he would like to have himself paraded in print; sufficient is it to say, that he was a gentleman and a sailor.

CHAPTER XVIII.

OWHERE in the world can be found a more admirable site for a city, in all the particulars of a magnificent and picturesque scenery, than on the broad estuary of Sierra Leone. Twenty miles in length, and varying in breadth from ten miles at its entrance, between Leopard's Island, on the north, and Cape Sierra Leone, on the south, to four miles at the Island of Tombo, where it terminates, it presents, on either shore, a variety of natural features, which at once rivets attention and excites a mixed and highly pleasing emotion of the beautiful and the sublime.

In glowing terms, have travellers described the picturesque and Oriental character of the view—as rising from the water's edge, the town stretches up the surrounding hills, with its white dwellings and prolific gardens ; whilst in the distance, emerging from the high woods, appear the country mansions of the Europeans, with their projecting eaves and rows of green jalousies enclosing the shady verandas—affording the luxury of a mid-day walk in the open air. How is it possible for gloomy forebodings of disease and death to thrust themselves upon a stranger, who, for the first time, looks upon this enchanting scene—upon the glowing bosom of the estuary, scarcely rippled by the light airs and gentle tides of these latitudes, the quiet Bullom shore, the bold sweep of that amphitheatre of mountains, gaping with enormous ravines and dark valleys, and clothed with never-fading forests ! Yet in this very excess of beauty germinates the seeds of the pestilence. So bountiful is nature, that the first showers of the wet season convert even the public ways into fields, and cover them with a rich mantle of herbage. From the decomposition of this exuberant vegetation is supposed to arise the deleterious miasma, so powerful in its influence upon the unacclimated constitution of the European visitor. If such is the case, what is its nature or essence?

Is it a gas? The theory has many and able advocates, but if true, chemical analysis ought to be able to detect it. Is it an effluvia or odor? Possibly, but how is it that in many cases it produces no effect upon the sense of smell? Is it animalcular? The speculation is as old as the times of Lucretius and Columella, and it certainly accords the best with what we know of the laws by which malaria is governed. But may it not be vegetable in its composition, as well as in its origin, and consist of the germs of the vast variety of fungi! These germs, imperceptible to the sense, and inappreciable by the most delicate analysis, are known to pervade the air in the greatest abundance. Perhaps their quantity may regulate the intensity, and their specific character the form of disease. This suggestion is, as far as I know, original, and seems to me as plausible as either of the others. It may pass for what it is worth.[*]

The greater portion of the population of Freetown consists of liberated Africans, who have been rescued from Spanish and Portuguese slavers. The white residents are few in number—scarcely a hundred—most of them the officials of the different colonial departments, such as the legislative council, the vice-admiralty court, and the mixed commission for the adjudication of captured slave-ships.

From a number of these gentlemen I received treatment that was but a continuation of the politeness and kindness of the officers of the brig, and my companions came in for their share of attention. Offers of service, advice, with invitations to breakfasts, dinners, and suppers were poured upon us. A bill upon a Liverpool house for one hundred and fifty pounds, which I luckily happened to have upon my person when leaving the slaver, furnished a highly satisfactory test of the sincerity of these proffers. The bill was readily cashed at the commissariat department.

But it is not my intention to detain the reader with all the little details of my short sojourn in Sierra Leone, and I must hurry on to my departure, touching, by the way, only upon one event—my separation from Kaloolah and Enphadde.

Long and anxious were the consultations before it was finally settled that we should part—I to return to home and friends in the far West; Enphadde and his sister to seek, amid the dangers and difficulties of African

* It is, perhaps, unnecessary to say that the writer could not, by any possibility, have heard of the speculations of Professor Mitchell upon the same subject. It does not, of course, diminish the credit due the Professor, for his recent able and conclusive exposition and development of this theory of malaria, that the idea should have occurred several years since to Mr. Romer, or that it should have been made the occasional subject of conversation and investigation by the editor for ten years past.—*Note by the Editor.*

barbarism, their native country in the East. The prospect for them, however, wore not so gloomy an aspect as might at first be supposed. Enphadde, as I have said, seemed to have a very definite idea of the relative situation of the Quorrah and Framazugda, and he was confident that if he could reach the banks of that river in the kingdom of Bambara, of which country he had heard, he could make his way through Houssa to the great city of Sackatoo, from thence to Mandarra, where a short space of three or four hundred miles farther, in a southeasterly direction, would bring him to the confines of his own country. The journey was long, and filled with dangers, but it was some encouragement to reflect that Denman, Clapperton, Lang, etc., had found comparatively but little difficulty when once in the interior, and that chiefly arising from the jealousy of the white man, or the unfavorable influence of the climate upon the European constitution. To neither of these would Enphadde be exposed, especially if, as he proposed, he should darken his and his sister's skin with the juice of some of the various coloring nuts always at hand.

Closely we pored over the map of Africa, until Enphadde had made himself master of all the geographical information it could afford. Much useful knowledge was also acquired by repeated conferences with some intelligent Mandingo traders. A kaffila of these people was expected to start in a short time for Bambara, and with them it was proposed that Enphadde should make the first and most dangerous part of his journey through the country of the Timmanees. It was considered essential that he should assume the character of a merchant, and for this purpose a stock of goods was necessary. These, thanks to my bill of exchange, were easily obtained. The assortment was principally composed of beads, rings, small mirrors, coral, paper, knives, linen, scarlet cloth, gold lace, and a variety of small wares. As an assistant in the business of the journey, we selected a native of Koollah, who, about a year before, had been brought into port in a slave-ship. The fellow had acquired a high character for honesty and industry, and, like many other liberated slaves, was accumulating money; but the desire of revisiting his distant home was too strong for him to withstand the temptation of company and protection the whole distance. He acceded, with apparent delight, to Enphadde's proposal, and in all his actions and words evinced so much openness and candor, that I felt satisfied that my companions had made in him an important acquisition.

Appropriate and comfortable clothing was purchased for them all, and to Enphadde's accoutrements I added a stout cutlass, a pair of double-barrelled pistols, and a portable compass. To Kaloolah's charge was entrusted a small spy-glass and a compact and convenient form of tinder-box. The first, perhaps, might be useful in discovering danger in time to avoid it—the second would always secure a means of protection against the dangerous inhabitants of the forest. To the Koollah I made a present of a musket, with which he promised to perform wonders in the way of guarding Kaloolah from enemies of every kind. Nothing that I could think of, likely to facilitate their journey or insure their safety, was neglected. The whole plan of the expedition was thoroughly digested, and every conceivable combination of circumstances considered and, as far as possible, provided for. My directions, reiterated again and again to Enphadde, were that, as far as possible, he should conform to the manners and customs of the countries he had to pass; that Kaloolah should travel with her face concealed as closely as could be done without exciting curiosity and suspicion : that he himself should adhere strictly to the character of a merchant; and that while, on the one hand, he should not be too chary of his presents to the officials of the different countries on his route—on the other hand, he should avoid any thing like a careless prodigality, or an appearance of inattention to his mercantile interests. Enphadde was quick, shrewd, and bold, and I felt confident that he would act up strictly to my numerous suggestions; and that in any extraordinary cases he would find the necessary resources in his own wit and courage. Had he been unencumbered with his sister, I should hardly have felt a doubt of the successful termination of his journey. As it was, I had strong hopes that their safe return would, erelong, cause the hills of Kiloam to resound with the songs of joy and rejoicing.

And why did not I accompany them? That is precisely the question that was so often asked by Kaloolah. And a difficult question it was to answer—at least to her satisfaction—in fact, I could hardly answer it to my own. On the one hand was the strong temptation to enter upon the exploration of the mysterious regions of Central Africa—the curiosity to see and examine the productions, the scenery, and the manners and customs of the country of which my companions were the representatives. The interest, even affection, which they had excited; and, added to all, the natural promptings of an adventurous disposition. On the other hand was an almost irresistible longing to revisit once more the scenes of my youth. An indefinite, and therefore exaggerated, idea of the difficulties and dangers of the adventure—a little of that inexplainable but exceedingly natural and common irresolution so often felt, especially by the inexperienced, at the threshold of any important undertaking ; and a doubt as to the propriety of continuing my relations to Kaloolah, which it was beginning to be quite evident were fraught with trouble to her, if not to myself. But more than all in determining my course was the discouraging influence of ill health. The remnants of the Congo fever still hung about me, inducing a degree of mental and corporeal lassitude, and repressing that elasticity of spirit which, in full health, would have converted dangers into pleasures, and obstacles into arguments for pushing on. These sensations of depression and weakness grew daily stronger and stronger in the bright but pestilent air of Sierra Leone. I longed to escape to a colder and more congenial climate ; and, as it happened, a vessel for Liverpool was lying in port, almost ready to sail. Should I forego the opportunity, it would be some time before another would occur. Suddenly summoning resolution, I sought the captain, and made an agreement with him for the passage.

The pallor of death overspread the features of Kaloolah when I announced to her that I had made arrangements to sail in the next ship. She uttered no sound—not a sigh—not a tear ; but the fixed eye, the quivering lip, the bloodless cheek, and the shrunken rigidity of her whole frame indicated the intense emotion within. For a moment she stood thus, erect, and the next the spasm passing, my outstretched arm was hardly in time to save her from falling to the ground. Gently laying her upon the green sward at the foot of a waving palm, I knelt by her side. She did not faint—I was in hopes that she would. Shocked and frightened, I knew not what to say or do. I screamed to Enphadde, but he was far down the hill-side. I shouted to some negro women for water, but they paid no attention. I rubbed her hands, raised her head, and turned her face to the cool sea breeze that came up from the broad estuary below, and at last did what was the very best thing to do—I raised her in my arms, pressed her to my heart, and kissed her pallid lips.

For a few minutes she struggled with the tide of feeling that had been so suddenly thrown back upon her heart. She grew in years as I gazed. When I first saw her, she was a child—an artless, fascinating child—and now! It seemed as if at one bound she had reached the verge of womanhood.

She bent forward her head, covered her face with her hands, and burst into a passionate flood of tears. I felt relieved. Her tears were to me like the rain-drops to the mariner in a hurricane—the presage of a calm. " 'T is well," thought I, and I drew my breath more freely ; " 't is well the heavy night dews, dropping from the bended flower, relieve it from the weight that endangers the stem."

She raised her head. " Kaloolah ! " said I.

She sprang into my arms, and buried her face in my bosom.

" Kaloolah, you love me ! "

" As I love nought else in this world," she replied.

" And I—I, Kaloolah ! "—I was about to add some protestation of affection, but would my feelings towards her warrant it ?—were they those of strong abiding love? Were they other than fraternal ? Other than a sympathy for her misfortunes, an admiration of her simplicity—her innocence ? I knew not ; but even if they were, would it be right to express them ? I thought of my mother, and fancied that I could almost hear her words, My son ! my son ! amid the sighs of the gentle sea-breeze that swept through the rustling palm-tops.

" And Enphadde ? " said I.

" Will journey more easily without me—he will reach home in safety, and gladden the eyes that now weep for him.

" And you, Kaloolah ? "

" And I—I—," passionately exclaimed Kaloolah, " am your slave—I follow you—where you go I will go—your country shall be my country."

" Impossible ! Kaloolah. Enphadde will never go and leave you behind. Without you, how would he dare meet the eyes of that white-haired old man who sits mourning for his youngest child, his best beloved daughter in the halls of Kiloam. Think of your cousins, Kaloolah. Think of the playmates, and friends, and servants who all loved you so much. Think of the hall of crystal, the court of the fountains, and the broad, shady gallery that looks down upon the joyous and magnificent city. Think of the pleasant walks in the royal gardens upon the banks of the Wollo. Think of your favorites, the flowers, the birds, the diamond fish, and Gogo, your golden-haired ape, who would mind no one but you, and who was so graceful and so sensible. Think of all the beautiful things that you have so often talked with me about. You cannot leave them all. You will return to them. Your sisters, Kaloolah, are sad ; your presence will change their tears into smiles. The streets of Kiloam are in gloom, for there is grief in the palace of Selha Shounsi, the father of his people ; your return will fill them with the voices of gladness. The hall of crystal will again glitter in the light of the festival—the water will again sparkle and play in the court of the fountains—the drooping flowers will raise their bended heads—your silent pets, the birds, will resume their songs—the diamond fish will flash their silver light from the lowest depth of their marble pools ; and Gogo—sensible Gogo—will cease to pine when he gambols once more in the footsteps of his mistress."

As I spoke, Kaloolah withdrew herself from my arms. Calmly she drew up her slight and graceful figure to its full height, while a sparkle of feminine pride beamed from her eye.

"Enough," she said. "I understand you. You love me not. You would be burdened with me no longer. I forgot that I was to you but a useless slave. I fancied that I was a princess of the long line of Shounsi —forgive my foolishness——"

"Kaloolah!" said I, reproachfully, taking her hand.

Her countenance fell, she grasped my hand in both of hers, and tears again started to her eyes.

"She sprang into my arms, and buried her face in my bosom."

"Forgive me," she sobbed, "you have been too kind to me. I obey you—I go with Enphadde, but—but—those pleasant scenes you have spoken of, Jon'than——'

"What of them?" I demanded.

"I shall never see them!"

"Nay, nay, Kaloolah, think not so. Enphadde feels confident of re-visiting them."

"He may—he will, but unless in company with you, Jon'than, I shall never see them. They are here, Jon'than, and here," pointing her hand to her head and heart; "but we look upon the realities together, or I shall never see them."

" A foolish fancy, Kaloolah. Why should you think so?"

" I know not why, but so it is. Yet mention it not to Enphadde—I would not discourage him in the attempt."

" Perhaps you will tell a different story when I visit you a year or two hence in Framazugda," said I.

" How! What mean you?" exclaimed Kaloolah.

" That, perhaps, I will yet undertake to visit your country. It is possible, I will even say probable; but it would only be in hopes of finding you."

" Oh, Jon'than, if that could be so! but I cannot hope it."

" It shall be so—I feel that such will be my destiny—be assured that I shall make no resistance to the march of fate." As I spoke the resolution, full-formed, sprang into life. I felt its invigorating influence. Why should I not give Kaloolah the full benefit of it.

" I will certainly make the attempt to reach Framazugda," said I, energetically.

" When?"

" Ere the almond-trees have three times strown, with their silver leaves, the garden walks on the Wollo."

" You promise?"

" No circumstances that I can control shall prevent me from being there. I promise."

" Oh, Enphadde!" exclaimed Kaloolah, throwing herself joyfully into the arms of her brother, who was advancing to join us. " Jon'than will come to us. We shall see him again—he has promised to join us erelong in Framazugda."

" God grant it," replied Enphadde. " No stranger could bring such light and joy to the court of Selha Shounsi."

We seated ourselves upon the sloping green sward, and for an hour discussed the pleasant and newly opened prospect of a future meeting. Uncontrolled by reason, hope revelled wild and free, indulging in the most delightful vagaries. An event really so improbable seemed to grow more and more simple and feasible the longer we considered it. Kaloolah, so far from dreading now the journey, was anxious to set out at once that she might be at home to receive me.

Unfortunately, the kaffila of Mandingos would not be ready to start for two or three weeks, whereas, in a day or two at most the ship in which I was going would sail. This would be a lonely interval of time for them; but there was some encouragement in the reflection that it was short, and would soon pass.

Again and again had I to repeat the promise of coming to Framazugda. Kaloolah dwelt upon it every hour of the three days that elapsed before my departure, and at the last moment she exacted its solemn renewal.

"I shall watch the fall of the almond's silver leaves," were her last words; "the fourth time, and you come not, they fall on my grave. Farewell!"

"Farewell, Kaloolah!"

Gracious heaven! I like not, even now, to think of the horrible choking sensation with which those words were pronounced. Not ten miles from land, and I would have given the world to have returned and linked my fate indissolubly with hers. But it could not be, and well it could not. Mysterious agencies were weaving the threads of destiny far more skilfully than we could have done had we had complete control of warp and woof.

CHAPTER XIX.

OUR ship was old, leaky, a dull sailor, and heavily laden—qualities that illy accorded with the pretensions of her high-sounding
name—the *Duke of Wellington*. The crew consisted of eight
men and two boys, and a more lubberly set, with the exception
of one fine white-headed old seaman, named Jack Thompson, were never
berthed in a forecastle. Bad as they were, however, it must be said in
their favor that they were fully worthy of their officers.

The latitude of Cape Verde was reached on the eighth day after leaving Freetown, but our course had been so far to the west that we did not
get sight of the cape. In fact, according to the calculations of the captain, we had been compelled to give it altogether too wide a berth, and
he consequently gave orders to haul the ship's head more towards the
African shore, as soon as the wind permitted. It was evident that, missing a sight of the cape, he was all abroad as to his longitude, and well he
might be, for he had nothing but a very loose, inaccurate dead-reckoning
to depend upon. During his own watch, the log was never thrown—a
drunken guess at the ship's way serving instead—and in the mate's watch,
the reckoning was kept with hardly more accuracy.

One evening, a few days after our departure, the ship was standing
westerly, with the wind from the north, and the mate was heaving the
log, when, as I came upon deck, I heard him say "Seven knots and a
half," and immediately he proceeded to note it down upon the log-slate.
I looked aloft and around—the wind was light, the ship close-hauled, and
apparently moving very sluggishly through the water. "Seven knots
and a half!" I exclaimed. "It is impossible that she can be going so
fast."

"Oh, yes, sir," replied the old sailor whom I have mentioned. "She
is going that—here—" and he put his finger to his eye, and nodded his

head towards the mate, who had stretched himself out for a doze upon the hen-coop. "Some craft sail very fast, sir, with three sheets in the wind. What they don't go ahead is made up in the spinning round."

"Let us try a cast of the log," said I; and calling one of the boys to relieve him at the wheel, the old man held the reel for me. The marks upon the line indicated a rate of about four miles and a half.

"Not so much out of the way as I thought," said the old man. "Only three miles! that's nothing to some of the captain's guesses. I should n't be at all surprised to see the skipper put her any time dead to windward at the rate of twenty miles an hour. According to the rule of mathematics that he uses sometimes, he could do it just as easy as he could say 'How do you do?' to the bottom of an empty rum bottle."

"And what rule may that be?" I inquired.

"A rule in compound addition and multiplication, sir. It's simple enough, but 'taint every one who can work it like he can. He adds his own particular lee-way to the lee-way of this lubberly old tub; throws in her way through the water, and multiplies the sum by the number of horns he took before breakfast. The product is the number of knots that we've cheated the wind out of."

"And by such a rule, how long will it be before we reach Liverpool?"

"The Lord knows, sir. If the skipper has many sober fits we may box about the ocean a long time; but, if by good luck, he should keep himself dead drunk the whole voyage, as he did coming out, we shall have a chance to hit our port and float in."

Previous to this conversation I had paid but little attention to the ship's reckoning, but from this time it began to be a subject of much interest. Its manifest inaccuracy could not but excite some little anxiety, which was not diminished by being shared with my new friend, Jack Thompson. With the captain, any kind of conversation in relation to it was perfectly impracticable. "He was satisfied as to the ship's position"; "could attend to his own business"; "did n't want the advice of any one." And when I proposed to adjust his quadrant, swore that adjustment was all fudge, and that he could take the sun near enough for his purposes without any such nonsense.

For several days the ship had been heading to the northeast. Our latitude by observation was about 20° N. and our distance from the African coast, according to the captain's computation, a little over two hundred miles. I grew more and more uneasy. My mind was constantly haunted by vague ideas of the dangerous rocks and shoals, and the strong and irregular currents by which so many ships had been swept to destruction ; and of the cruel fate of their crews—hurried into hopeless captivity among the Arabs of the desert. My fears compelled me to speak once more to the captain.

"Blast my eyes!" he exclaimed, "do you take me for a fool? do you think that I don't know all about the Arguin bank, and the Blanco reef, and the currents, and all that? You can't tell me any thing, sir, that I don't know."

"Well—but captain," said I, as deprecatingly as possible, "suppose that we try a lunar observation. There is a good opportunity now, and if you and Mr. Brown will take the altitudes, I will measure the lunar distance, and work the problem."

"Blast your lunars!" he replied; "they are all humbug. I would n't give a rope's end for a bushel of them. I never knew a fellow that meddled with lunars and chronometers, and such nonsense, who did n't run his ship ashore in the end."

That evening I remained upon deck until a late hour, listening to some rather tough yarns of my forecastle friend. The mate, as usual, was asleep upon the hen-coop ; the captain was preparing himself for his watch on deck, and a fresh tour of duty at the brandy bottle in his berth below.

My mind was busy with thoughts of Kaloolah. I thought of her as threading with weary steps the wild forests of Central Africa,—crossing the swollen streams, and ascending the pathless hills,—enduring fatigue, and encountering danger,—exposed to insult, and threatened each instant with slavery and perhaps with death. The unpleasant revery was interrupted by a low soughing sound, that appeared to come from directly overhead. I stopped short in my walk, listened intently, and again heard it, but it was so faint as to be scarcely perceptible.

"Did you hear that?" said I, advancing to the old sailor at the wheel. "Listen!"

"I can hear nothing," he replied after a moment's pause,—and neither could I from where we stood, but by stepping a few feet forward, toward the starboard gangway, it came again. Entrusting the wheel to his companion, the old man joined me.

"Well, I declare," he exclaimed, after listening for a few moments, "that is curious. If I did n't know that it is the wind eddying around in the belly of the sail, I would swear that there were breakers aloft,—it sounds just like the surf at a great distance."

"Perhaps it is the sound of the surf which, striking against the sail, is reflected down to us ; such a thing may be. Had I not better speak to the mate?"

" No ; there 's no use in that ; it 's nothing but the wind—and, besides, you could never make him hear it."

The sounds came fainter and fainter and less frequent, and at last died away entirely, which the old man explained by the wind's veering a point or so—not a very satisfactory explanation, for, as the vessel luffed in a corresponding degree, the wind must have struck the sail at the same angle ; whereas, were the sounds the reflected notes of a distant surf, they might well cease from the change in the relative position of the plain of the sail. However, there was but little use in expressing my apprehensions to either captain or mate. The idea of hearing breakers overhead would have been scouted as an absurdity, or laughed at as a capital joke, according to the captain's spiritual barometer—a dozen glasses above comfortable, it might be " devilish funny " ; a few glasses short of that mark, and it would be a " blasted humbug," and any one who believed it " a lubberly fool."

I retired to my berth a little before twelve o'clock. At the expiration of the mate's watch he came below and awoke the captain, who turned out in rather a surly humor, to judge from the growling and muttering, at some undefined object of objurgation, that he kept up while putting on his clothes. As he mounted the companion-way the mate turned in, " all standing," or, in other words, with his clothes on ; and, resuming the slumber that had been interrupted merely by the change of the watch, the cabin was all quiet again, save the heavy tramp of the captain's feet overhead, as he lazily paced up and down the deck.

Suddenly there came a loud shout from the forecastle, and the noise of many feet moving aft.

" Breakers ! breakers ahead ! breakers on the weather-bow ! " shouted several voices, and all was in an instant hurry and confusion.

Jumping from my berth, I rushed upon deck, closely followed by the mate. The night was dark, the wind moderate, and blowing about five points on shore. Ahead, and on the larboard bow, a line of light flashed through the gloom, and the roar of the surf rose and fell upon the fitful blasts of the breeze.

Both officers and men were completely paralyzed by surprise and fear.

" Wear ship ! " I shouted, seeing that it was apparently clear water on the lee-quarter. But the helm was already jammed hard down, and the ship was coming to the wind. A dozen contradictory orders were issued by captain and mate. The ship, never very active at the manœuvre, now refused to come round, missed stays, fell off, and gathered stern-way.

" Wear her round," was now the word, but such confusion prevailed that hardly an order was given or obeyed in proper time. It was with difficulty that I could get the fore-top-mast stay-sail hoisted or the spanker brailed up. No one seemed to have any idea of what to do or how to do it, except Thompson, who jumped forward to obey my orders, reiterating them at the same time in a tone that began, at least, to command attention and obedience—but attention and obedience were now too late.

The after sails were shivering, and the head yards were still sharp aback, when a heavy swell, subsiding beneath us, let the ship down upon the rocks with a shock that threatened dislocation to every bone in our bodies. The next wave knocked her stern quite round, and, raising us, threw us with another tremendous thump higher up, with our broadside to the sea. She heeled over towards the shore and settled down so solidly as to be hardly moved by the succeeding waves. With the exception of the main-top-mast, all our spars remained standing, and their weight, and the action of the wind upon the sails, which were still flying, served to hold the ship down in her inclined position. The captain proposed to cut away the masts, which would have lightened the ship and allowed her to roll off seaward, when she would have sunk, or thumped to pieces in a very few minutes. It was only by the most authoritative interposition, in which I was warmly seconded by Jack, that the execution of the order was prevented.

All that we could do or say, however, was insufficient to prevent active preparations for going ashore, which could be indistinctly seen, like a black line, at some thirty or forty rods' distance. I represented to the crew the almost certainty of being swamped if they attempted it in the darkness of the night—the little danger there was of the ship's breaking up before daylight, as the tide must be ebbing, and her position becoming more and more stable and secure ; and that, if the boat were lost, our only chance of escape from death or captivity among the merciless inhabitants of the desert, would be destroyed.

" Get out the boat ! get out the boat ! we 'll go ashore," was echoed by all hands, and foremost by the captain and mate.

The boat was soon under the lee of the ship, and the men crowded into her, all except my friend Thompson, who indicated his determination of sticking to the ship. We felt alike as to the stupidity and folly of the act, and the worse than stupidity that had brought us into our present situation. The captain was the last who entered the boat.

" Will you come with us ? " he asked, while holding on in the main-chains.

" Never ! " exclaimed Jack, with indignant energy : " I 've followed you far enough; I 've no disposition to go with you to the place where you are now going."

"What place is that?" demanded the captain.

"To hell—in five minutes—with the blood of a dozen men on your drunken soul!"

The captain sank into the boat, which immediately pushed out from the lee of the ship into the raging and roaring waters.

"There he goes, poor devil," muttered Jack. "It 's no time to bear ill will to any one, but I do wish that his owners at Liverpool were along with him. More than half the blame rests at their door for intrusting the ship to such a stupid sot."

"You are right, Thompson," said I, "it 's no time to bear ill will or bitter feelings. Let him go; we 've got enough to do to take care of ourselves——"

"Enough to do!" interrupted Jack. "What can we do, but wait the breaking up of this old tub? The stern boat is stove, and the long boat that they 've gone off in is by this time no better! However, if you can propose any thing, I 'm agreeable. I see that you 're the chap to work out of a scrape, if any one can, and whatever you say I 'll lend a hand to do."

"Well then, listen to me? Do you know where we are?"

"Why, on the desert, somewhere about the middle of it, I suppose."

"You are right; we are somewhere near, if not directly upon Cape Barbas. The nearest places, where we could find any assistance from Christians, are Portendik, about three hundred miles to the south; and Mogadore, more than five hundred miles to the north. The distance either way is a perfect desert, without vegetation, without water, at least that we could find, and inhabited by tribes of wandering Christian-hating savages. You see that our chance of reaching either place by land is rather small."

"You may say that," said Thompson, "what with the heat, and the sand, and the thirst, and the merciless Arabs, we should stand no more chance than a short-tailed whale in the Norway whirlpool."

"Our next chance is, that the captain and crew have got safe on shore, and if so, the boat will enable us to reach the Canaries."

"Belay that," interrupted the old man, "there 's no use talking about it. There is n't the ghost of a chance. If you depend upon that, we had better make up our minds to give ourselves up to the Arabs at once."

"I don't depend upon the poor chance of finding that the boat is safe. There is still another and a better chance. This coast from Cape Blanco to Cape Bojador is the resort of fishing-vessels from the Canaries. They are large polacca-rigged boats of from a hundred to a hundred and fifty

tons, and they remain on the station for some time. They generally
anchor close in-shore, and sometimes they land and carry on a small trade
with the wandering natives. They don't go north of Bojador, because
there the inhabitants have small boats in which the Moors would come off
from the shore and attack them; and they never go much south of Cape
Blanco, or the bank of Arguin. A little north of the cape is their favorite
ground. If we could get on board one of these fishermen, we should be safe."

"Aye, if we could; but without a boat, what can we do?"

"We can try, at any rate," I replied. "In half an hour it will be daylight, when we shall be able to see our way to the shore. If we can contrive to make a landing, and take with us water and provisions, we shall
probably be able to find some place in the neighborhood where we can
secrete ourselves until the Arabs have paid their visit to the ship.
When the coast is clear again we can then watch for a fisherman, and
perhaps attract his attention by some kind of signal. If we can find a safe
hiding-place for a week or two, I am convinced that Providence will send
us the means of escape. If not, when our water and provisions are
exhausted, we can take the chance of pushing out to sea on some piece
of a wreck, or give ourselves up to the Arabs."

Jack approving my plan, without more words we addressed ourselves
actively to the proposed preparations. The position of the ship favored
our exertions; she was careened towards the shore, with her stern somewhat elevated, so that the sea was prevented from dashing over her deck,
except just at the bow; while the stern being raised, prevented the water,
with which the ship was filled, from standing above the floor of the cabin,
and enabled us to get at any thing we wished in the steward's pantry, and
the bread-lockers.

Our first care was to collect all the bottles, jugs, and demijohns that
had withstood the shock of the ship's striking, and fill them with water
from the casks that still remained safely lashed to the booms. A ten-
gallon keg of brandy, which was the cause of all our misfortunes was
emptied of its remaining contents, and devoted to the same purpose.
The beef and pork, that happened to be in the harness casks on deck, we
divided into two or three lots, which we wrapped in canvas covers. We
did the same with a barrel of ship biscuit, and with several miscellaneous
articles, such as clothing, instruments, a few nails and spikes, which we
thought might perhaps come in play, and a few pieces of small cordage.
My idea in taking these last-mentioned articles was, that in case we could
do nothing better, we might perhaps construct a raft out of the spars
and pieces of timber which would come ashore from the wreck.

CHAPTER XX.

BY the time we had finished our preparations it was quite light, allowing us an opportunity in observing, with the desired distinctness, the perils and horrors that environed us. We found that the ship had struck upon the rocks at the bottom of the little bay, or indentation in the line of breakers, and that consequently we were considerably nearer the shore than we should have been had she gone on a hundred yards farther, either above or below. Directly in front of us, and not more than thirty rods off, rose a perpendicular cliff of dark, ragged rock. At this point the base of the cliff was washed by the sea; but we observed with pleasure that, at a short distance, in a northeasterly direction, the wall of rock withdrew itself, in an irregular curve, from the water, leaving a long beach of sand. Between the ship and the shore was a line of naked rocks, which, at high tide, were so situated as to be washed with the whole force of the surf. Beyond them the water, at low tide, was quite smooth, and apparently not of much depth. An opening at some distance to the right of the ship's position, afforded the only practicable passage for a boat to the shore. I pointed it out to my companion.

"The fools," he exclaimed, bitterly, "if they had waited till daylight they need not have splintered their boat, and dashed their bodies upon those black-looking rocks. But some men are doomed—if God wont kill them, they will kill themselves."

Fastening a line around my body, I jumped overboard, and stretched out for the reef. A minute or two sufficed to carry me within reach of a jagged point of rock, which I succeeded in grasping—retaining my hold while the following swell dashed over me; upon its subsidence I gained a footing and reached, not without some severe bruises, a higher point of the reef. Pausing merely to haul taut the line and fasten it around a point of a rock, I stepped into the water on the other side, and found, as I expected, that it was possible to wade without much difficulty to the base of the cliff, and by diverging a little to the right, gain the narrow beach of sand.

Making my way back to the reef, I found Jack ready with the line rove through a pulley at the end of the fore-top-sail yard to veer away the bundles that we had prepared. Hauling down the line on deck, he attached in turn a jug of water or a bag of bread, and hoisting it to the yard-arm, veered away; as he veered I hauled, and in this way succeeded in bringing the various articles within reach without touching the water. As they arrived I detached the bundles from the line, and wading with them ashore, deposited them safely upon the sand. There now remained only the old man. I made signs to him to lash himself to the middle of the line, the same way as he had the keg of water, so that he could veer himself away, while I hauled him in. Stationing myself as far out as I could, and yet retain a firm footing, I prepared to receive him. He was almost within my grasp, when the reflux of the wave tore him away, but the next moment a huge swell threw him into my arms, and rolled us over upon the jagged bed of rock. Happily no bones were broken, but the blood streamed from numerous cuts upon our hands and bodies.

Casting off the line, so that the Arabs might have no reason to suppose that any one had had communication with the shore, we crossed the water to the main beach. Here we found ample evidence of the melancholy fate of our companions. Fragments of the boat were scattered along the sands, and just at the water's edge was a large white object that sluggishly rolled up and down the inclined bank— one moment at rest upon the bare sand, and the next, sprawling and bobbing about in the returning water.—It was the mutilated corpse of one of the boat's crew.

At a little distance above high-water mark we proceeded to make an excavation in the sand, in which we deposited a keg of water, with a package of pork and biscuit, and our bag of nails and cordage; carefully effacing our footprints, we returned to the edge of the water, where any tracks would soon be washed out by the rising tide, and loading ourselves with our remaining provisions, set out for a hiding-place for ourselves. We carried an earthen jug, half a dozen junk bottles and small copper tea-kettle filled with the precious element; together with about twenty pounds of ship biscuit, a few pounds of pork, and a dozen or two of raw potatoes. In addition to my share of the burden, I also charged myself with a spy-glass, compass, and an old musket.

"I pointed it out to my companion."

The sun was now about three hours high, and peering over the lofty bank, threw his burning rays upon us. The shade at the base of the cliff invited us, but we dared not quit the margin of the beach, for fear of leaving the impression of our feet in the sand. The heavy night-dew which had laid the dust on the heights above, had now evaporated, and a strong land-breeze springing up, clouds of silicious particles came eddying down from the top of the cliff. The volleys were composed of an almost impalpable powder, that filled our mouths, ears, and eyes, mingled sometimes with small, round grains, that made the skin of our faces and hands smart severely. The heat was intense; the perspiration poured from our faces, and, catching the flying particles, rolled down our cheeks in arenulous ridges and streams.

About a mile from the ship we came to a long ravine that opened up the bank for some distance. It was very rough and irregular, and we could not see its termination, but we concluded that it must afford a passage to the top of the bank. Our first impulse was to ascend it, but, upon consultation, we decided that as it would probably be the passage by which the Arabs would descend to the ship, it would be better to push on beyond it to some broken rocks which we could see about half a mile off.

We resumed our march, and soon arrived at a spot where the bank came down again, almost close to the water. Along the base were several huge pieces of rock, which had evidently been detached from the face of the cliff. One of these had fallen so as to leave a small triangular space, elevated about twenty feet, and exposed to observation only from the sea, while at the same time it was concealed from above by the projection of the overhanging cliff. With some difficulty we clambered over the fragments of rock, and deposited our burdens upon the small bed of sand which partly filled up the crevice. For some distance farther on, the narrow space between the bank and water was so covered with heaps of large stones, that we had no fear of any one making the attempt to pass in front of our hiding-place.

We had now a *point d'appui* for our further operations; and after resting ourselves, and examining with the glass the beach, and the crest of the cliff on either hand, as far as we could see, we concluded to set out again, and explore the country on top of the bank. To attempt the ascent along the ravine I have mentioned, would take us too far from our cover; we were compelled, therefore, to seek a path nearer, but much more difficult. The bank that we had to clear was fully a hundred feet in height, and rose in some places perpendicularly, in others inclined, at an angle of several degrees towards the sea. The geological composition of the rock, however, favored us, consisting of strata of calcareous and silicious sandstone, separated by layers of quartz sand, which had become disintegrated by the action of the sea air; there were numerous horizontal crevices and ledges, by which we could gain a foothold on the face of the cliff. In the upper strata particularly, the calcareous prevailed over the silicious in the formation, and there were numerous holes which had formerly been filled with some pure calcareous material, which, having been decomposed, had been forced out by the wind. These holes assisted us much in drawing ourselves up from ledge to ledge. It was trying work in the hot sun, but at last our exertions were rewarded with success, and we stood upon the top of the bank.

What a sight met our eyes! A boundless earth-ocean, with its rocky islets and billows of sand! A dreary waste, with no green thing to relieve the dismal uniformity—no sight or sound of even the meanest specimen of organic life! Overwhelmed with the terrible sublimity of the scene, we remained for some minutes mute, motionless, straining our eyes across the undulating lines of low hills, or watching the wild gambols of the whirling clouds. " *Bahar billah maia!* " well have thy savage inhabitants named thee, thou " arid sea of sand !"

Keeping our way as much as possible between the sandhills, we started off for a rocky elevation about half a mile inland, which promised a more extended horizon. As we advanced, we found that in some places the ground was hard, and covered by a layer of silicious pebbles; in others, the bare rock showed itself, with its upper surface worn as smooth as glass by the attrition of the moving sand. In some spots this rock was an agate-looking limestone, beautifully mottled and veined, and susceptible of the highest polish. At the base of the crag which we proposed to ascend, we were gratified by the sight of several stunted thorn bushes, if a gratification that can be called which only served to impress more forcibly the idea of barrenness and sterility.

I was stooping to examine their withered leaves and sturdy spines, when I was startled by an exclamation from my companion. The old man pointed to a dark object, moving among the sand hills on our right. Upon applying the glass to my eye I saw that it was a man mounted upon a camel. He was moving slowly down to the edge of the bank. We watched him, keeping ourselves well concealed, and saw him make his way nearly to the crest of the beetling crag, when he dismounted and walked forward on foot. He soon caught sight of the ship, and running back, mounted his camel and came down towards us on a long swinging trot. When he had arrived at a point opposite the ship, he dismounted again, and advanced forward, but this time with more caution, crouching low, and near the edge throwing himself on his face and slowly drawing himself along the ground. For some time he remained, peering down upon the ship, then mounting his camel, he moved still farther towards us, and stopped at the head of the ravine; here he halted for a few minutes, as if in doubt; but at last wheeling his beast, he urged him forward at a rapid rate, in an east-by-south direction. His course slanting inland from the coast, which here trended from west-southwest to east-northeast, carried him within a few rods of us, but throwing ourselves flat on the ground behind a hillock, we escaped his observation.

" Crouching low, and near the edge throwing himself on his face."

We watched him until he was out of sight, when we mounted the crag, and discovered that his course lay toward a distant range of black hills, which we concluded afforded a refuge to his family or tribe.

"He's a rum-looking bird, he is," was Jack's commentary upon the fellow's appearance, as we saw the fluttering rag that was bound round his head disappear in the distance.

"Yes, a rum-looking bird indeed, and in an hour or two he'll be down upon us with his whole flock; we must be travelling back to our retreat."

"Do you suppose, Mr. Romer, that God made this country himself?" inquired Thompson, as we struggled back through the sand.

"Why not, as well as the rest of the world?"

"Because the Bible says that he looked at all he had made, and pro-

nounced it good. Now He never could have said that of this country.
A poorer piece of land I never laid eyes on. You don't need a mark of
the cloven hoof to know it for the 'devil's own.' I 've heard tell," he
continued after a pause, "that the inhabitants here are man-eaters. What
do you think, Mr. Romer?"

"That there is no truth in the report. Their religion would keep
them from cannibalism. They would no more touch a man's flesh than
they would pork."

"I don't know about that. If they don't eat each other, what else
have they got to live on. I 've heard some folks say that there are no
such thing as cannibals anywhere in the world; but I know better. I 've
been among the New Zealanders, and there they use each other for fresh
grub, as regular as boiled 'duff' in a man-of-war's mess. They used to
eat their fathers and mothers when they get too old to take care of themselves; but now they 've got to be more civilized, and so they eat only
ricketty children, and slaves, and enemies taken in battle."

"A decided instance of the progress of improvement and the march
of mind," said I.

"Well, I believe that is what the missionaries call it," replied Jack,
"but it 's a bad thing for the old folks. They don't take to the new
fashion—they are in favor of the good old custom. I never see'd the
thing myself, but Bill Brown, a mess-mate of mine once, told me that when
he was at the Bay of Islands he see'd a great many poor old souls going
about with tears in their eyes trying to get somebody to eat them. One
of them came off to the ship and told them that he could n't find rest in
the stomachs of any of his kindred, and wanted to know if the crew
would n't take him in. The skipper told him that he was on monstrous
short allowance, but he could n't accommodate him. The poor old fellow, Bill said, looked as though his heart would break. There were plenty
of sharks around the ship, and the skipper advised him to jump overboard,
but he could n't bear the idea of being eaten raw."

We had reached the edge of the bank, and paused to take another look
over the arid expanse.

"This is a good moral, Mr. Romer," exclaimed Thompson.

"How so?" I demanded.

"Why, I never had any thing that made me feel so like a parson in a
hurricane—ready to get right down on my knees, and say 'Good Lord,
deliver us.'"

"We may well pray for his help," I replied, "for without it we stand
but a poor chance of deliverance from our present difficulties."

" You 're right, Mr. Romer; if a poor fellow needs a lift from Providence anywhere, it is on such a piece of land as this. Afloat with plenty of sea-room, I always feel independent, and just as though I could veer and haul for myself; but here, bless my soul! unless God lend a hand, a fellow can neither tack ship, nor wear, heave-to, nor scud."

With a good deal of difficulty we succeeded in descending the path that we had come up. We reached our retreat thoroughly exhausted by the heat and the exertion. Having arranged that we should keep watch and watch, Thompson stretched himself upon the ground to take what he called his watch below, while I stationed myself so as to command a view of the mouth of the ravine.

CHAPTER XXI.

THE sun was about an hour high, when two half-naked figures presented themselves among the fragments of rock at the bottom of the gorge. One of them I instantly recognized as the fellow we had seen, by the rag around his head, which was so tied as to allow the end of it to fall down partly over his face. The other one had no head-gear, and his only protection from the rays of the sun was a thick mop of short grisly hair. Their only garments were ragged shirts of cotton, once, perhaps, white, but now of a dirty brown. Their complexions were swarthy, almost black, which, however, we had afterwards opportunities of observing, was in a great measure, owing to a thick coating of dirt. Their forms were of the middle height, light, and exceedingly spare ; and they evinced wonderful agility in slipping from rock to rock down the declivity.

As soon as they reached the sand they started off on a swift run towards the ship. In a few minutes they were followed by two more men, and these by several other parties, among whom five or six women made their appearance. As they came upon the level ground, each in turn stretched out at full speed, until at last more than forty ragged shirts were streaming along at intervals, from the ravine to the wreck.

They were soon all collected in a group, at the base of the cliff, where it came down to the water's edge, opposite the ship ; and from their rapid motions and vehement gestures, we concluded that they were discussing the interesting question of the best means of getting at the prize. Parties of them continually waded from the shore to the reef, and back again, but without, apparently, being able to devise any plan for passing the barrier of breakers.

" It 's plain enough," remarked my companion, " that there 's none of the Sandwich Islander breed about these fellows. Why, I 've seen women in the Pacific miles out to sea, swimming about with their young ones on their backs. These chaps are nothing but land crabs, and they'll never lay claws on that ship until she breaks up, and comes ashore herself."

The Arabs seemed to have come to the same conclusion ; for quitting the reef, they seated themselves in a circle upon the sand, while the women were employed in picking up the fragments of the boat, and branches of dried sea-weed, with which to make a fire. As the fire could not be needed for warmth, and as they most probably had no provisions that required cooking, we concluded that it was for the purpose of burning the splinters of the boat, so as to extract the iron nails. For two or three hours after the darkness of night had closed over sea and shore, the bright flashes of flame streamed upward from the wild bivouac, and, dying away, left us to our speculations for the morrow, or to such slumber as might be supposed would visit our eyes in the vicinage of such neighbors.

About the middle of the night, the wind, which had been blowing for several hours a fresh breeze directly on shore, increased in violence, rolling the surf in with such force, that at high tide we were drenched with the spray. We comforted ourselves, however, with the reflection that the old ship must inevitably go to pieces, and that the sooner the Arabs got possession of her fragments, the sooner they would leave the coast clear for our operations.

The morning dawned, and, agreeably to our expectation, the ship was no longer in sight. But, as the light grew stronger, we could perceive that the beach was covered with broken spars, pieces of timber, casks, cabin furniture, sails, and clothing, and we observed with dismay, that a large fragment of the rudder, with the iron pintles attached, was thrown upon the rocks, almost at our feet.

The savages were actively at work, running up and down the sands, securing pieces of clothing, canvas, and cordage, and occasionally quarrelling, and even fighting among themselves for the possession of coveted articles. A seaman's chest had come ashore, at not a great distance from our hiding-place. It was discovered by one of the women, but before she could open it the crowd collected around from all quarters, and then such a scrambling for its contents ; every article had a dozen hands on it at once. Knives were drawn, and blows made, apparently with desperate determination. One fellow had succeeded in securing several check shirts, which he threw into the arms of one of the women, and flourishing his knife, energetically expressed by the most frantic gestures his resolution to defend them to the death. At this moment the grisly-haired old fellow came up, running like the wind, and dashing him aside, struck the woman a blow on her breast, knocked her down, and seizing the shirts, thrust them into the arms of another woman. He then made a bound at a fellow who had got possession of a sailor's jacket, and compelled him to relinquish it, and was equally successful in an attempt upon a red woollen cap. I concluded that he must be the admiralty judge, for certainly no one could have made a more striking practical application of the laws of *flotsam and jetsam.*

Next to pieces of sail-cloth and clothing, the article of most value to them was the iron, and to get at this, they had no other means than to haul fragments of the wreck into piles, and set them on fire. This was laborious and slow work, and the day passed before they had half finished it. All night the fires were kept burning, and in the morning the search was resumed for fresh material. Several times parties came within a few rods of us, but each time something attracted their attention, and prevented them from continuing their researches in our direction. We could not flatter ourselves, however, that we should long escape detection. From the moment that we first saw the rudder on the rocks below us we had given up all hope.

In view of our inevitable fate, I occupied a portion of our time in impressing upon my companion certain rules for his conduct, and in giving him all the information that I thought might prove serviceable to him in case we were separated. I did not conceal from him the sufferings to which he would probably be subjected; but at the same time I encouraged him to hope that, like a good many other unfortunates, we might live to return to civilized life. I urged upon him that in no case, however strong the inducement, must he turn Mahometan—that, as a renegado, his life would be fully as uncomfortable, and that then all hope of redemption would be destroyed. That he must steadily deny all knowledge of any mechanical employments, and persist, in spite of suffering and punishment, in refusing to make himself of any value to the Arabs as a slave. I also told him that if he could persuade his masters to take him to Sweirah (the Arabic name for Mogadore), his ransom would be readily paid by Mr. Wiltshire, the English consul, with whose name all the inhabitants of the desert were perfectly familiar. Jack promised to remember and obey my injunctions; and—having agreed between us to say nothing of our buried provisions, for fear that our captors would suspect that we had also concealed money, and resort to torture to force us to disclose it— with as much resolution as we could command, we awaited our fate.

We had not long to wait. The sun was not an hour above the horizon, when one of the stragglers of the party came down to within a few rods of us. He was a young man, apparently not more than twenty years of age, but he had the true truculent scowling look of the Bedouin, that at first sight made him appear about forty. He got sight of the rudder, and immediately ran towards it. While stooping to examine it he did not observe us, but upon raising his head, there we were seated upon the rock, a little elevated, not more than a dozen yards off, and looking down directly upon him. Never was there presented a more striking picture of astonishment and terror. His eyes started from their sockets, his short stiff hair erected itself like steel-filings on a magnet, the blood forsook his swarthy skin, leaving it of a dirty yellow, and his lips curled themselves up in a rigid cataleptic grin. For some moments he stood still, unable to move, until I made a motion to rise, when he gave two or three convulsive jumps among the rocks, reached the sand, and started up the beach, yelling as if he thought a legion of fiends were at his heels.

"The game is up now," said Thompson. "What shall we do?"

"Make sure of one good drink of water," I replied, "and then march out and meet them."

Taking the old musket in my hand I stepped forth, followed by Thompson, and gained the sands. The alarm had spread: the Arabs were running from all quarters. As we advanced, those nearest to us retreated, evidently in so much consternation that, had we followed them up briskly, we should have been able to drive them from the field.

When we had advanced a short distance, we stopped and waited a few minutes until the Bedouins, recovering from their surprise, moved down in a body towards us, halting in apparent doubt and hesitation, when within fifteen or twenty rods. I immediately moved forward alone, again stopped, and, bowing low in token of submission, exclaimed: "*Salam Ailekom!*" This salutation in their own language seemed to puzzle them exceedingly. I happened to remember a few words of Arabic that I had seen in some old narratives of shipwrecks; so after bowing once more, I exclaimed: "*Fine Sheikh!*"—Where is the chief? A movement in the group indicated that the old grisly-haired fellow was a man of authority. Making a signal for him to come towards me, I threw aside the gun, and again bowed. The gun seemed to have been the cause of their hesitation; for the instant it was out of my hands they rushed up like so many tigers. Offering no resistance, I was at once borne to the ground by the force of numbers; and it seemed for a few minutes as if the whole party were bent upon piling themselves upon my body. Their knives gleamed before my eyes, and grazed my skin in several places; and each moment I expected was to be my last. The metal buttons of my pea-jacket were cut off in a trice, my pockets torn out, and my clothes rent in numerous places in their eagerness to find money. There was not much about me to gratify their cupidity, and, in a few minutes, I was allowed to rise and look around. Thompson, I saw, had been treated in like manner, or worse; the remnants of his garments presenting a more dilapidated appearance even than my own.

A furious discussion now commenced, as to the right of ownership of our persons, in the course of which we were most unceremoniously hauled, and pulled about by the contending claimants, and several times threatened with instant death. For full half an hour the contest raged with unabated fury; more than once I expected to see them come to blows, when most probably our lives would have been sacrificed in the melée by the jealous disputants. At last a kind of compromise was effected, and the war was ended without bloodshed.

We were now seated together upon the sand, and the Bedouins huddling around began to question us about the ship. They soon found that my knowledge of Arabic extended only to a few words, but they could not conceal their expressions of wonder that I could speak even those. They first wanted to know if I was the "*rais*," or captain; to which I replied "*la*," or no, and here our verbal conversation, for want or words, had to close. By signs I explained to them, that excepting Thompson and myself, the crew were all drowned; that the ship had been to the negro country for wood and oil, and that she had no money on board. I mentioned Sweirah, and Mr. Wiltshire, and undertook to persuade them to take us there for ransom. But little attention was paid to my representations—our captors continually recurring to the subject of the ship and her cargo. It was with difficulty that I could satisfy them that she had not had money, and that we had not buried some of it in the sand. They tried my companion, but he had heard my answers, and an energetic "*La! Lazah!*" was all they could get out of him.

At the conclusion of the consultation, which lasted two or three hours, the grisly-haired fellow, whose name I ascertained was Hamet Askeiff, intimated to me by a kick in the ribs that I was his property, and that I must rise, and prepare to ascend the bank. The preparation consisted in packing on my back about fifty weight of iron bolts. My companion received a like intimation, couched in similar terms, and his back was loaded with a similar burden. "*Bomar! bomar!*" shouted our masters, at the same time giving us a few hearty thwacks with a large stick, and off we started, accompanied by five or six of the men and two or three

THE HIDING-PLACE DISCOVERED.

women. The ascent through the ravine, under our heavy loads and in the hot sun, was laborious enough. Several times Thompson lost his footing and fell, when he was compelled to rise again amid a shower of execrations and blows, and upon attempting to assist him my back came in for a liberal share of the same kind of compliments. Fortunately, I had been allowed to retain my pea-jacket, which served as some protection, but Thompson had been stripped of all except his canvas trousers and tarpaulin hat, and his naked body suffered not only from the blows, but from the intense heat of the sun. We were near the top of the bank, when Jack became utterly exhausted by the exertion. Our masters were a little distance behind.

" Mr. Romer," he exclaimed, drawing with laborious effort his breath, " I can't stand this any longer."

" We must, we can't help ourselves. Come on, hold out for a minute more and we shall be at the top."

" No, no, let us dash these villains down the rocks, and then rush down upon their friends at the beach. Better die at once by their knives, than be murdered this way. I'll carry my load no farther ", and my companion threw his burden from his back to the ground.

Without stopping to answer him, I seized his load, and staggered forward and upward as fast as I could under a hundred weight of iron. He started after me, calling out for me to stop and give him back his burden, but I persevered, and we reached the level ground together, and at the same moment with our masters. Here a shower of blows, equally distributed, rewarded Jack for dropping his load, and me for picking it up.

Five or six camels were standing at a little distance, each one with his fore-leg doubled up, and tied with a rope of hide, so as to prevent them from wandering. One of these was selected, the iron placed upon his back, and one of the Arabs mounting him, the word " *bomar* " was again sounded, and we all started off across the desert, in the direction of the hills that we had seen on the first day in the southeast.

For three long hours we pursued our weary way in the broiling sun, over loose sand hills, into which our feet sank deep at every step, until we came to a small rocky plain, and beyond that to a range of rock hills, two or three hundred feet in height. At the foot of one of these we found several huts, constructed of stone piled up on three sides, about four feet high, and covered with a skin, or an awning of coarse dark cloth. Here we found a number of women and children, who gathered around us, at first in silent curiosity, but soon they got bolder, and began to annoy us with their impertinent familiarities. They examined our skins;

felt our persons; pulled our hair and ears, and closely investigated the mystery of our clothing. My pantaloons, in particular, excited their wonder, and the question was often asked how I got into them, and whether I had been put in, and then sewed up in them. Their attentions, however, were not confined to these pleasantries. Several of the women amused themselves by spitting upon us, throwing sand in our faces, and cursing us in a profusion of unintelligible gutturals.

"*Sere! sere!*" I exclaimed, jumping to my feet, and assuming as fierce a look as possible.

At this Arabic exclamation, equivalent to "go away," or "clear out," our tormentors rushed from us, screaming with affright; but in a few moments they returned, and became more abusive than ever. Our lives were even in danger from the stones with which they had armed themselves, when Hamet fortunately made his appearance, and I called to him to come to our assistance. "*Aghee! aghee!* Hamet Askeiff!"

He ran up, laughing immoderately at my pronounciation of the words, and at our distresses; but at last he condescended to interfere, and our tormentors were driven off.

At sunset several loaded camels came in from the wreck, and with them most of the party that we had left behind on the beach. The camels were unloaded, and turned loose to browse upon a few stunted thorns. A mixture of water, camel's milk, and the meal of a kind of millet, was prepared by the women, and furnished the only refreshment; after which the Arabs disposed themselves for a regular council. A bright fire, made of splinters of the wreck, and dried thorn-bushes, threw up its light and illuminated the swarthy faces of about thirty Bedouins, who squatted in a circle around it. Pipes were produced, filled, and passed about from mouth to mouth. The whole scene brought strongly to my mind certain descriptions of Indian councils in my own country, but there were many points of dissimilarity. There was a lack of that gravity and dignity so generally attributed to the conduct and manners of the aborigines of America, and there was certainly but little resemblance between the blank desert waste, and the thickly wooded covers and green prairies of my own distant land.

We were ordered to take our seats within the circle, and then commenced a repetition of the same questions that had been put to us at the beach. As soon as an opportunity occurred, I brought forward the subject of taking us to Sweirah for ransom, but it was received with no better favor than in the morning. They seemed to be much surprised that I should know any thing about Sweirah, and could point out the direction in which it lay, but they gave us to understand, in the most

decided manner, that there were insuperable obstacles to taking us there.
Hamet, drawing his knife, placed the point of it against his breast, intimating that he would run upon it in going to Mogadore, from which I
concluded that his band was at feud with some of the northern tribes.
In the course of the conversation, the word Hoden was frequently mentioned, and also the word Waladah. I knew that Hoden was supposed
to be a town or station, and was generally put down, probably without
much accuracy, to the southeast of us. I could form no idea of the
position of Waladah, but it was not difficult to understand that it was a
place where it was proposed to carry us for sale as slaves. In such a case
all hope of redemption was at an end, and the only chance of ultimately
regaining our freedom would be in making ourselves thoroughly acquainted with the language, so as to be able to avail ourselves of any
favorable circumstances to escape. To acquire the language perfectly, I
at once resolved should be my chief object. Once master of it, so as to
pass for an Arab, I could not see how my masters would be able to prevent me from regaining my freedom. The future was dark and indefinite,
but not without a few feeble gleams of hope that forbade utter despair.

I communicated my suspicions and plans to Thompson. The old
man shook his head despondingly.

"It may do all very well for you, Mr. Romer, but it wont answer
for me."

"Why not?" I replied, as encouragingly as possible.

"Why, just look at the difference between us. You propose to make
yourself a regular Arab. Well, you're young, and with your spare figure,
dark complexion, and black hair and eyes, in a short time you will look
like an Arab, but what shall I do, with my light skin and blue eyes.
Besides, I am too old to learn the language. I might, perhaps, learn to
parly-voo-fransay through my nose, but I can never get the knack of pulling my words up by the roots, from the pit of my stomach. No, I feel
that I shall kill two or three of these chaps before long, and that 'll be
the end of me."

I endeavored to comfort the old man, and to inspire him with a more
hopeful idea of his future fate, but fatigue, hunger, thirst, and the pain
of his cuts and bruises conspired to depress his spirits, and he refused to
entertain the belief that he had any prospect of life, much less of liberty.
We were stretched side by side upon the sand ; a heavy dew was falling,
and the night wind grew quite chilly. My pea-jacket, which I had taken
off, and stretched over us, afforded an inadequate protection ; but, notwithstanding all the disagreeable and painful circumstances of our situation,
tired nature exacted from the "restorer" the tribute of her oblivious sweets.

CHAPTER XXII.

A Scanty Breakfast—Watering the Camels—A Change of Humor—Plaguing the Women—
Judicious Flattery—A Pigeon-Wing in the Desert—Working the Pumps—Starting for the
Interior—Suffering by the Way—Character of the Country—Instinct of the Camels—The
Wells of Ageda.

T early dawn we were aroused, and about a pint of milk and
water, in which had been mixed a handful of barley-meal, was
given to us for our breakfast. We begged loudly for more,
and at last succeeded in getting a part of one of our biscuits,
which we shared between us. We found our palates not quite so dainty
as the day before, and the ill flavor of the putrid water no longer excited
so much disgust.

Most of the Arabs immediately started for the beach, after giving us
to understand that the next day we were to take up our line of march
for the interior. One reason for moving so soon, we found to be the state
of the wells, which were unusually low for the season, and which promised
in a day or two to fail entirely. We were taken to these wells, and compelled to assist nearly the whole day in drawing water. They were situated at a little distance from the camp, at the bottom of a cleft in the hills,
and consisted of two or three natural holes of great depth. A stake was
made fast across the mouth, with a rude kind of pulley attached to it;
through this a rope, with a goat-skin bucket at the end, was rove. By
the aid of the rope, an Arab descended to the bottom, and filled the
bucket with the water that slowly percolated through the chinks, from
some hidden reservoir. When the bucket was filled we walked away with
the other end of the rope, and drew the bucket to the top, where it was
emptied into a large calabash by the women, and supplied to the camels.

As soon as the first camels had been watered they were dispatched to
the beach, and, with an appearance of haste, in the movements of their
masters, that induced us to think that the scanty supply of water was not
alone the cause of our departure. Besides their desire to get us at once to
market, we concluded that they had fears of a visit from some of their enemies, or perhaps, friends, who might wish to come in for a share of the spoil.

I had made up my mind to take my fate as easily as possible, and to waste no mental energy in useless repinings. Nothing that I could say, do, or think, could, for the time, alter my destiny, and therefore why trouble myself with fears, hopes, and regrets, which could have no influence in furthering my chief object. There were but two great facts in relation to my situation, worthy of serious thought—one, that I was a prisoner, and about to be sold into slavery, in which state I should be compelled to remain for a year, or perhaps two; and the other, that I was bound to recover my freedom. That my master could not keep me for ever was a settled point—a fixed fact, that admitted of no dispute. How or by what means my escape was to be effected, it was impossible to say; that was a question that time alone could determine, but, until time did so, I was resolved that I would not give myself any trouble, but take things easily, and bide the march of fate. Providence, and my own stout legs and arms, I felt to be a good dependence.

As soon as I had formed this resolution, a kind of reckless jollity took possession of me, which, at first, excited my companion's surprise, but which, before long, exerted an infectious effect upon his feelings. The change in our humor at once made a decidedly favorable impression upon our masters, and before nightfall we had fairly gained an immunity from the wanton annoyances and insults which we had to endure the day before. We might have tried to excite their sympathies for our distresses in vain, but as soon as they found that we were perfectly reckless, impudent, and independent, they began to entertain for us a degree of respect.

Acting up to the design I had formed of learning the language as soon as possible, I lost no time, but at once commenced an energetic and thorough course of practice—asking the names of every thing I could see, repeating their phrases, and shouting out the words that I had mastered, right or wrong, to the utter astonishment and, at the same time, to the high amusement of our masters. I joked, laughed, and scolded with the women, ridiculing some and flattering others, and instantly retorting any abuse in their own terms, eked out with voluble English and Spanish. Several times I received some hard knocks from the enraged women, but, by skipping about here and there, and dodging around and under the camels, I generally contrived to elude them. There was one skinny old hag, with whom, in the course of the day, I had a good deal of amusement. She seemed at first to have taken a particular dislike to Jack, and was every moment attacking him with words and blows, until I contrived to draw her rage upon myself, and at last worry her into terms. I mimicked her motions and words, and retorted her curses, until, almost bursting with passion, she would rush at me with a heavy stick, when away I would skip, cutting up all kinds of queer antics amid the immoderate laughter of the other women and of the few men who were looking on. No one seemed to enjoy the fun more than the wife of Hamet, who, as it was easy to perceive, was as delighted at the old hag's disappointment and discomfiture, as at my capers.

For the twentieth time the old lady came at me, with the kind intention of knocking out my brains, expressed in every movement and feature. Exerting my agility, I sprung up, and seizing the hump of one of the tallest camels, drew myself on to his back. The astonished animal hopped about upon his three legs, while I, vaulting from side to side as my pursuer came round, looked down with the utmost complacency from my secure elevation. When the old lady's breath was pretty well exhausted I finished the performance by jumping down, and cutting a regular pigeon-wing in the sand. The most vigorous and graceful *pirouette* of a Vestris or Taglioni never excited greater admiration and applause. The men laughed heartily, while the women and children fairly shrieked and yelled with delight, and when Jack Thompson capped the climax with a double-shuffle, I was really afraid that fat Mrs. Askeiff would go off in a convulsion. This would have been a sad misfortune, for, from the instant we had seen her round, fat, and comparatively good-humored face, we had marked her out for a patron and friend. Luckily an opportunity offered itself for a piece of judicious flattery, privately administered, which completed the favorable impression that my saltatory exertions had commenced. Passing my hands up and down, at a little distance from my own person, to indicate her obesity. I bowed, smiled, and exclaimed "Beautiful! very beautiful!" If she had been brought up in an English boarding-school she could not have comprehended more readily my words. It would be hard to say which was swallowed with the greatest avidity, the delicate compliment or the bowl of milk and meal with which it was repaid.

At sunset our master, Hamet, with the other men, returned from the beach. After conversing for a few moments with the women, and giving some directions about the camels, he beckoned me to follow him, and together we moved out from the camp. Turning behind a rock that concealed us from view, he stopped, uttered a few words, and pointed to my feet. His words were worse than Greek—pure Arabic—and his motions perfectly incomprehensible. He repeated his orders, and at last, with an expression of angry impatience, he began to move his own feet. The idea broke upon me; he had heard of my pigeon-wing, and was determined to have a private rehearsal for his own particular amusement. Was ever any thing more ridiculous? A captive in the hands of barbarians, amid the sands of the great desert, to be taken out behind a rock and required to cut a pigeon-wing for the amusement of an old surly Arab! Hamet waited until my risibles had composed themselves, when he again gave the signal, and the performance commenced. Once, twice, three times—and then gravely indicating his satisfaction, he signed me to follow him back to the huts. A rather large allowance of milk and a whole biscuit testified to the liberalizing influence of the pigeon-wing upon his heart.

"Seizing the hump of one of the tallest camels, drew myself on to his back."

"Well, if that is n't the rummest go I 've heard of," exclaimed Thompson, when I explained to him the cause of Hamet's unexpected liberality. "I 'm glad he did n't call on me for a double-shuffle, for my soles wont stand it many times; and if we are to get our living by dancing, what are we to do when our shoes are gone? I 've known fellows to keep themselves above water by working their pumps, but I had no idea that the same thing could be done on dry land, or I would have brought along an extra pair."

Before daylight the next morning preparations were commenced for the journey. The skin and cloth coverings of the huts were taken off and packed away; the cooking utensils secured, and the camels saddled and loaded. Three of these animals were furnished with panniers, in which rode the smaller children and two or three women, among whom, of course, was Mrs. Hamet Askeiff. The other women, like ourselves, were compelled to walk.

The first day's journey, after leaving the hills, was over a flat pebbly plain, perfectly destitute of vegetation, except now and then a thorn-bush and a few roots of the *salcornia*. We passed the skeleton of a camel, and not far from it we observed the tracks of an animal of the cat kind. Our direction was about east-by-south, and we travelled at least twenty-five miles. My companion was exceedingly distressed, and with difficulty kept up with the body of the caravan. Not unfrequently his motions had to be quickened by applications of the stick. Being younger, and of a spare make, and, at the same time, more accustomed to pedestrian exertion, I did not suffer nearly as much.

At sundown we encamped on the open plain, with nothing in view but the sky above and the vast expanse of low sand-hills around us. The camels were unloaded, two or three small tents erected, and, after evening prayers, every one received his allowance of meal and water. Thompson and myself got each about half a pint. We begged lustily for more, but received only an intimation that we had already had more than we deserved. Kind Mrs. Hamet, however, took compassion on us, and slily slipped into our hands a few dates, as dry and as hard as so many pebbles. We swallowed them whole upon a suggestion from Thompson, that " in that way they would last the longer, and our stomachs would have something to gnaw upon for a week."

After prayers, and their make-believe ablutions, our masters disposed themselves for a smoke and a talk. The tobacco-pouch was produced, and the pipe carefully filled, lighted, and passed round. Thompson succeeded in begging a mouthful of the weed. The Arabs watched him as he rolled it up and thrust it into his mouth, when they burst out into an unanimous expression of disgust and contempt.

" Look! " they exclaimed, " at the Kaffirs! see how they pervert God's gifts! Tobacco was made to smoke and to snuff, and the infidel dogs (God's curse upon the whole race!) put it in their mouths and eat it. But what can you expect of fellows who never pray and who eat pork! Faugh! *Mashallah!* Blessed be God, they 'll all roast yet! "

Before sunrise the next morning we were again *en route.* The character of the country differed but little from that of the day before, with the exception that there was a larger portion of rough and rocky surface. Our shoes suffered severely, and by the time we had reached our camping ground we were but little better than barefoot, and with a sad prospect of sore feet before us. In this particular the third day fully realized our expectations. The heat of the burning sand, and the sharp points of the jagged rocks, made it impossible for us to keep up with the caravan. We pointed out to our masters the cause of our loitering, but they only laughed and urged us on with sticks and stones. At last my companion gave out entirely; his feet were so lacerated and swollen that he swore he could n't and would n't move a step farther. The Arabs, finding that it was really impossible for him to move, made him mount on the hinder part of a camel, where he had to keep himself from slipping off backwards by holding on by the tufts of hair on the hump. The rough skin, sharp bones, and heavy motion of the animal soon made this mode of travelling as distressing as walking. More than once he was about to throw himself off, upon the ground, to die; and nothing but my encouraging exhortations prevented him from obeying the dictates of pain and despair.

At night there was a discussion among our masters concerning us. My progress in the language enabled me to comprehend the general drift of the conversation, from which it appeared that we were bound for some place by the name of *Quahlet*, but whether it was the Walet of Mungo Park, or the Qualet of Callie, or, as was most probable, a different place from either, it was impossible to say. A few days, however, five or six at furthest, would, perhaps, elucidate the question; so, dismissing the subject, I composed myself, as tranquilly as possible, to sleep—to sleep, but not to dream; the exigencies of exhausted nature frequently forbid an indulgence in such luxuries. Nowhere can I recollect that I enjoyed more profound repose than during this first journey in the desert. Queen Mab, if she ever drives her team of atomies in that quarter of the world, never seemed disposed to pay me a visit, or if she did, found sense, feeling, and fancy all engaged, and was denied admission.

The country, as we advanced, continued to present the same appearance, a vast plain of sand-hills, until the sixth day, when we entered upon a more rocky, and irregular tract. Large masses of a reddish granite were scattered about in all directions, sometimes so closely together as to leave room for not more than one loaded camel at a time to pass.

Emerging from this sea of rock, we encamped upon the edge of a plain of yellow sand. The ground was hard, the sand-hills few and small, and the scene agreeably relieved by several patches of vegetation. A number of acacias were in sight, and close around our camp were numerous bushes, upon which the camels were turned loose to graze.

In the course of the next day we saw several gangs of camels, some

with loads, moving under the guidance of their masters, and others quietly browsing upon the thorn-bushes that grew at distant intervals. Towards nightfall two horsemen were seen skirting the edge of the horizon.
The air was so clear that we could see the slender shafts of their long
spears, drawn like black lines upon the sky. Hamet pointed to them and
exclaimed " Ostrich hunters ! "

We resumed our march again early in the morning, and pressed on
with rapidity during the greater part of the day. From the motions of the
camels alone, it was easy to perceive that we were approaching water.
They no longer straggled wide, or stopped to crop the stunted bushes,
but with outstretched necks toiled on at a rate which made it extremely
difficult for me to keep up with them. A ridge of low, whitish-looking
hills indicated the position of the wells, which, even at the distance of
ten or fifteen miles, had sent their grateful odors to the keen senses of our
thirsty beasts.

About three o'clock in the afternoon we came upon the brink of a
steep precipice, about fifty feet in height, inclosing on three sides a small
irregular basin, of perhaps twenty acres in extent. We halted and looked
down upon the busy scene below. At the bottom of the basin were
numerous pits, and around three or four of these were collected crowds
of camels. There were at least three hundred in all, attended by fifty or
sixty men and women. We noticed also several horses and mules. Hamet
happening to be in very good humor, condescended to inform us that
these were called the wells of Ageda, and that they were the only wells
within five days' journey, and furnished all the water for the town of
Quahlet, which was half a day farther to the east.

By making a slight detour we reached a place where the shelving
precipice allowed our camels to descend without going round to the head
of the ravine, through which the camels below were ascending and descending in long strings.

The path was difficult, and in several places the animals had to jump
from rock to rock, a distance of six or eight feet, but, under the skilful
guidance of our masters, the descent was accomplished in safety, and we
stood at the bottom of the basin amid the group around the wells.

CHAPTER XXIII.

SALAM Ailekom! Ailekom Salam!" was reiterated a hundred times between our party and the strangers, accompanied with the almost interminable string of compliments, inquiries, and good wishes which Arab etiquette prescribes for a friendly greeting. The ceremony through, and the excitement created by our appearance somewhat abated, we were allowed to approach the wells and commence drawing water for our camels.

When we had finished, instead of keeping on to the town, our masters made preparations for spending the night upon the spot. A fire was kindled, and, after evening prayers, a large bowl of cooscoosoo prepared of which we got a small portion, and found it delicious. It consisted of flour, rolled into small round grains, and was cooked by putting it into a kind of earthen colander, with holes pierced in the bottom. The colander was then fitted into the mouth of an earthen pot, which contained a little water, with part of a kid cut in small pieces. The steam, as it arose, ascended through the holes in the bottom of the colander, and made its way through the mass of cooscoosoo, which, when sufficiently cooked, was turned out into a large dish, a cavity made in the middle of the pile, and the contents of the pot poured into it. A dozen dirty hands were at once thrust into the dish, and, by a dexterous twist, the yellow grains were rolled into good-sized balls, and jerked into the mouth with wonderful rapidity.

Fortunately, in the dish prepared for Hamet and his immediate friends, there were a few grains more than was necessary to distend their stomachs to within the smallest possible distance of the bursting point, so we were allowed to finish the dish, or, as Hamet facetiously expressed it, to swallow our "share."

The night passed pleasantly; the weather was serene, and the high banks on either side protected us from the wind. Several parties, with their camels, remained upon the ground, and numerous camp-fires threw their flickering lights upon the wild and uncouth groups of animals, and upon the rugged boulders and precipitous ridges of the deep basin. Until late at night the Arabs remained assembled in front of our tents, where they were amused by the performance of a professsional story-teller, who recited his tales with much spirit and energy—imitating the voices of the different speakers, gesticulating and grimacing with great freedom, and accompanying himself with frequent emphatical blows upon a tambourine. His longest story was a peculiar version of the " Forty Thieves." In the main, he adhered to the plot as we have it in the " Arabian Nights"; but there was an infinity of detail that the Eastern *raconteur* had not dreamed of, and which, perhaps, the more polished taste of Yeman would have rejected as puerile and tiresome, but which seemed to constitute the chief charm of the story to the unrefined auditors of the Sahara.

The next morning, at sunrise, as we were getting ready to set out for Quahlet, three or four horsemen dashed up to the wells at full speed, shouting at the top of their voices, " *Fine Nazarin ?* " " Where is the Christian ? "

We were pointed out to them, when they galloped toward us, jumped to the ground, and, leaving their horses unattended, advanced close to us, and began a minute inspection of our persons. They were horrible-looking fellows, worse, even, than our masters, or any Arabs we had yet seen. Their forms were literally nothing but skin, sinew, and bone. Their eyes, deep sunk in their heads, emitted a lurid light, and a dark scowl was carved in permanent lines upon their sharp angular features. Each one wore a *haick*, and over it a *jallabeah* of coarse woollen, resembling, in shape, a shirt with a hood attached to it. Their horses had very much the look of their masters ; at first sight they would have been taken for broken-down hacks, but, upon closer examination, the clean limbs, small head, clear eye, and expanded nostril, would have indicated their descent from the famous *Sh'rubah Er'reeh*, or " wind drinker " of the desert, so called, partly as a metaphor for speed, and partly because of a habit they universally have, of thrusting out their tongue, with a peculiar noise, when running.

After the new-comers had examined us to their satisfaction, they withdrew with our masters, and commenced chaffering about our price. In an hour or two it was announced to us that I had been purchased by the strangers, but that Thompson must accompany his first masters to the town, where he would be sold to a Moor, who wanted to take him on to some place still farther in the interior. I heard the name Al Araiouan pronounced, but I could not make out distinctly whether that was the place where the Moor, whom the new-comers represented to be ready to purchase Thompson, resided or not.

The news that we were to be separated occasioned us the greatest distress. There is nothing like a partnership in misfortune to originate and strengthen a feeling of friendship; and nowhere, perhaps, could a slight acquaintance ripen into intimacy more readily than amid the desolation of the desert. The old man fairly wrung his hands in despair when informed of our doom. He urgently joined me in my entreaties to my new master, that he would also purchase him, but without success.

"Never mind," said I, "we will meet yet, and that too under more favorable circumstances than at present. Keep up a good heart, as I shall, and trust in Providence. I feel perfectly confident that we shall together escape from these miserable wretches. And it will not be a great while either before we do so."

"I hope so, but I must say that I don't see much chance of it. However, God bless you, Mr. Romer, and I hope he'll restore you to freedom, whatever he does with old Jack Thompson. When you get clear, if you will recollect to write, or send word to the old woman in Liverpool—you know the street,—you will do me a favor. But you wont forget it, I know. God bless you, my boy! Good-bye!"

We held each other by the hand. Our masters made a movement of impatience. "God bless you! Good-by!" I exclaimed, and dropping his hand, turned to conceal my tears. Upon looking around, Thompson was at some distance, slowly following the camels of Hamet. He looked back, waved his hands in adieu, and then steadily plodded onward.

Seldom has my heart felt more heavy than at that moment. It was not merely the peculiar circumstances of our position that made the parting so hard. There were points in the character of Jack that had served to create a strong feeling of attachment and respect. I should have parted with him, under any circumstances, with regret; judge then of my feelings, when bidding him adieu, probably for ever, amid the wilds of the Sahara.

Leaving the hills, my new master, whose name I was informed was Sidi Mohammed ben Alum, turned off in a direction due north, accompanied by one of his companions; the rest of the party setting off at full speed towards the southwest.

My feet were in such a condition that, although I had bound them up in strips of clothing torn from the skirts and lining of my pea-jacket, I walked with pain, and with difficulty kept up with my master's horse, whose pace was restrained to the slowest rate. After moving along in this way for two or three hours, Mohammed began to get impatient, and finding that his curses had no effect in quickening my motions, he asked me if I could ride. His surprise was great when I replied in the affirmative. "How is it," said he, "that you who always live in houses upon the water, should know how to manage a horse?"

Nothing could be more admirable than the steadiness and ease with which the gaunt half-starved animals beneath us kept up their stride. Going ahead with a long swinging gait seemed positively more natural and less fatiguing to them than standing still; and for four or five hours we kept under way at different rates of speed, according to the nature of the ground, but without once fully stopping to breathe.

Our way lay over an extensive plain, covered in some places with loose flints, and scattered here and there with thorns. From this we passed through a long valley, overgrown with thistles, and again an open tract of moving sand, beyond which we came to a range of rocky eminences, at the base of which was situated a *douah*, or village, composed of about thirty tents, arranged in two parallel lines. For a distance of several miles around, the plain was covered with scattered thorns and thistles.

As soon as we came in sight of the *douah* a number of black slaves ran forward to meet us. Taking hold of Mohammed's foot, as it was turned up along the horse's flank by the short stirrup, they applied their heads to the sole, and repeatedly kissing the hem of his *haick*, welcomed him back with a profusion of compliments. The women and children too, came forward, and repeated in a very submissive tone their greetings. Mohammed's wives arranged themselves before him, crossed their arms upon their breasts, and bowed. He advanced towards them and held out his hand; they all touched it and then applied their own hands to their mouths, heads, and breasts. The whole ceremony was well calculated to make an impression upon strangers, and, had I not already learned that appearances were not to be relied on, I should have gathered the idea that Mohammed was a good husband, kind father, and humane master; and that his polite dependants were really glad to see him back. My hesitation in admitting the evidence of this excessive ceremonial politeness saved me from a great mistake, for a more complete devil in human form, and one more generally hated and feared in all the relations of life, it would have been hard to find even among the inhuman fiends of the Sahara.

It would occupy too much space were I to note the course of my life from day to day from this time forward for several months. The time, although fertile in events of interest to me, would seem monotonous and tiresome to the reader if dwelt upon in all its details. It is sufficient to say that I was soon established in all the duties and privileges of a slave. The duties consisted mainly in watching the camels while feeding—driving them to the hills, and collecting the roots of a kind of thorn for fuel. The privileges consisted in sleeping outside of the tents, exposed to the sand winds and the chilly dews, and supping once a day upon the refuse of the meals for the black slaves, who, being believers, were entitled to, and received a degree of favor and consideration that no Kaffir could expect.

Notwithstanding my sufferings and privations, my health continued good. Every ounce of superfluous flesh being gone, my frame rapidly became hardened to the sinewy consistence of a Bedouin's body, and soon acquired a wonderful power of enduring fatigue, hunger, and thirst. My progress in the language was rapid, so much so, that before the year was out I spoke it fluently. I felt that my capacities for action were nearly reaching their perfect development, and that in a short time it would be necessary to mould into some degree of form and consistency the vague plans which had been revolving in my head. As I frequently had to drive the camels a distance of two days' journey, and remain alone with my gang in the plain, sometimes four or five days, I had abundant opportunity for meditation, while, by close attention to the conversation of the Bedouins, I was able to pick up a great deal of information in relation to the desert, without exciting their suspicion.

One of the most serviceable accomplishments, I knew to be the art of writing charms for the cure of diseases, or for the protection of the wearer from all evil influences. These charms invariably consist of verses from the Koran, which are frequently written upon scraps of paper, and worn about the person, at other times written with chalk upon a board. The chalk marks are then washed off, and the water drunk by the patient with the usual reverential expressions of faith in the unity of God and the sanctity of his prophet. As it was impossible for me to learn to read and write the Arabic, I adopted the plan of copying repeatedly all the charms that came in my way, until I had fixed the turn of each letter in my mind. In this manner I accumulated quite a stock, which, without knowing the meaning of any of them, it was in my power to reproduce at any moment.

I resolutely persisted in making myself of as little use to the Arabs as possible. I could do nothing well, except watch and drive the camels.

There was some danger, however, of carrying the thing too far, and I took timely warning, from a remark that I accidentally overheard Mohammed make, to the effect that he had a great mind to sell me to the workers of the salt mines below Quahlet. This idea was warmly seconded by several of his friends, particularly by an old *talb*, or priest, who had been the most strenuous in his exertions to convert me to the true faith.

"The *Nazarin* is good for nothing, why have him about. The sight of him is bad for the eyes."

I took the hint. I had no idea of being sold into the salt mines, where my personal movements would be restrained so as to render escape perhaps impossible, and I at once resolved that the old priest's eyes should no longer be troubled with the sight of me. Fortunately events occurred a day or two after that enabled me to carry my long-cherished designs into execution.

CHAPTER XXIV.

T was one evening, at the close of the nineteenth month of my captivity, that, being at some distance from the camp, a dark speck appeared upon the distant horizon, which my keen and practised vision at once discovered to be a camel. I supposed, at first, that it had a rider, and that it was, perhaps, the *avant-coureur* of a party who were coming to visit us; but upon watching the animal for a while, it became evident that there were no others in company, and that he was without a master. Upon coming to this conclusion I started off for the animal with all speed. Could I have been seen streaming along, bare-foot and bare-legged, with a dirty piece of cotton around my head, and the rags and tags of a tattered haick fluttering in the wind, not one of my Christian friends would have dreamed that I was aught other than a genuine wild Arab.

The last rays of the twilight lingering over the scene sufficed to satisfy me that no Arab was near, so making the camel kneel, I mounted him, and directed his course towards the camp. The animal was much fatigued and evidently in want of water; but the readiness with which he stretched out at the word of command, into a long, rolling, jolting, but rapid pace, showed that he was of a better breed than the ordinary pack camel, and that he had, at least, some of the blood of the high-bred dromedary, so much valued for their extraordinary bottom and speed.

Before coming in sight of the camp, I took the precaution of stopping and hiding a bag of dates that hung at the saddle-bow in a secret hiding-place, where I had already accumulated several articles that might some day come in play, such as a large water skin, a wooden bowl, and a small bag of meal. It must not be supposed that I had been able to obtain these articles without a good deal of difficulty. My stock of food, small as it was, required months of gradual accretion—every handful that I could save, or steal, being carefully added, until the bag acquired a weight, which, expressed in the equivalent of sustentation, might be safely put down as equal to at least a month above the point of actual starvation.

It was quite dark when I rode up to the tents, and threw myself from the camel. Most of the men were away upon some expedition, but those who were at home, including my master Mohammed, immediately gathered around.

"You have done well, *Roomah*," said Mohammed. "He has lost his master. We must take care of him. What is one man's misfortune is another man's good luck. Blessed be the name of the Prophet! Let us see what God's gift is worth."

Torches were lighted, and the Arabs commenced an examination of the animal. At once several voices exclaimed, "*A heirie! a heirie!*" Sidi Mohammed evinced the highest exultation, and all the party manifested their satisfaction at what they unanimously pronounced to be a piece of good-fortune. The camel was examined with the closest attention, and his points discussed with as much interest as were ever those of a race-horse by a party of turf-men. There seemed to be no doubt that the animal was a *tasay heirie*. For the first time in his life, Mohammed spoke pleasantly to me.

It may be well to explain that a *heirie* is of a peculiar breed of camels, famous all over the desert for their great endurance and wonderful speed. They are to the common camel what the racer is to the cart-horse, and as much pains are taken to preserve the purity of their blood as are ever bestowed upon the thorough-bred champions of the turf. As in the case of the race-horse, there are certain points, consisting mainly in the greater fineness and compactness of the frame, by which the breed can be at once recognized. Of course there is a great deal of difference in the powers of different animals, depending upon some accidental peculiarity of structure, and perhaps upon a greater or less taint of common blood; but it must be a very poor *heirie* that cannot far surpass, in the important qualities of wind and speed, the best of the ordinary camel. Inferior *heiries*, called *talayeh*, will perform three moderate days' journey in one, or about sixty miles a day; and this they can do for several days in succession. A better class, denominated *sebay*, will go seven days' journey in one, or a hundred and twenty miles; and the fleetest, called *tasay*, have been known to go at the rate of nine days' journey, or a hundred and sixty miles per day.

A *heirie* of this last kind is of course rare, and exceedingly valuable, being worth three or four hundred times the usual price of a pack-camel.

It was expected by my masters that so valuable an animal would not be long without some inquiries after him, and the best means of securing him from his owners were openly discussed. The third morning afterwards, I was directed to ride him to a distant well, that was but little used, and where we should be but little likely to meet any other families of the oasis. I had just ridden up on my return, when a couple of horsemen belonging to our family or douah, dashed into camp from the wells of Ageda. They looked at the camel with some surprise, asked a few questions, and then announced that his owner, with a large party of friends, was at no great distance behind—that they had met them in the basin af Ageda, where they made a great ado about their loss—that the animal had wandered from them while on their way from Hoden to their home in the oasis of Bahga, and that they were determined to search the whole length and breadth of the oasis of Quahlet to find him.

"God send them good eyesight; they will need it to find him," exclaimed Hamet.

"Selme! Fatimah!" he continued, calling to his wives, "bring the dates! bring some bread and a skin of water, quick! hurry! Here, Roomah, fasten these articles, and now you and Soonshoo mount and take your course to the 'devil's mouth'; when you get there, make the heirie lie down in just the spot where we found our stray camel the other day. You and Soonshoo will keep watch over him, and don't you stir until I come. I will be with you as soon as these people are gone."

Obeying the order we mounted the kneeling heirie. As the director of his motions I occupied the front seat, with my legs closed upon his neck, while Soonshoo, a little bandy-legged black slave, was a-straddle behind the hump, and holding on by the long hair.

In about an hour we came to the spot where I had concealed my stock of provisions. Little Soonshoo's eyes opened with astonishment when he saw the articles. "Ah, *Roomah*," he exclaimed, "what an admirable thief! you beat us all. We steal only a little milk or a few dates, but you steal things by the bagful. But what are you going to do with all these articles?"

"I'll show you, you little rascal," said I, attaching to the saddle my bag of meal, dates, and my goat-skin bottle. "Come, mount. Do you see those milch camels yonder? The fellow in charge of them is stowed away under some thorn-bush, sound asleep, I'll venture to say; we'll have our fill of milk for once, if we never do again."

In a few minutes we came up with the group of camels grazing, and, dismounting, we tied up the foreleg of our heiric and proceeded at once to milking the flock. I gave Soonshoo the wooden bowl, while I milked directly into the mouth of the skin. He imagined that we were only to help ourselves to a drink; but when he had filled the bowl, I turned it into the bottle, and, to his utter astonishment, directed him to fill it again.

"But Mohammed! What will he say? He'll break every bone in our bodies!"

"Never mind Mohammed," I replied. "I'll take all the beating. Fill the bowl."

"Well do our masters call you the son of *Eblis*," replied Soonshoo. "Where will your courage stop? You will dare some day to steal the haick from Mohammed's back. But mind, if this is known, I shall put all the blame upon you."

"Yes, and the first thing you do will be to tell of it, in order to have me flogged. I know you, you little black rascal; but never mind, milk away, I'll take all the blame."

Two hours brought us to the "devil's mouth," where we were to secrete ourselves. The "mouth" consisted of a few low rocks at the commencement of an extensive reach of loose sand, which was utterly destitute of vegetation.

The little black shouted, pointed to the rocks, and vehemently insisted that I was making a great mistake in altering my course. "Stop! *Roomah!*" he exclaimed, "there is the 'mouth.' Why don't you hold up? Son of Satan, you are going out into the open desert! Stop, I tell you, Kaffir! dog! I'll have you flogged till there's as many holes in your skin as there is in my *cousab*."

Finding that his cries received no attention, and that I steadily persisted in pushing out into the desert, the fellow let go his hold, and, at no little risk to his bones, allowed himself to slip down from his elevated position and roll heels over head upon the sand. I immediately stopped the heiric and made him kneel, at the same time sternly ordering Soonshoo to remount. "Mount, mount, you little villain! Do you hesitate? Look at this." and I flourished my camel goad around his ears, making him dodge and hop about with extraordinary agility for such a corpulent and sturdy subject.

"Mohammed shall know this," he shouted, "you son of *Shetan!*"

"You are mistaken," I replied, "I'm *Shetan* himself. Mount, mount quickly! You wont? Well, I must make you." Catching him by the back of the neck I shook him a few times, and then gave him a kick that lifted him fairly on to the back of the kneeling camel. "Now, be cautious, and keep your seat; if you tumble off again I'll put the evil eye on you, and change you into a baboon."

At the end of about two hours, having, as near as I could judge, made some fifteen miles from the "devil's mouth," I halted and dismounted. Making Soonshoo do the same, I untied the bottles of milk and water, and poured out a portion of both, until the bowl, which held nearly a pint and a half, was filled to the brim. Into this I threw a handful of meal, and told Soonshoo, who was holding the bowl, to drink. Fear

" Good-by, my dear Soonshoo ! "

checking his usual greediness, he obeyed with a timid air, and after a few swallows handed the bowl towards me.

"Drink it up! finish the whole of it; you know that's the way you have always done whenever our mistress gave you any thing to share with me. Drink it all, you'll need it before you get home."

"In the name of the Prophet, tell me, O *Roomah*, where you are going to take me. Let us go back; there is nothing before us for forty days but the broad desert. If we go far into it we shall be lost; I will say nothing to Mohammed about coming here, or about milking the camels, or about—— "

"No lies, you little villain! save your tongue until you get to camp,

and then you may tell Mohammed what you please. Here, take these
dates, and tie them up in a corner of your *cousab*."

Securing all my bottles and bags, and tightening the girths of my saddle, I mounted my camel and made him rise, leaving the black standing
upon the ground and looking on with the strongest expression of astonishment depicted in his sable visage

"Good-by, my dear Soonshoo; I sha'n't see you again, so take good
care of yourself. You know your way, it's a straight course back to the
'devil's mouth.' By the time you get there it will be quite late, and
your short legs will be very tired, so you will have to go into the sand
hollow between the rocks and take a good long sleep. The next day you
can set out for the camp, which you will reach by sundown. If you are
thirsty to-morrow you can milk the camels, you know, if you come across
any, and put the blame all upon me. When, you get in you must bid
Mohammed adieu for me. Tell him that if he wants to see me again he
must come to Sweirah—that if he had taken me there himself he should
have had a large ransom in powder, cloth, and guns; but that he would n't
believe my word, and I must now look out for myself. Give my love to
our mistresses, and if Fatimah inquires after me, tell her that I shall
always think of her as one of the most ugly, loathsome animals that
Allah ever suffered to creep about upon the face of the globe. Tell her that
if I do go to hell, as she has so often predicted, it is some consolation to
know that she has got no soul and can't come there too. Good-by, Soonshoo: You must ply your legs, my little friend, or you wont get sight of
the rocks before dark. Good-by!"

I waved my hand to the stupefied Soonshoo, and then adjusting myself in the saddle, gave the word to my gallant heirie, who started off at
a pace that would have tasked a good trotter on a smooth road, to keep
way with, even for half an hour. On looking back, I could see the black,
standing, for some time, in the position that I left him in; but, at last,
apparently awaking to the reality of his situation, he turned, and with
desperate energy commenced running in the direction of the "mouth."
He soon tired of that gait, and the last that I could see of him he was
trudging along more slowly, most probably pondering the wonderful
story he had to tell of the son of Shetan, who had carried him off nearly
two days' journey into the desert, and had left him to find his way back
on foot.

Instead of continuing my course to the north, as soon as Soonshoo
was fairly out of sight I hauled my heirie's head around due east. My
object had been to impress the black, and through him, his masters, with

the idea that I had started for Sweirah or Mogadore, in the southern extremity of the kingdom of Morocco, and thus throw them off my track, should they, as they most probably would, undertake to follow me. Mohammed would readily credit the idea; in fact, had I been going that route, it would have been impossible, by any doublings or maskings, to make him believe that I had taken any other, and this was one reason why I had deemed it best to merely make a feint at Sweirah, but, in reality, to plunge into the midst of the Sahara. Besides this, there were insuperable objections to continuing my course towards Mogadore; it was in that direction that the owners of my camel resided; there was, also, much risk of falling in with some of my old friends belonging to the family of my first master, Hamet Askeiff; and there was the small chance of making my way alone, without suspicion, through the populous districts on the northern border. My true plan I concluded to be, to press on easterly until I reached some of the great caravan tracks, in the neighborhood of which I might find a residence, until an opportunity presented of joining a kaffila going north, and thus, as an obscure individual member of a great multitude, emerge from the desert at some point on the coast of Barbary, as Fez, Tunis, Tripoli, or, perhaps, Cairo. Such a course would be divested of all ground for suspicion, and would leave Mohammed and his friends completely at fault.

It was with an indescribable rush of feeling—a perfect whirlwind of emotion—that I wheeled my heirie short round, and shouted a few encouraging words to the willing beast. There was something in the idea of unrestrained freedom—something in the all-pervading sense of dependence upon naught save the blessing of God, and my own strength and courage, that overbore fear, doubt, hesitation, and suppressed all contemptible repinings and all the agitations, even of hope. There was no moving object in sight. Around lay the desert, and before me stretched its interminable wastes, where for hundreds of miles no green shrub grew, where the foot of no living thing, save that of the occasional wanderer, had ever printed its moving sands. I was alone, but I was free! Once I was alone upon the sea, but how different this solitude of the desert. There I was the slave of circumstances, here their equal; here was action, energy, volition. If conquered in a contest with fate, there was the pleasure of fighting, if not the joy of victory. One case required patience and fortitude, the other simply courage. Ah! how much more pleasant to attack and repel, than to await and endure.

The rapid motion of my heirie exhilarated me. To skim along on a dromedary, at a steady pace of ten miles an hour, produces a feeling as near to that of ubiquity as it is given to man to know. On horseback one may attain a greater speed, but it is for a short time, and there is the disagreeable sense of exhausted wind and tired muscles—a sympathetic feeling of the fallibility of horse-flesh. By steamer or rail-car one may travel much faster, but in straight lines, and on given courses. Stick to the track is the law of such motion, and a sense of confinement the result. But with the lithe frame and indefatigable sinews of a thorough-bred dromedary beneath you, and the broad desert around you, there is, besides the full joy of rapid motion, a deep sense of freedom in azimuth that is perfectly enchanting, and a most refreshing feeling of reliance upon the inexhaustible energies and unfailing wind of the animal you bestride. You need not trouble yourself about your beast. Be assured that he can stand it as long as his rider. Be assured that he will almost jolt the heart out of you, make your chylopoietic viscera "*chassez* and cross over," and semi-luxate every bone in your body, before he will give out. "I 'm a man," gasconades a Bedouin. "I can back a heiric at full speed for a week!" There is meaning in the boast. "It takes a man," thought I, as I tightened my sash, pulled a piece of haick around my face to keep off the sand wind, and took a steady strain upon the halter that served to support my heiric's outstretched neck and head—"It takes a man, and there is deep pleasure in feeling equal to the demand."

For three hours we kept under way, until just at nightfall we arrived at a small hollow—where grew a few bushes—the extreme outposts of the oasis. Here I decided to stop for the night, and allow my heiric an opportunity of nibbling a few mouthfuls, the last that he would most probably get for many days.

THE first glimmerings of morning twilight found me mounted, and at least an hour's distance from my resting-place in the sand hollow, where I had halted my dromedary the night before. The short-lived crepusculum was soon succeeded by the full light of the sun, who rose from his bed of sand with a remarkably lurid and bloated countenance, that seemed to indicate any thing rather than a pleasant night's repose. Instead of looking like a bridegroom, fresh from his chamber, he had much more the appearance of an old debauchee, who had been keeping late hours and bad company.

As he rose the wind rose: the sharp, fine grains of sand flew with such force as to make the skin tingle severely where they impinged, but it was some comfort to reflect that the wind would have the effect of obliterating our track. As we were travelling directly against it, some part of its force was due to the velocity with which we moved. More than once we were compelled to abate our speed, and even to stop and turn our backs to it, until the whirling gust had swept past.

As the day advanced, the fierce red sun shot down his burning rays, heating the naked plain and the dusty air almost to a furnace heat. In the intervals of the gusts the surface of the parched ground glimmered, and glowed through the refracting currents of the air, like objects seen through the waving vapor surrounding a hot stove-pipe, and suggested, more than once, the idea of the country schoolhouse in winter, the huge stove with its basin of water on top, its piles of green wood drying beneath it, and the shivering, red-cheeked, and red-nosed urchins arrayed in rows around it. But, as has been frequently observed, a man can't hold fire by thinking of the frosty Caucasus; so neither could my recollections of red noses and cold feet, or any of the "please-let-me-go-to-the-stove-and-warm-myself " associations of boyhood modify the oppressive influences of the sun, wind, and dust.

Something crackled beneath the feet of my dromedary ; it was the fleshless skeleton of a camel, half buried in the sand—some luckless wayfarer, who had, at last, succumbed to the depressing power of heat, thirst, and fatigue !

Towards night the wind ceased entirely, but, although a perfect calm prevailed, the atmosphere remained filled with particles of dust, which seemed to have been so finely comminuted as to have lost the property of weight. The atmosphere overhead had a peculiarly hazy and purplish appearance ; huge currents of slow-moving air crept like monstrous ghosts, with grotesque forms, and with mysterious movements, along the surface. The sun sank down, but long before he reached the horizon his fiery face was merged in the glowing wall, that, like a great rim of red-hot copper, bounded the vision on every side.

At dark we encamped on the open plain. I allowed myself not half a pint of milk and water, but I could not resist the temptation of washing the nostrils of my heiric, and squeezing a few drops of the precious fluid into his mouth. According to my reckoning we had made about ninety miles. It would not have been difficult, despite the wind, which is always a great drawback, to have made at least twenty-five miles more, but, after having obtained a good offing from the oasis, I had judged it best to husband the powers of my heiric, and, accordingly, had reduced his pace to one at which he would be the most likely to hold out the longest.

Early in the morning we were under way again. The weather was similar to that of the day before, with the exception that the wind did not blow quite so hard, and there were longer intervals of dead calm. The surface and soil were somewhat different, the sand hills were not so high, there was a greater proportion of pebbles and angular fragments of stone, and in some places a stratum of dark granite showed itself above ground, either running along in level plains, or shooting up in irregular and jagged pinnacles of from five to fifteen feet in height. At one spot these were so numerous and so uniform in size, as to put me in mind of a ploughed sandy clearing, with the dark stumps standing in it. Several fragments of skeletons were passed, and, moving rapidly among the rocks was an enormous serpent, full thirty feet in length. As I was wholly unarmed, prudence prevailed over curiosity, and the monster was allowed a wide berth, of which he gladly availed himself, to make his escape.

Encamped again at night on the open plain, having made about one hundred miles. The evening breeze came fitfully, and with a peculiar heaviness, that was attributable more to its electrical state than to any change in temperature. For several hours there was a succession of flashes of electricity, without thunder. Any one would have sworn that we were about to have a shower, but, before morning, all indications of it had disappeared.

The third day passed with no unusual occurrence. Nothing could be more disheartening than the baleful aspect of the sky, as the sun went down behind the sand-hills in the west. Words will not convey an idea of the scene, or of my sensations, or, at least, it would require too many of them to do so; and if, therefore, the reader has any curiosity upon the subject, the best way of gratifying it is to imagine himself on a sandy plain, and, for firmament, a huge red-hot potash kettle inverted over him. My poor dromedary seemed to feel the depressing influences of the weather. When we stopped, which we did after having achieved a distance of one hundred miles, he evinced a degree of restlessness and irritability, that alarmed me not a little for the state of his health.

According to the most accurate computation that the circumstances of the case would permit, we had travelled a distance of three hundred miles from the douah of Sidi Mohammed, and were now somewhere near the usual caravan route, from Timbuctoo to Taffalet, in Morocco; and within at least three days' journey, or sixty miles of the town of Toudeney, where is a great salt mine, and in the neighborhood of which are the wells of Teleg. To the south lay the town of El Arouan, five or six days' journey; to the east, about the same distance, the oasis of Mabewah, inhabited by the *Wolled slem er'rife;* to the northwest, I supposed, was El Kabla, the oasis of the *Wolled D'leime.* It will be seen that I had a pretty general idea of the geography of the desert, as understood by the Arabs; but, for more particular information respecting my position, and the exact bearing and distance of places, it would be necessary to seek information of some one better acquainted with the immediate localities. This I hoped soon to be able to do, as I was confident that there were human beings within at least fifty miles of me.

The morning of the fifth day dawned with a still more lurid and threatening aspect than had been worn by either of the preceding ones. Shortly after sunrise the wind increased in violence, lifting immense clouds of sand, and hurrying them with a gyratory motion across the plain. For some time we struggled on, but in a few hours the sun became hidden and the horizon completely shut out. The movements of

my beast plainly indicated his desire to stop, and as the only object of
moving now was the chance of falling in with travellers, I judged it best
to obey the dictates of his instinct. No hill, rock, or bush was there to
afford us a shelter, and as the wind momentarily increased in force, we
were compelled to crouch, as best we might, before it on the open plain.

Darker and darker grew the scene. Thicker and thicker came the
clouds of sand. Fiercer and fiercer howled the sweeping blast. A few
dim rays of yellowish light alone had power to penetrate the dense
masses of dust that enveloped us. My heirie buried his nose in
the sand, finding it easier to breathe beneath the surface than above it,
and wrapping my face in my haick, I followed his example. The oppression of the chest—the accumulation of sand in the lungs and air passages—the heat—the thirst—were terrible.

It required frequent exertion to keep from being buried alive. Every
little while a solid sand-hill would be hurled upon us to a depth of three
or four feet, when we would have to struggle up from it in utter darkness, and shaking it off, resume our prostrate position. I lay close by
the side of my heirie, with the halter in my hand. Upon rising and
giving his head a slight pull, he would surge forward and backward, and
heave himself up like a ship after having been boarded by a heavy sea,
and then immediately settle down again to his former place without
stirring from his tracks.

The feeble glimmerings of light died away, and it was night; but
there was no moderation in the force of the gale. The light returned,
and I concluded that it was again day; but fiercer flew the sands, and
louder howled the whistling blasts. I had tasted nothing now for nearly
twenty-four hours, not even a drop of water. With my eyes shut, I felt
for the skin, and untying its mouth took about half a pint. It was evident that the water was evaporating beneath the extreme aridity of the
air! "O Thou, who holdest the wind in the hollow of thy hand, save
me! save me!"

Notwithstanding the sip of water, which was all that I could allow
myself, the sensation of thirst grew in fierceness. Without the practice
and the training that I had had under the privations and sufferings of
the oasis, it would have been ungovernable. What reason, thought I,
to thank God for all things; even for the barbarities of Mohammed and
the hatred of his wives! Besides the sensation of thirst, there was the prostration of strength, the exhaustion and agony of obstructed respiration.
An occasional low moan from my companion added to my own sufferings
the awful apprehension of losing in him my only earthly dependence.

Night again came and passed, and no change in the force of the wind, although it had varied in direction, until about the middle of the forenoon, when suddenly it fell to a light breeze, and in a few minutes to a perfect calm. The reader may imagine my physical exhaustion, upon rising and looking around once more upon the open day. But after clearing out my air-passages, eyes, and ears, getting a good drink of milk and water, and inhaling a few mouthfuls of the comparatively clear air, my strength began to return. My friend and companion was also much weakened, but after performing the same kind offices for him that I had for myself, and giving him about a pint of water, he recovered rapidly, and in two or three hours was quite ready for a start.

At the north there was something that appeared like a range of small hills, and towards them I directed my course, but my heirie seemed to be of a different opinion, and resolutely persisted in turning his head to the southeast. Recollecting the wonderful stories told by the Arabs, of the camel's power of discovering water at a distance, I concluded that it would be best to let him have his own way. We moved off at a slow and steady pace for three hours, through an unvarying succession of sand-hills without seeing any thing to attract attention, except a few scattered twigs of thorns, which had been torn off by the wind. It was now about an hour to sunset, and, exhausted as I was, I felt it almost impossible to keep my seat any longer, so selecting a spot to stop, I halted my beast and dismounted. Imagine my consternation when while standing carelessly by his side, he suddenly jerked his halter from my hand and started off at a sharp trot. Away he went at the top of his speed, and away went, with a startling whir, the flock of hopes that, through all difficulties and dangers, had hitherto nestled around my heart. I pressed after him with desperate energy, when suddenly he disappeared entirely from sight. The view was quite uninterrupted clear to the horizon, and it was not easy to imagine what had become of him, until upon arriving upon the brink of a deep hollow of some thirty feet in depth, and about ten acres in area, I saw him slowly moving about with his head close to the ground. To descend the declivity and secure the fellow was the work of an instant. Having tied up his foreleg, I had leisure to look around while seating myself upon the ground to recover my breath, and was at once convinced that the hollow contained water, the scent of which had led my heirie into his alarming but lucky escapade. The formation of the ground favored the idea, and if any further proof were wanting, there were signs around of its having been, not long since, visited by camels.

Upon examination, it was not difficult to select from several indications, but principally from the dromedary's movements, a spot beneath a small ledge of rocks as the place where it was most likely that water would be found. The sun was still above the horizon, though, of course, his level beams could not reach the bottom of the pit. There was light enough, however, for the time, and by a little exertion perhaps something might be done before it was quite dark, so turning to with my wooden bowl for a shovel, I commenced throwing out the sand from beneath the ledge. At a depth of four or five feet a little moisture began to show itself, and upon penetrating a foot or two farther the water began to percolate slowly through the bottom and sides of the pit. Helping myself to a good draught, and my heirie to about a dozen bowlsful, merely to take off the edge of his appetite, I secured him so that he could not get into the well, and stretched myself upon the ground, when my eyes were almost instantaneously closed in a sound sleep.

In the morning, after making a thorough ablution of my person, and eating an unusual liberal breakfast of meal, dates, and sour milk, the important and laborious operation of watering my heirie commenced. As the water ran but slowly, and there was nothing but a small bowl in which to deliver it, it was quite late in the forenoon by the time we had made a finish. There were, however, no reasons for hurry. One day's rest, after a sand-storm, was little enough to recruit exhausted nature, and it was not until the next day that we got underweigh.

"And which way now, my friend?" said I, in accordance with the Arab's habit of continually talking or singing to his camel. "Which way now? Oh, thou bird! thou beauty! Choose for thyself. Oh, thou who drinketh the wind! who swalloweth the ground! who killeth with the blows of thy feet both time and space! choose for thyself, for if one course does not answer we will make another, returning in time upon our track to the cool well for a starting-point. The southeast? Well, away!—lu-lu! lu-lu—away!"

Three hours' travel, with a good look-out all around the horizon, and no sign of a human being! The reappearance, however, of the desert-thistle in patches was a cheering indication, especially to my companion, who eagerly browsed upon the tough leaves and thorny branches. Upon remounting him, after having allowed him two or three hours for his meal, we altered our course a little more to the east.

Shortly after, while winding along between the sand-hills, my attention was attracted to a dark and motionless object projecting from the side of one of the hills. Upon approaching, it proved to be a camel with a heavy pack upon its back, and on looking around, at some little dis-

A LOADED CAMEL BURIED IN THE SAND.

tance, there were indications of several more. The animal had been dead not more than two or three days, for there was hardly a sign of putrefaction, and the ravens had not yet had time to pay the body a visit. The conclusion was irresistible, that it was one of a caravan which had been overwhelmed by the recent sand-storm.

The load of the poor beast was composed of several bales, or packages, of a moderate size and light weight. Upon opening them, there appeared on one side a number of pieces of red and blue cloth; a package of Fez caps, and several fine closely-woven haicks, in the manufacture of which the Moroccans excel. On the other side were packages of coral, glass, and amber beads—the latter exceedingly valuable for rosaries,—a dozen or two of small mirrors, and a case of long Spanish sheath-knives. But by far the most interesting objects to me were several pairs of pistols, single- and double-barrelled; half a dozen canisters of best English powder, so highly valued by the Arabs for priming, and a mahogany case with the key attached to the lock. Let it be recollected that my chief trouble had been the want of arms, and the delight may be imagined with which, upon opening the case, my eyes fell upon a double-barrelled gun, of French manufacture. Had I needed any guaranty of the value of the article, after closely inspecting the elaborate and careful finish of all its parts, it was to be found in the name of "Le Page, Paris," engraved upon the locks. The gun was furnished with all its appurtenances, such as flints, flask, and bullet-moulds, and, in addition, a bag containing four or five pounds of leaden balls; an exceedingly lucky circumstance, as without it the gun would have been comparatively useless.

It was quite late before my examination of all the packages was finished, giving me good opportunity, during the night, of making my plans for a disposition of the treasure. In the morning, as soon as it was light enough, I commenced operations, by taking the gun from its case, putting its parts together, and laying it aside; the case was buried deep in the sand, so that no Arab, finding it, might suspect that it belonged to my gun, and that, consequently, I had examined the camel's pack, and had secreted any of its contents. I then selected a pair of English double-barrelled pistols, and a long sheath-knife, filled the powder-flask, and made up a pouch of bullets from the large bag; a few pieces of amber and coral, by way of ready money, completed my personal equipment. I had a strong disposition to rig myself out in an entire new suit, but prudence advised sticking to my old rags and tatters, for a while at least, or until it had been ascertained how much temptation to robbery and murder the virtue of my next friends could withstand.

The remaining powder and ball, with two pair of pistols, three knives, four haicks, sashes, and caps, half a dozen small mirrors, and all the coral, amber, and glass beads, were made up into a secure and compact package. The remainder of the goods I re-arranged as they were before, leaving them half buried in the sand, for the benefit of the next comer.

Securing my pistols, powder-flask, and coral upon my person, and fastening the package upon my heirie, I mounted, gun in hand, and set out. Fortune, as if determined to smile her sweetest, conducted me, a little farther on, to another member of the unfortunate kaffila, to whose saddle-bow was attached a large bag of dates. There was no use in stopping to examine the dead animal's load. My outfit was complete. I needed nothing else. I was richer than Crassus or Crœsus—I had enough. There were but three articles besides those with which I was supplied, for which I could have found use—a compass, pocket-sextant and a spyglass. As it was hardly probable that any one of these would be found in a camel's pack in the desert, I merely stopped to secure the dates, remounted, and went on, meditating, by the way, the truth of the old adage, " it is an ill wind that blows nobody any good," and deeply pondering the mysterious orderings of Providence, of which the misfortunes of the kaffila, and my consequent good luck, afforded such a striking example.

CHAPTER XXVI.

FTER a hard ride of several hours we emerged from the sand-hills, and arrived at the borders of an extensive plain that was covered with pebbles and flints of a large size, and which was traversed by a serrated chain of gentle elevations. Arrived at a suitable spot, a slight depression of the ground, screened from observation at a distance, I dismounted, and using the wooden bowl, scooped out a hole in the ground large enough to contain the package of articles selected from the dead camel's pack. My object in doing this was to secure my treasure from the cupidity of the people I was approaching. I had fears that even my heirie and gun would prove a strong temptation to a violation of the laws of hospitality. Having deposited, therefore, the package, and with it the bag of dates, the ground was filled in, the pebbles spread over it, and a careful note made, in my mind, of the appearance of the spot and its bearing from the hills.

Upon remounting my heirie and issuing from the hollow, I was not a little startled at the apparition of two moving figures at a very little distance. It took a second look to convince me that they were ostriches, and not men. As soon as they caught sight of me they took to their heels, and by their watchfulness and timidity, afforded a still further proof that the neighboring country was inhabited.

The rough, pebbly plain extended, on the side that we were approaching, quite up to the foot of the hills. Reaching these I dismounted, and ascended their acclivities on foot, for a *reconnoissance* of the country beyond. Upon gaining the summit, one of the most charming views in the world burst upon my sight. Lying under the lee of the hills, and protected by them from the blasting southeast sand-winds, there stretched a magnificent expanse of gently undulating stony surface, more than half of which was covered with a pleasing variety of thorns and brambles.

Where the bushes could not grow, the naked granite rocks, or perchance a patch of dark sand, served to relieve what would otherwise have been a monotony of beauty. A few scraggy acacias, with two or three stunted date palms, materially added to the picturesqueness of the view. Several camels and a flock of goats were scattered over the plain. I stood entranced, so much so that it was some time before I observed at my feet a douah of a dozen tents. Apparently none of its inhabitants had yet got sight of me.

Hastening at once to my heirie, and mounting him, we took our course through a hollow between the hills, and debouched on the other side, in full view of the douah. According to the etiquette in such cases, I moved up to within thirty or forty rods of the tents, and then dismounting, stood motionless until it pleased the sheikh of the douah to take some notice of my presence. I had not long to wait. In a few moments a white-bearded old fellow, in a greasy haick, stepped forth from one of the tents, and came towards me. When within half a dozen yards, he stopped, and after a moment's scrutiny saluted me with *Salam Ailekom!*"

"*Ailekom Essalam,*" I replied.

"Is it peace?" he demanded.

"It is peace," I replied.

Upon this we advanced towards each other, touched our hands together, and then applied them to our lips. This was repeated half a dozen times, each time both of us making an effort to kiss the other's hand, which was modestly withdrawn, as if the honor was considered too great to receive. The courteous contest would have lasted a long time, had I not at last cut it short by grasping a portion of his dirty haick, and applying it to my lips. All this time there was a rapid interchange of complimentary questions.

"Are you well? how are your friends? How are all the people of the west? How is our Lord Muley Abderrhaman?" The last question is a compliment that an Arab of the western part of the desert seldom fails to pay to the emperor of Morocco. A compliment which he can well afford to pay, inasmuch as he never pays any thing else.

Our greetings over, Sheikh Ali ben Hammadow conducted me to the douah, where I was introduced to his sons, and half a dozen other men, by the name of Ishmael El Drebbah, or Ishmael the marksman. My story was soon told. I represented that I belonged to the *Beni Zebis*, a tribe of *Mongearts*, in the neighborhood of Cape Bojador, and that I was almost the only one living of my immediate family, which had been nearly extirpated in a death feud with a family of the *Beni Zosh*. That recently I had taken signal vengeance for the death of my relatives, by murdering my chief enemy, with two of his wives and three of his children, besides killing several camels and maiming a slave belonging to his brother, and firing several stacks of barley the property of his cousin; and that to avoid the fury of his friends, I had taken my heirie and fled.

Sheikh Ali complimented me upon the virtuous resolution and courage thus displayed, and invited me, with many protestations of undying friendship, to make his tent my home. He informed me that the country was called the Waddy Messir, and that it contained numerous douahs, inhabited by the members of his tribe—the *Beni Hareb*. I also gathered from the

" *Salam Ailekom !*"

conversation of those around, that my entertainer was both a *sharife* and a *hadji*—that is, one claiming descent from the Prophet, and one who had made the pilgrimage to Mecca. Upon the whole, I rather liked his appearance, but there was something exceedingly repulsive and sinister in the manners and appearance of his sons and other relations.

At night Ali's wives presented us with a large dish of cooscoosoo. With a " *Bishmallah crrachman crrachman !* "—In the name of God, all powerful and merciful!—I thrust in my hand and made a hearty meal. " *Elhamed lilah !* "—God be praised !—I exclaimed, finishing, and throwing myself upon the ground just within the edge of the tent, but in such a situation that I could command a good view outside. In a few minutes my eyes closed in a pretended sleep. A number of suspicious circumstances, which it is needless to particularize, now occurred to convince me that some of the Arabs, with Hassan, the Sheikh's oldest son, at their head, were plotting mischief. Until late at night, my weary and anxious watch was kept up; at last all was still, and slumber was about settling, with its heavy weight, upon my eyelids, when my attention was aroused by a slight rustling movement close to the edge of the curtain dividing the tent. It was so dark that the bodies of Ali and several of his sons, who were stretched in the same apartment, could not be distinguished; but my ears were so close to the curtain that it was easy to perceive that it had been raised, and that somebody was creeping from beneath. Cautiously, and without the least noise, my knife was drawn from its sheath, and held in my right hand, while my left was outstretched upon the ground towards the raised curtain. Slowly the moving body drew itself towards me, stopping often; and although the distance from the curtain to me was not more than three or four feet, taking at least twenty minutes to creep it. Imagine my anxiety and suspense. At last a hand was laid upon my arm, and passing downwards, my hand was gently pressed by a set of small fat fingers, that, it was plain enough, belonged to no man, and which, upon second thought were clearly referable to no woman about the encampment, except to Ali's youngest wife. A prompt attack! thought I, recollecting several amiable glances which the young Arab beauty had bestowed upon me. But I was doing the benevolent Mrs. Ali, in my thought, a great injustice.

A gentle pressure of my hand, as if to see whether I were awake, was returned on my part, and was followed by a low "Hish!" and my visitor reached forward, so as to bring her mouth close to my ear.

"Listen," she said, "but don't speak. You are in great danger. Hassan and his brothers have resolved to murder you. There are but two ways in which you can escape; take your choice. You must give your heirie to Ali, and your gun to Hassan, and all will be well. If you wont, you must stay by the tent until I get a chance to drive your dromedary up into the gorge of the hills, and when I give you the signal, you must wander towards him, and without losing an instant, mount and be off. Hish! Don't speak."

Forbidden to speak, it was yet necessary to make my visitor some acknowledgment of her kindness. Her lips were in tempting proximity—I recollected that they were smooth and pouting, and enclosed a row of pearly teeth—so turning my head, I brought my own lips smartly in contact with them. A stinging slap in the face, and then a sound like a suppressed laugh, and a parting squeeze of the hand, showed that Mrs Ali, while she could resent any thing of impertinence in the kiss, was not wholly insensible to its propriety as a token of gratitude, and an expression of my perfect comprehension of her plans. In the morning it was pleasant to find, from her good-natured smile, that the rather ill-timed compliment, upon the whole, had not been taken amiss.

The loud voice of old Ali, in the muezzin's usual form of invocation, resounded through the douah, calling the faithful to morning prayer. After which I arose, stepped forward in front of the tent, and speaking to Ali in a loud tone, invited him and all within hearing to listen to me. I then commenced—addressing my discourse chiefly to Ali. I observed that "hospitality to the stranger was the great virtue of the Arab character; that it was enjoined by the Koran, and universally practised and esteemed, except by unbelievers and idolaters. That the life and property of one to whom we were offering the rights of hospitality were, and ought to be, held sacred."

To this proposition Sheikh Ali audibly assented, while Hassan and his companions looked on, with increasing marks of surprise.

" Now you must know that here, in your family, there has been formed a determination to violate my rights, and to disgrace the character of the true believer. You need not ask me how I know it, I am a learned man, a doctor—a *Tibeb—El Hackem.* I know the secrets of the earth and the air, and should I not know such a thing as this? I do not accuse you, but I ask you how will Allah look upon the man who violates his law by the murder of a guest?"

" It shall not be," said the old man, jumping to his feet, and striking his staff violently on the ground. " It shall not be. Am I not master here? I say it shall not be."

" I know it," I replied. " It shall not be ; I have not spoken of it so much for my sake as for yours. I need not explain how the plot must have failed, but I will show you how Allah was prepared to punish the crime, had it been consummated. Listen to me, and mark how wonderful are the ways of God, and what risks we run when we deviate in the slightest degree from the plain track of the law! Your best heirie is lame—I can cure him. If I had been murdered last night, you would never have ridden him again. Your brother is sick—I am *Tibeb*—with the blessing of Allah I can cure him—without my skill he will soon die But listen still further! Listen, and open your eyes with wonder at your stupidity and God's goodness. My gun and camel, and this old haick, are all the property that could be got by taking my life, while with me would have

perished the knowledge of the spot in the desert where lie, overwhelmed
with the sands, the richly laden camels of a kaffila from Teffilet. You
would have robbed a poor man, and at the same time have destroyed the
only guide to wealth that will make your family the richest in the desert."

This announcement caused an immense sensation. The Arabs jumped
to their feet, and crowded around me, each one protesting that I was the
best fellow in the world—that I was their friend and guest, and that they
never had an idea of harming a hair of my head. Old Ali embraced me
several times, and even the truculent lout, Hassan, had the impudence to
offer me his hand, and to swear by every hair in the tail of Mohammed's
camel that my life, in his eyes, was more sacred than his own! It was
not my policy to push matters too far, so I accepted Hassan's apologies
and protestations, with an intimation of the possibility of having mistaken
his intentions; but to all questions as to the locality of the buried caravan,
I refused to reply until all was ready for a start, when I would show them
the way. The whole ordering of the business I at once took upon myself,
with the purpose of establishing, as far as possible, habits of command
and obedience, which might be available at some future time. A strong
power is frequently built up on a series of small and opportune demands
and submissions. The first links are so silently and smoothly forged as
to excite no observation, until at last compliance becomes a stringent
custom, and exaction, oppression, and tyranny, a right.

At night, the camels having been watered, and everything prepared, we
set out—crossing through the hills, and striking out into the flinty plain
on the other side. Our party consisted of twenty men, and ten or twelve
camels. Ali, Hassan, and myself were mounted upon horses. They
were truly gallant animals—not to the eye, for they were nothing but
animated skeletons,—but their speed and bottom were wonderful, and
they were even able to go two or three days without drink. Hadji Ali
loudly vaunted their qualities, assuring me that they were of the pure
blood of the *Frafiye*—the best family of the *Koheije* in Yeman, —and that
he could produce their pedigree for more than two thousand years. " But
know, O my worthy friend Ishmael, that dear to me as is the animal you
bestride, if thy report of the kaffila prove true, he is yours. I will pluck
him from my eyes, I will tear him from my heart. Thou shalt have *Ayoud.*"

CHAPTER XXVII.

 NEED not dwell upon our expedition. Suffice it to say that it was quite successful. We found the camels as I had left them, and, upon a close search of the country, discovered half a dozen more, with their valuable loads, and in several instances the remains of their unfortunate masters. After an absence of twenty days, we returned to Waddi Messer, bearing with us an amount of wealth that more than realized the expectations my report had excited.

Shortly after this, the water of the wells beginning to fail, it was resolved to break up the douah, and remove to the well of Boulag, about forty miles to the northwest, and not far from Toudena, to which town the Arabs proposed to carry their goods for sale, to the salt traders going south. With wonderful despatch the tents were struck, and, with the household utensils, packed upon the camels. The goats were collected and driven ahead, preceded by Ali and myself on horses. A long train of camels, some of them piled up with women and children, followed the goats, and a party of five or six horsemen brought up the rear. We encountered several douahs, by whose inhabitants we were politely greeted, and, in several instances, hospitably entertained. On the third night we fell in with a family, *en route*, like ourselves. We encamped together, and having purchased two kids and a sack of rice, I issued a general invitation to a feast. My wishes were admirably seconded in the department of the *cuisine*, by young Mrs. Ali, and in two or three hours after sunset, the senses of my dark, dirty, and hungry guests were delighted with several dishes of smoking pilaw. "*Bishmalla!*" I exclaimed, "in the name of God, fall to," and upon the word, at least forty hands were plunged simultaneously into the smoking messes. An exhibition of manual and mandible dexterity followed, which lasted about fifteen minutes, when repeated exclamations of "Thank God!" and "Glory to his Prophet!" indicated that there were limits to the capacity of even an Arab's stomach. Generally, the Bedouin is extremely abstemious; but occasionally, and especially when he can gratify his appetite at another man's expense, he will demonstrate the possession of a talent for *gourmandize* that would comport with the umbilical expansion of a Samoied or an Esquimaux, but which one would hardly expect to find within that spare and attenuated frame, in which it lies, most of the time, in abeyance.

After supper pipes were produced and passed around, and the conversation became general and animated. The subject of horses and camels was discussed—the state of the markets at Sweirah and Timbuctoo was introduced, with the rate of a camel's freight across the desert, and the prices paid for protection through the different tribes. Several stories of family feuds, and among them the one that I had invented, were told. These were received with applause in proportion to the atrociousness of the revenge. It being a subject of regret that there was no professed story-teller present, I volunteered to give them the story of Aladdin and his lamp. My offer was received with a round of compliments, which, upon the conclusion of the story, were renewed. "*Bishmalla!* what a man he is! what generosity—what courage—what wit! He feasts our bodies and souls. He tickles our hearts as well as our stomachs. His story is fit sauce to his feast, and his feast was worthy of a king."

It was five or six days before we reached the well of Boulag, which we found already surrounded by several families, but there was water enough for all, and our tents were erected without any objections from the first comers, who were all either relations or friends. We were now a large and formidable party, consisting of at least two hundred men, and numbering a hundred horses, full five hundred camels, and a goodly number of goats. The women and children were in fair proportion. For the latter there was a regular school, where they were taught to read the Koran. The plan of instruction consisted in practising, simultaneously, in their loudest voices, a portion of the sacred book, written on a board. It was not a little amusing to see fifty or sixty boys squatted upon the ground, each one with his board, and all of them violently working their bodies backwards and forwards, as if upon the industrious flexure of their vertebral articulations depended the proper articulation of their words.

I was not a little surprised to see so many artisans in full employment. A number of weavers were daily engaged in turning into cloth the yarn of camels' and goats' hair spun by the women. Saddle- and bridle-makers were busy with harness for horses and camels. Blacksmiths had enough to do in furnishing bits and shoes. They were exceedingly skilful: with a small charcoal fire, and a bellows made of a couple of bladders, they contrived to do very difficult work, with neatness and despatch. There were even jewellers, who exhibited no small degree of taste and dexterity in the manufacture of gold and silver rings, ornaments for the hair, and studs for headstalls and reins.

It soon became known that I was a Tibeb, and the fame of the cure effected in the case of Hadji Ali's brother, brought me repeated applications for medical advice. As the cases where my medical skill was invoked were mostly either imaginary or such as required time, the expectant plan, luckily, inasmuch as there were few or no medicines to be had, was the true plan; but instead of the bread pills of the allopath, or, what is the same thing, the infinitesimal doses of the homœopath, my usual prescription was a written charm. It was wonderful, the success that attended my practice. Pity it is that I have not preserved a record of my cures, and that I am unable now to present a detailed statement of all the pathognomonic signs, and therapeutic indications that were met and fulfilled by this one infallible specific. Science suffers—and, still more, bequacked Christendom suffers—for then had the medical quidnuncs revelled in a new system of practice with a hard name, and the credulous public had tickled itself for a time, at least, with the beauties of *epardo-pathy*. A course of Koran would have become, perhaps, in time, the fashionable alternative, and the writings of the Arabian prophet, turned to their true account --that of an universal panacea,—have been swallowed throughout Christian lands without stirring the bile of a sound orthodox faith.

But it was as a *raconteur*, rather than as a physician, that my reputation attained its widest range. Fortunately, the Arabian Nights was a book that had been a favorite, and my memory was charged with the whole stock in trade of the beautiful Scheherazade. Every evening, when in camp, it was the custom to assemble in the centre of the douah, and there, squatted in a circle upon the ground, listen to the song or story, which, however often repeated, seemed never to tire. My stories were received with particular favor, for the reason that, in addition to all the fanciful embellishments of the Eastern authors, I did not hesitate to add a few grotesque inventions and ridiculous exaggerations of my own. The fame of our entertainments soon spread, and attracted visitors from the other douahs; so that, not unfrequently, there was an audience of two or three hundred. Among these were always three or four good singers, with a stock of songs that seemed perfectly inexhaustible. The singer generally accompanied himself upon a rude guitar, or a tambourine, and frequently several instruments would join in the chorus. The airs were, most of them, exceedingly monotonous, and the words and sentiments had hardly more variety. Nine tenths of all the songs were on the subject of love, in which were invariably introduced the horse, the heirie, or some allusion to the happy lot of the Bedouin. A few were exclusively patriotic, and devoted to celebrating the pleasures and comfort of the desert, and the courage and independence of its inhabitants. Of these latter, the following may serve as a fair specimen : —

THE SONG OF THE BEDOUIN.

Like a star peering out through the folds of thick night,
    An oasis gleams 'mid Sahara's drear wilds,
Dispersing the gloom with its emerald light,
    And cheering the waste with its soft sunny smiles.
Here the tent often folded, now firmly pitched stands,
    With the voices of childhood the green Waddy rings ;
The pure water bubbles from 'neath the fierce sands,
    And, loudly exulting, the wild Arab sings :

" What reck I of all the dull pleasures of town ;
    Of life's feeble joys, crushed and cramped within walls ;
Of the Mufti's weak laws, or the Kadi's stern frown ;
    The bazaars, and the baths, or the base traders' stalls !
No, alone in the desert, so boundless and wild,
    The pleasures of freedom the bold Bedouin finds,
Fierce pleasures, and meet for Sahara's own child,
    Who roams o'er her sands as uncurbed as the winds.

" My camels are strong, and my heiries are fleet ;
    Ever saddled and ready my ' wind-drinker ' stands ;
I call him—he comes, and I vault to the seat,
    Now away, and away o'er the fierce burning sands !
With what thrilling delight do my quick pulses beat,
    As like to some wild flying demon in wrath,
My gallant steed swallows the ground with his feet,
    And swift as a bird, through the air cleaves his path !

" Ha ! a dark moving object far distant I see ;
    Along the horizon it rushes with speed :
Come, come, my brave courser, my trust is in thee—
    That ostrich shall honor thy blood and thy breed.
We near him ! We near him ! Ah, laggard, 't is vain
    That with rapid feet casting the dusty clouds back,
In circles wide wheeling, thou scourest the plain,
    For Ayoud, untiring, is close on thy track !

" We near him ! We near him '—in vain all his speed,
    In vain all his strength, all his wiles, all his art :

STORY-TELLING.

One more spring ! one more stride ! and the slender jereed
  Is brandished aloft, and flies straight to his heart.
Stately bird of the desert, thy plumage so bright,
  So soft, and so graceful, and light as the air,
The markets of Sweirah shall fill with delight,
  And in far Kaffir lands wreathe the brows of the fair.

" Why trembles my courser ? Why snuffs he the air ?
  Why pales the bright sun in the brightness of noon ?
'T is the breath of Azrael—prepare, oh ! prepare,
  For the poisonous blast of the purple simoon !
Down, down in the dust, and hold tightly the breath,
  Till the dark desert demon has fiercely swept past—
He has gone—he has gone—the dread angel of death
  Has flown on the wings of the hot scorching blast !

" To horse ! now, to horse ! Mount, mount, every man !
  Send the word through the tribes with the speed of the light,
The merchants of Houssa, Tombûte, and Soudan,
  With their rich laden camels are heaving in sight.
Behind the dark sand-hills we quietly sit ;
  Hush ! hush !—not a whisper.—Now, now we 're away !
With the blood on our rowels, and foam on the bit,
  With a rush like the Siroc we dash on our prey.

" At the gleam of our spear-points the battle is won ;
  The brave who resist are borne earthward and slain ;
The cowards are scattered like mists by the sun,
  And their bales of rich merchandise cumber the plain.
There are cottons of Nyffe, and cloths of Bornou,
  The jelib, the haick, the bornouse, and kaftán,
Rings, anklets, and bracelets from famed Sackatoo,
  And jewels, and ingots from golden Soudan.

" Now, glory to Allah ! who sends us the prize ;
  To Allah, unstinting, who loads us with spoil ;
Unto Him, who each want of His children supplies,
  And rewards thus so freely their faith and their toil,
And to Him, who is seated at Allah's right hand,
  To God's holy Prophet let all glory be :
And glory, O glory, thou dear desert land !
  For thy joys, though they 're few, are the joys of the free."

My skill as a marksman contributed not a little to the consideration
and influence that I was acquiring ; with this disadvantage, however, that
it excited more jealousy and envy than my other accomplishments, and
gave me two or three strong personal enemies. Among these, the principal one was the truculent Hassan, son of Ali.

A source of considerable anxiety was the constant apprehension of the appearance among us of some one of the family of my old masters, by whom my person might be recognized as that of the fugitive slave. The dread of such a misadventure compelled me to the precaution of scrutinizing any new-comers before showing myself, while it very much interfered with the pleasures and comforts of my situation, and very much strengthened my determination to avail myself of the first opportunity of returning to civilized life. Sometimes, however, I had a mind to set out for the south and visit the negro countries, and even attempt penetrating the Djebel Kumri—the Arabic name for the Mountains of the Moon—and seeking, among the transmontane table-lands of that mysterious chain, the native land of Kaloolah. On the one side, there was the strong desire to revisit old friends and old haunts; an intense curiosity as to what had taken place during my absence; a wish to relieve the anxiety that I knew must be felt respecting me; and a disposition to relate to sympathizing ears the curious adventures that I had encountered: on the other hand, was the unquenched thirst for adventure; the glittering allurements of a *terra incognita;* the ambition of being the means of solving some of the great geographical problems which had for so long a time excited the interest of the scientific world; and, more than all, the hope of again seeing Kaloolah, whose image neither shipwreck, nor slavery, nor the fierce storms, nor the wild freedom and excitement of the desert had banished from my mind. · It was thus, halting between two opinions, that I remained three or four months at the well of Boulag, little dreaming that circumstances were maturing that would turn the scale in favor of the south, and leave country, home, and kindred dangling in the distant perspective.

CHAPTER XXVIII.

NE day the news arrived in camp that a caravan from Tim-
buctoo was attempting the direct northern route, without
having made the usual terms with the leading men of our
tribe. As this was the caravan that I had been so anxiously
expecting, it was not a little disappointment to learn that owing to the
foolhardiness of its conductors, who believed that the oasis of the Messer
had been deserted for the valleys of Hareb and the plains of Tuat, the
expedition would certainly fail; and that, instead of having an opportunity of joining the kaffila, I should probably see it attacked and
plundered—a catastrophe that might have been easily prevented by the
payment of the usual tolls to the wild masters of the country through
which it had to pass.

"To horse! to horse!" was the word that passed from one extremity
of the oasis to the other with the rapidity of the wind. Each green
waddy, from a distance around of a hundred miles, poured forth its
horsemen; all rushing, with the instinctive eagerness of the Ishmaelite,
at the first intimation of spoil. The rendezvous was appointed at Boulag,
and when all were collected we numbered over four hundred mounted
men, the whole under the command of Sheikh Mahmoud Eben Doud
Skein, the acknowledged senior chief of the whole tribe.

The sheikh, a little withered fellow, was nearly ninety years of age,
but he sat his horse with the grace and vigor of early manhood, and
evinced an uncommon degree of vivacity and energy in all his movements.
The first day of his arrival he dashed into the encampment, with a few
followers, at full speed; checked his horse instantaneously, bringing his
haunches almost to the ground, and then forcing him to perform a number of lofty croupades, marked upon his sides with the points of the
heavy iron spur the initial letters of the Mohammedan confession of faith.

Jumping from his horse, the old fellow seated himself upon the ground, and quietly enjoyed the expressions of admiration which his performance called forth. His orders were given with promptness and precision. Scouts were despatched to watch the movements of the kaffila; which was struggling along at the slow pace of the loaded camel; and, in the meantime, arrangements were made to meet our prey at the well of the *Waddy el bahr nile*, or the valley of the dry river, which was about three days' journey to the southwest.

Besides Mahmoud, there were several other sheikhs of nearly equal authority; the most active of whom was Kaid Hassen iben Salech el Achmer, Sidi Achmed iben Ali el Hammr el Schare, and Hammed iben Omar el Busroche. The last was particularly celebrated in the *Lab el Barode*, a game of which the Arabs are extravagantly fond. It consists in several horsemen placing themselves in a line abreast, and dashing forward for a few rods, all the while twirling their muskets in the air, and sometimes throwing them up and catching them with great dexterity, At the end of the course the horses are instantaneously checked, the muskets brought down and fired over the head of the crouching steed, the animal recovered with a single demi-volte, wheeled and walked slowly back to the starting-point.

At length all our preparations having been completed, and having obtained accurate information of the movements of the kaffila, we set out, and in three days, without any adventure of interest, reached the banks of the rocky ravine, where we proposed to conceal ourselves. Next day we remained quietly crouching among the sand-hills, bordering a flinty plain of several miles in extent—the hot sun beating down upon our unsheltered heads, and occasional eddies of impalpable dust making respiration, which, in a pure air, is decidedly the most pleasing function of the body, a positive misery. A few dates, equally shared between man and steed, and a single sip of water, afforded the only refreshment that my hardened and abstemious companions required. For myself, anxiety for the doomed caravan wholly occupied my mind, but none of the numerous plans that occurred to me seemed to promise any hope of averting its fate. It had advanced so far that even a knowledge of its danger would come too late—too late to escape, but, perhaps, not too late to effect a compromise, and prevent an attack.

Seeing no other plan, I had almost made up my mind to jump upon Ayoud, and dash out at any and all risks, when messengers arrived with information that at once excited a commotion in our ranks. Orders were passed to mount, and taking up our line of march in an oblique direction towards the level plain we had crossed the day before, we slowly and cautiously wound among the low sand-drifts. The greatest care was taken to conceal our movements, not a man was allowed to ascend the rifts, which compelled us to make large detours to get round them, and in several places orders were passed for the men to dismount and lead their horses, until a higher cover had been attained.

The sun was about three hours high when we reached a position just at the edge of the plain, and where we were protected from view by a long rift of sand and a few irregular rocky eminences. By stretching our necks a little, we had a good view of the plain, quite to the distant horizon. All eyes were at once directed to the left, where, emerging from the sand-hills, were to be seen numerous groups of men and camels. No order appeared to be preserved in their line of march, the different parties straggling over a space of a quarter of a mile in width and nearly two miles in length, with wide intervals between the groups. One after another, the heavily laden " ships of the desert " worked their way out from among the sand-hills on to the plains, until at last there appeared an almost interminable array of full fifteen hundred camels, accompanied by five hundred men and numerous slaves. Slowly the straggling trains toiled on towards us, in a course that would bring them past our cover at the distance of less than a quarter of a mile. Already the guides and foremost groups had passed by, and, from their motions, were evidently about to halt for the night, while from the advancing parties could be heard the monotonous chant with which the Arab encourages the footsteps of his weary beast. At this moment the signal was given, and in a solid mass we rushed upon the plain, deploying at full speed, as soon as we had cleared the sand-hills, into a long line, two deep. This manœuvre was executed with unexpected precision.

About fifty of our men were armed with guns, and these occupied the front rank ; the remainder were armed with spears, which, with wild shouts, were twirled high in the air above their heads. " *Allah Ackbah ! Allah Ackbah ! Allah illah Allah ! Rasoul Mohammed Allah !* " was loudly shouted along the ranks, mingled with the strongly aspirated and encouraging " *Hah-hah ! Hah-hah !* " of the Arabic horseman to his steed. It was easy to perceive, however, that, amid all the bustle and excitement, there was an intentional illustration of the adage, " the more haste the less speed," and that, notwithstanding our yelling and spurring, we were far from charging at our fastest pace. Our horses were forced into lofty and violent action, while in reality they covered the ground slowly, and by this plan the panic was allowed time to spread, and afforded to many an opportunity of flying, who would otherwise have fought in sheer desperation.

The instant our first shout broke upon the stillness of the plain, the whole kaffila halted in consternation. Shouts of fear and rage answered our battle-cry, mingled with the loud yells and curses of the camel-drivers, and the shrieks of the women and children, who formed part of the riches of the caravan. The few who were in the van goaded their weary beasts into a trot, and pressed onwards, regardless of those behind, while those in the rear collected their beasts and turned back among the sand hills, from which they had just emerged. Others, who were too far advanced to escape, deserted their property, and fled wildly on foot across the open country, while others stood their ground and made what preparations they could for resistance. These last, however, were few in number, and they had hardly time to uncover their long guns or to unsheath their scimitars before we were upon them.

Without combination or order, they could make but little resistance, and in a few minutes they were all overpowered, disarmed, and compelled to seat themselves upon the ground, while the victors proceeded to collect the spoil. The last rays of the short twilight of southern latitudes were now illuminating the scene, showing with wonderful distinctness the wild groups of horsemen, as they galloped about after the fugitive camels. In a few moments the glowing red was succeeded by the cold gray of night, and the Bedouins began to gather in with the animals they had captured, leaving fully one half of the scattered caravan to make its escape under the friendly cover of the darkness. It was arranged to bivouac upon the spot, and await the light of day for an examination of our plunder. The slaves, most of them women and children, were placed in the centre, around these the loaded camels were made to kneel, while outside, and surrounding all, the victors stretched themselves upon the ground, each one beside his steed, and with his arms by his side ready for use. A guard was stationed over the prisoners, and sentinels were posted far out on the plain as a precaution against attack, although there was but little danger to apprehend from the scattered and flying fugitives.

Gradually, one after the other, the chattering Bedouins had sunk back upon the ground, and wrapping their faces in the folds of their haicks, were resigning themselves to rest. The cries of the children and the moans of the women slowly subsided, when they found that their captors were not the desert demons with which their imaginations had been filled. A few low voices in conversation, in the liquid languages of the Soudan, rose and fell upon the gentle night wind, interrupted, perhaps, now and then, by the deep guttural exclamation of an Arab voice at a restive camel. One of these animals exhibited signs of restlessness, and, rising to his feet, evinced a disposition to press in upon the enclosed slaves. Leaving my horse at a little distance, securely picketed by a short cord and a strong wooden peg driven into the ground, I strode forward, and with some little difficulty reduced the animal to obedience; but, as he still evinced symptoms of disquiet, instead of returning to my steed I threw myself upon the ground at the side of the camel, and between him and a closely hooded figure that I supposed to be some female slave of a higher class than the other half-naked blacks.

The noises of the wild bivouac grew less and less; the night wind swept by with a more gentle sigh; the sky was cloudless, and the bright stars peered down like angels' eyes, with a peculiar earnestness and intentness, as if their wondering owners were trying to pry into the deep physical and still deeper moral mysteries of this strange world. "Look on! Look on!" I muttered, half-aloud, imagination lending plausibility, for the moment, to the forced conceit. "Look on, ye host of sparklers! your pure natures must ever find a puzzle in the changing and commingling threads of vice and virtue that make up the web of human life." I gazed upward, steadily, in a deep and absorbing revery, and as I gazed the stars seemed to grow brighter and larger, and to pour into my soul a flood of radiance that slowly etherialized each material portion of my frame. He who has ever drunk in the spiritualizing influences of nature in any of her highest moods, will understand the sensation with which I gazed, while almost a conviction sprang to my mind that some truth might yet be found lurking beneath the rubbish of rejected astrology. "Bright and beautiful beings!" I exclaimed, "it cannot be that all the beliefs respecting your aspects and influences, once so firmly and so generally held, were utterly vain and untrue. Say, were all the dreams and dogmas of astrology, from the first, the offspring of ignorance and chicane, or were they the relics of a higher astronomy that flourished ere the world grew old? Oh! if the science were true, and I were but master of its arcana, how would I question you! I would make you prophesy of the future, but not until you had satisfied me as to the present and the past. I would ask you of other scenes and fairer lands. I would ask you of friends— and above all, I would ask you of Kaloolah—sweet, gentle, artless Kaloolah!"

At this instant I heard my own name pronounced in a low, soft tone, but with perfect distinctness. "Jon'than Romer!" were the words that seemed to float upon the air directly above me. I could not but smile at the intensity of imaginings that could thus so impudently attempt an imposition upon my senses, but at the thought the words came again, and with a clearness of enunciation that made me start almost with alarm lest my senses themselves might be joining in the league against my reason. " I like to give fancy fair play," said I to myself, " but this is carrying the joke a little too far," and sitting up I gave myself a shake, as if to arouse the sleepy understanding to a proper watch and ward over the portals of the mind.

" Jon'than Romer! " said the voice, and this time in tones that could not be misunderstood for the delusions of fancy. " What mystery is this? " said I, starting and turning towards the figure that I had taken for a negro slave. " Can it be—Kaloolah? Did you call me? Kaloolah! " The reclining figure raised itself from the ground, and stretching forth both arms, whispered low, but distinctly, " It is I—Kaloolah. Oh! Jon'than! " Her further words were cut short by a choking inspiration, and she would have fallen, but I was at her side, and she buried her face in my bosom.

For some moments we sat without speaking ; indeed words would have been inaudible amid the deafening reverberations of our beating hearts.

I turned back the folds of her head-dress and exposed her face to the bright rays of Arcturus, who was peering down from the zenith. There could be no room for doubt. 'T was she! Kaloolah! I pressed her closely to my breast. For a moment she lay, unresisting, in my embrace, and then gently disengaging herself, she drew her hood over her face and sat erect. Still all was silence; how long it might have lasted I know not, had it not been broken by a sob, followed by the least faint tinkle of a silvery laugh. I caught her hand, and drew her again towards me. It was necessary to sit very close, and whisper low, to avoid attracting attention from the drowsy slaves, or the more distant but wakeful Bedouins.

" Tell me, Kaloolah, how is this? How do I find you here—in this wild spot, and in such a guise? "

" I come, as you see— a slave. Such have I been almost from the time we parted ; but you, Jon'than, how came you here? "

" Ah, mine is a long story ; tell me first how you came to recognize me, and to call my name? "

" The heart, the heart—Jon'than, has keen senses. I saw you as you stood over the wounded man, and turned aside the swords that were seeking his life. The idea that it was you was too improbable for belief, but the fancied resemblance made my heart give one bound, and then fall cold and dead as a stone. Again, when you came here to the

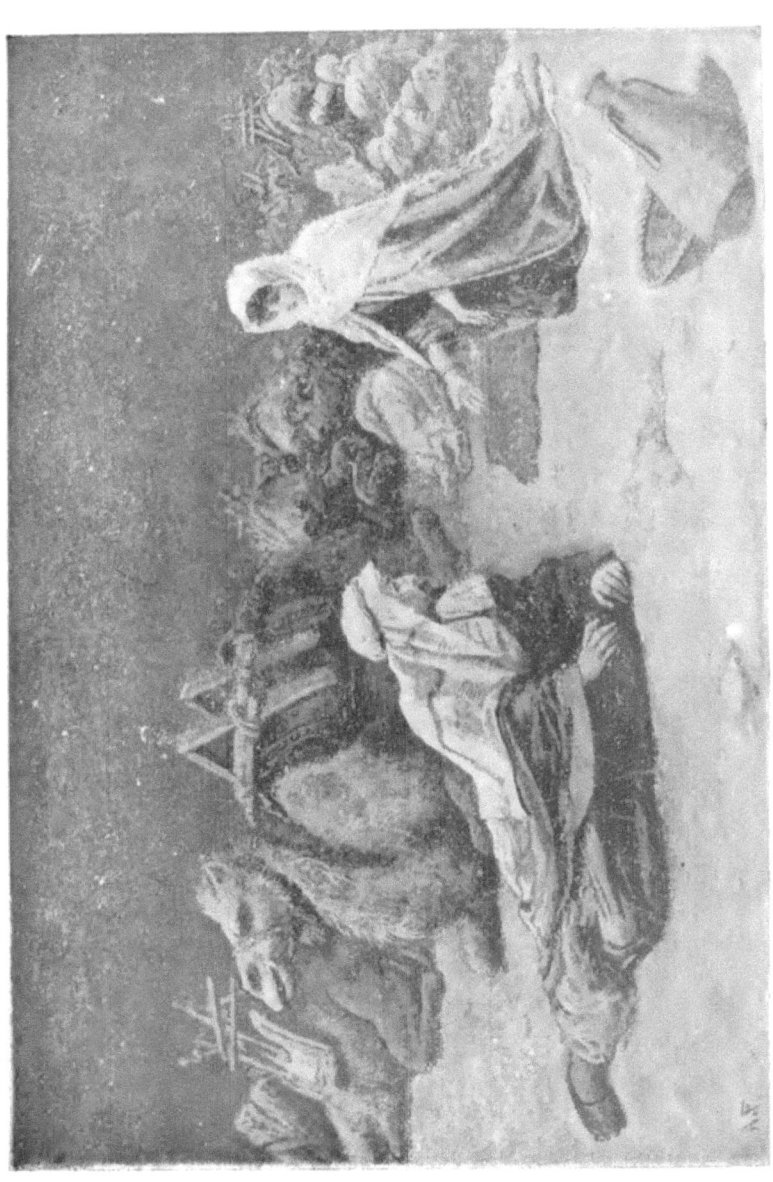

"... The reclining figure raised itself from the ground, and, stretching forth both arms, whispered low but distinctly: 'It is I! — Keturah. Oh! Jon'than'"

camel, that voice roused every thought of you, but I could not, for a
moment, really believe that it was you. After quieting the camel, you
threw yourself upon the ground, and at last I heard you muttering words
that sounded like English. How my heart struggled with its rushing
tide. I pronounced your name—an Arab would not have noticed the
sound—you started. I repeated your name; you answered me, you
called me Kaloolah. Ah, tell me, do I dream, or is it all true and real?
Tell me that you are Jon'than, that fancy does not deceive me."

In answer to my questions, Kaloolah now related her adventures after
leaving Sierra Leone. Her story was long and interesting, but for reasons, that perhaps the reader is fully prepared to appreciate, it must be
condensed into the fewest possible words.

Leaving Freetown, the Mandingo kaffila, with whom, it will be recollected, Kaloolah and Enphadde were to travel, made its way through the
country of the Timanees. Beyond this the road became exceedingly
rough and difficult, until they had reached Kissa, where the kaffila halted
for two or three weeks. Up to this time, Enphadde and his sister had
travelled without much molestation, except from the occasional insolent
curiosity of the fanatic Foulahs, who, however, when assured that the
white people were not Christians, allowed them to pass without detention. At Kissa, however, symptoms of difficulty began to show themselves. For some time they were closely confined, while councils were
held respecting them. The party of Mandingos, who had sworn to protect them, now deserted them, carrying off a large portion of their property, and leaving them to the tender mercies of the rapacious king and
nobles of Kissa. After much difficulty and trouble, Enphadde succeeded
at last in procuring permission to set out on his journey for Timé. Two
surly Foulah guides were obtained, by whom the travellers were conducted to a small village nearly four day's journey beyond Kissa. The
village was situated upon the banks of a pleasant stream, and consisted
of about thirty mud huts, affording accommodation to a pastoral and
inoffensive people. The appearance of the travellers excited no little
surprise, but they were received with kindness and hospitality. A hut
was assigned them on the banks of the river, and provisions supplied them
in abundance.

In the evening Enphadde was sent for, to visit the chief of the village.
During his absence, Kaloolah, allured by the beauty of the night and the
rippling of the water, stepped from the door of the hut to the edge of
the stream. For some minutes she stood gazing in a deep revery upon
the bosom of the star-lit water, when she was suddenly seized from

behind—a cotton *paigne* thrown over her head and twisted almost to suffocation. Her hands and feet were then tied together, when she was lifted up, carried a short distance down the stream, and deposited in a canoe. In a short time the canoe stopped, the muffler was taken from her face, her limbs freed, and with a rough grasp upon her shoulder, she was forced forward at a rapid pace through a tortuous and tangled forest-path. About midnight they arrived within sight of a fire, kindled at the base of an impending rock. Here they found a party of four females, recently captured, and in course of the night were joined by two more of the slave-hunting gang, who brought with them a boy of about five years of age.

Before daylight the whole party set out at a rapid pace in a direction nearly due north. For twenty days they continued their journey, barely stopping for sleep and meals, and carefully avoiding several villages, that Kaloolah could see in the distance on either hand. Several times they encountered bands of travellers and wild beasts, but met with no molestation from either. At last they reached a large and populous town, which proved to be an extensive slave-mart. Here the females were exposed for sale—the blacks readily finding purchasers; but the whiteness of Kaloolah's skin, and her slender figure, worn down by her long and fatiguing journey, were deemed objections, and it was some time before a purchaser could be found. At last, however, she was bought by a Madengo merchant, who was about to start with a number of slaves for the great city of Jennie, on the Niger.

In this large and flourishing city Kaloolah remained for about a year, as a slave in the house of Hamadow Kinka, a rich Foulah, a relative of King Sego Ahmadow, and a devout believer. Not content with performing the duties enjoined by the Koran, this pious Mussulman, in his reverence for the words of the sacred book, had bowed in humble submission to its less stringent suggestions. With him, permissions were recommendations, recommendations commands; and four wives in consequence rivalled each other in their attempts at his domestic felicity. To one of these ladies Kaloolah was particularly assigned, but the repugnance she evinced to the duties proposed to her soon reduced her from the light but disgusting offices of lady's maid, to the more fatiguing but dignified labor of the household drudge.

To assist at the toilet of civilized beauty; to adjust the graceful drapery; to tint, with the hues of health, the delicate cheek; or to braid the glossy ringlet; is an employment that, in numberless instances which might be mentioned, fairies, and queens, and illustrious ladies of all ranks have condescended to, without derogation to their dignity and grace ; but to perform the like offices for an Ethiopian belle—to rub in the rancid mutton-tallow and palm-oil, with which her whole person has to be anointed ; to drape her reeking form in dingy and unctuous finery ; or to wield the fan for hours over her heavy post-prandial slumbers ; all this is a very different matter. The truth of this observation will explain the feeling of pleasure with which I found that Kaloolah had chosen the hard lot of an out-door slave ; and excuse the particularity with which I take leave to state that her chief employment was to bring water in a calabash for

" Her chief employment was to bring water in a calabash."

domestic purposes from the river, and that she never assisted in anointing or abluting either of the obese beauties of Kaid Kinka's harem.

It happened that in her visits to the river, Kaloolah's appearance attracted the attention of an old Moor from Morocco, who had crossed the desert to Timbuctoo on a trading speculation, and thence had pushed on up the Niger to Jennie. He was now about to return, and after making some inquiries, proposed to Kinka to purchase her with the intention of taking her home with him, where her white skin would be no objection, and her peculiar beauty would be better appreciated. " Who knows," thought the old speculator, " but that she may find favor in the

eyes of Muly Abderrhaman himself, and if so she will prove one of the
best bargains that I have yet made."

In a few days after this change of masters Kaloolah and the Moor
embarked in one of the large boats employed upon the river for the
famed city of Timbuctoo. There were forty or fifty other slaves, with a
dozen or more negro and Moorish traders, besides a crew of fifteen or
twenty men, and a heavy cargo of rice, millet, butter, honey, onions, pis-
tachios, colat-nuts, preserved fruits, and manufactured stuffs.

Without incident, except the forcible exaction of tribute by a party
of Tuaries, the travellers reached, after a voyage of a month, a small
village, and landing, proceeded over fields of sand, about an hour's journey to the great city of Timbuctoo. During her short residence in this
city Kaloolah was closely housed, so that she had hardly an opportunity
of making any observations as to the size or general appearance of the
town. She noticed only that the streets were narrow; the houses low,
mostly of one story; that the city appeared to stand in a plain of sand,
and that it had no walls. Ten days after her arrival, her master announced
that a caravan was ready to start, and that she must prepare for a journey across the great desert. But little preparation on her part was
necessary, her whole wardrobe consisting of a long, loose cotton robe, a
cotton kerchief tied around the head, and falling over the face like a veil,
and a thick woollen haick in which, at pleasure, she could wrap herself
from the fierce rays of the sun, or the keen airs of the night. As her
beauty was the chief subject of the speculation, it of course was for the
interest of her master to treat her with kindness, and to afford her all
possible comforts in her wearisome and fatiguing journey. A matting of
coarse wool was provided for her repose at night, and the large pannier
in which she rode was so stuffed and slung as to render comparatively
easy the heavy paces of the camel.

In six days the caravan halted at El Arouan, a town in the midst of
the desert. Here it rested about a week, when it resumed its march, and
toiling on from well to well, a weary journey of twenty days, had at last
fallen into the ambuscade, which the attempt to avoid the usual tribute
had provoked. For a second time, under circumstances of peculiar
interest, at least to us, Kaloolah had been thrown, as it were, into my
arms.

CHAPTER XXIX.

IT was about a week after the events described in the last chapter, that two travellers might have been seen *en route* across the yellow plain, billowed by arenulous waves, that, sun-tipped by the level light, glowed coppery and carbuncular as the noses of a bivouac of gigantic Bacchuses. Both were mounted upon camels. One, perched upon his high and narrow saddle, with his feet upon the animal's neck, after the usual manner of "camelestrians." The other seated in a pannier, which was balanced by a weight of provisions, water, and baggage. The difference in position would at once have indicated the difference of sex, and it needed not the gun, slung across his back, and only partially concealed by the folds of his haick—or the long, slender spear, serving also as a goad for his companion's beast—to enable any one to pronounce as to the respective gender of the parties.

Of course, the reader understands that the two were no other than Kaloolah and myself; and it is unnecessary, therefore, to stop longer than to explain that it was the enmity of Hassan, and the jealousy of Mrs. Ali, that had caused our precipitate flight. Upon the division of the spoil, on the morning after our attack upon the caravan, Kaloolah had been assigned by lot, to an old Arab, who, satiated with the pleasures, yet hardly inured to the pains, of a well-stocked harem—and, withal, having certain notions of female loveliness, to which Kaloolah's classic features and slender figure did not conform—was exceedingly chagrined at the turn of fortune, which threatened to throw into the wrangling elements of his domestic felicity a feminine superfluity—or, as he expressed it, "another tongue in his tent."

"*Bishmallah!*" he exclaimed; "God is great!—but this is a small thing! She is not a man; she is not a black; she cannot work; but wont she eat and talk! They all eat and talk! I take a club sometimes and knock them down; beat them; break their bones; but they still eat and talk! God's will be done; but it is too much! To put such a thing upon me for my share! She is good for nothing: I cannot sell her!"

"Yes, you can," said I. "I will give you these *tobes*," showing him three or four cotton garments, which had fallen to me as my share of the spoil.

The old fellow eagerly accepted the offer; and the bargain was concluded, with all legal forms, just as Hassan interfered with a higher offer: but he was too late.

Upon returning to the douah at Boulag I purchased a small tent for Kaloolah, to which she closely confined herself, in order to escape the insult, and even violence, to which she was liable on account of her white skin, and her ignorance of the dogmas and forms of the Mohammedan religion. Nothing, however, could save her from a great deal of annoyance and discomfort. In addition to this there was the settled enmity of my old enemy, Hassan, with whom I had already had several altercations; and who, as was frequently intimated to me by several of his friends, and even by old Ali himself, only waited a convenient opportunity of carrying his designs against me into execution, without danger to himself. In my case—a stranger, without relations—there was no blood-avenger to fear, and nothing but a wholesome respect for my personal prowess held his hand from immediate attack. Such a state of things was far from pleasant: not that I had the least fear of the fellow—for a constant reliance upon my own personal resources had almost extinguished the feeling—but the uncertainty as to the time of his intended attempt was exceedingly annoying. The necessity of keeping a vigilant watch was exhausting in the extreme. But little refreshing is sleep when the head is pillowed upon pistols, and the hand relaxes not its grasp upon the yataghan. Had it not been for Kaloolah, the temptation would have been almost irresistible to settle the doubt, by provoking a rencontre, and deciding the question, as to his life or mine, upon the spot. As it was, however, prudence dictated an immediate flight—a course that was still further indicated by the sudden and distressing development of love, and its common attendant, jealousy, in the bosom of the young wife of Ali. Truth, not vanity, induces me to mention my unintended conquest. Respect for the sex, however, and a sentiment of gentlemanly delicacy, which the reader will appreciate, prevents me from dwelling upon the story at length. It was wrong, undoubtedly, in Seffna to love any other than her old, rugose-faced, white-bearded husband; but it is not for me to blame her. One thing, however, in her conduct can hardly be excused.

True, I might have treated her affection with more tenderness; I might have nursed the gentle flowers of passion, instead of turning away from their fragrance; I might have responded to that " yearning of the soul for sympathy "—have relieved, with the food of love, " the mighty hunger of the heart "; but all this and more that I might have done, but did not do, gave her no right to throw stones at Kaloolah.

These last—the stones I mean—could be received only as an intimation that it was best to take our departure at once, and as I had made all preparations—having bartered Ayoude for a heirie, which although far inferior to my own, was still a good traveller, and having provided a store of provisions and water—we silently left the douah just after nightfall, and proceeding to where I had stationed the camels, mounted, and set out with our faces towards the south.

The rising sun found us many miles from Boulag, and not far distant from the range of hills where I had first come upon the douah of Sidi Hadji Ali. It will be recollected that in a small hollow of the desert-plain, stretching off from the base of the hills, was deposited the greater portion of the treasure that I had selected from the lading of the dead camel, and a slight deviation from our true course brought us into the immediate neighborhood of the spot. Still it required a close observation, and an attentive comparison of the salient points, if salient they could be called, when all but the distant hill-tops was nearly unvarying uniformity, to hit upon the exact place, and it was not until the sun was several hours high that we directed the steps of our camels down the sides of the familiar-looking depression.

Making the camels kneel, so that we were secure from observation, while Kaloolah kept watch upon the edge of the hollow, I turned to, and with the blade of my spear soon succeeded, much to my satisfaction, in disclosing the buried package. Upon examining the powder, pistols, and other articles, they were found uninjured by their temporary inhumation, and after replenishing my flask and pouch with the munitions of war, I remade the package and placed it upon the back of my heirie with a sentiment of confidence in fortune that was peculiarly refreshing. I knew that the fickle goddess had a strong liking for me, but should she attempt to play any of her coquettish tricks, had I not the means and the will to compel her favors? " Yea, verily," thought I to myself, " I will woo her as the heroes of Valhalla wooed their brides, sword in hand, with the stern word and the strong arm! Am I not rich and well armed, and ready to buy or fight my way through the darkest portions of the Ethiopian world? What more can I ask? Hurrah for Framazugda!"

" Hurrah for Framazugda!" said Kaloolah, repeating the exclamation that had unconsciously escaped me, and at the same time thrusting her tiny hands from the folds of her haick, and waving it with inimitable grace.

There is nothing more fascinating in female manner to many tempera- ments than that compound expression of tenderness, interest, and mirth, expressed, though but poorly, by the term " archness." When founded on a delicate appreciation of the ludicrous, yet modified, and accompanied by a deep sympathy with the sentiments to which it is a response, it goes at once to the core of the heart. The proudest man bows without a mur- mur to the implied superiority; the most sensitive man fears not the gentle smile, or laugh, when accompanied by the eager eye, or the blushing cheek.

" You laugh at me, Kaloolah," said I, " but I will show you that mine is no idle boast. You shall once more see the flowers and the fields of Framazugda."

" I am certain of it, Jon'than, or else I could not laugh."

" And why are you certain?"

" Because you promise it. What you undertake, you will accomplish. What you promise, you will undertake."

" But it is a long road, and, as you well know by experience, it is filled with dangers. Have you no fear?"

" None while I am with you, Jon'than. The noon-day sun suffers no shadows. You are my sun; in the light of your eyes dangers draw off like the wild beasts from the traveller's fire; they may threaten, and growl, but they dare not attack me."

Nothing strengthens a man more than the confidence of others in his capacity to do, and it may be judged, therefore, that it was with a very comfortable share of determination that, placing Kaloolah in her pannier, I mounted my heirie, and gave to our camels the signal to set out.

Our route for several hours lay over a hard pebbly plain, bounded to the south by a belt, or rather bed, of reddish sandstone, beyond which came again an interminable extent of shifting sand. At sundown we halted for the night. The camels were secured; a small tent of goat- skins, as a bed-room for Kaloolah, was speedily pitched, into which I in- sisted she should retire as soon as we had partaken of our frugal supper of dates, sour milk, and barley meal. She protested that she was not sleepy; but it was easy to perceive that the heavy, jolting trot of the heirie had greatly fatigued her, and that repose was necessary if we wished to husband that essential element of success, her health and strength. I had but to throw myself on the ground and intimate my desire to sleep to secure obedience to my injunctions. Kaloolah withdrew to her tent, and I saw no more of her until the gray and purple coated *avant-couriers* of Apollo's chariot announced that it was time to be up and away.

Six days passed, in which time, according to my calculations, we had measured off and marked with the broad, spongy feet of our camels a hundred and eighty miles of sand. A few trifling desert incidents alone served to vary the monotony of the way—the blanched skeleton of a camel—a flight of vultures—an ostrich—the tracks of a recent traveller, and a few straggling and struggling thorns. One of these latter, a stunted but sturdy little fellow, stood solitary, without a companion, directly in our path. I drew the rein of my heirie to allow him to crop its leaves.

"No, No!" exclaimed Kaloolah; "do not harm it. 'T is but a mouthful, and existence must be sweet, or it would not cling to life so bravely. Let it live on. Why should we be more cruel than the winds and sands of Sahara?"

"A very pretty sentiment, Kaloolah; but like a good many pretty sentiments, it will hardly bear to be carried very extensively into practice. You think of the useless little bush, while you forget the poor heirie."

On the morning of the fourth day we had a fine opportunity of viewing, in immediate succession, some of the most interesting phenomena of the desert. There first appeared on our left hand several gigantic pillars of sand. At one time we counted a dozen. Sometimes almost stationary, yet with a very evident rotary motion, at others trailing over the ground with an irregular pace, and swaying backwards and forwards, and gliding round and round each other in all possible curves, they could not but suggest the ideas of dancing giants and demons—thus taking the mind back through all the apocryphal histories of tall men, from Teutabochus to Polyphemus, unto those authentic times when "there were giants in those days," and revealing to fancy's vision a pretty fair glimpse of an antediluvian quadrille.

As the sun rose in the heavens the whirling pillars slackened in their gyrations, and one after the other diappeared, to be succeeded by that most curious phenomenon, the mirage. Not a breath of air disturbed the profound calm of the plain, though in the upper regions of the atmosphere there floated lazily a few vapory films, attenuated to the verge of impalpability. Around, all was still—the stillness of the desert—a stillness which, if the reader will pardon the paradox, one can hear—when silence becomes audible—when the impact of the sunbeams upon the sand becomes a sound—when the auricular nerves, unsupported by their accustomed stimulus, vibrate without sound, producing a sensation as if one were listening to the very first beginning of a mighty, ever-threatening, never-coming noise—a noise that you can hear and cannot hear at the same time. Suddenly there was a glancing, gleaming, and quivering close to the surface of the plain, which increased as we advanced, until we were presented with a wavy and somewhat indistinct view of a large sheet of water. Gradually the scene became more clear and steady, until at last there lay stretched before us a beautiful lake, than which no lake ever seemed more inviting or more real.

"Wollo, Wollo!" exclaimed Kaloolah. "How beautiful. Let us hurry on. One bath in that clear water will give me strength for a thousand miles. Oh! I wonder if we shall find in it the azure-leafed lotus that grows in the Wollo?"

Poor Kaloolah! what a disappointment when she learned that the whole was an illusion, and saw in a few minutes the enchanting scene dissolving away. For some time we rode on in silence, with the veils of cotton cloth drawn over our faces to ward off the light and heat. Upon looking forth again not a vestige of the lake was left, but an exclamation from my companion attracted my attention to several dark specks in the sky. They were elevated at about an angle of forty-five degrees, and showed themselves a little to the west of the point whither we were tending. The spots were in motion relatively as to each other, and were also moving very slowly across our path. It was easy to perceive that they were the inverted and magnified images of camels, and that in number they were just sixteen.

It was not until two or three hours had passed that the real causes of this desert Fata Morgana appeared on the verge of the horizon. Urging our beasts into a more rapid pace, in about an hour we came up with them, and found that they were traders coming from the northeast, and proceeding south like ourselves; but that, disappointed in finding water where they had expected, they had been compelled to change their course to due west, in hopes of discovering an old neglected well.

"Where are your companions?" I demanded. "There were sixteen of you."

The travellers answered that a party, with the fastest camels, had been dispatched to look for the wells. My knowledge of their numbers excited the greatest astonishment, and at once elevated me in their estimation to the rank of a magician.

The story that I was moving to the Negro country on account of a blood-feud, and in the expectation of trading advantageously a few rosaries of coral and glass, was readily received and credited, and it was at once settled that I should join their party, at least as far as El Garwan, a salt mine, about five or six days distant. The agreement was mutually advantageous. The travellers were not sorry to have their forces strengthened by the addition of one well armed man, especially as we were now coming into the immediate neighborhood of a tribe of Tuarics. These savages, bold, rapacious, and predatory, are afraid of nothing but fire-arms, and my gun added an effective fourth to the strength of our party. For my part, I cared but little for protection, but I wanted guides; and hence my willingness to accommodate my motions to the slow paces of a loaded camel.

Two of the party returning and informing us that they had been successful in their search, we moved off in the direction indicated, and, about sundown, reached the well, which, when cleaned out, yielded a full supply of very pure and sweet water. Around this " gem of the desert " we encamped ; the camels were watered—a fire of dry brambles made— some water boiled in an earthen jar, and into it infused, by the old chief, with an air of wonderful importance and gravity, about half a teaspoonful of green tea.

" Taste this," said he, offering me some of the colorless infusion ; " it is the great medicine of the *Nazarius*. It comes from the other side of the earth, where the sun never shines ; and men find it only by creeping about on their hands and knees, with lanterns hung around their necks."

" Oh, Hahnemann ! " thought I, " what a humbug is thy doctrine of infinitesimals ! It may do when the patient needs no medicine, but not when he is dying for a full, strong dose ! Oh ' for an honest Christian cup, big, black, and steaming with odors, consecrated to the worship of the Dii Penates, and suggestive of the sweetest associations of home ! "

CHAPTER XXX.

"EL Garwan! El Garwan!" shouted my companions, as a collection of clay houses and low round huts broke upon our view. Situated in the open plain, with no green thing about it, nothing could be more dreary and unpicturesque. The movable douahs of the Bedouin seemed, in comparison, almost beautiful; yet here could be found men—some of them from the semi-civilized towns of the Mediterranean states—who, for the sake of money, were willing to spend their lives in this awful, miserable, hot, dry, dusty and dirty hole. "Drop a dollar into a potter's furnace, and you 'll burn a Barbary Moor to death," is an adage of the Bedouin, which, if any one believes to be an exaggeration, can be verified by a visit to El Garwan.

The whole trade of the town consists in salt, which is dug up in large, hard lumps of pure sal-gem, from a depth of five or six feet below the surface. The work is wholly performed by slaves, who also cut the lumps into pieces of a uniform size, and generally ornament them with some rude, fanciful designs. So compact is the salt, and so dry the air, that houses are sometimes built of pieces of it, which are found to be as durable as those constructed of rubble work, or of sun-burned brick.

Having hired a house—consisting of only one apartment, about four feet wide, eight feet long, and as many high, into which Kaloolah withdrew from the heat of the sun, and the impertinent observation of a crowd of vagabonds—I went out to take a look at the slaves in the salt-pits, in the expectation that there might be some Christians among them, to whom I could afford relief. I had not forgotten Jack Thompson, and there was a bare possibility that he might be among them. A thorough search, however, dissipated the hope, and, in answer to my inquiries, I was assured that there were no slaves but the wooley-headed, ebony-skinned beings before me.

"But are there no Christians?" I demanded.

234

"None now," replied my informant; "we often have them, but they are not good for much; they cannot stand the heat."

"You are right," I replied; "they are worthless dogs for work, but they bring good ransoms at Sweirah. If I could come across any, I would purchase them for that purpose."

"Well, I will tell you where you can find one. About three days' journey to the west is Marbash, and there I know that they have a Christian slave, for I saw him working in a salt-pit, not one moon ago."

"How old is he?"

" Mounting, so as to overlook the wall," etc.

"He is not young—his hair is gray; but I should think that he has twenty years yet in his body."

The description given me by my informant answered very well for Thompson; but I knew that there were too many Christian prisoners in the desert, who were supposed by their friends to have been lost at sea, to feel much confidence in finding him in the slave at Marbash. Whoever he was, however, he was evidently some one demanding my services, and I at once resolved to visit him, and, if possible, purchase him of his barbarous masters.

Returning through the narrow and filthy streets, to the door that opened into the little court in front of my house, I was struck with the appearance of a ragged and squalid figure that accosted me for alms. A few woollen tatters hung about his person, which was thickly bestudded with sores; a brown rag was tied around his black, bullet head, and the ends brought down so as partially to defend his eyes, which were disgustingly inflamed. His form was emaciated, and he walked with a feeble and tottering gait. His age was about thirty. Such figures are common enough in any Mohammedan town, but there was something in this fellow's appearance that at once arrested my attention. There was a familiar look about him, and there was a melancholy twinkle at the bottom of his dark gray eye, that spoke of a soul not yet broken down by the frowns of fortune, or driven into the Mussulman's usual refuge—a stupid indifference to life, with its miseries and its pains.

He said he had not tasted food for several days. His looks were sufficient proof of the fact ; so slipping three or four *feloos*—a copper coin—into his hand, I told him to go and purchase bread.

An hour or two afterwards, as I was standing in the little court, which was separated from the street by a low wall, I was startled by a voice, singing in a low tone a verse or two of the well-known Irish song, the "Exile of Erin." Mounting, so as to overlook the wall, I saw the beggar, seated on the ground beside the wicket, apparently awaiting my exit. In the meantime he was amusing himself with singing and talking to himself, and in poking a pile of offal with his staff. There was no one but myself within hearing ; but, even if there had been, he need hardly have feared to discover his secret thoughts and feelings, inasmuch as he was speaking a language that no citizen of El Garwan could have understood. My surprise may be imagined, when I heard the fellow talking in good, plain English, though with certain peculiarities of accent and pronunciation that spoke strongly of that gem of the ocean, the Emerald Isle. His words ran nearly as follows :

"Sure, it 's in luck you are to-day, Mr. Hugh Doyle ! 'T aint every day that yer stomach has a chance to cry enough, in the face and eyes of a calabash of milk and meal. Will ye be aisy now, an' maybe I 'll get ye some more from the same place. Ah, Hugh Doyle ! Hugh Doyle ! do ye remember the time when ye 'd hardly say thank ye for a meal of parates and meat ? and now ye 're starving to death !—And don't ye deserve it, ye vagabond ? Did n't ye desart yer country in anger, and have n't ye renounced your God in fear?—Are ye a true man, Hugh Doyle? Divil the bit of it! Ye 're a cowardly, lying, skulking thief of a renegado!— Can you pray? Yes, ye can, to Allah and Mahomet! Allah, Allah, Allah! Mohammed rasoul Allah! And is that yer creed? Ye 've sworn it, ye villain! Holy Mother of God! ye 're damned, Hugh Doyle! All the praists in the world, with the Pope and his cardinals at the back of 'em, could n't absolve ye! And how have ye bettered yerself? When a slave, ye were worked and baten, but ye were fed. Ye chose to make a hathen and a beggar of yerself, and now ye 're starving to death! Ye have the lot of Lazarus in this world, without a chance of his fate in the next; and all becase ye are not a true man. Ochone! Ochone! I mourn for ye, Hugh Doyle!"

The beggar bent his head in silence. A few low sobs came from his breast, which was evidently filled with emotions deeper and stronger than would seem to be indicated by his deliberate, audible self communings. With his thin hand he passed a portion of his tattered garments across his eyes.

In a few minutes he raised his head, and commenced singing: "'There came to the bache—' ah! if I could only get to that same bache!—seems to me if I could see the ocean on'st more I could die content. Sure I could look across it as aisy as across the lake at Bournboy, and see the green hills of Erran and Derrymorn. Sure I could pick up its drops in my hand and ask them, did they know any thing of the water of Cavan? Had they ever fallen in rain upon the Ballyneegeerah? Had they ever hung in dew diamonds from roses of Eneskillen? Had they ever been scattered from the daisies by the light steps of the 'Pride of the Borne?' ——————Och, Bessy, mavourneen, why, why did ye smile on Teddy Moffat and frown black as night on Hugh Doyle? Could ye see me now, but little would ye drame that ye saw the boy ye drove to list in the marines—————I was mad—————Ye thought I would n't, but I did, and here now sits Hugh Doyle among haythens, himself as big a haythen as can be found in the four quarthers of Asia, Africa, and Amir-ica—————Och, Hugh, you vagabond (bad luck to ye, I would say, but sure, ye 've enough of that same), ye 've desarted yer country, ye 've changed yer religion, ye 've sold yer soul for nothing at all. Small price, ye may say; and so it would be for a dacent soul, but yer's is worth no more, and ye can't complain, for has n't the divil paid ye up like a jintle-man, and a man of his word?—————Hugh, Hugh Doyle, ye 'll starve in this world and roast in the next, ye poor, mane, unfortunate vagabond!"

"Hugh Doyle!" I exclaimed in a loud voice from the top of the wall directly over his head, "Hugh Doyle, are you a true man?"

"Holy St. Patrick! what is that!" said Hugh, jumping to his feet with an agility hardly to be expected of his feeble frame.

"Hugh Doyle!" I repeated, sinking my head instantly behind the wall, "are you a true man?"

"Sure I am—Hivin presarve us, but this is a manifestashun! Maybe it is the saint himself—sure I am, your reverence. No, no, I was—that is, I will be. Och, help, your reverence, a poor cratur who has drained the cup of misfortune, and has been living upon the dregs for the ten years past—a poor divil, your honor, who has had to keep a mortal long Lent without fish—whose tay has been nothing but adversi-*tay*, with not the laste dash in the world of sugar or crame——"

"Come in," said I, pushing open the gate, and addressing him in Arabic.

He entered, and looked around with an air of bewilderment that was truly comical, and that served to heighten the tragic interest of his appearance by contrast. He could see no one but, as he supposed, a grave Mussulman, who commenced asking the particulars of his history, to which he at once replied in voluble and exceedingly pure Arabic.

Divested of its unessential details, Hugh's story was short. He was born in the county of Cavan: had received some education: had got into some love difficulties; had enlisted in the marines, and been sent to sea in an armed brig, which had been wrecked upon the coast of the Sahara. With a portion of the crew he reached the land: was soon discovered by some of the tribes who wander up and down the coast in search of wrecks; seized as a slave, carried into the interior, and sold. In a short time the cruel treatment he was compelled to endure on the one hand, and the promises and persuasions of the Arabs on the other, induced him to renounce his religious principles and profess a belief in the creed of Mohammed. For a little while he enjoyed a benefit in the change. The luxury of proselyting—one of the highest in the world, and one for which every sect has a taste—cannot be had every day, and the Arabs were willing to pay for it in charity to the convert. But with the novelty of his conversion abated their sympathy in his fate, and soon the contempt invariably felt for any one who changes his opinions or renounces his principles from the force of external circumstances, began to manifest itself in their conduct. They had saved his soul, why should they bother themselves about his body—they had put him into the path to paradise, he must pick out for himself his way in the world. He had no means of obtaining a living. Nominally free, he was yet jealously watched, at least until the deficient charities of a poor, selfish, and cruel people had allowed his health and strength to sink below the possibility of an attempt at escape.

"You would like an opportunity of escaping from this horrible hole, would you not? You've had enough of the Prophet and his followers. Nay, nay," I continued, speaking for the first time to him in English, "speak the truth, Hugh Doyle."

The poor fellow, pale and trembling, sunk upon his knees.

"You wonder who I am—no matter, you'll know one of these days. I've only time now to talk about your case. You would leave this place, and no wonder, for any change in your condition must be for the better. Listen then, obey my orders implicitly, and you shall go with me; fail in any one particular, and I cast you off to die the death of a renegade."

There was no danger that Hugh would intentionally disobey any of my directions, but there was much risk from the excitement of newly awakened hope, and the inconsiderate levity, sometimes an ingredient in Irish character. It was safest, therefore, to take advantage of the mystery in which, to his apprehension, I was enshrouded, to enforce obedience, compel caution, and concentrate his attention to the object in view, and the means of attaining it.

"You have been at Marbash?" I demanded.

"Sure I have," replied Hugh, "'t was there that I lived better nor three years. I remember it well. If I had now all the blood in my body that was drawn from my back, and buried in the salt-pits there, I should be a strong man."

"Do you think that you could find your way back?"

"As asy as point out the course of the sun in broad day. 'T is a wide path, and no turns in it."

"Well, then, listen to my plan. I intend going to Marbash, and shall want a guide, and some one to look after the camels. We must contrive it so that you will be the man. I will go into the street just before starting, which will be in two or three days, and commence bargaining for a guide. Numbers will propose, but I shall offer so little that no one will accept the terms. In the midst of our wrangling you must come forward and offer your services, when I will at once strike a bargain with you, and we will mount and be off."

Hugh seized the hem of my haick, and pressed it to his lips, while sobs prevented a reply.

"Well, what do you say. Do you hesitate?"

"Hesitation! yer honor; would a man hesitate to draw his hand from the fire? Oh, no, 't is only the suddenness of it—like a flash of lightning to a man who has lost his road in the night—t' is the unexpectedness of it."

"We will start in two days," I continued. "This will give you some time to recruit your strength, which you will do rapidly upon full meals, as you are suffering wholly from want of food. But it will not do for you to be seen with money, and to avoid all suspicion, we must have but little communication with each other; you will, therefore, come here at night, and you shall have a supply of cooscoosoo and milk. In the meantime be careful that you do or say nothing that will attract attention; follow your usual habits, and mind how you ever address me in English."

Having reiterated my directions in the minutest manner, and enforced upon him the necessity of extreme caution, I opened the door of the court for him to pass into the street. Closing the gate, and stepping to the spot where I could overlook the wall, I saw Hugh stop for a moment, cross himself, clasp his hands together, and, raising his face, mutter some prayerful ejaculation. He then marched off with quite a firm, almost stately, step, down the street for a few paces, and then pausing, again looked back. I threw open the door, and beckoned to him.

"Is this the way," I exclaimed, in a stern tone, "that you obey my directions. Pray standing, cross yourself, and march off as if you were the kaid of the town!"

"Sure I forgot——"

"How dare you forget. Have you performed the part of a half-starved beggar for ten years, and yet you cannot continue to do so for two days longer? Go, sir. I shall keep watch of you, and if you venture to attract attention, by word or deed, or by any alteration in look, manner, gesture, or gait, I 'll leave your fleshless bones to be buried in the sands of El Garwan. No words! be off, and thank God—secretly, mind you—that there was no Moor within sight when you chose to insult the Prophet with your Christian prayers in the streets of a Mohammedan town."

Without a word Hugh slunk away, but it was easy to see, that, however he might imitate it, his gait had no longer the natural and painful slouchness of one without hope.

CHAPTER XXXI.

HE two days passed without any adventure of interest. By a liberal but judicious distribution of alms to the poor, presents to some of the chief men, with medical advice to all who asked it, I had thoroughly engratiated myself with the inhabitants of the town, none of whom offered any opposition to my taking Hugh with me to Marbash, or expressed any doubt of our return. Indeed, how could they, when we left behind, as security, an old camel and three or four loads of salt.

These two days had done wonders for Hugh ; had afforded a necessary rest to Kaloolah, and had prepared our animals for a long stage of a hundred and fifty miles which we had yet to pass before reaching the southern borders of the desert. The two animals that I had added to my party were both heiries, and although hardly equal to the one ridden by Kaloolah, and far inferior to mine, were yet strong, active, and very fleet as compared with the common camel. Hugh mounted one, the other was laden, for the time, with an extra supply of provisions and water, and, as quietly as possible, at early dawn we set out for Marbash.

It was not without some little emotion that at about sunset of the second day I saw a few dark spots in the distance, which Hugh asserted were the two or three dozen hovels that composed the town of Marbash. No one, who has not experienced the feeling, at a distance from home, and in barbarous lands, can understand the force with which a man is attracted towards one of his kind with whom he has any community of religion, language, or habit. The bands of human sympathy are strong and all-pervading ; but, unfortunately, nations have stretched them to a degree of tenuity which prevents them from always being seen or felt. When removed to a distance from the repelling forces, man finds himself attracted to man in a proportion compounded of his distance from old stupid conventionalities and selfishisms, and his nearness to his sympathizing kind.

The next morning we mounted and rode into the town. There were not more than a dozen inhabitants to be seen. Most of the houses were in ruins, or half buried in the sand. Once a place of some consequence by its trade in salt, it had been almost depopulated by the superior attractions of the mine at El Garwan, and by the frequent visits of a tribe of marauding Tuaries.

Without circumlocution I stated the object of my visit. The consequence was, as we have anticipated, that the master of the slave at once made up his mind to demand four times as much as his market value. " He is a wonderful slave ! is he not ? " exclaimed the fellow, appealing to the bystanders, who answered with an assenting " *Yea ! yea !* "

" He has all the knowledge of the Christians. He is as strong as a lion. He is as—— "

" Bah ! " I exclaimed, cutting short his list of good qualities ; " we understand all that. For work he is not worth the salt that he eats ; but I want him to take to Sweirah. If he is an Englishman I will give you a good price : if not, he wont be worth taking as a gift ! "

A short walk brought us into the salt-pits. At the first glance I recognized the familiar form and face of Jack. He was working, together with half a dozen negroes, breaking up, with a kind of small spade, the sal-gem into large square pieces. In appearance, he had altered but little. If any thing he looked in rather better condition than when we parted at the well of Ageda.

As we approached he looked up at me, and gave a sudden start ; but as I met his glance with a cold, steady, and unmoved look, his countenance fell, though still retaining traces of astonishment and dubitation. His master took no notice of his emotion, and in a few moments we walked off to conclude, if possible, our bargain. Expressing myself satisfied with his appearance, and with the Moor's assurance that he was an Englishman, I made an offer which, after some chaffering, was accepted. Certain legal forms had to be gone through with—a *talb* or scribe was called to make out a bill of sale and a receipt. While waiting for this I directed Hugh to take the two camels and to mount Jack upon one of them, and set out from the town. In a few minutes I also got under way with Kaloolah, and followed at some distance behind, until we had got beyond the view of the inhabitants of Marbash.

" Jack Thompson, ahoy ! " was my salutation as we rode up on a sharp trot beside him. " How are you, my old friend ? Do you know me ?

Nay, Nay, hold on; if you lurch so you 'll be overboard. Steady man. Mind your helm. If you yaw your craft about in that way you 'll broach to, or come by the lee, and have your decks swept before you know it ! '"

" Bless my eyes ! Mr. Romer ! Good heavens ! Oh, dear me, can it be ! " and the old man wrung my hand while tears started from his eyes and trickled down his weather-beaten face.

His emotion was infectious. Kaloolah's eyes were distilling the diamonds of sympathy. Hugh's inflamed eyes were overflowing, and there was a very perceptible sense of moisture in my own.

" 'T is only the last drops, yer honor ! " said Hugh, pointing to his eyes. " Sure, when the heart is filled with grief it overflows, and its waters are bitter ; but when ye put a big joy into it the grief is forced out, and its last drops are sweet. Oh, there 's all the difference in the world between the top and bottom of sorrow."

" Don't think that I 'm astonished to see you, Mr. Romer," interposed Thompson. " I knew that you would come ; I have dreamed it a hundred times. If it had n't been for the thought of you I should have bilged and gone down long before this. I am flat aback with joy, but not with surprise."

" Well, file away again, Jack, and let us know how you have got along since we parted. But come, while we are talking we may as well be moving. We must put thirty miles between us and this spot before night. Hugh Doyle, you will attend to this lady's camel. Forward ! "

As we rode along, Jack and myself exchanged the histories of our adventures ; but, as the details of his desert life would be wholly without interest, it is needless to note the long, rambling conversation in which they were told. His had been the monotonous life of a slave in a salt mine, undisturbed by events of higher importance than occasional beatings, frequent attempts at proselyting, and once a change of masters, and a journey from the Waddy Sebah to Marbash.

Our conversation was interrupted by the appearance of a company of Tuarics, who were mounted upon heiries, and armed with their usual weapon, a long lance. Handing my spear to Hugh, and my knife to Jack, I unslung my gun, and held it conspicuously, with the muzzle projecting above my head. The Tuarics upon sight of our party changed their course, and came towards us at a rapid pace. There were but six of them, and, armed as we were, there was but little to fear. Still, a battle was to be avoided, if possible, and as nothing invites an attack so much as an appearance of hurry and fear, we closed up our ranks in compact order, and moved on steadily, but with slow and deliberate steps. Something in our motions or equipment evidently had a discouraging effect; for, after advancing so closely that I was just beginning to entertain the question of emptying a couple of their saddles before allowing them to come any farther, they halted, and, after a brief consultation, wheeled their heiries and made off.

"Perhaps," suggested Kaloolah, "they intend to follow us with a greater force."

"No danger, yer ladyship, of that," said Hugh. "It is aisy to see that those fellows are a long way from home. Their beasts are leg-weary; and, do ye see, they are as gaunt as greyhounds? They have n't tasted water for a week."

We encamped a little before sunset, in order to have light for selecting an outfit for my companions from my stores. Each was furnished with a new *suilham*, cap and turban, a pair of pistols, with a supply of ammunition, and a small quantity of coral, amber, and glass beads, which, as having a readily exchangeable value, would answer for money, in case any thing should happen to separate us.

When the division was made, and our packages done up and stowed, I addressed my companions, explaining to them my determination to proceed due south, through the Negro countries of Africa; that it was a long journey, filled with difficulties and dangers, and that I had no wish to take them with me against their will. I told them that, according to my calculations, we were not far from the southern borders of the desert, and about seven hundred miles from the Atlantic coast: that, if they chose to undertake the journey across the desert to Mogadore, it was very possible they would succeed; and that, in such case, they were quite welcome to the animals they were riding and to the articles that had just been distributed between them.

"Bless my eyes, Mr. Romer, you ain't in earnest!" exclaimed Jack.

"Ye may say that!" interposed Hugh. "Holy St. Patrick! Lave ye, is it? I 'll tell you, on'st for all, Mr. Romer, it can't be done! Ye may say the word, and I 'll creep on my knees; but, by jappers! I 'll follow ye. A purty business we should make of it, to start for Mogadore, full fifteen hundred miles, and us not knowing a foot of the way! To be sure, Mr. Thompson might tell the pints of the compass, and so could I, for that comes natural to all men; but how could we get our latitude and longitude?—us, who have n't been university-bred, and don't understand fluxions and logarithms, and other mathematics?"

"And what do you say, Thompson?"

"Say? What should I say, except that it will be a hard blow that

makes us part company again? I agree with Mr. Doyle, that it would be
sheer nonsense for us to attempt to work a back traverse without you.
No, no; drive ahead, I say! When a ship gets on a reef, it 's the best
plan, sometimes, to crack on all sail, and force her over into deep water.
Who knows but that we may come out at the Cape of Good Hope, yet?
But, at any rate, whether I 'm ever to see blue water again or not, I shall
keep in your wake. You 've youth and strength, and wit and luck, on
your side, and, in future, I sail under your orders."

"Well, my friends!" I exclaimed, "I am not sorry that you so readily
make up your minds to go with me. In fact, it would be very foolish for you
to do otherwise; and I only made the proposal in order to give you a fair
chance of choosing for yourselves. It might be possible for Hugh, speaking the language as he does, to get through; but for you, Jack, the
chances would be that you 'd run aground before the voyage was half over.
For my own part, I am glad of your company. You will be able to render
me the greatest assistance; and, if this lady ever sees her country again,
she and her friends will be under no small obligations to you."

"Will she? By the powers, I 'm thinking that it is just the revarse!
'T is we that are under obligation to her, for permission to tread in her
footsteps."

"I 've been thinking, Mr. Romer," interrupted Thompson, "that, in
our situation, a good look-out is one of the greatest of virtues. Now,
you 're the captain of this crew, and it wont answer for you to keep
watch: or, rather, you are supposed to be on the watch all the time: so
I think that Mr. Doyle and myself had better keep watch and watch.
He 's been to sea, and knows what that is. If he 'll call himself the
starboard watch, I 'll take the larboard; or *vice varse;* it 's all the same
to me."

To this proposal Hugh readily assented, and even warmly insisted
upon it, when I suggested that his strength would hardly permit him to
keep watch, for several days yet. It was astonishing what wonders five
days of food and hope had done for him. He was no longer the same being.
There began to be a degree of steadiness and strength in his gait, a certain smile round his lips, and a pleasant light in his eye, that indicated the
workings of a renewed spirit; and, as well, the full and happy operations
of the digestive organs. Even his sores had put off their indolent and
malignant character, and were rapidly assuming a healthy appearance.
So much for good food, and plenty of it! It is a great thing, a plenty
of good, plain, wholesome food in this world, and not without its influence
in the next. If any one doubts, let him ask the starving millions, who

are suffering the pangs of hunger—who are dying of diseases engendered of famine—who are grovelling in the mental and moral debasement of deficient nutrition—and what will be the answer? Why, that a starving stomach permits no moral sense, no religious sentiment—that you must fill that organ before you can touch the heart—before you can make the consolations of religion, the incitements of virtue, the hopes of heaven, any thing better than miserable and empty sounds, signifying nothing.

CHAPTER XXXII.

The Limit of the Desert—Hugh's System of Fortification—A Herd of Gazelles—Character of the Country—Encamping in the Shade—Gazelle Stalking—A Pleasant Meal—Jack's Song—Hyena Music—A Fresh-Water Lake—Bathing—A Visit from a Crocodile—A Characteristic Proposition—Leeching a Camel—A Negro Ploughman—A Chase and a Capture—Hassan and the Tuaries—A Supply of Provisions—An Addition to the Party.

FIVE days of weary travelling, and the character of the country began to change. The sand-hills no longer lay so heavy nor so steep; the desert-thistle began to appear in great abundance, and, farther on, numerous specimens of the acacia, and a tree bearing an agreeable red fruit, like the cranberry; tracks of the jackal and panther were noticed, and several flocks of gazelles scoured the plain as we approached.

"It will not be long, now, Mr. Romer," said Hugh, "before we come upon the inhabitants of these parts. God send us a safe deliverance from them, if they are Tuaries!"

"Amen!" exclaimed Thompson. "If what the Moors and Arabs say of that people is true, we shall have good reason to call upon God for help."

"No croaking, my men," I replied. "You ought to know the Moors too well to take their word for any thing. We know that they will lie; what the Tuaries will do, we have yet to learn. The Tuaries are no worse, I'll answer for it, than fifty other nations that we shall have to pass before we reach the end of our journey."

"Don't you think, yer honor," said Hugh, after a pause, "it might be as well to fortify ourselves a little, in case of accidents?"

"Fortify ourselves!—with what?"

"With a full male. Do you see that?" pointing to a herd of thirty or forty gazelles. "There's not a jintleman's park in Ireland, or England either, that has a finer taste of venison than this same country, and divil the game-keeper within twenty miles of us!"

"You seem to think of nothing but eating."

"And with rason, yer honor. Is n't every man born to ate a sartain amount in this world? and have n't I starved so long that I must make my jaws do double duty to make up for lost time? Sure, I 've enough to answer for, without laving the world with a long account of unaten dinners upon my conscience! But it 's not for myself that I spake, yer honor; it 's for her ladyship. The laste taste in the world of flesh would do her a power of good. Beauty can't live upon air, nor upon date-stones, baring the leather-skinned beauty we have left behind us. Sure, one Christian faste would give her ladyship a dale of strength, and put us all in good heart to meet any vagabonds of Tuarics that may cross our path. Look, yer honor, what a nice shade from the hot sun beneath this clump of trees! and here, too, is green herbage for the poor bastes to moisten their mouths with; and see, there is dry sticks enough for a bonfire! Sure, if ye would move along to the back of that hillock, ye could get a shot at those beauties!"

The country presented somewhat the appearance of an open heath. The soil was thin, but sufficient to support an amount of vegetation that, after the perfect nakedness of the desert we had just left, struck us as being almost grandly rich and luxuriant. A dozen trees, at least, besides those by which we had stopped, dotted the extensive landscape: hundreds of low bushes, with dark green foliage, enlivened the scene: and here and there, over broad patches, a few gallant grasses and mosses held, in the chains of vegetation, the roving sands.

We dismounted; the camels were unladen, and turned out to graze. Kaloolah's tent was pitched, and Hugh and Jack set about collecting sticks for a fire. Giving them the strictest orders not to wander far from the camp, and to keep a good look-out around the horizon for visitors, I took my gun, and started off towards the herd of gazelles, who were quietly dozing beneath the shade of a group of acacias. Making first a large detour, in order to get to windward of them, I crept down slowly towards them, and, by taking advantage of all the little inequalities of the ground, was enabled to approach within shooting distance without exciting any alarm. For the last hundred yards I was compelled to crawl slowly along the ground. Upon rising to get a fair view of them, the whole herd started to their feet, and stood, for an instant, trembling with excitement at the unexpected apparition. I marked a fine fat fellow, and fired. On the instant, they bounded into the air, and upon descending again, commenced kicking the ground from beneath them, in a succession of wonderfully vigorous and spiteful jumps. Higher than all jumped the one that had been hit, but he did not cover so much ground, and, after a few bounds (the convulsive efforts of departing vitality), he fell lifeless upon the plain. Under Hugh's energetic superintendence, a large fire was awaiting the result of my expedition. It did not take long to dress the animal, portions of whose carcass were soon roasting, frying, and stewing before a fierce fire of dry sticks. When done, I served up a portion to Kaloolah, upon a platter of fresh leaves, and was exceedingly gratified to see her, although endowed with as much real delicacy as any heroine of romance, make a good, solid, sensible meal, like any other hungry traveller.

We had, of course, no forks; but despite the manipular necessities of the case, Kaloolah managed her meal with singular dexterity and grace. There is hardly a prettier sight, thought I, than to see a pretty woman eat. True, in the verdancy of youthful sentiment, many a one has shrunk from the profane association of ruby lips with the processes of mastication and deglutition, but a little more experience, and there comes to a man the conviction that women, however angelic, are not wholly spiritual in their natures, and that food is essential to all of the sex, as well as to grandmothers and old maiden aunts. With this conviction, he learns to extract pleasure from what at first gave him pain. The prickle that pierced the tender papilla of his unsophisticated sensibility becomes a pleasant morsel to the hardened and practised camel's-tongue of true taste, and he no longer sympathizes with the pseudo-sentimentalists, who would wreathe, as it were, with cypress and yew the portico of the temple of Love—forbid the burnt-offerings and libations, and literally starve to death the enchanting beauties that minister at the altars.

As the sun went down the air became quite cool, making our bright fire as pleasant to feel as it was to see. What with the refreshing coolness, the flashing fire, the full meal, and the fact of having arrived at the borders of vegetation, my party were all in high spirits--the animated conversation, and the loud laugh, indicating an elevation of feeling that was quite gratifying, knowing as I did the many dangers we had to encounter, and the necessity of a good *morale* to meet them successfully.

Withdrawing a few yards into the shade of a clump of trees, I took a look at the scene. It was striking and picturesque. Kaloolah sat on a piece of carpet at the door of her goat-skin tent beneath the scanty branches of a scraggy acacia—on either hand at a respectful distance sat my two followers, dressed alike in their new Moorish garments, with the exception of the turban—Hugh having laid his aside; and Jack's twist being a kind of *ad libitum* performance, it is impossible to describe.

For some time Hugh entertained Kaloolah with a number of Irish melodies. They sounded curiously enough, those familiar airs, as they floated away on the night wind of the desert. Could they have caught the ear of some adventurous Clapperton, or Lang, how they would have excited his astonishment and stirred his heart.

Hugh rose to his feet and made a low salaam—" May it plase yer ladyship," said he to Kaloolah, " to open that half-blown rose of a mouth of yers, and favor us with a song."

As soon as she could make out his meaning, Kaloolah complied—singing several pleasant little songs in her own soft language. When she had finished she intimated a desire for Jack to give her a taste of his musical quality. Nothing loth, Jack struck an attitude and began. It was only a common sea song, and could be considered appropriate to time and place only by contrast ; but as I lay at some little distance in the shadow of the trees, his voice came over me like a nor'wester. He sang with unction, and his damp tones, redolent of spoon-drift, fairly brought the brine to my eyes.

THE HURRICANE.

The mercury fell so far and fast,
  Our skipper's cheek grew pale,
" Lay up ! Lay out ! " he sternly cried,
  " Furl every stitch of sail ;
Pass double gaskets, fore and aft ;
  The hatches close secure ;
Trice up the ports—the guns run in,
  And lash them firm and sure."

Our skipper spake unto a crew
  Of joyous hearts, and free
As ever, in a right trim ship,
  Sailed o'er a tropic sea.
And while he spake, the sun his rays
  Poured down like melted gold,
And lazily our gallant bark
  In noon-day calmness rolled.

But as our crew sprang up the shrouds,
  They saw, with vague surprise,
The yellow sun grow dim and red,
  And one dark cloud arise—
That swiftly to the zenith swelled
  And spread around, o'er all
Old Ocean's slowly heaving breast,
  A black and dismal pall.

And then a moan crept o'er the sea,
  Beneath the breathless air.

And came, as if from out the deep,
  The wailings of despair.
While higher yet—and higher yet
  The long and placid swell,
On which our bark had gently rolled,
  Now, surging, rose and fell.

And tossed her wide—stripped to her spars
  Of every rag of sail,
And all prepared, alow, aloft,
  To battle with the gale.
One moment thus we silent lay,
  When sudden through the gloom
We heard the whirlwind's awful roar,
  The crashing thunders boom.

And at the sound the demon blast
  Leapt on our quivering bark,
And bore her down till her yard-arms
  Bestirred the waters dark.
" Hard up ! Hard up ! Starboard your helm,"
  Our skipper fiercely cried.
" Hard up it is," the straining men
  In shrieking tones replied.

But still on our broadside we lay,
  Amid the wild uproar,
And buried deep in showers of drift
  That hurtled fiercely o'er.

"Ho! axes for the mizzen-mast,"
  Our first lieutenant cries.
"Hold on! hold on! One moment hold!"
  Our skipper brave replies.

And then with trumpet to his lips,
  High rising o'er the gale,
He sends along our anxious decks
  His steady, cheering hail:
"Ho! forward, there — the fore-shrouds
    man,"
  And as his voice thus rung,
Twice fifty true and gallant men
  Into the rigging sprung;
And there, 'mid driving foam and spray,
  With desp'rate grasp they clung.

Hurrah! her head pays slowly off
  Before this added strain,
"Hurrah! Hurrah! Ease down your
    helm,
  She rights—she rights amain."
And quick before the demon blast,
  Who, mad at loss of prey,
Now louder howls—now fiercer chafes,
  Our good ship gathers way.

And through a seething sea of foam,
  And 'mid the driving rack,
She swiftly flies, with no sails set,
  To urge her on her track.
With no sail set!—but hark! that sound!
  It is the main-course driven
From out the double gasket's gripe,
  And into fragments riven.

With no sail set, but hark! again,
  A top-sail breaks away,
And whipt to ribbons, in a breath,
  Far out the streamers play.
But still both brace and stay hold true,
  And still our spars stand strong,
And still, amid the wild uproar,
  Our staunch bark howls along.

But swiftly now the raven clouds
  From the dark furrows rise,
And fast before the struggling light
  The storm-king shrieking flies.
And now, thank God, with stay-sails set,
  And helm held hard-a-lee,
Our brave old ship—laid timely to,
  Safe heads the surging sea.

Never, perhaps, were stomachs more thoroughly astonished than were ours at this sudden change from a hard, meagre, vegetable diet, to a full meal of animal food. They took it quietly, however, and a good night's rest showed that, if surprised, they were far from displeased. A solid breakfast, after the same fashion, completed Hugh's plan of fortification, and, mounting, we moved on, prepared for the worst, confident that only with life could we be deprived of the invigorating influences of a glorious "feed," and the pleasant reminiscences of a roasted gazelle.

During the night, the hungry growl of the hyena rose several times upon the air, and, shortly after getting under way, a party of the gaunt, grinning beasts flitted across our path, in the purplish gray light of early dawn. Hyenas are not very interesting or companionable animals, and their voices are not generally considered musical; but, under the circumstances, we were pleased to meet with them—the silence and lifelessness of the desert had given us a fellow feeling for any and every form of animal life.

We had been in the saddle but two or three hours, when our attention was aroused by the shouts and gestures of Jack, who had ridden on some distance in front. As we neared him his excitement appeared to increase; he waved his hands for us, and eagerly pointed to some object ahead. A long way off, we could hear his stentorian shout of "Water! water!" and, as we came up, a charming scene broke upon us, as suddenly as if created by the wave of an enchanter's wand. The main feature was an extensive sheet of water, that stretched away from our feet to the base of a range of low blue hills. The shores were, apparently, marshy, and the lake of no great depth, inasmuch as numerous sand-bars and mud-flats showed themselves above the water. Countless flocks of aquatic fowl blackened its surface, and far out was a moving object, that we concluded to be a man in a canoe; he was standing up, but whether paddling or poling his boat we could not decide.

We soon stood upon the flat shore, and convinced ourselves, by copious draughts, that it was no mirage. After satisfying our own appetites, and allowing our camels to drink their fill, it was resolved, unanimously, that we should indulge in the luxury of a bath. The propriety of ablution, in our case, will hardly be disputed by any one who recollects the mode of life we had been leading; the scarcity of water in the desert, and the complete exclusion of our skins, for so long a period, from its clarifying influences.

Around a projecting point, covered with thick brushes, lay a beautiful little bay, which I selected as a bathing spot for Kaloolah. The beach was shelving and sandy, the water shallow, and a single broad-leaved palm tree threw its shade upon shore and lake. Leaving Kaloolah, with special directions not to venture far out for fear of crocodiles, or hippopotami, I returned to a little knoll that commanded a view of all the approaches to the spot. Further down the beach, Hugh and Jack had selected a bathing-place, and were soon busily engaged in unearthing their long-buried cuticular strata.

For some time I sat watching the movements of the distant boatman, who seemed, from his motions, to be spearing fish—or noting the manœuvres of the vast squadrons of water-fowl—or gazing at the odorous, and infinitely varied beauties of the lotus fields, that lay basking in the full sun upon the surface of the water. Suddenly there came a shrill shriek from Kaloolah, and in an instant she darted into view, and ran rapidly along the shore. Her loose robe of cotton draped itself round her limbs, and somewhat impeded her movements, but still two to one on her would have been a fair bet, had even Atalanta, or swift Camilla been in the field. Without stopping, however, to admire her graceful paces, I rushed to the shore, and soon ascertained the cause of her alarm

As I came in sight, Kaloolah turned quickly, and finding herself, as the phrase is, " more frightened than hurt," she uttered a laugh, and pointed to a youngster of a crocodile who had come out of the water, and while she was dressing had advanced unperceived, until close enough to seize her haick as it lay upon the sand. The fellow was making off with his prize, when I rushed at him, and succeeded in seizing him by the tail. The water was about knee deep, and as the thief was strong and active, though not more than six or seven feet long, the splashing that incontinently took place may be more easily imagined than described. Kaloolah seemed to enjoy the terrors of this novel aquatic combat, for, although frequently exhorting me to let the fellow go, she laughed long and loudly at our grotesque struggles. At one moment I would drag the monster out, high and dry, when, like a very Antæus, he would gather fresh strength from contact with the ground, and walk off into the water in spite of my best exertions, all the time retaining a firm hold of the haick. At last, however, finding that it was impossible for either of us to get the advantage, we concluded to compromise matters, and upon his surrendering the haick I gave him his tail, with which he industriously paddled himself off into deep water. The haick was of course somewhat injured in the contest, having numerous marks of the monster's teeth, but as Hugh observed, " It was such a blessing that Kaloolah's body was not wrapped in it when the marks were made," that the injury to the garment could hardly be considered a matter of regret.

It was now my turn to bathe, so intrusting Kaloolah to the ward of Hugh and Jack, I sought a retired spot and plunged in. It was not advisable to venture far out, lest some saurian *spes gregis* should take it into his head to resent the insult that had been just offered to one of the youngsters of his flock.

While preparing to remount, Jack made a characteristic proposition. It was neither more nor less than that we should give up travelling by land, and embark upon the lake.

" Embark in what ? " I demanded. " What kind of a craft do you propose ? "

" Why, surely," he replied, " we shall be able to find something that we can make a raft of at least. Or, why could n't we make a signal to that fellow, and get him to take us on board ! "

Thompson was really in earnest, and I had to explain to him that the lake was most certainly not the expansion of a navigable river, and that it could be nothing more than the marshy terminus of a few short water courses from the distant hills, to convince him that his proposition was impracticable. "The boat you see yonder," I continued, "is probably a small 'dug-out,' carrying only one man, and it is doubtful whether the water is deep enough to float a large craft. In fact, in a few days it is quite probable that the whole lake will disappear—"

"In which case," interposed Hugh, "we shall cut a mighty quare figure, all illigantly wrecked upon the rocks of a mud-bank, and without the laste drop of water around us in which we could swim to the shore."

We had proceeded but a few paces on our course when my heirie began to give symptoms of uneasiness. He turned his head about, and champed his teeth as if in pain, and at length blood was observed to issue from his mouth. Our alarm may be imagined ; a worse accident could hardly befall us than that one of our beasts should give out. We held an anxious consultation. At last I bethought me of making a close examination, and endeavoring to ascertain the cause and nature of the complaint, and commencing with his mouth, our investigations were at once rewarded with success.

"I see him! I see him!" exclaimed Hugh, and suiting the action to the word, he plucked from beneath the heirie's tongue a monstrous leech, which the poor beast had taken in with the water of the lake. The alarming symptoms exhibited by my heirie were at once removed. With a deep sense of joy and thankfulness, we speedily reformed our line of march—Jack leading, in what he called "the cat-head watch," while Hugh spread himself well out on our left flank ; our right being covered by the lake. This triangular disposition of our forces was the best we could adopt to guard against surprise, and to command an extensive view of the country, which, as we advanced, became more and more irregular in its surface, and more thickly dotted with trees.

We moved on for about half an hour, when suddenly Jack stopped, and upon coming up to him, he pointed to the tracks of men and camels. The tracks were numerous, and of different ages, some of them appearing quite recent, and some of them several days old.

We moved on again, but in a few minutes our motions were arrested by a signal from Hugh. He was near the crest of a low ridge of ground, about half a mile off on our right. We saw him dismount, and leaving his kneeling camel, creep cautiously along to the top of the ridge. In a moment he returned and made motions to us to join him. Upon coming up, Hugh informed us that he had been startled by the sounds of a human voice, and that upon creeping to the top of the hill he had discovered a black man ploughing in the field beyond. As he spoke a loud shout came over the crest of the ridge. I at once dismounted, and crept up high enough to obtain a view of the fellow. He was a stalwart black, quite naked, with the exception of a waist-cloth of blue cotton tied round his loins. He was engaged in lazily turning up the thin soil for a crop of some kind of grain. A crook stick of timber cut from the trunk, and one of the branches of a small tree, answered for a plough; to this rude instrument were harnessed a couple of small cows, by means of ropes of hide fastened to their horns. The furrows, or rather scratches, made by this machine, were not more than two or three inches deep. It was evident that we had arrived in a country in which geoponics, as a science, had been stationary since the days of the first tiller of the earth.

Having ascertained that the ploughman was alone, I directed Hugh and Jack to await my motions, and remounting my heirie, urged him across the rounded ridge at his best paces. The negro soon got sight of me, and instantly started off at full speed, but my beast was altogether

" He suddenly stopped, and poising a light spear, expressed, by his gestures, a very decided disposition to assume the offensive."

too fleet for him to escape. Finding that we were gaining upon him, he suddenly stopped, and poising a light spear, expressed, by his gestures, a very decided disposition to assume the offensive.

It was impossible to persuade him that my intentions were not hostile, and it was only by pointing my gun at him that I could make him throw away his spear and go back with me. He could speak only a few words of Arabic, but when Hugh addressed him in Tuaric he answered readily, and upon assurance that we wanted nothing of him but a little information in relation to the country, he laid aside his fears and became quite communicative.

He informed us that we were about sixty days' journey east of Timbuctoo, and that we were clear of the desert, and just upon the edge of a country inhabited by Tuarics, but that at present most of the men were away, engaged in an attack upon a large negro town in the southwest, the inhabitants of which had refused to pay the customary tribute. We could not have arrived at a more fortunate moment.

It was exceedingly gratifying to find from the man's replies that my calculations, as to our position, were not more than fifty miles in fault. We were a little farther east from Timbuctoo than by my estimation, but that might be explained upon the ground of the strong probability that the city is situated at a less distance from the ocean than is generally indicated upon the maps. At any rate we were just where I wished to be, and so near to our estimated position, as to warrant a very comfortable degree of confidence in the correctness or my dead reckoning for the future.

The negro informed us that Agades, a large caravan station, was due west of us, from whence a frequent communication was kept up with Sackatoo, the great capital of Houssa, and with the flourishing city of Kano, visited and described by Captain Clapperton. Our informant seemed to understand the country well. He told us that he belonged to a tribe of Kerdies, or Kaffirs, inhabiting a chain of hills in the south of Mandara; that he had been captured, and taken from place to place until he reached Kano, where he lived for three or four years, until purchased by a party of slave-dealers to be taken across the desert. On their way from Kano to Agades they were attacked by the Tuaries, and he thus came into the hands of his present masters.

Upon asking him the bearing of Sackatoo, he pointed to the southeast. He said that by taking this course we should get clear of the Tuaric country in three days, and that when once among the negroes, travelling would be comparatively safe, and that it would be easy to fall into some of the Kaffila tracks leading to Sackatoo. In reply to questions about a guide, he shook his head, and intimated pretty plainly that the less we had to do with his masters the better—that our best plan was to push on as rapidly as possible, giving a wide berth to any Tuaric village we might encounter, for, although the warriors were away, the women, children, and old men were not to be despised. There was but one objection to this plan, and that was, that our provisions were nearly exhausted. Upon mentioning this we were astonished by an offer from the negro to bring us a supply of meal. He took us to a rising ground and showed us a collection of mud and stone huts covering the slope of a hill about two miles off, promising that if we would encamp in the hollow and keep out of sight, he would go and get some provision and return in the course of the night. As an earnest of his intention, he insisted upon milking his cows into our bowl and giving us a good draught all around. There was an air of openness and honesty in the fellow's face and manner that would perhaps have induced us to confide in him, even had we not been so situated that it was impossible to do otherwise.

The sun was just setting when we finished our conversation, and we at once commenced unlading our camels and preparing to encamp, while the negro, who gave his name as Hassan Haboo, unyoked his team, and driving them before him, set off for his village. As soon as he was out of sight we replaced the loads and led our camels to another hollow about a quarter of a mile off. Here I resolved to leave Hugh and Jack with Kaloolah, while I kept watch at the first place; by this plan, if Hassan intended treachery, we should discover it in time to escape.

Never was suspicion more unjust. It was near midnight that my anxious ear detected the sound of footsteps. By putting my ear close to the ground I could distinguish the dull heavy tread of a camel mingled with the lighter foot-falls of his master, and in a few minutes they appeared in sight upon the crest of the hill. Descending into the hollow the stranger halted, apparently in doubt at not finding the objects he sought. As he was alone there could be no doubt that it was our new friend Hassan; so, without further hesitation, I rose from my cover and joined him.

He had brought with him a camel well laden with barley-meal, rice, and a quantity of hard bread, unleavened and baked in cakes of a rhomboidal shape. He had also a jar of honey, another of butter, and half a dozen strings of *kabobs*, which are small pieces of meat strung alternately, fat and lean, and roasted by twirling them before the fire, carefully baisting them the while with butter, and flavoring them with salt and the bruised seeds of a species of pungent pepper.

Without giving us time to make any disposition of the provision, Hassan insisted that we should mount and set out; and when it was objected that we could not find our way in the dark, he announced his determination to act as a guide. To all our questions his replies were vague and indefinite; but still there was something in his manner—an air of sincerity, and an unaffected expression of uneasiness and fear that compelled me to follow his advice.

The loads were put upon our beasts, and, leading them by their halters, Hugh and Jack brought up the rear, while, with Kaloolah, I kept close to our guide in order to have an eye upon his movements. The night was cool and pleasant, though the stars twinkled but dimly to eyes accustomed to the eager lustre with which they look down upon the desert. A soft southern zephyr, laden with moisture and melancholy, came noiseless, but with a capacity and a longing for sound, until catching the echoes of our footsteps it bore them murmuring with joy away. There was something in the scene, the time, the weather, the stealthy pace of our little party, the silence enforced by our guide, and our ignorance of what we had to fear, that made me feel, to say the least of it, uncommonly queer.

Hassan led the way, without once stopping or hesitating, and at the first blush of daylight he set us the example of mounting his camel, and still pressed on. It is singular, thought I, as the sun rose over a line of distant highlands, revealing a broad and smiling prospect of grass-covered, grove-besprinkled hill and plain; it is singular that the fellow evinces yet no disposition to leave us. At that moment the idea occurred to me that Hassan had joined us with the intention of escaping from his masters, the Tuarics, and that our chief danger was the danger of being pursued and caught with him in company. Calling Hugh to me, I rode up to Hassan, and questioned him, when he at once admitted that such was the case. He said that he had long resolved upon flight, and when he found that we were going in the direction of his country, he had made up his mind on the spot to go with us. That as for being pursued there were only a few old men and boys to pursue us, and that he had managed matters so that his flight would not be suspected for a day or two, when he would be beyond reach.

"Do with me as you please," he continued, taking my hand and putting it on the back of his neck. "I am your slave, but I can never go back."

The fellow, as a guide and as a stout addition to our little force, was worth running some risk for; so we determined, without much hesitation, to enlist him into our ranks, and to accept his supply of provisions without inquiring too curiously whether he had been fully justified in stealing them or not.

BY THE EDITOR.

The editor here takes the liberty of condensing into a few words six long chapters of Mr. Romer's manuscript, which are devoted to a description of the five months' journey through the negro countries that lie between the northern frontiers of Houssa and the extreme southern boundary of Mandara.

Our travellers passed through the Tuaric country in safety, owing to the absence of the greater portion of the population. When they reached a little town called Dirkim, they exchanged their camels for four fine horses and two pack mules. From this place they proceeded under a succession of guides to Sackatoo, the capital of the Fellatah dominions. Here Mr. Romer disposed of a portion of his goods at an advantageous rate, and purchased three Moorish muskets and a quantity of cowrie shells, which were the current coin of the more southern country. He also purchased a bright-eyed young negress to serve as an attendant to Kaloolah. Four months after leaving Sackatoo, they reached the Kerdie country to the south of Dah Koollah. Here they found an agreeable change in the character of the land. There was every indication that they were not more than three or four hundred miles from Framazugda, Kaloolah's home. From this point we must let our author speak for himself.

CHAPTER XXXIII.

Forest Sights and Sounds—Kaloolah's Feelings—The Great River—A Fine Prospect—The Froalbell—A Strong Camp—Constructing a Raft—A Stroll in the Forest—A Lion in the Path—The Boa—Crossing the Yah'nil Nebbé.

OR a long time had we pursued our way through the sombre forest, all silent—subdued in spirit, and disposed to bow reverentially to receive the blessings which the religious old trees, with outstretched arms seemed invoking upon our heads. From all sides arose curious and horrid noises, that, like the grotesque grinning faces of Gothic architecture, served only to increase the pervading solemnity—the screeching of parrots, paroquets, and an infinite variety of birds unknown to naturalists even by name; the chattering of myriads of monkeys; the occasional laugh and growl of animals of the hyena family; the wild rush and whir of startled deer, harts, roebucks, and the gliding, rustling sound of huge snakes, moving along the ground, or around the gigantic trunks, and among the verdure of the gnarled branches.

"You are silent, Kaloolah; what are you thinking of?" I demanded.

"I am not thinking." replied Kaloolah, "I am only feeling."

"And how are you feeling, pray?"

"As I did once when I stood in the inner hall of the great mound temple of Kiloam. There, however, all was silence—with nothing to disturb the sense of God's presence and power but here—this—oh, this is horrible!"

"What is horrible? This shade—this gloom—"

"No, no; not the forest; not this cool shade; not this pleasing gloom, but these sounds that so mock and threaten as we go—these gibbering fiends, up there in the trees, that grin upon us so. Oh, how pleasant it would be to have this shade to ourselves—to be able to move beneath this umbrageous canopy without being annoyed and startled by such terrible sights and sounds—so strange, yet so familiar—familiar, yet none the less horrible. They do not frighten me so much

"You are silent, Kaloolah!"

since I know, Jon'than, you can protect me, but they somehow frighten my heart."

"Indeed, Kaloolah, so young, so innocent, and yet thy heart has recollections of grinning faces, and mocking voices, that the noises around us revive! Courage! we shall soon be through this wood. —— Well, Hassan, what now?"

"The great river is in front of us," replied Hassan; and in a few minutes we emerged from the dark forest, and stood upon its banks. There lay the broad stream, some fifty or sixty feet beneath us, and beyond it a vast expanse of open, rolling country, dotted with clumps of trees, and undulating with rounded hills, through which opened up long vistas of surpassing beauty. In the middle ground the hills grew more varied in their forms, and more abrupt, serving to link, by an easy transition, the milder beauty of the river's bank with the lofty grandeur of a chain of towering mountains in the background.

From the foot of the bank upon which we stood extended a wide beach of dark, gray pebbles and sand. It took us some time to find a spot at which our animals could descend. From the beach the view was much restricted of the country on the other side of the river, but the loss was made up by the pleasing outline of the bank, and the magnificence of the masses of rock and verdure that towered above us behind, and extended as far up and down as the eye could reach. Gigantic flowering creepers, splendid specimens of the rock-hugging ceres, and a magnificent flower, like the morning-glory, but as large as a man's hat, and of a brilliant blue and gold, covered and concealed the angular points and rough projections of the cliffs. Among these, as in the forest we had passed, revelled a thousand different kinds of birds of the most glorious plumage: little paroquets, bedecked in all the prismatic colors; humming-birds; golden and purple wood-peckers, and a little bird that Kaloolah clapped her hands at the sight of, and called the *kinkapal*, or gem-bird. Around its head and neck were little tufts of plumage of different hues, that reflected the sunlight as brightly as a brilliant of the first water. The wings and body were of a plain gray, while the head and neck were clothed as with a little casque and corselet of diamonds, rubies, and opals. Here, too, floated several specimens of the *froulbell*, a bird which may justly be pronounced one of the greatest ornithological curiosities in the world. Its body is about the size of a wren, and without wings, but from every point on its surface comes out the most delicate feather streamers, a foot or more in length. Wonderful is the delicacy and lightness of this large mass of plumage in which the little body of the bird is concealed. The finest feathers of the ostrich, or the bird of paradise, are coarse in comparison. The outer extremity of each feather is of a pure white, but towards the body glow the brightest hues of green, blue, purple, and gold, so that the wind, parting the masses of graceful plumage as the bird floats slowly along, reveals each moment new combinations of color to the delighted eye. But not the least curious part of the froulbell's structure is the machinery with which, in the absence of wings, it is furnished for locomotion. The bill is simply a tube, open at both ends, and extending directly through the head, so that one orifice is directly in front, the other behind. From the middle of this tube, or from the top of the head, rises a hollow, cartilaginous globe, capable of expansion and contraction ; this communicates with the tube, in which are two valves, the one in front opening towards the globe, the one behind, away from it. When the globe is expanded a vacuum is produced, and the air rushes in through the valve in front. When the globe contracts, this valve closes, and the air is forced out through the other valve behind ; and thus, by an alternate action of suction and propulsion, the froulbell is able to move along slowly, when the wind is not too high. The flexibility of the neck enables the bird to direct the tube to any angle of elevation, and thus, aided by the legerity of its plumage, to ascend to any height, although it generally flies low in search or small insects and animaculæ, which, when sucked into the globe, are retained in the convolution of a lining mucous membrane, and afterwards transmitted into the stomach. The passage of the air through the valves occasions a pleasant flute-like sound, which varies in tone and quality with the size of the bird and the rapidity of its motion.

But it was no time for ecstasies over the beauties of the animal and vegetable kingdom, with a broad and rapid river in front of us, and with no means at hand of crossing it. Again and again I questioned our two guides, but they were firm in the assertion that we should have to travel several days before encountering a Kerdie village, and that then we might not find either ford or ferriage. The only plan was to make some kind of a boat or raft upon which we could carry our luggage, and to swim our horses across, despite the danger of attack from the crocodiles, with which the river appeared alive. As this would require some time, preparations were made for a more permanent encampment than usual.

A little rocky peninsula jutted into the river, and was connected to the main land by a narrow isthmus. The sides were quite steep and jagged, rising about five or six feet in height, or enough to protect us from the visits of the river monsters, while a large fire upon the narrow neck afforded a full defence toward the land. The area of the peninsula was just sufficient to accommodate our party, beasts and all. Here we picketed our steeds, pitched Kaloolah's tent, and arranged our baggage. The rest of the day was consumed in building a shanty of bushes, cutting fodder for our horses, and collecting firewood.

We passed a pleasant night, although, had not our ears been hardened by our long and intimate companionship with wild beasts of every description, we should perhaps have been disturbed by the loud whining and plashing of the crocodile, the deep breathing and floundering of the hippopotamus, the bark of the jackal and hyena, or the thundering roar of the lion that occasionally reverberated along the cliffs, startling for a while to silence the inferior beasts. We slept, however, with an unusual feeling of security. Our position was a strong one, in fact perfectly impregnable—a real little Gibraltar of an encampment to our prowling and growling foes.

The next morning we started in search of some kind of material for a raft. We had not gone far up the stream when we came across a large hollow tree, about fifty feet in height, without branches, except near the top, where it put forth ten or twelve arms, somewhat resembling the sturdy and awkward-looking limbs of the dragon-tree. It was little more than two feet in diameter, and although decayed near the roots, so as to expose its hollow-heartedness, is still seemed to enjoy a vigorous old age.

"There," said Jack, "that would be just the thing if we had it down, and cut up into three or four lengths, with any way of stopping the ends."

"The easiest thing in the world. You see to getting it down, and I will find something with which to cover the ends. Or, rather, as we shall need lashing to hold the pieces together, you shall manufacture the necessary rope out of the skins that I will furnish, and Hugh shall superintend cutting the tree."

Leaving Kaloolah and her maid in charge of Jack, and Hugh with the two guides hard at work upon the tree, I took Hassan with me, and moved into the woods in search of skins. Nothing of sufficient size could come amiss, and it took but a short time to shoot and flay more than twenty animals, among whom hardly two were of the same species.

By sunset Hugh had the tree down, and Jack had twisted a large quantity of rope. The tree had now to be cut into three pieces of about twelve feet in length, the openings at the ends to be secured with skins, and the logs got into the water and firmly lashed together into a raft. Without any of the proper means and appliances, this was a work of time, and it was not until the fifth day that the raft was ready for its burden.

It was early on the morning of the sixth, that, accompanied by Kaloolah, and the lively Clefenha, I ascended the bank for a final reconnoisance of the country on the other bank of the river. It was not my intention to wander far, but allured by the beauty of the scene, and the promise of a still better view from a higher crag, we moved along the edge of the bank until we had got nearly two miles from our camp. At this point the line of the bank curved towards the river so as to make a beetling promontory of a hundred feet perpendicular descent. The gigantic trees grew on the very brink, many of them throwing their long arms far over the shore below. The trees generally grew wide apart, and there was little or no underwood, but many of the trunks were wreathed with the verdure of parasites and creepers so that the forest vistas were often shut off by immense columns of green leaves and flowers. The stems of some of these creepers were truly wonderful: one, from which depended large bunches of scarlet berries, had, not unfrequently, stems as large as a man's body. In some cases one huge plant of this kind, ascending with an incalculable prodigality of lignin, by innumerable convolutions, would stretch itself out, and, embracing several trees in its folds, mat them together in one dense mass of vegetation.

Suddenly we noticed that the usual sounds of the forest had almost ceased around us. Deep in the wood we could still hear the chattering of monkeys and the screeching of parrots. Never before had our presence created any alarm among the denizens of the tree-tops; or, if it had, it had merely excited to fresh clamor, without putting them to flight. We looked around for the cause of this sudden retreat.

"Perhaps," I replied to Kaloolah's inquiry, "there is a storm gathering, and they are gone to seek a shelter deeper in the wood."

We advanced close to the edge of the bank, and looked out into the the broad daylight that poured down from above on flood and field. There was the same bright smile on the distant fields and hills; the same clear sheen in the deep water; the same lustrous stillness in the perfumed air; not a single prognostic of any commotion among the elements.

I placed my gun against a tree, and took a seat upon an exposed portion of one of its roots. Countless herds of animals, composed of quaggas, zebras, gnus, antelopes, hart-beasts, roeboks, springboks, buffalos, wild boars, and a dozen other kinds, for which my recollection of African travels furnished no names, were roaming over the fields on the other side of the river, or quietly reposing in the shade of the scattered mimosas, or beneath the groups of lofty palms. A herd of thirty or forty tall ungainly figures came in sight, and took their way, with awkward but rapid pace, across the plain. I knew them at once to be giraffes, although they were the first that we had seen. I was straining my eyes to discover the animal that pursued them, when Kaloolah called to me to come to her. She was about fifty yards farther down the stream than where I was sitting. With an unaccountable degree of carelessness, I arose and went towards her, leaving my gun leaning against the tree. As I advanced, she ran out to the extreme point of the little promontory I have mentioned, where her maid was standing, and pointed to something over the edge of the cliff.

"Oh, Jon'than!" she exclaimed, "what a curious and beautiful flower? Come, and try if you can get it for me!"

Advancing to the crest of the cliff, we stood looking down its precipitous sides to a point some twenty feet below, where grew a bunch of wild honeysuckles. Suddenly a startling noise, like the roar of thunder, or like the boom of a thirty-two pounder, rolled through the wood, fairly shaking the sturdy trees, and literally making the ground quiver beneath our feet. Again it came, that appalling and indescribably awful sound! and so close as to completely stun us. Roar upon roar, in quick succession, now announced the coming of the king of beasts. "The lion! the lion!--Oh, God of mercy! where is my gun?" I started forward, but it was too late. Alighting, with a magnificent bound, into the open space in front of us, the monster stopped, as if somewhat taken aback by the novel appearance of his quarry, and crouching his huge carcass close to the ground, uttered a few deep snuffling sounds, not unlike the preliminary crankings and growlings of a heavy steam-engine, when it first feels the pressure of the steam.

He was, indeed, a monster!--fully twice as large as the largest specimen of his kind that was ever condemned, by gaping curiosity, to the confinement of the cage. His body was hardly less in size than that of a dray-horse; his paw as large as the foot of an elephant; while his head! —what can be said of such a head? Concentrate the fury, the power, the capacity, and the disposition for evil of a dozen thunder-storms into a round globe, about two feet in diameter, and one would then be able to get an idea of the terrible expression of that head and face, enveloped and set off as it was by the dark frame-work of bristling mane.

The lower jaw rested upon the ground; the mouth was slightly open, showing the rows of white teeth and the blood-red gums, from which the lips were retracted in a majestic and right kingly grin. The brows and the skin around the eyes were corrugated into a splendid glory of radiant wrinkles, in the centre of which glowed two small globes, like opals, but with a dusky lustrousness that no opal ever yet attained.

For a few moments he remained motionless, and then, as if satisfied with the result of his close scrutiny, he began to slide along the ground towards us; slowly one monstrous paw was protruded after the other; slowly the huge tufted tail waved to and fro, sometimes striking his hollow flanks, and occasionally coming down upon the ground with a sound like the falling of heavy clods upon a coffin. There could be no doubt of his intention to charge us, when near enough for a spring.

And was there no hope? Not the slightest, at least for myself. It was barely possible that one victim would satisfy him, or that, in the contest that was about to take place, I might, if he did not kill me at the first blow, so wound him as to indispose him for any further exercise of his power, and that thus Kaloolah would escape. As for me, I felt that my time had come. With no weapon but my long knife, what chance was there against such a monster? I cast one look at the gun that was leaning so carelessly against the tree beyond him, and thought how easy it would be to send a bullet through one of those glowing eyes, into the depths of that savage brain. Never was there a fairer mark! But, alas! it was impossible to reach the gun! Truly, "there was a lion in the path."

I turned to Kaloolah, who was a little behind me. Her face expressed a variety of emotions; she could not speak or move, but she stretched out her hand, as if to pull me back. Behind her crouched the black, whose features were contracted into the awful grin of intense terror; she was too much frightened to scream, but in her face a thousand yells of agony and fear were incarnated.

I remember not precisely what I said, but, in the fewest words, I intimated to Kaloolah that the lion would, probably, be satisfied with attacking me; that she must run by us as soon as he sprang upon me, and, returning to the camp, waste no time, but set out at once under the charge of Hugh and Jack. She made no reply, and I waited for none, but facing the monster, advanced slowly towards him—the knife was firmly grasped in my right hand, my left side a little turned towards him, and my left arm raised, to guard as much as possible against the first crushing blow of his paw. Further than this I had formed no plan of battle. In such a contest the mind has but little to do—all depends upon the instinct of the muscles; and well for a man if good training has developed that instinct to the highest. I felt that I could trust mine, and that my brain need not bother itself as to the manner my muscles were going to act.

Within thirty feet of my huge foe I stopped—cool, calm as a statue; not an emotion agitated me. No hope, no fear: death was too certain to permit either passion. There is something in the conviction of the immediate inevitableness of death that represses fear; we are then compelled to take a better look at the king of terrors, and we find that he is not so formidable as we imagined. Look at him with averted glances and half-closed eyes, and he has a most imposing, overawing presence; but face him, eye to eye; grasp his proffered hand manfully, and he sinks, from a right royal personage, into a contemptible old gate-keeper on the turnpike of life.

I had time to think of many things, although it must not be supposed, from the leisurely way in which I here tell the story, that the whole affair occupied much time. Like lightning flashing from link to link along a chain conductor, did memory illuminate, almost simultaneously, the chain of incidents that measured my path in life, and that connected the present with the past. I could see the whole of my back track "blazed," as clearly as ever was a forest path by a woodman's axe; and ahead! ah, there was not much to see ahead! 'T was but a short view; death hedged in the scene. In a few minutes my eyes would be opened to the pleasant sights beyond; but, for the present, death commanded all attention. And such a death! But why such a death? What better death, except on the battle-field, in defence of one's country? To be killed by a lion! Surely, there is a spice of dignity about it, maugre the being eaten afterwards. Suddenly the monster stopped, and erected his tail, stiff and motionless, in the air. Strange as it may seem, the conceit occurred to me that the motion of his tail had acted as a safety-valve to the pent-up muscular energy within: "He has shut the steam off from the 'scape-pipe, and now he turns it on to his locomotive machinery. God have mercy upon me! —He comes!"

But he did not come! At the instant, the light figure of Kaloolah rushed past me: "Fly, fly, Jon'than!" she wildly exclaimed, as she dashed forward directly towards the lion. Quick as thought, I divined her purpose, and sprang after her, grasping her dress, and pulling her forcibly back, almost from within those formidable jaws. The astonished animal gave several jumps sideways and backwards, and stopped, crouching to the ground and growling and lashing his sides with renewed fury. He was clearly taken aback by our unexpected charge upon him, but it was evident that he was not to be frightened into abandoning his prey. His mouth was made up for us, and there could be no doubt, if his motions were a little slow, that he considered us as good as gorged.

"Fly, fly, Jon'than!" exclaimed Kaloolah, as she struggled to break from my grasp. "Leave me! Leave me to die alone, but oh! save yourself, quick! along the bank. You can escape— fly!'"

"Never, Kaloolah," I replied, fairly forcing her with quite an exertion of strength behind me. "Back, back! Free my arm! Quick, quick! He comes!" It was no time for gentlenesss. Roughly shaking her relaxing grasp from my arm, she sunk powerless, yet not insensible, to the ground, while I had just time to face the monster and plant one foot forward to receive him.

He was in the very act of springing! His huge carcass was even rising under the impulsion of his contracting muscles, when his action was arrested in a way so unexpected, so wonderful, and so startling that my senses were for the moment thrown into perfect confusion. Could I trust my sight, or was the whole affair the illusion of a horrid dream? It seemed as if one of the gigantic creepers I have mentioned had suddenly quitted the canopy above, and, endowed with life and a huge pair of widely distended jaws, had darted with the rapidity of lightning upon the crouching beast. There was a tremendous shaking of the tree-tops, and a confused wrestling, and jumping, and whirling over and about, amid a cloud of upturned roots, and earth, and leaves accompanied with the most terrific roars and groans. As I looked again, vision grew more distinct. An immense body, gleaming with purple, green, and gold appeared convoluted around the majestic branches overhead, and stretching down, was turned two or three times around the struggling lion, whose head and neck were almost concealed from sight within the cavity of a pair of jaws still more capacious than his own.

Thus, then, was revealed the cause of the sudden silence throughout the woods. It was the presence of the boa that had frightened the monkey and feathered tribes into silence. How opportunely was his presence manifested to us! A moment more, and it would have been too late.

Gallantly did the lion struggle in the folds of his terrible enemy, whose grasp each instant grew more firm and secure, and most astounding were those frightful yells of rage and fear. The huge body of the snake, fully two feet in diameter, where it depended from the trees, presented the most curious appearances, and in such quick succession that the eye could scarcely follow them. At one moment smooth and flexile, at the next rough and stiffened, or contracted into great knots—at one moment overspread with a thousand tints of reflected color, the next distended so as to transmit through the skin the golden gleams of the animal lightning that coursed up and down within.

"Over and over rolled the struggling beast."

Over and over rolled the struggling beast; but in vain all his strength, in vain all his efforts to free himself. Gradually his muscles relaxed in their exertions; his roar subsided to a groan; his tongue protruded from his mouth, and his fetid breath mingled with a strong sickly odor from the serpent, diffused itself through the air, producing a sense of oppression, and a feeling of weakness like that from breathing some deleterious gas.

I looked around me. Kaloolah was on her knees, and the negress insensible upon the ground a few paces behind her. A sensation of giddiness warned me that it was time to retreat. Without a word I raised Kaloolah in my arms, ran towards the now almost motionless animals, and, turning along the bank, reached the tree against which my gun was leaning.

Darting back, I seized the prostrate negress and bore her off in the same way. By this time both females had recovered their voices, Clefenha exercising hers in a succession of shrieks that compelled me to shake her somewhat rudely, while Kaloolah eagerly besought me to hurry back to the camp. There was now, however, no occasion for hurry. The recovery of my gun altered the state of the case, and my curiosity was excited to witness the progress of deglutition on a large scale, which the boa was probably about to exhibit. It was impossible, however, to resist Kaloolah's entreaties, and after stepping up closer to the animals for one good look, I reluctantly consented to turn back.

The lion was quite dead, and, with a slow motion, the snake was uncoiling himself from his prey and from the tree above. As well as I could judge, without seeing him straightened out, he was between ninety and one hundred feet in length—not quite so long as the serpent with which the army of Regulus had its famous battle, or as many of the same animals that I have since seen; but, as the reader will allow, a very respectable sized snake. I have often regretted that we did not stop until at least he had commenced his meal. Had I been alone I should have done so. At it was, curiosity had to yield to my own sense of prudence, and to Kaloolah's fears.

We returned to our camp, where we found our raft all ready. The river was fully half a mile wide, and it was necessary to make two trips; the first with the women and baggage, and the last with the horses. It is unnecessary to dwell in detail upon all the difficulties we encountered from the rapid currents and whirling eddies of the stream; suffice it that we got across in time for supper and a good night's sleep, and early in the morning resumed our march through the most enchanting country in the world.

CHAPTER XXXIV.

THE first day there appeared no signs of human life. Countless herds of wild animals roamed over the plains. Sometimes we were completely surrounded, as far as the eye could extend, with herds of quagas, gnus, antelopes of five or six different species, buffalos, wild boars, giraffes, ostriches, and elephants. Each moment as we advanced we started from their lairs, in the crevices of the calcareous rocks, or from beneath the thick herbage, the leopard, the hyena, and the lion. The prestige, however, of the latter had departed— he was no longer the unconquerable, and, except at night, we had no fear of an attack. The elephants and wild buffalo were much more dangerous, and repeatedly we had to make large detours to avoid them.

Several times we mistook a collection of lofty ant-hills for human habitations, and as often did we fancy the figures of the tall ourang-outangs, who stalked about upon the edges of the cliffs, to be those of men.

On the second day we entered a valley, through which meandered a shallow tributary of the *Yah'nil nebbé*, the great river that we had just crossed. The scenery along its banks was singularly picturesque and imposing. Sometimes the valley spread itself out so as to leave a space for fertile savannahs along the river's banks, where grew clumps of palms, with a peculiar variety of the baobab, and a tree that I took to be a species of the Indian banian. Numerous fruit-bearing trees were scattered about; one of them producing a fruit like a large green-gage, but without a seed stone. The flavor was delicious. Another, producing a fruit about a foot long and an inch in diameter—it consisted of a brilliant scarlet rind, containing a transparent pinkish fluid, with the *bouquet* of *Chateau Margeaux* and a taste resembling champagne punch. It was precisely similar in its effects to the latter drink. Luckily we were cautioned in time by Kaloolah, and indulged no further than to a little pleasant elevation of the spirits.

The fifth day we got sight of several stone huts erected upon the jutting promontory of rock that overlooked the level savannah. The inhabitants did not await our arrival. I rode forward alone, and made signs to them. The men stopped, and poised their spears, while the women continued their retreat. Upon attempting to approach them they also took to flight, and disappeared in the deep gullies and dense jungles.

As we advanced, clusters of huts became more frequent; in fact the country seemed quite populous, but it was impossible to get speech with any of the people. The only conclusion we could come to was, that they took us for a party of slave-hunters, and that our guns excited their alarm.

We were now thinking about encamping for the night when Hugh rode up and informed us that just beyond a thicket of acacias he had discovered a walled town upon the slope of a hill. We spurred forward, and upon emerging from the wood there lay an open plain about a mile broad, covered with tall grass, and beyond it a town of about fifty houses.

We had hardly entered the plain when we heard the sound of drums and wooden horns. Several horsemen appeared, galloping across the field, and men could be seen running about upon the slope of the hill and the tops of the houses and walls.

We advanced steadily to the foot of the hill. A straight path led up to a wooden gate which was closed and defended by towers on either side. In these towers and along the walls were stationed men and women, armed with spears and bows, which they flourished over their heads with furious gestures and cries, intended to intimidate us and encourage themselves. It is to be hoped that they succeeded better in doing the latter than they did in their attempts at the first.

Halting at a proper distance, I directed Hassan to ride forward and make signals of friendship to them. He advanced until within a bow-shot, when he dismounted, and laying his gun upon the ground, pointed to it. He again advanced a few steps forward, bearing a staff with one of Kaloolah's linen garments tied to it for a flag. The shouts and gesticulations recommenced, and, the arrows beginning to fall about him, Hassan was compelled to make a rapid retreat.

"It is clear enough they don't like a black skin," exclaimed Jack; "suppose I give them a look at the red and white paint of my figure-head. Perhaps they have a taste in colors."

Dismounting and taking the emblem of peace in his hand, he went forward on foot. Arrived to within a proper distance, he commenced a long oration in the language of signs. There was a copiousness and profusion of imagery in Jack's style that would have made his fortune in pantomime. It had its effects upon the inhabitants of the town. A man was lowered over the wall, which was not more than twelve feet high, by a rope. He came towards Jack, when the two saluted each other with a profusion of gestures— the stranger repeatedly putting his hand upon his head and bowing, while Jack, doffing his straw hat, grasped his fore-lock and scraped his foot in true quarter-deck style.

We were growing a little impatient at the length of the colloquy, when Jack made a sign to us to advance. As we came up, the natives, who were now increased in numbers, by the addition of five or six from the walls, stood their ground and gazed at us with a peculiar expression of interest. At this moment Kaloolah threw back her veil. The movement quite delighted them, seeming to inspire them with confidence in the honesty of our intentions. " Framazug! Framazug!" they exclaimed, and two or three running towards the gate, which was now partially open, returned with an old man, who at once addressed us in the Framazug tongue.

Nothing could exceed the delight of Kaloolah when she heard his words. She pressed forward, and at once engaged the Kyptile in a most animated conversation. They talked so rapidly that it was with difficulty that I could follow them.

It appeared that these were a people very friendly to the Framazugs, from the borders of whose country we were now distant only about ten days' journey, and that Kaloolah's father was still alive. As to any thing further in relation to the internal affairs of Framazugda, the speaker knew nothing.

Two dignified personages, armed with whips of bull's-hide, with which they kept back the crowd, now invited us, in the name of the *Matcham* or king of the town, to enter and enjoy the hospitalities of Soconale. We found his majesty seated on a stone bench, just within the gate. There was no attempt at royal display. Two or three elderly men, probably cabinet ministers, sat on either side of him ; and half a dozen tall fellows, with spears and large shields of bull's-hide, seemed to act as guards. The king was quite old, and, unlike many of his subjects, was very fat. Our conversation lasted until it was dark. Torches were then produced, and the old king waddled before us up a broad, straight street, until we came to an enclosure, surrounded with a picket fence, in the centre of which stood a large one-story stone house. Here the Matcham informed us we were to take up our quarters.

In front of the entrance to the house a large fire was blazing. From several huge earthen pots issued clouds of promising odors. The stone floors were covered with matting, new and clean, and from the roof our beds were suspended with ropes—there was first a heavy wooden frame, upon which was spread to the thickness of a foot a layer of the freshly hatchelled fibres of a kind of *spartum* or rush, and over this a fine flexible mat of the same material. Soft, yet cool, there were never beds more luxurious— too much so for us; and for the first two or three nights we were com-

" The stranger repeatedly putting his hand upon his head and bowing."

pelled to give them up and sleep on the stone floor. So much for the power of habit! Strange that such a power should be so much neglected, and that many sensible people, parents and teachers, should confine themselves to the prevention of bad habits, caring nothing for the inculcation of good, and imagine that they can make up for the latter by a stuffing of principles. "Good principles are very well; but good, strong, positive habits are better," I exclaimed, throwing myself upon the stones, where in a few minutes we were all in a sound and refreshing sleep.

In the morning we had a message from the king inquiring after our healths, and shortly he himself appeared, followed by two or three servants bearing a fresh supply of provisions. The remains of our supper were removed, and a profusion of good things arranged for breakfast upon small wooden tables, standing about a foot high from the floor—fresh eggs, milk and honey, rice cakes, wheaten bread, with a great many dishes and fruits that no Christian ever heard of before. In the centre of the table was an immense egg-shell, about a foot in diameter, which, furnished with a rim and feet of gold, answered for a punch-bowl. Into this the Matcham emptied the contents of several of the red peduncles of the good and evil tree which I have mentioned. A servant now presented a bouquet of flowers, from which the Matcham, selecting three, gave us each one. They were in color of a deep orange varied with blue. The calyx was about the size and shape of a small tea-cup, and situated at a right angle to the hollow stem, which served as the handle of a dipper, and which, passing through the side of the flower down to the bottom, answered, also, the purpose of a straw in a tumbler of mint-julep. The dew was still on them, and an enchanting fragrance was exhaled from the little vermilion, lily-shaped anthers, that far surpassed the mingled perfumes, while it excited the heart-filling memories, of musk, patchouli, and *eau de cologne*. Following the example of the Matcham, we dipped our flower-cup into the egg-shell and finished our breakfast by sucking up two or three draughts of nectar, such as was never offered by Ganymede to Jove.

After breakfast we walked out to see the town. There was nothing, however, of much interest in the view. The houses were all of one story, generally surrounded by a stone fence, and scattered around without any regard to regularity, except on the borders of the large avenue which ran from gate to gate.

The inhabitants were a different race from any that we had yet seen. They had none of the negro characteristics. Their skins were of a light copper color, their hair straight and flowing, and their noses aquiline. Their dress consisted mainly of a loose shirt of linen, confined to the waist with a woollen sash. Sandals of untanned skin protected their feet, and strips of feather-cloth adorned their heads and necks.

After our walk we stopped at the palace and were invited to a seat beneath a shady arbor in front of the porch. Several dignitaries of the court here joined us, while the curious crowd stood around at a little distance.

The Matcham informed us that he was hereditary ruler, not only of Soconale, but of several other towns to the south. He represented the country, between his dominions and Framazugda, to be thinly inhabited by other tribes of the same people, who all lived in walled towns, and who were more or less dependants of the great Sultan Shounsé, whose power, however, was inadequate to their protection from the attacks of a very barbarous white people who lived about ten days' journey east of his, the Matcham's towns.

" And what is the name of this people? " I inquired.

" They call themselves the Jalla," replied the king. " They are exceedingly cruel and ferocious, but we don't dread them much, because they can't make thunder and lightning. It is the negroes from the north who are our worst enemies. Once upon a time my people, the Kyptiles, were very numerous, and inhabited the plains all along the Yah'nil Nebbé. But the negroes began to come across and seize our people, and carry them away. We couldn't stand before their guns : and after fighting with them for a great many years, we were compelled to fly higher up, and build our towns with walls. Even now they frequently come in large parties and traverse our country quite to the borders of Framazugda.

" To the southwest there used to live a very good people, who were negroes ; but other blacks, with fire-arms, came upon them, and have taken possession of their country, and have extended their conquests clear up the hills to Framazugda, so that we have now the Jallas on the east, the Manda and Koolla blacks on the north, and the Phollo and Foota Jal negroes on the west. Our only friends are the Framazugs on the south."

After condoling with the poor old king upon the threatening aspect of his foreign relations, we took our leave, and retired to our quarters.

It was nearly a week before the hospitable king and people of Soconale would consent to our departure. We were compelled to demand an audience of leave, at which I distributed a quantity of beads, coral and amber, to the different dignitaries of the court. To the king I gave a brass basin that I had purchased at Sackatoo, a silk tobe and cap, and a pistol with a few charges of powder. The latter was received with an expression of reverence and awe, that I felt sure would soon elevate it into an object of adoration.

Outside the gate we found our escort drawn up for us. It consisted of a dozen men, well mounted upon small black horses, and armed with bows and long spears. Besides these there were two mounted guides, one of whom was the old fellow who had acted as our interpreter ; and three men, on foot, each leading a buffalo, by a rope through his nose. The huge packs of provisions that towered from the backs of these animais, proved that the worthy Matcham did not intend that we should starve by the way.

With the king at their head, the whole population of Soconale accompanied us to the banks of a little stream; here our final adieus were exchanged. Shall I confess it? it was with moistened eyes, and a yearning at the heart that I waved my hand to the simple and affectionate Kyptiles, and spurred up the steep banks of the rippling brook. If Framazugda had not been before me, I could have accepted the king's urgent invitation to stay with them, and defend them against the Mandi and the Jalla.

CHAPTER XXXV.

The Djébel el Kumri—Slave-Hunters Abroad—The Footas and Their Guns—Jack's Opinion of the Footas—A Plundered Village—Military Precautions—A Kimboo Scout—An Accession of Strength—Midnight Musings—Planning an Ambuscade—Caught in Our Own Trap—A Charge and Repulse—The Kimboos' Revenge.

EN days brought us to the base of a lofty chain of mountains—a spur of the Djébel el Kumri, or *Lunæ Montes*—stretching to the southwest. On either hand the peaks shot up to a very great height, and were covered with snow; but in front of us, to the south, they fell away, so as to withdraw their fir-covered summits from the region of perpetual congelation. Along the base of these lesser peaks our route lay on the fifth day after leaving Soconale. A beautiful plain extended as far as the eye could see to the west; several rivers meandered through it, and, away in the distance, a broad silver lake glittered in the noontide sun. This plain, once populous, was now, our guides informed us, almost uninhabited—the Foota Jals having nearly exterminated the Kerdie population.

At the banks of a large river, flowing in a northerly course, our route turned, due south, into the mountains. A succession of beautiful valleys opened up an easy and pleasant path. As we advanced, we fell upon a broad trail of men and horses, going south. We followed it for several hours, until we came to the remains of a village, which had all the marks of a recent fire. The blackened stone walls were standing, but the woodwork and thatched roofs were gone. There were no living beings in sight, but, upon riding up to the top of the hill, upon which the village was built, we discovered half a dozen bodies, horribly mutilated, and within the huts, the half-roasted remains of several more. The bodies were neither Kyptiles nor negroes, but apparently mulattoes, or a mixed race.

Thus, then, was confirmed the story which some herdsmen had told us the day before—that several parties of slave-hunters were abroad. Our Kyptiles were terribly frightened. "We shall all be captured and killed!" exclaimed Sooloo Phar, the captain of our escort, in a very doleful tone.

277

"Silence!" I exclaimed, with a voice and look that made Sooloo almost jump from his saddle. "Are you a man, and frightened before you see your enemy? What are you afraid of? Are we not twenty well-armed men?"

"But they are armed with guns!" replied Sooloo. "If they were Kerdies, or even the fierce Jalla, I would show you what a Kyptile can do! But these are Foota Jals, and who can stand before their guns?"

"That, for their guns!" I exclaimed, snapping my fingers with as contemptuous an expression as I could conveniently assume. "That, for their guns! Have not we guns, too? and, besides, your bows and spears are not such poor weapons in comparison. Charge a party of these Foota the same as you would a party of Jalla, and you will find that they will run like sheep. Come, move on : as for hiding ourselves, or turning back, I would n't think of the thing if a thousand Footas were in the way! Ask Mr. Thompson, there, he knows all about guns, what he thinks of turning back, because there is a chance of meeting with a party of slave-hunters, armed with their rusty old guns, and powder that wont send a bullet as far as you can throw a long spear?"

"My opinion!" replied Jack, "my opinion is, the Footas may go to the devil! If these gentlemen are afraid of their guns, suppose you let Hugh and myself ride ahead, and when we get sight of those land-sharks we 'll take their guns away, and put plugs in their muzzles, tie up their triggers, and empty their pans, and then our friends here can ride up, and have a fight upon equal terms."

Jack's quizzical proposition, when translated, with all gravity, into the language of our friends, seemed to please them mightily, and, added to my own assurances, restored a degree of confidence that made them quite willing to push on. There could be no doubt of their natural courage, and their readiness to fight on even terms; but it was difficult to shake off their overwhelming apprehension of fire-arms. Although somewhat accustomed to our guns, they could hardly be persuaded to touch them; and when we rested them upon the ground, at our halting-places, our guards would place themselves at some distance, and eying them with an air of veneration, mutter charms and prayers. I almost wished for a brush with a party of slave-hunters, in order to disabuse them of their paralyzing prejudice.

Upon dismounting, and closely examining the ruins, and the decaying bodies, it became evident that not more than three days had elapsed since the visit of the Footas; and that, consequently, their parties had not yet returned from the south, in which direction a broad trail indicated that they had gone after firing the village. It was necessary to move with caution to guard against surprise. Jack, with one of the guides and two other Kyptiles, led the way; Hugh and two Kyptiles brought up the rear; while, with Hassan, Kaloolah, and the main body of the army, including the buffaloes and baggage, I occupied the centre. Nor were our flanks neglected. A scout moved along the river's bank, so as to command a view of its rocky bed; and another kept even pace with us, among the rocks and bushes of the hills on our left.

A circumstance soon occurred that proved the value of my precautions. It was gratifying, inasmuch as I was beginning to reproach myself with excess of prudence, and to fancy that I was humbugging myself, with an idea of danger and responsibility, into a very unnecessary and romantic display of strategic generalship, in a remarkably small way. Watching the motions of the scout, who was about a quarter of a mile from us, on the elevated ground to our left, and at the base of a steep range of rocky hills, we saw him stop, and, in a few minutes, make a signal, by stretching out his arms. Riding at full speed towards him, I perceived that, in front of him, and between us, was a deep rocky gully, and that he was pointing to a clump of palm-bushes, that grew on the side towards me. As my horse flew by the bushes I got sight of the object indicated, and wheeling my steed instantly, was, in another jump, right over the crouching body of a man. The poor wretch expected nothing but instant death.

He was a tall, well-made young mulatto, of a light yellow complexion, and with thin lips and prominent nose. His dress consisted of a ragged linen shirt, with the eternal red sash, and around his shoulders some tatters of a robe of bird-skins; his thick bushy hair was cropped close behind and on the top of his head, but was allowed to grow long in front, and to project horizontally, like a shaggy pent-house, over his eyes—a style of head-dress which, as may be supposed, was decidedly more of the useful than the ornamental.

When assured that he was among friends, he readily told his story, in the Kyptile tongue, with which he seemed perfectly familiar. He said that he belonged to the village that we had seen in ruins; that the Footas surprised the town when many of the men were away, and had slaughtered all the males and infants, and driven off the women and children that could walk; that, upon the alarm being given, the men, who came running to the town, were attacked by parties of Foota horsemen, and cut down, in every direction, in the fields; not more than thirty, out of a village of three or four hundred, had made their escape.

He could give no definite idea of the number of the Footas, but from his replies I gathered that they were about two hundred, mounted, one third of whom might be armed with guns. He said that, higher up the country, he had seen towns on fire, and that the Footas were burning and slaying in every direction. In answer to my inquiry, as to what he was hiding behind the bushes for, he replied that he had been placed there by his comrades, to watch for the Footas, who, having gorged themselves with spoil, must now be upon their return.

"And what to do?" I demanded. "Would you attack them?"

For an instant the fellow's eye gleamed like a tiger's, and a convulsion of rage and anguish passed over his features, but his countenance fell, and a melancholy shake of his head was his only reply.

"Have your countrymen no weapons?" I continued. "Have they no hearts—no courage? Are you all cowards, that you thus suffer your wives and children to be carried off, without resistance?"

"We have weapons," he replied; "bows and arrows, and shields, and spears, and we have got strong arms and stout hearts; but what can we do against the lightning-irons of the Footas?"

"Have your people the will to do any thing, if I show them the way?"

"My countrymen have no wish to live," he replied. "Give us thirty Foota lives, and take ours when you will."

"Go, then, collect your countrymen, and bring them to me this evening. I will pitch my camp in that grove, and will wait for you. We'll see if we can't teach these Footas a lesson that they will remember! Go, bring your friends, and let as many as possible come mounted, and all of them fully armed."

The fellow started off upon his mission with alacrity, while we moved up into a small thick grove of trees, and prepared our camp for the night.

Two or three hours after dark our outposts heard and answered the signals agreed upon. Our messenger had collected about forty of his countrymen, one third of whom were mounted. They were a dejected, miserable-looking set of men, and, at first, could hardly comprehend my intentions. But when made to understand that we would go with them against the Footas, and attempt the rescue of their wives and children, their spirits revived, and their countenances expressed a degree of animation that proved they wanted only a leader, and more confidence in themselves and their weapons, to become fully a match for their cruel foes.

In a rocky hollow our camp-fire burned brightly, and before it and upon the glowing coals roasted the carcass of a wild hog and several specimens of smaller game. It was a pleasure to see our half-starved visitors eat. After their appetites were satisfied, I took their leading men aside and held a long consultation.

In reply to questions, they informed me that at about half a day's journey up the country, the hills came down nearly to the bank of the river, leaving a long, narrow defile, through which the Footas would have to pass upon their return. From their description I was convinced that it would be just the place for an ambuscade. The only question was, could we reach it before the Footas should have passed. The strangers assured me that they knew, from the smoke of the burning villages, that the enemy were now engaged in the valley, beyond the pass, and that if we pressed forward we should be in time to occupy it, as the Footas would, necessarily, move very slowly, laden, as they were, with spoil, and having to drive before them their numerous captives.

"And you, Kaloolah, what do you say? Shall we go on and meet these Footas, or shall we try to hide ourselves until they have passed? We cannot turn back, for there is a large party in our rear."

"Oh, let us go on and meet them," replied Kaloolah—"think of the women and children—"

"But suppose they should prove too strong for us. What would be our fate? Have you no fear?"

"Have you any fears, Jon'than?" demanded Kaloolah.

"None, if we can cross the little prairie before they emerge from the hills."

"Let us on then—my heart knows no fear when you lead the way; but, Jon'than, if the Footas should prove too strong for us; they will never make you a slave. You will either escape or die, wont you, Jon'than?"

"Certainly, I shall never be taken alive."

"And I," replied Kaloolah, "I shall go with you. In either case, Jon'than, I go with you!"

Hugh and Jack expressed themselves in the most emphatic manner in favor of a brush, and even Sooloo Phar, when he found, as he did from our visitors, that another body of Footas were in our rear, so that there was no turning back, declared his readiness to fight. It was refreshing to find such a degree of unanimity, and so much spirit and confidence—thanks to our four guns.

The chief of a hundred fights may sleep on the eve of a great battle, but I felt no disposition to close my eyes. I don't choose to dwell upon my anxieties and sense of responsibility; but the reader will

readily understand that, considering the disparity of force in men and
weapons, and the important issues at stake, it is no reproach to my coolness or confidence that I felt rather wakeful. The great heroes of
history have played the game of war upon a grander scale, but never with
stronger feelings of interest in the result. "No!" I exclaimed, as I was
pacing up and down before the flickering fire, in an oratorical tone,
that started Hugh and Jack from their slumbers, and which would have
brought three rounds in Tammany Hall,—"No! a prospect of the biggest
empire that ever dazzled the vision of blood-stained ambition could add
nothing to the interest of a contest when the issues are victory and
liberty on the one hand, defeat and slavery on the other!"

"Was yer honor spakeing to us?" demanded Hugh.

"Yes, yes! Up, up! It is time to start. I see the first blush of
daylight, and the sun, you know, gives short warning in these latitudes."

The word was spread throughout the camp, and in ten minutes the
whole army, now amounting to about sixty-five men, was ready to start.
A scouting party of our new friends, the Kimboos, led the way. Close
behind I followed with a small party of Kyptiles, and at a little distance
in the rear came the three guns and the infantry, cavalry, and baggage in
close order.

The sun had risen a couple of hours when we came to a great plain
intersected by several streams, and encircled by bold and lofty hills. In
shape it resembled an ellipse, our path corresponding to the conjugate
diameter, which might be about eight miles. The transverse diameter was
fully twenty. The surface, which appeared quite smooth and level, though
we afterwards found some considerable elevations, was covered with a
rich clothing of grass. No trees, however, afforded a shelter from the sun
or a cover from the enemy.

For a few minutes I hesitated about committing my party to the open
prairie, and proposed that we should skirt the circle of hills, where we
could, if attacked, make a better defence against the enemy's cavalry ; but
the Kimboos assured us that this was impossible by reason of several
deep and impassable ravines which projected far out into the plain. Our
only chance was to take the direct route along the banks of the river, and
to press on so as to reach the pass before the Footas.

We stopped a few minutes for breakfast and to water our horses, and
then, leaving the friendly cover of the trees and rocks, launched out into
the open plain.

While toiling on through the rank herbage, occasionally descending
into water-gullies and crossing the beds of several small streams, my eyes

were not idle, and I noted several places where the nature of the ground would have aided in a defence against cavalry. This was encouraging, as I had expected to find the plain a perfect flat, and without shelter of any kind.

It was within about a mile of the rugged hills that rose abruptly from the further side of the plain to a height of a thousand feet that we passed a little peninsula of land, made by the confluence of a creek with the main river. I did not take much notice of it at the time, as we were so close to the mouth of the defile, and all eyes were strained in the direction of the hills. In a few minutes more we should know our fate. There were yet no signs of the Footas. We pressed on, our hearts beating high with a hope which was destined to a most cruel disappointment.

Our advance guard of mounted Kimboos were observed to stop, and the next minute wheel their horses and gallop towards us. It was easy to see, at a long distance, that they were the bearers of bad news. Upon coming up they informed me that from the crest of a low ridge of ground about half a mile beyond, a large body of Footas might be seen reclining in the shade of the hills, and that another party were just debouching from the defile into the plain. While speaking, a party of two or three horsemen appeared in sight, and galloped down towards us. When within fifty rods they wheeled their horses and went back at full speed.

We were fairly caught in our own trap. In a few minutes the whole body of the enemy would be down upon us, and in the open plain, where my frightened troops could scatter and run, there was no chance for a successful resistance. The danger was imminent. Fortunately there was no time lost. My decision was made at once, and, riding back, I gave orders to retreat upon the peninsula already mentioned, which was a little distance in the rear and on our right hand.

This tongue of land was made by a creek with a wide bed and steep banks, some twelve or fifteen feet high, which, running in a line perpendicular to the main river until within a hundred feet, suddenly turned at right angles, and, running parallel with the river, emptied into it three or four hundred feet below. The promontory was considerably elevated, so that when we reached it, which we did in about ten minutes, we could command a view of the hollow way in which the Footas were moving. We could perceive a large party, which was gradually increased in number by flying horsemen, from the crowd in the rear. These were coming towards us.

Dismounting my men at the entrance to the point of land, I sent Kaloolah and her maid in to its farther extremity, together with our baggage and our horses. By rolling down the banks a few loose stones, I shortened the breadth of the narrow isthmus from one hundred to eighty feet. This line I filled up with a rank of twenty-five men, making them kneel and present their spears, with the butts resting upon the ground, after the manner of the rows of an infantry square. Behind these I placed another rank of twenty-five men, with their long spears projecting over the heads of the first.

As soon as my men caught the idea, they formed the lines as accurately and as quickly as if they had been veterans. The whole operation did not require five minutes. The Footas were now close by, and coming on at full speed; but I knew the necessity of an appearance of coolness to encourage my men, and deliberately passing up and down in front of them, I adjusted the spear heads to their proper elevation. When all was arranged I made a brief address, to the effect that if they were perfectly steady the Footas could do them no harm: " They cannot get upon our flanks, and you will soon see that they dare not attack us in front. Keep cool, and stir not, and we will give these Footas a reception they little dream of. But if you do not stand firm," I continued, going at once to the very foundation of discipline, "if you do not stand firm, you see this," showing them one of my pistols, "well, I shall keep it charged, and will blow the brains out of the first man that moves from his position; so mind you, if the Footas are in front, recollect I 'm behind you, and I never miss my aim."

Stepping within the ranks, I took my station in line with my three musketeers and a dozen archers, giving them the strictest orders not to fire a shot or draw a bow until I gave the word.

On came the Footas, whirling their guns and spears above their heads, and yelling like so many fiends. There were at least a hundred and fifty of them, and one third were armed with muskets. These came first, followed by the spearmen, the whole squadron moving without any other effort at order. As they came on, the nature of the ground compelled them to crowd together, and when within a few rods of us, they were so huddled up as to very much interfere with each other's movements; but still they kept at full gallop, and for a few minutes I was apprehensive that, not knowing their danger, and ignorant that military etiquette requires that cavalry should check their horses in front of a square of infantry, they might spur on and ride us down before they could be made to understand their mistake. It was pleasant, therefore, to see the front rank beginning to draw reins, while the rear ranks were closing up in great confusion, and forming a fine compact mass of human flesh for my batteries.

"Oh! for a long eighteen," exclaimed Jack to his companion, "and a stand or two of grape-shot!"

"You may say that. There could n't be a more beautiful chance for mince-meat. But look, here comes their broadside! I wonder when the captain is going to give us the word!"

"Steady, men! steady! now," I exclaimed encouragingly to the kneeling ranks, "recollect, the first man whose spear-head wavers shall have a bullet through his head!"

The Footas were now five or six rods off, when they simultaneously brought the butts of their long guns against their breasts and fired, but with a very bad aim, or rather without any aim—many of them who were in the rear firing their guns into the air. The balls whistled over our heads, but not a man was struck.

"See," I exclaimed, "their guns do you no harm. Steady there! keep in your places and hold your spears firmly! Recollect, the man who stirs from his position or whose spear-head wavers, I'll shoot right through the head!"

It must not be supposed that, during this time, the Footas had come to a halt. They had merely slackened their speed to deliver their fire, and then, calculating upon the usual paralyzing effect of their volley, they spurred up, expecting us to give way. On they came until within ten feet of our spear heads, when the front ranks recoiled as suddenly as if they had breasted a rock. There was something in our motionless ranks that they could not comprehend, and they would willingly have turned back, but that was not so easy, as those in the rear came pressing on, yelling and flourishing their swords and spears, and crowding up in constantly increasing confusion.

Our enemies were not a bad-looking set of men. They were well formed, good riders, and mounted upon small, active horses with the high-peaked Moorish saddle, which was generally furnished with red housings. Rings and plates of silver and gold hung from various parts of their half-naked bodies, and relieved the dense jet of their skins, while their faces were constantly lighted up by their white flashing teeth and eyes.

"Back! back!" pressed the astonished leaders; but still the movement of the whole mass was towards us.

"Are you all ready? take good steady aim; and you, Jack Thompson, cover that fellow in front of you with the leopard skin!"

"Aye, aye, sir? I've been drawing a bead upon him for this last five minutes!"

" Fire, then ! "

Bang ! went my three muskets simultaneously, and at the same instant twanged the bow-strings of Sooloo Phar and his Kyptiles.

Not a shot was thrown away, which, as soon as I saw, I threw in my reserve fire, and knocked over a couple of prominent-looking individuals with ostrich plumes in their hair.

Our guns were discharged now as fast as we could load and fire, while Sooloo Phar kept up an effective and continuous flight of arrows.

The enemy were completely panic-stricken and thrown into the utmost confusion. They fought and struggled with each other ; horses reared and plunged, and several were forced down the precipices on either side. For some minutes they seemed utterly incapable of making any properly directed efforts to escape, while we continued to pour in our fire with the utmost coolness and precision. At last they got their horses' heads round, and began to make off, many of them severely wounded, and leaving about thirty-five men, most of whom had muskets, dead upon the ground.

At this instant the idea of charging the Footas in turn flashed upon me, and, without hesitating an instant, I gave the order to mount. A number of the Kimboos rushed out, and seized the riderless horses of the Footas, while the others, with the Kyptiles flew to our steeds, which we had turned loose behind us. In less time than it takes to tell of it, we were all mounted, and, spears in hand, ready to launch upon the flying and frightened foe.

Giving Kaloolah and Clefenha in charge of Jack and Hassan, with strict orders to follow our motions, a little in the rear, I shouted the word to charge.

" Forward, and keep close order ! Ride together, men ! Close up, close up ! Keep together ! Hold in there, in front, or I 'll send a pistol ball after you ! "

There was no need for words of encouragement ; a complete reaction had taken place, from the extreme of fear to the extreme of confidence and courage ; and my men would have charged a thousand Footas, for whom they now felt almost as much scorn and contempt as they did hate. Vengeance ! vengeance ' almost streamed in a visible streak from the strained eyes and dilated nostrils of the Kimboos.

" Ha, ha ! Ha, ha !" laughed the old Kyptile guide and interpreter, who rode by my side on the flank of the column ; " Ha, ha ! the spears are thirsty ; the bows and the guns have had a good drink of blood ; but the spears of the Kimboos are dry ; they 'll drink the Foota River up."

The Footas had separated into several small parties, some of them flying back to their companions who were left in charge of the slaves, but the larger party, numbering perhaps fifty, drawing off along the banks of the creek, until we set out, when they too turned their horses' heads to the south, to regain their reserve body. It was our object to intercept them. Every nerve was strained for that purpose, and it was soon evident that we should succeed.

We were close to them when they halted, some wheeling their horses to turn back, some proposing to go across the plain to the east, and some few, apparently, making indications of resistance. It was at this instant of hesitation that we drove in upon them at full speed. Heels over head went men and horses, and even several of our own men were dismounted by the shock. The Footas could make no resistance. In five minutes forty saddles were empty, and the light spears of the Kimboos were dripping with blood.

Those who escaped took their way towards their camp, and at full speed we followed them. By the time we came to the ridge, beneath which was the Foota camp, I had succeeded in again forming my men into close order. Below us were our enemies, apparently in the greatest consternation. They had drawn themselves in front of their crowd of captives, to the number of seventy or eighty ; and as we came down upon them they fired an irregular volley, as much at the fugitives before us as at our ranks. Before they could load again we were upon them, and then commenced a similar scene of unresisting slaughter as that which had just been enacted.

The Footas were flying like scud in a gale, and the Kimboos were pursuing and spearing them down without mercy. Satisfied that there was no danger of their rallying again in force, I drew off my Kyptiles and rode on to the captives, when we dismounted and cut the bands that confined the limbs of the males. There were between two and three hundred prisoners, the greater number of whom were women and large children. The smaller children, the sick and the aged, had all been slaughtered by the Footas. Who could wonder at the pertinacity with which the victorious Kimboos kept wheeling and circling in all parts of the plain, like kites o'er their quarry, and pouncing with relentless fury upon their unnerved and scattered foes.

CHAPTER XXXVI.

HAD the reader, about ten days after the battle, been perched, with a good telescope in his hand, upon the snow-covered summit of the great volcano that, rising far above its compeers, served as a beacon to the country for a hundred miles round, he might, perhaps, have seen a large party, some mounted and some on foot, winding its way upward and through a beautiful country of hill and dale, wood and open plain. But the reader, under such circumstances, would have been, probably, profoundly ignorant of the character and object of the travellers, whereas, now, it is hardly necessary to inform him that the party consisted of neither more nor less than myself and companions, accompanied by about a hundred guides and guards from the last town.

We had got again into a district inhabited by Kyptiles, and had been, of course, well received by the Matcham and his people. From all the villages that we passed, the people came out with presents of melons, grapes, figs, small loaves of hot wheaten bread, smoking dishes of meat, fish, and vegetables, and that greatest of all luxuries, pure water, iced with snow from the hills. Invitation upon invitation poured in upon us to stop and refresh ourselves, but the nearer we approached the confines of Kaloolah's country, the more anxious was she to press on. The lofty peak of the flaming Kebbi was a familiar object to her, and recalled in their fullest force the associations of kindred and home.

At night we encamped with the volcano in full view. About one third of the way up its rugged sides was spread a dark forest of cypress, fir, and pine. Between this and the region of snow was a brilliant zone of electric light. Through the night the lightning played in broad sheets of

"The great volcano, that, rising far above its compeers, served as a beacon to the country for a hundred miles round."

flame over the rugged rocks, flashing far upward on the snows above, and illuminating the dark wooded slopes and ravines below; while above all streamed upward the lurid flames of the peak.

At length the morning dawned of the day which, before its close, was to bring us to the banks of the Nourwall, a stream separating the Kyptiles from Framazugda. No sleep had visited my eyes, an indescribable whirl of emotions had compelled me to pace away the midnight watch in front of our camp-fire. Hugh and Jack were alike wakeful, and till a late hour were anxiously listening to the stories told by our guides of the wonders that were in store for us.

Kaloolah stepped from her tent, with her hood drawn closely around her face. Kebbi was flaming up at the moment famously, as if in rivalry of the blushing morn, that came bounding along the tops of the hills. I took Kaloolah's hand, and, bidding her good morning, pointed to the peak--but she averted her head and made no reply. Her steed was ready, and without further words I tossed her to the saddle. I could feel, however, that she was somewhat heavier than usual; that her touch upon my shoulder was not so delicate—the pressure of her little foot not so light and springy.

"Are you ill, Kaloolah?" said I, resting my arm upon the high back of her saddle.

She suddenly threw herself forward upon my shoulder and sobbed violently.

"Are you ill, Kaloolah? Unhappy? Tell me what disturbs you."

"I don't know, Jon'than; I have been dreaming of Enphadde, and----"

"Believe me, we shall find him safe. How happy he will be to meet you!"

"It may be, but even if I were sure of his safety, I think that I should weep this morning. Why? I know not, unless it is because we were so gay yesterday."

"And why not be gay to-day? by night we shall have reached the end of our journey; and are we not assured that there is no danger in the way?"

"Ah, that is what makes me sad. Our journey has been long and wearisome and dangerous, but still I do not wish it finished. I could think of nothing all night but the past, and there were moments when I almost wished that we were back in the desert. But here come the sun; heed not my foolish tears, they will dry in his beams like dew on the flowers."

But despite the enlivening influences of the sunlight, it was not until late in the day that Kaloolah's spirits recovered their usual joyous elasticity.

As we rode along our guides entertained us, as had been their custom, with stories of the land we were about to enter ; in which it was easy to perceive that there was no disposition to sacrifice the wonderful to precision and truth. This, however, did not surprise me, as most of the stories, especially those relating to the capital, purported to be only at second-hand—not one of our escort having visited the great city of Kiloam.

" And how is it," I demanded, "that none of you know much of Framazugda from personal observation ? Is there not a constant communication kept up between your countrymen and the Framazugs ? "

" The Framazugs do not like the visits of strangers," was the reply. " 'T is true that we are now upon good terms, and our people even pay a trifling tribute to the Emperor Shounsé as an acknowledgment for the protection that he has afforded us against the Jalla ; but for many centuries the Kyptiles and Framazugs were bitter enemies.

" You must know that the Kyptiles came from the north many hundred years ago, but still long after the Framazugs, who, coming from the east, across a great water, had taken possession of the country. Our people displaced a portion of the Framazugs and drove them south into their present country, where the main portion of them had taken up their residence. From that time there was a constant succession of wars along the borders, which interrupted all communication."

" But how is it," said I, " if the Framazugs are so rich, and learned, and numerous as you say they are, that your people were able to war with them upon equal terms for so long a time ? "

" They had enemies on every side of them. Away to the southwest of them are deserts, inhabited by a wild people called Jiggers. They ride upon birds, like an ostrich only ten times as big. These birds can run like the wind, and they have wings with which, although they cannot fly, they can skip along over rocks twenty feet high, with a man on their backs. Beneath their bills they have a large bag, in which they carry water for a long journey ; and at night, when the Jigger encamps, he makes the bird brood upon the ground with outstretched wings and tail, beneath which he and his family find shelter. The Jiggers have always been terrible enemies to the Framazugs.

" Besides these there are the Jouaks who inhabit the hills and mountains on the southeast. They are a wild race, who are covered all over with hair, go naked, and fight with clubs. These people often descend into the plains of the Framazugs, destroy the crops, and carry off the inhabitants, whom they are said to eat. The Jouaks are horrible-looking wretches—their under lips hang quite down to their breasts, and constantly drop blood; their teeth project and are filed to a sharp point, and from the corners of their mouths stand out tusks as large as a wild boar's."

"Next to these comes a country of swamps and marshes, inhabited by terrible animals, part man and part beast. They have the heads and breasts of men, and the bodies and tails of serpents, and when they come out from their swamps the breath of their armies poisons the air for miles round."

"Then in the northeast, just beyond those hills, are the Jalla. For many years they pressed upon the Framazugs, until about five years ago, they made their way by exterminating whole tribes of Kerdie blacks, to the borders of the Kyptiles. 'T was then that we found it best to come to terms with the Framazugs, and make common cause with them against the enemy. In a few years we had additional reason to cultivate peace with our southern neighbors; for the Kollah and Mendi negroes, armed with lightning sticks, came upon us from the north, and drove us from the banks of the Yah'nil Nebbé, killing the Kyptiles and carrying off the Kerdies who were living among us, and ravaging our country so that this portion which we are now traversing is the only part that has escaped their visitation; and now the Flahhas and Foota Jals are enclosing us on the west!"

"High time," I observed, "that you and the Framazugs should make friends, when you are completely surrounded by such enemies."

"So our people thought; and, notwithstanding our many wars, the Framazugs were very willing to make peace with us, for although they are a brave people, they are not fond of war—they much prefer to build great houses, and plant gardens, and make fountains, and dance, and feast, and bathe. The Jalla and the Koola made us peaceable, and then came the Footas and made us firm friends. Two or three times the Emperor Shounsé has sent armies to the assistance of the Kyptiles against the Jalla and Foota."

"With what success?"

"Perfect success against the Jalla: they have been defeated several times, and prevented from coming down from the passes of the mountainous country that you saw on your left after crossing the Yah'nil Nebbé. But against the Footas we could do nothing. They can bring large armies of twenty and thirty thousand men into the field, all armed with guns; and before them the combined forces of the Framazugs and our people have always been compelled to fall back. The Footas have continued to advance, until, within a year or two, they have established themselves all along the banks of the Queal from Lake Tsamsa, which is in Framazugda, to the Yah'nil Nebbé. Ten days in that direction is the lake, and just where the Queal issues from it the Footas have built a large walled town, from whence they send out their plundering expeditions."

For several hours we had been riding through a rough and rocky district, in many places almost bare of vegetation, and apparently destitute of inhabitants, when suddenly we came upon a wide plain that, at first sight, seemed one bed of the richest-hued flowers. What was our surprise when we found that the dazzling dyes were owing to myriads of snails that covered the stocks of a species of coarse furze. Beyond the plain the ground became low and marshy, and covered with clumps of mangroves, canes, and large tufts of bog grass, that grew to the height of ten feet. We passed several deep pools, made, as our guides assured us, by a very large creature with one horn. We heard the noise of some animals floundering and wallowing in the mud among the reeds. I supposed them to be hippopotami, but was undeceived by the sudden appearance in our rear of a monstrous rhinoceros. The Kyptiles passed on, while I stopped to take a better look at him. In a few minutes half a dozen more made their appearance. Riding a little too close, one of them took offence, and instantly charged me. I wheeled my horse among the bushes, and fired at the monster, within a few feet of his tough hide, as he dashed by, but without apparently making the least impression. The fellow and his companions were about twice as large as the ordinary rhinoceros—their horns were fully six feet in length, and their hides thick in proportion. They were truly great game; but, to enjoy the sport, one ought to hunt them with a battery of flying artillery.

Overtaking my party, we debouched from the marsh, crossed a narrow strip of firm and open ground, and came upon the hard sandy beach of the river. A little rocky island, two or three rods from the shore, was covered with the stone huts of fishermen. Several canoes were drawn up on its banks, and the rocks were covered with large hand-nets. A number of tawny fellows, dressed in red cotton shirts, were basking in the sun, with the thorough *poco curante* air of their profession. Our arrival excited some sensation, and in a few minutes the little island was alive with women and children.

Across the stream (which was about three hundred yards broad) the bank rose abruptly, by a succession of steep terraces, and was crowned with several buildings, connected by crenelated curtains, and defended by several low battlemented towers. The terraced ascent was without trees, or an unevenness that could serve as a cover to an attacking party, and thus corresponded to the *glacis* of modern fortification. No part of the town was in view, as it occupied a slope of the hill that fell away from the river, and the road to it led along the base of the castle bank, and up around a ravine, through which ran a small stream into the Nourwall.

Far down the river, on the same side on which we were, was a height of ground, upon which a shattered wall and falling towers indicated the position of a town, which, for some reason, had been abandoned. Two

" *I wheeled my horse among the bushes, and fired at the monster.*"

or three boats were moving about on the water, with low, straight bows, and high arched and carved sterns, that came up and turned over forward, like the acrostolicon of the ancient trireme. These served for orna-ment, and also answered to suspend an awning of red cotton that was stretched on a framework of reeds.

We soon opened a communication with the island. A boat was launched, and three fellows stepping into it, with one push sent it across to the beach. They evinced no little surprise when they saw Kaloolah and heard her speak ; but my appearance and manners seemed to puzzle them the most. It was curious to witness the respect with which they looked upon our guns—the first that they had seen.

They offered, at once, to take our message to the governor of Garazha, requesting permission to enter the Framazug territory: intimating, however, that it was not customary to admit strangers without a good deal of delay, and that we should, probably, have to wait where we were until the next morning. The idea was not a pleasant one, inasmuch as we should have to encamp upon low flat ground, exposed to the visits of the crocodiles and hippopotami of the river on the one side, and the rhinoceri and elephants of the marsh on the other. A dozen large fires would be necessary, and there was no fallen timber anywhere near.

We watched our three messengers (who refused to permit any one of my party to accompany them) until they landed, and, drawing up their boat, proceeded beneath the terraces, which began now to be covered with spectators, around by the ravine, and so out of sight. It was full an hour before they returned, when they came accompanied by forty or fifty people, and getting into their boat, pushed off. At the same instant, from the smaller stream, there shot out into the Nourwall a large wide barge. It was rowed, or rather paddled, by twenty men, in two rows, all of them in red shirts, and wide-brimmed, high-peaked, palm-leaf hats. In the stern-sheets, beneath the red cotton awning, reclined an elderly man, dressed in loose flowing robes of white and blue, and a cap of feathers that gleamed like a casque of burnished silver and gold.

He landed, and, in quite a haughty manner, commenced making a few inquiries, and ended by informing us that the dagash, or governor, could not send his boats for us until the next morning, and, in the meantime, we must stop where we were.

I was not a little provoked, both at the interruption and at the old fellow's manner. There was an assumption of superiority that I felt strong disposition to put down on the first favorable opportunity, which was not decreased upon learning that he was nothing more than a kind of captain of the port.

"Can we find a place to sleep among those ruins on our right?" I demanded.

"Oh! no, no!—impossible!" chorused the whole body of fishermen, in which they were joined by the Kyptiles. Even the old Framazug shook his head, and the faces of his crew showed that they agreed with him.

"Why not?" I demanded, somewhat astonished at the outbreak of voices.

" Why ? because that is the Whamba Donga's own town ! It is a thousand years ago that the people of Garazha wished to build a town, and they chose that spot ; but every night the tools with which they worked were carried over the river, to where Garazha now is, by spirits. They persisted, however, until they had got one of the towers done, when Whamba Donga took up his residence in it, and played so many diabolical tricks upon the builders that, at last, they were compelled to give up, and leave the place to the demons, who have ever since had possession of it. Any one who ventures among those ruins after dark is strangled and eaten by Whamba Donga and his imps."

" More likely by lions and leopards from the jungle," I replied. " Come ; I 'm not afraid of Whamba Donga. Let us go and find some snug corner where a single fire will protect us!" But not a Kyptile would consent, and, to my utter astonishment, even Hugh and Jack seemed to think it better to run our chance with the rhinoceri and elephants in the open ground, than to provoke the devil by an invasion of premises which he had held in fee simple for a thousand years.

" Well ! then we must cross to Garazha ! "

" Impossible ! " replied the captain of the port : " the governor says that you can't enter until to-morrow."

" But how can we remain here, when these fishermen say that this bank at night is covered with wild animals, and that they dare not set foot upon it after dark. We have no wood, and we shall need several large fires, not so much to protect ourselves, as to secure our beasts ; and besides, we are in want of food. We must cross the river."

" Impossible ! " replied again the captain.

" No, sir ! " I exclaimed, striding up close to the astonished official, and backing him with a number of majestic flourishes to his boat, " it is not impossible. We will cross ; back, sir, and tell the dagash that Dr. Jonathan Romer, one of the sovereigns of the great republic of the United States of America, demands immediate admittance. Tell him, too," said I, pointing to Kaloolah, " that his master's daughter, the most illustrious Princess Kaloolah Sem Shounsé, is here, and that she orders him to send boats for us without delay. Tell him that if he hesitates we will swim our horses across and push on to Kiloam in despite of him ! "

The announcement of Kaloolah's birth and rank created no small sensation. Making a low salaam, the old Framazug jumped quite nimbly into his boat, and pushed off without saying a word.

It was not long before he reappeared, followed by several large boats.

Upon landing he informed us, in quite a subdued manner, that he had been directed to take us across. Our horses were first embarked in a large scow, and then we took our places beneath the awning of the captain's barge.

On the other side we found quite a crowd, and were received by several officers, habited like the captain, in loose robes and feather caps. The common people were all dressed in red cotton shirts and palm hats. It will be recollected that, for almost every thing curious and strange, I had been prepared by my long conversations with Kaloolah, her brother, and the Kyptiles ; and that, therefore, there was nothing in the universal red to surprise me, knowing, as I did, that that was the natural color of the Framazug cotton.

Mounting our horses, we were conducted a few rods along the beach, and then, turning at right angles, were led up the bank of the small brook, that was fringed with alders, willows, and magnificent oleanders in full bloom. The road ran along between the bed of the stream and the wall of the town, until it stopped at a wide machicolated gateway.

A company of horsemen were waiting to receive us. Within the gate a band of fifty musicians had been stationed ; and the instant we appeared trumpets sounded, drums were beaten, and cymbals clashed, and wild barbaric strains of harmony floated upon the air, startling our steeds, and producing in me a degree of " all-overishness " that was quite refreshing. I should be doing injustice to my feelings, to compare them to any thing else than those which must have agitated the breast of Alexander upon his triumphal entry into Babylon. I looked at Kaloolah, and fancied that she had grown two inches taller. A tear stood in her eye, her lip trembled, but her head was well back, her breast thrown forward, and she sat her horse with a graceful and dignified firmness that I had never before noticed.

Slowly we moved up a wide straight street, lined on either side with stone houses, which were generally of two stories, and furnished with deep receding balconies, and shaded with rows of majestic trees. The street was well paved and clean, but the cross streets were noticed to be small, unpaved, and dirty. Accustomed, as I had been, to the disgracefully paved and filthy streets of New York, and of various Portuguese, Moorish, and negro towns, it was not for me to deny any portion of credit due to the municipal government of Garazha, for keeping even one street in passable order.

We arrived at the foot of the hill, upon which was the castle and residence of the governor. A winding road led upward. As we ascended we had a fine view of the town below us, and of the rich valley beyond the walls, across which the setting sun was shooting his level beams.

We passed through an arched passage and rode into a wide, open, elliptical court. A large fountain was playing in the centre. A row of copper brackets, all around the wall, a little higher than a man's head, supported earthen vases in which grew the richest flowers, new to me, and exhaling perfumes to which my olfactories were wholly unaccustomed. Several pairs of carved and painted folding doors opened on either side, and a row of lattices above the flower-pots looked down into the court from the second story.

We were now requested to dismount, and were conducted across the court through a wide door, and domed hall or ante-room, into a large square apartment. The room was carpeted with a thick covering, which, as I afterwards learned, was made by first spreading the floor with melted asphaltum, and then dotting it with variously colored cotton and wool. Several round windows of rock crystals, set in copper frames, looked out upon the river, and admitted the last beams of the sun. At the upper end of the room, beneath the windows, were five or six figures of lions crouching. These were lion skins stuffed with wool, and intended for seats. In the corners were large flower stands, and depending from the ceiling was an immense bouquet. The walls and roof were richly ornamented with what any one would have taken for fine gilding, but which was nothing more than a mosaic of pieces of the glittering skins of serpents.

There was no one in the room when we entered, and the officers who ushered us in, instantly disappeared. Directing Hugh, Jack, Hassan, and Sooloo Phar to arrange themselves near the entrance, I led Kaloolah to the upper end of the room and looked out upon the river, where boats were now bringing the main body of my Kyptile guard.

We stood thus, for a few minutes, when the wide doors were flung open—two officials entered, followed by a venerable, dignified man, with a long white beard and with no covering upon his head but a single plume of the froulbell gracefully interwoven with his gray locks. He was the dagash !

With Kaloolah upon my arm, I advanced towards him. He turned so as to bring the light full upon her face, looked steadily at her for a moment, and then attempted to prostrate himself before her. But Kaloolah was too quick for him—she darted forward and seized his hand.

" Rise," she exclaimed with a royal air, " rise, worthy Lord of Goul ; the old confidant and friend of Shounsé must not kneel to his daughter."

If the dagash had had any doubt before of the identity of Kaloolah, it was now removed, and he threw himself upon the floor in a perfect agony of loyal and affectionate respect.

At last we got the old gentleman on his feet again, and Kaloolah, taking his arm, made him conduct her to the lions. She seated herself upon the back of one of them, and, obeying the courtly wave of her hand, the dagash and myself followed her example.

As Kaloolah sat thus, talking with the respectful official, there was surrounding her, and pervading every look and action, that *maintien* of high breeding—that certain indescribable something beyond what is expressed by the mere term refinement—that air of lofty self-possession, of habitual repose in a serene social atmosphere, above the reeking fogs and fumes that envelop the struggling vulgar, little and great, which is, to men who can appreciate it, so overwhelmingly fascinating, and without which physical beauty and all feminine attractions are like jewels without gold, lacking in a finished and elegant setting. Hitherto Kaloolah had not had the advantage of having been seen through the magnifying glass of the imagination. She had been too near to admit of it, but now that there was evidently a distance growing between us, my fancy begun to have more scope. For the first time I took a look at her through my mental telescope, adjusting the focus for parallel rays, and putting on a high power, so as to fill the field of view with her manifold perfections. As I sat and watched her lithe figure, swaying with every emotion—one tiny hand half hidden in the lion's mane, the other gracefully moving in expressive gesture—her black eyes now beaming, now melting—her fruity mouth—her rich hair waving in clustered ringlets—and her laugh and voice, so eminently persuasive and thorough-bred in its simple and earnest *abandon*,—as I sat, and with sharpened senses drank in all this, a slight feeling of anxiety, for the first time, came over me. It was difficult to repel the idea, that perhaps this star, now culminating so brilliantly in the zenith of love, might turn out to be a comet moving in a path of such eccentricity and inclination as to put the chance of its intersecting my orbit again, out of the question entirely.

CHAPTER XXXVII

Garazha—A Ride—Supping in a Cavern — New Notions of Noses — A Sumptuous Repast — A Hunt—Rousing a Lion—A Desperate Ride — The Cha Donga-troll — Death of the Lion — Large Birds' Nests — The Semper-sough—Waiting for News—The Change in the Princess.

Y means of posts at short intervals it was possible to convey a letter from Garazha to Kiloam, and receive an answer in three days. It was settled, that, in the meantime, we should take up our residence in the castle and await the orders of the court.

Every thing was done that the worthy dagash could do, that would minister to our comfort and pleasure. A fine suite of rooms, looking out upon the river were allotted to us. Those on one side of the central saloon were occupied by Kaloolah and Clefenha, the others by myself and attendants. Numerous servants were appointed to wait upon us, and we had but to express a wish and it was gratified.

In the afternoon we took a ride beyond the walls. We passed through groves of banian, tallipot, and acacia, and cultivated fields enclosed by lofty hedges of cactus, and over meadows enamelled with the iris, daffodil, lotus, crocus, narcissus, and a dozen flowering bushes, trees, and creepers that put my slight smattering of botany completely at fault. On our return we visited a magnificent limestone cave. Numberless large and lofty rooms, ornamented with stalactites of dazzling whiteness, were lighted up with lamps of hippopotamus oil. We passed through them until we came to a chamber three hundred feet long, about one hundred feet in breadth, and about sixty feet in height to the lower points of the stalactites with which the roof was incrusted. Innumerable lamps, concealed in the crevices and angles of the roof, lighted up the place with the brilliancy of day. A small stream of cool water ran through the centre of the room ; and along its bank, as if growing from the marble beds, were arranged masses of fresh flowers. A band of music struck up as we entered—its wild strains rolling and reverberating among the arches and interstices of the fretted roof with wonderful effect. We were conducted to the upper end of the room, where a row of calcareous concretions slightly fashioned by the hand of man, served for tables and seats; and here, again, were flowers

"Truly, princess, your people have a taste for flowers!" I exclaimed.

"It is their passion," replied Kaloolah. "The dagash will tell you that it is universal, and that a Framazug could as well do without food as without flowers."

"Ah! yes," said I, "they are very beautiful, and afford great delight by their brilliant colors and graceful forms, but I cannot understand the expression of ecstatic pleasure with which your people seem to inhale their fragrance. Tell me," said I, turning to the dagash, "to which of the senses, sight or smell, do flowers chiefly address themselves?"

The dagash looked at me for a moment as if he thought the question a very simple one.

"To the smell surely," was his reply. "To the sight, it is true, they give exquisite pleasure; but the sight cannot be cultivated so highly as can the sense of smell. Numberless as are the combinations of form and color, and keen as may be the appreciation of visible beauties by an educated eye, they are as nothing to the rich melodies and infinite harmonies of scentdom—to the million correspondences and differences—chords and discords that address themselves to the exalted sensibility of a highly cultivated nose."

"A cultivated nose!" I exclaimed. "Do you mean to say that you have any systematic methods of training noses, and thus artificially developing their natural capabilities?"

The dagash gave me another look of astonishment, as much as to say, what on earth were noses in your country made for?

"Certainly," he replied; "what sense more worthy of it? What sense will better repay the labor? What sense is capable of affording more exquisite delight? Through what sense is the mind more ecstatically affected? Can it be, that in your country its supremacy is not acknowledged?"

"In my country," I replied, "the sense of smell is thought to be a very useful sense; but no one ever dreamed of undertaking by a course of training to develop its latent capacities."

"How is that? Do you not cultivate the eye, the ear! why not the nose?"

"I don't know; unless it is that in our cities, particularly the great commercial capital that I came from, there are not unfrequently odors that would render the exercise of a delicate nasal sensibility any thing but agreeable. It may be that a secret conviction of expediency has held the higher and more refinable powers of the olfactories in abeyance."

" Shocking ! " exclaimed the dagash, rapidly running his nose over a large bouquet in zig-zag and irregular lines, like a dog when hunting a quail field.

" The worthy dagash has not been far enough from home to learn that a bad smell is not the worst evil in the world," said Kaloolah, laughing. " If his nose had been compelled to endure all that mine has, he would have got used to perfumes that the bare intimation of now makes him shudder ! "

" Unfortunate daughter of the great Shounsé," exclaimed the dagash, " and did you encounter many bad smells ? "

There was something in the old man's tone and look of respectful pity that made me, too, feel sorry for Kaloolah's nasal afflictions, and I rapidly ran over in my mind all of the principal stenches that we had been called upon to endure, to see if there were any that some exertion on my part might not have dispersed or neutralized. " No," said I, upon reflection, " I am free from reproach. A gross of the best double distilled cologne could not have saved us; but, most illustrious princess, I can readily understand now what you must have suffered."

A crowd of servants in the universal red cotton shirts and feather-cloth jackets now came bearing trays of roasted meats, fish, flesh, and fowl. To these succeeded vegetables, most of which were new to me. Among others was the custard plant, belonging to the cucurbitaceous family, and numerous specimens of the *solanum* genus—one a magnificent variety of the *lycopersicum*, and another a large *tuberosum* growing above ground, that far surpassed the ordinary potato. A dessert of fruit, flowers, and conserves followed, with the delicious juice of the red pepper-looking pendants of the champagne-punch tree. The fruit that most excited my admiration was a large purple gourd, something like an egg-plant. These were served up, embedded in snow. Upon slicing off the top there appeared a pink-colored fluid of the consistence of thick cream, which was scooped out, and eaten with spoons, fashioned from the dazzling white teeth of the hippopotamus.

" How beautiful is nature in this country," thought I. " Delicacies that in poorer countries are the products of art, here grow spontaneously. Champagne and ice-cream ! Well, I should n't be surprised to be offered a finishing glass of natural maraschino."

Our repast finished, we were conducted to our horses just as the last beams of the setting sun were gilding the silver snows of the distant mountains. As we came out I noticed that the long low entrance was plentifully encrusted with saltpetre—an observation that was afterwards to prove of the greatest utility.

On our way home the conversation turned upon fire-arms, and the dagash and his officers expressing a wish to see an exhibition of their power, it was decided to make a hunting excursion to the other side of the river the next day.

A hurried breakfast, *al fresco*, in the court of the fountain, and we descended by a steep path along the terraces to the shore of the Nourwall. We crossed in company with the dagash and his officers, and found assembled, on the other side, a body of two hundred men, all armed with bows and arrows and long spears. Suspended from different parts of their persons, each one wore what looked at first to be small wisps of straw, but, upon closer examination, they proved to be bunches of dry rushes, soaked in some very inflammable fluid. These were intended as a means of defence against the rhinoceros, and were to be used by attaching them to the end of the spears, lighting them by mean of a match, carried for that purpose, and presenting them, in full blaze, to the eyes and nose of the attacking animal. The rhinoceros, upon receiving such a salute, turns and runs, when the spear is instantly thrust into a tender place in the lower part of his body, and the animal, after running a few rods, and dashing, in his stupid rage, against trees and rocks, and sometimes giving with his monstrous horn a death-thrust to his nearest relatives, falls and expires. The sport requires skill, activity, and nerve. The hippopotamus is sometimes killed in the same way, when caught on shore in the daytime, but with the elephant the plan does not answer; with his trunk he dashes aside the blazing fagot, and presses on to the charge. Fortunately his skin is not so thick as that of the rhinoceros, and poisoned arrows bring his stately carcass slowly but surely to the ground.

We had not proceeded far down the river when we roused from his lair a huge lion, who, after looking at us contemptuously for a few minutes, bounded off and hid himself among the ruins of Whamba Donga's town. The Framazugs evinced no disposition to follow him, and for that very reason I was determined to see something more of his majesty.

Putting spurs to my horse, I breasted him directly against a hill, over which the lion had disappeared. The dagash and all hands called and shouted after me, but supposing that they were expressing their fears of the lion, or of Whamba Donga, I drove the heavy Moorish spurs into my active little steed, and dashed with a wild Arabic yell up the hill at full speed. The top was reached, and there, yawning directly under my horse's nose, lay a ravine, two hundred feet wide, and sheer down fifty or sixty feet deep. There was no room, or time, to check or turn my horse, or throw myself from the saddle. The motion was too swift—our momentum too

" Straight and swift as is an arrow he sped along the cracked and jagged wall.

great. A yard farther, either to the left or the right, and we must have gone headlong over the precipice, but directly in front of us ran a ruined wall, less than three feet wide, across the ravine. It was broken away in several places, and divided by wide cracks, where the stones stood trembling for a fall. Without the slightest feeling of hesitation—without the smallest movement of restraint, I swerved my horse a little, and with a fresh touch of the spur, leaped him on to the crumbling and narrow path. Straight and swift as an arrow he sped along the cracked and jagged wall, dashing aside the loose stones, toppling over large masses of masonry, and, at the end, safely leaping a chasm of ten feet between the wall and the bank.

I wheeled my steed, and looked back, but not without a shudder, and a feeling of thankfulness at my lucky escape. The Framazugs had reached the top just as my horse was climbing along the wall, and, upon seeing me rein up safe and sound upon the other side, they set up a great shout, and moved in a body down toward the river, where there was a path across the ravine.

In the meantime I amused myself in examining the wall. It appeared to be very old, and to have been intended as a foot-way, or as a support to an aqueduct. Upon inquiring of the Framazugs, none of them knew any thing about it, except that it was built by the founders of Whamba Donga's town—and that it was known as *Cha Donga-troll*, or the Devil's bridge. His infernal majesty, it had always been supposed, possessed the exclusive right of way—a right which my safe passage across seemed to render somewhat questionable.

While looking up the ravine, where the banks became more shelving, I saw a large animal lazily bounding over the loose stones of the bottom and slowly ascending the side on which I was standing. It was the lion. The few palmettos and tufts of flowery shrubs that grew in the crevices of the rocks were insufficient to conceal him for more than a moment from sight, and I watched him until he reached a platform of rock, some ten or fifteen feet from the top of the bank. A small camphor-tree, with its pointed and warty leaves, that, waving in the breeze, reflected with varying effects the light from their green and yellow-tinted upper and under surfaces, grew upon the very edge, and threw a shade upon the rock below. The lion paused, snuffed the air, stretched himself like a cat, gave two or three tremendous yawns, and then leisurely laid himself down for a snooze, with his head towards the inclined bank.

As soon as he had settled himself for his siesta, I dismounted, and crept along the bank, until within about three rods of him. Crouching low, I could see his whole carcass except his head, and, of course, without being seen myself. The question now was, whether upon raising my eyes so as to get a view of his, he might not start before a sure aim could be taken. There was no use in mentally revolving a point that could be settled only by experiment; so, raising my person to its full height, I looked the monster in the face. He did not appear to notice me; his eyes were open, but there was no "speculation," at least, as to the price and qualities of man's meat, in them. I raised the gun slowly to my shoulder, and deliberately looked along the sights right into the monster's eye.

Ha! there goes a lurid flash across that yellow optic wave upon wave of pinky light, like the vibratory flashings of the aurora borealis; like the half-advancing, half-retreating colors of the dawn; like the deepening blushes of beauty when awakening to the first consciousness of the heart; like the pulsatory gleamings of a puddling furnace on a foggy night; or like the glowing light of a kettle of melted potash in the depths of a dark forest. He 's waking up. He begins to fancy that he sees something. It would not be safe to calculate upon that eye remaining where it is more than the thousandth part of a second longer. So, lightly on the trigger!

The sharp report startled the sleepy rocks, and set them a screaming and yelling, as if each one was bound to prove his descent from the identical stone into which, according to Ovid, Juno turned her loquacious handmaiden. At the same instant the lion tore up the bank with a furious bound, and rolled over and over upon the level ground in the agonies of death. I jumped aside as he came up, and, with my gun still to my shoulder, was about to give him the contents of the other barrel behind his forelegs, when it became evident that it was unnecessary. Tumbling about for a few moments without consciousness, and in the exercise of mere muscular contractility, he sank to the ground and died, about as soon, perhaps, as it was possible for such an enormous mass of tough vitality to die.

At this moment the dagash and suite came up—admiration and astonishment depicted in their faces, and expressed both by gestures and words. "*Balak wen! g'rh'sah hoo-hoo wadden!*" "What a man! What courage, to attack a lion!" exclaimed the dagash, and "*Balak wen! g'rh'sah hoo-hoo wadden!*" replied the officers and men, whose admiration seemed to be equally divided between my ride across the Donga-troll, and the death of an animal that they had never dared attack except in large parties, and even then at a great risk of life. As it was an object to acquire a reputation for hardihood, I affected to look upon the performance as a matter of course, and, with a politic disingenuousness, did not explain that my ride had been involuntary, and that my attack upon the lion had been by stealth, and not an open, fair fight.

While riding along upon the banks of the stream, my motions were arrested by the voice of Hugh, who was floundering out of his path among the tall reeds of the marsh. "Come here, yer honor! here's something worth looking at! Did yer honor ever see any thing the likes o' that?" said Hugh, pointing to two birds' nests, built upon the ground, of canes and reeds, interwoven with dry grass and the fibres of the spartum. Each nest was about ten feet in diameter, and four feet deep. Upon inquiring of the natives, they were represented to belong to a monstrous bird with a body as large as an elephant, and standing almost twenty feet high. From the description it appeared that the animal must belong to the flamingo family—but as to the size, we could not but think that the Framazugs were exaggerating; yet there were the nests, large enough to couch an elephant. I will only add, that all doubt has been since removed, and that I have had opportunities of verifying the existence of an animal, alongside of which the Arabian roc would sink into insignificance, and which is as large as, if not larger than, the monstrous bird of New Holland, whose existence has been put beyond a doubt, by the frequent discovery of nests, twenty-five and thirty feet in circumference. I need say nothing further here, inasmuch as a full description will form one of the most striking features of my proposed work upon the natural history of Framazugda. In that work, too, will figure to better advantage, in full detail, the many curious smaller animals that we encountered, not forgetting various specimens of flying serpents, a large winged alligator, and an animal that I at once recognized as a dragon, from its correspondence to the descriptions in that standard work, "The Seven Champions." Another animal will demand a prominent place, although here I may merely mention it. It is an amphibious polypus. If the reader will conceive a large cart-wheel, the hub will represent the body of the animal, and the spokes the long arms, about the size and shape of a full grown kangaroo's tail, and twenty in number, that project from it. When the animal moves upon land, it stiffens these radii, and rolls over upon the points like a wheel without a felloe. These arms have also the capability of a lateral prehensile contraction in curves, perpendicular to its plane of revolution, and enable the animal to grasp its prey, and draw it into its voracious mouth. It attacks the largest quadrupeds, and even man himself; but if dangerous upon land, it is still more formidable in the water, where it has been known to attack and kill an alligator. This horrible monster is known by the name of the *Semper-sough*, or "snake-star," and is more dreaded than any other animal of Framazugda, inasmuch as the natives have no way of destroying it, except by catching it when young in cane traps sunk in the water, and baited with hippopotamus cubs. Fortunately it is not very prolific, and its increase is further prevented by the furious contests that these animals have among themselves. Sometimes twenty or thirty will grasp each other with their long arms, and twist themselves up into a hard and intricate knot. In this situation they remain, hugging and gnawing each other to death, and never relaxing their grasp until their arms are so firmly intertwined that, when life is extinct and the huge mass floats, they cannot be separated. The natives then draw the ball ashore, cut it up with axes, and make it into a compost for their land.

Crossing the river, we retired to the castle, where we waited with no little impatience until sundown, for the arrival of a messenger from Kiloam. None came, and even the dagash could not conceal his surprise and disappointment.

" Perhaps he has been delayed by some accident," I observed.

" No," replied the dagash, " it is hardly possible ; the runners go in pairs, and the day's journey is divided into twenty stages. The road is smooth, and there are never any accidents. I know not what to think."

" Well, I do," exclaimed Kaloolah, jumping up and clapping her hands with girlish glee, in utter contempt of all regal dignity, and to the great astonishment of the worthy dagash. " I understand ; Enphadde is coming, and the runners are stayed that he may announce himself. How long will it take him to come after receiving the news of our arrival ? "

" Four or five days ; depending upon the sharpness of his spurs."

" Then I 'm sure we shall see him in three days more ; but that will be a long time ; suppose that we set out to meet him ? "

Kaloolah's proposition was at once negatived by the dagash, much to my satisfaction. I was in no hurry, though, of course, full of curiosity ; for, somehow, there was something uncommonly pleasant in the view by moonlight, from the great terrace above the Nourwall ; and Kaloolah thought so too.

There could be no doubt that, whatever had been my feelings up to this time, I was now getting pretty deeply in love. The humbug of " fatherly care," and " brotherly affection," was all gone, and in its place there had got to be a most indubitable, love-like feeling of sympathy, anxiety, and respect. The change in me was but a natural response to a change I have already mentioned in Kaloolah's appearance and manners.

I remarked to Kaloolah how much she had altered : how suddenly she had assumed the *retenue* of womanhood. She playfully denied the charge. " At least," said she, putting her hand to her heart, " I have not altered here. Feel it ; its pulses are the same as when you threw it from you on the banks of the Sierra Leone."

CHAPTER XXXVIII.

Arrival of Enphadde—The Prince's Story—Setting Out for Kiloam—A Buffalo and His Trappings—A Weatherly Craft—Jack in the Howdah.

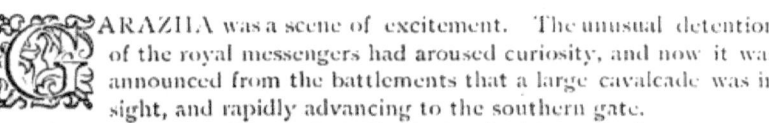

ARAZILA was a scene of excitement. The unusual detention of the royal messengers had aroused curiosity, and now it was announced from the battlements that a large cavalcade was in sight, and rapidly advancing to the southern gate.

" It is Enphadde, I know it is Enphadde," whispered Kaloolah, pale and trembling.

The door of the saloon opened, and there entered a tall, graceful figure, dressed in a blue shirt, and over it a closely fitting garment that came down to the knees, composed of fine feathers worked into a kind of cloth. The prominent color was a deep dazzling blue, bordered with a bright yellow. His legs were bare, except a garter of gold lace from which depended a heavy fringe like the bullion of an epaulette. Buskins of yellow morocco were laced to his feet, and on his head he wore a closely fitting green feather-cloth cap, with a fillet of gold and silver filigree, and a drooping plume of feathers of the froulbell.

Uttering a scream of delight, Kaloolah threw herself into the stranger's arms. It took me somewhat longer to recognize, in the full, manly figure, the stripling Enphadde. Disengaging himself from his sister's arms he flew towards me and gave me a most cordial embrace.

We shortly retired from the gaze of the crowd of officers, who filled the lower end of the long saloon, to the quiet of the terrace, where we seated ourselves upon the sward just as the sun was bidding good-night to the blushing clouds that hung in silent admiration of their own beautiful images, gleaming far down in the depths of the purple Nourwall.

As may be supposed, we had long stories to tell—many a question to ask—many a question to answer. Mine and Kaloolah's the reader understands. Enphadde's must be summed in three lines.

Upon returning to the hut and finding his sister gone, he rushed back to the head man and alarmed the whole village with his complaints and

307

lamentations. All hands turned out in search; which was continued during the night. It was at last concluded that she had been killed and carried off by some wild beast; in a day or two, however, it was known that a party of slave-hunters had been in the neighborhood and all doubts as to her fate were at once removed.

Grief so weighed upon Enphadde that he was unable to go on with the Mandingos, and for two or three weeks he remained, wishing and inviting death; his misfortunes excited the sympathy of the humane villagers, and he received the kindest nursing and attendance.

When able to walk he joined a kaffila going east. For about a month they got on very well; passing through several populous countries, until at last, while fording a broad stream, the kaffila was attacked by a party of armed negroes. The Mohammedan members of it were killed or dispersed, and the Kaffirs were seized as slaves. Great was Enphadde's joy when he found that his captors were marching him to the southeast. In fact, what seemed at first a misfortune, proved the safest and most direct means of his restoration to his own country.

Three weeks' travel brought him and his masters to a large town. Here he was exposed in the *socco* and immediately purchased by a slave-dealer, who put him, with others, on board of a large canoe and ascended (five or six days' journey) a stream running from the east. They then landed, and striking off through a hilly country in a southerly course, arrived in fifteen days at a small walled town named Bemnie.

There happened to be, luckily, in this town a party of Shemba traders, who had visited the country of the Foota Jals, where they had heard of the Gerboo Blanda, or white people of Framazugda. Enphadde's complexion and features excited their curiosity, and upon questioning him, and finding that he was the son of the Gerboo king they offered to purchase him, and take him home for ransom. For a whole lunar month they journeyed to the east, until they reached the first towns of the Footas, where his masters, either doubtful of his ransom, or tired of the long journey, sold him to a Foota chief, who promised to take him to Framazugda, but who, in the meantime, put him to work in his rice and cotton fields. Enphadde endeavored by promises of a high ransom to induce some one else to purchase him, but his master refused all offers. Finding, at length, that the Foota lord was too avaricious to part with his hopes of a splendid ransom, and yet too indolent to set about obtaining it. Enphadde secured a small bundle of provisions and a spear, and boldly plunged into a wild rocky country to the southeast.

For ten days he endured the extremes of hunger and fatigue, besides being several times attacked by wild animals. Once a lion bounded at him from the sedgy margin of a small watercourse. Enphadde had barely time to scramble to the top of a high rock, when the lion gave a jump, just reaching with his forefeet the edge of the rock, and slipping back without getting a foothold. The animal turned back, and deliberately placing himself in the same spot from which he had sprung, tried it again, but with no better success. Twenty times the creature repeated the experiment before he could satisfy himself that it was beyond his power. Unfortunately Enphadde had dropped his spear, or he might have easily put an end to the monster's saltatory exertions, by thrusting him while clinging to the edge of the rock. Upon finding that his proposed dinner was beyond his grasp, the fellow had the impudence to stretch himself out upon the ground and keep Enphadde broiling in the hot sun upon the rock until sunset, when, with a deep roar of disappointment and impatience that made the boulders in the bed of the river rattle like pebbles on the sea-shore, he bounded off in search of a less piquant but more come-at-able supper. Enphadde descended and secured his spear, but he thought it best to take up his lodging upon the rock for the night.

On another occasion Enphadde had succeeded in spearing a monkey, and, taking his prize to the bank of a stream, was busily engaged in rubbing two dry sticks together, in hopes of getting a fire, and making a comfortable meal, when he was alarmed by a wild rushing through the forest, and turning, he beheld himself enclosed by a legion of monkeys armed with sticks and stones. Discharging their missiles with wonderful precision and force, these infuriated animals closed in upon him. Enphadde used his spear vigorously—killing numbers, but not in the least deterring the rest. They swarmed upon him like vermin, and in a minute more he must have been overborne and killed, had he not staggered to the water and plunged in, with about forty monkeys hanging to him by their claws, tails, and teeth. The ferocious little devils were compelled to let go their hold and scramble back to the land, while Enphadde swam across to the other side. Covered with bruises and bleeding from a hundred wounds, and faint from want of food, he could just draw himself ashore, where he must have perished had he not been discovered by a party of negroes, and taken to their village.

He soon found that he was as much a slave as ever; but upon telling his story, they at once agreed to take him to the confines of his country and offer him for ransom. As soon as he was able to walk, they set out, and in ten days reached the river Queal. Ascending it to Lake Tsamsa, they arrived at the last town of the Foota Jals, named Goolah. From this place messengers were despatched across the lake to a Framazug town, and from thence word was sent to Kiloam, that the king's son, who had been mourned as dead, was alive, and to be ransomed for as many gold rings, of a certain thickness, as would cover to their tips the fingers of his master's hands. Commissioners were at once deputed to effect the ransom; who, when they arrived at the appointed spot for the ratification of the bargain, were introduced to a gigantic negro of Goolah, as the master of Enphadde. A delay of two or three days now occurred, in consequence of the commissioners not having more than half the requisite number of rings for his monstrous fingers. But at last a supply was procured—the giant's digits were sheathed in gold, and Enphadde was restored to the bosom of a doting father and to the affections of an admiring people. Great was the joy upon his return; but it was qualified by the profound regrets for the supposed cruel fate of his beloved sister. "Could we have known," concluded Enphadde, "that God had sent Jonathan again to your protection, how happy we should have been!"

"Poor Enphadde!" replied Kaloolah, "your fate has been the hardest; you have had no hope of my safety to support you, while I have been almost ever confident of yours."

"No," rejoined Enphadde, "we had no hope of ever seeing you again. Imagine our joy, then, upon hearing that you were here, alive and well, and that the preserver of both our lives was with you. 'Fly! fly! Enphadde,' said the great Shounsé, 'and bring her to my arms. And this noble stranger, conduct him in all honor, and quickly, too, for I long to testify my gratitude to the savior of my children.'"

Enphadde's story was finished—the fog-laden breeze began to steal across the bosom of the river, and the old dagash made his appearance, with many apologies for the intrusion, to announce that supper was waiting in the great hall. We entered amid a blaze of light, a burst of delicious music, and a shower of ecstatic odors, shaken from ten thousand flowers.

In his hurry to get back to Kiloam, the prince was anxious to obtain a remount of horses from Garazha, and set off the next morning. But the dagash told him that that was impossible. "There are hardly twenty horses in town, and to collect fifty from the country would take three or four days. In two days your own horses will have recovered from their fatigue, and, in the meantime, you will have to honor my poor quarters with your presence."

Enphadde was thus compelled to submit to a delay of two days, which was little enough time for his exhausted horses to recruit their

strength. The time, however, soon passed, and on the morning of the
third day we were all in the saddle, and, escorted by the dagash and most
of the inhabitants of the town, we emerged from the heavy stone gate-
way, and set out diagonally across the pleasant valley through which ran
the little tributary to the Nourwall.

A monstrous buffalo had been prepared for the use of the princess.
To a ring in his nose was attached a rope, by which he was led, although
he was so tame and well trained as to obey the slightest intimations of
the voice. Upon his back was erected a framework of canes, and this

*" Presenting a figure that would have furnished an artist with a good life model of Neptune on
the couch of Amphitrite."*

was covered with curtains of the finest muslin, worked in a kind of arabesque, with threads of gold, silver, and purple; within were cushioned
seats, upon which the rider might recline at any angle corresponding to
his or her notions of comfort or grace. Bands of glittering snake-skin confined the structure upon the back of the buffalo, whose horns, neck, and
tail were bedecked with garlands of flowers. The animal's gait was an
easy but rather ungainly amble, which he could continue for any length
of time, compelling his leaders and attendants, who ran by his sides
with bushes of fragrant herbs to keep off the flies, to move at a sharp
trot.

Notwithstanding, however, the fascinations of this bovine gestation,
Kaloolah expressed her preference for the saddle, and, after parting with

the dagash and his guards, she insisted upon mounting her horse and resigning the buffalo to Jack, who loudly expressed his delight at the change.

"Talk of horses," exclaimed Jack, "they are nothing to this ere craft. Why, when astraddle of one of these narrow-backed things, I feel like a lubber on a yard-arm. I roll, and pitch, and toss like a badly stowed ship; and every few minutes I fancy my ballast is about to shift, and that I shall be down upon my beam-ends. But here! Lord bless the two prettiest black eyes that ever looked out from an angel's head—and those are your'n, marm! I never see'd such a regular ship-shape ambulation on four legs afore. Why, I was once in an American brig out of New York—Mr. Romer's own city—and off the Horn we lay-to for two and thirty days in one steady gale. The wind blew so hard that it took six men and the cook to hold the captain's quadrant while he took the sun, and yet we never sprung a spar, opened a seam, strained a bulkhead, or shipped as much water as you could put in your eye and make anybody believe you had been crying. Now the motion of this craft is just like that brig, and if I had only a little sniff of tar and bilge water I could go to sleep and dream that I was in her, and once more fairly off soundings."

It will not be supposed that Kaloolah's knowledge of English was sufficient to enable her to understand all the delicate shades of meaning in Jack's sea-talk, but, somehow, they got on very well together. They had become great friends, and were very fond of holding long conversations, when Jack would spin his yarns with a profusion of gestures and grimaces that never failed to please the princess much, and which, not unfrequently, made it difficult for me to preserve a proper gravity of countenance.

At first I objected to the manifest impropriety of Jack's mounting the buffalo, but Kaloolah insisted upon it, and afterwards rode by his side, enjoying the unaffected delight with which he resigned himself to the rolling motions of the beast. Kaloolah's slightest wish was attended to with an air of deference and respect by her brother and guards that alone would have prevented me from interposing any serious objections to her will, and I was, therefore, obliged to permit Jack to occupy his elevated position, where he stretched himself out with the most *insouciant* air imaginable—presenting a figure that would have furnished an artist with a good life model of Neptune on the couch of Amphitrite.

CHAPTER XXXIX.

UR road for five days lay through an undulating country, that
grew more populous and more closely cultivated at every step.
On either side it was lined with a double row of fruit-trees, a
few only of which were familiar to me—such as the olive, the
almond, the orange, the fig, and the cactus opuntia or prickly pear. These
were all public property, and afforded the traveller both refreshment and
shade. The trees were very flourishing; and, upon inquiry, I found that
it was a matter of emulation among the owners of property along the
road as to which should thus present strangers with the most tempting
fruit. Between the trees were placed marble pillars, surmounted with
vases filled with fresh flowers. No higher compliment can be paid to the
owner's taste and horticultural skill than for the passing traveller to stop
and select the most beautiful.

The houses on either hand were mostly of stone—a yellow-tinted
marble,—and, although low, had a peculiarly light appearance. Generally
they were half buried in masses of rich verdure, which served to give
them a degree of breadth and dignity, and to very much assist their
architectural effects. Numerous aqueducts of freestone-work could be
seen crossing the country in every direction; and spanning the rivers and
watercourses were bridges equal in solidity and symmetry to the best
productions of Roman masonry. Lofty monuments, consisting of marble
pillars, carved into a series of globes, gradually decreasing in size from
the bottom to the top, and surmounted by a small plain cube of lava,
peered up from above the loftiest trees; and immense buildings, which
proved to be distributing reservoirs, into which the water is pumped for
the purpose of giving it sufficient head, crowned the summits of the hills
and frowned in massive majesty, like the feudal castles of Christian countries, upon the flowery dells and flowing streams below. Like feudal
castles? True, there was something suggestive of the association, but
how unlike in all important points. Both are elevated upon heights, and

generally upon the banks of rivers, but one is so elevated to afford a rapid descent to the pure water—to give force and pressure to the numberless refreshing jets and cooling cascades, and graceful fountains, the other to afford security to violence, vantage to rapine and slaughter—to give to human selfishness strongholds, from which, with irresistible momentum, it might descend and deluge the lower lands with blood. Suppose that all the dwellings of cruel, brutal, ignorant, short-sighted tyranny and superstition that dot the surface of Europe, had been for ages merely fountain-heads of water—prisons only for Undines and Nereids, who, when released from confinement, had danced and sung, ever and for ever appealing to the gradually deepening sense of the beautiful; speaking with a refining power to the delighted heart, and persuading from lavish Ceres and Pomona their choicest gifts to man. Suppose, still further, that instead of being mere reservoirs of water, these old castles, and towers, and convents, had been reservoirs of virtue—strongholds of honest human sympathy, whence had flowed all fertilizing and elevating influences: suppose, in other words, that all government, political, social, and religious, had not been perverted from its plain and inviting ends—the good of the whole to the sordid advantage of a part,—and what would now be the condition of Europe?—of the world? The wildest imagination can hardly compass the then glories of Christendom, with its ten or twenty thousand millions of happy and comfortable people.

And how has the world been thus cheated of its inheritance, and, possible, yet unborn, millions deprived of their rights in eternity, and the world overburdened with people, while yet not a thousandth part of its power of production has been developed? Is it the result of necessary pre-existent causes—the natural and inevitable evolution of the germs of evil, implanted from the beginning in the human heart—something over which man, from the laws of his nature, could have exercised no control? Or, is it the result of false teaching and bad habits—of imperious fashion —of long-continued and assiduous experiments in evil—of an industrious training in vice—of a diabolical combination of selfish men to trample their fellow-citizens beneath them, to degrade and beggar them, and to crush, with the iron heel of power, their generous impulses, their few and feeble, because unstimulated, aspirations for a nobler, and always nobler civilization? If the first, adieu to all the glowing hopes of the political reformer; if the second, who can set bounds to the constantly accelerated rush of political and social improvement?

But to return to my sheep, from which the water tanks have taken me a long way, and which were literally gambolling by my side. There were, as I have mentioned, several varieties of them, but the most curious was a long-wooled animal, about the size of a small cow, and furnished with monstrous udders of rich milk. Their backs were broad and soft, and more than once we saw a long-legged Framazug astride of one of them, and industriously drumming on its sides with his heels.

We passed through several villages and large towns, and saw others in the distance, and the places where we stopped for the night were substantial cities of twenty and thirty thousand inhabitants. From all these the people came out in crowds, saluting us with hearty shouts and a general waving of bouquets.

It was in the afternoon of the fifth day, after leaving Garazha, that our road lay up the steep sides of a range of hills, which for a long time had been seen bounding our horizon to the south. We were within a few rods of the crest of the hill. " Prepare yourselves," said Enphadde, " for a fine view. In a moment more you will see Kiloam. We are on the very brink of the great valley of the Wollosab ! "

At this instant our vanguard raised a great shout and flourished their spears over their heads. All stopped where the road made a sharp turn, and eagerly looked down at something on their left. Hugh stretched himself up in his stirrups, and gazed fixedly. Jack, finding the curtains of his howdah impede his view, jumped nimbly from the back of his buffalo and ran out to the side of the road ; and Hassan, as was his custom whenever any thing particularly pleased him, threw up the muzzle of his musket and fired it in the air. The instant he had done so I could see his eyes roll round towards me, as deprecating the anger that he knew he had justly aroused. " You 've fired your last charge of powder, my good fellow ! " said I, looking and speaking somewhat sternly to the frightened culprit. But at this moment my attention was drawn to the princess, by an exclamation from Enphadde.

Kaloolah was deadly pale. I thought she was about to faint, and jumping from my horse, flew to her side and lifted her to the ground.

" It will be over in a moment," said Kaloolah ; " direct our train to move on. We can overtake them in a few minutes."

" It is very foolish in me," said Kaloolah, " to feel so ! But when Enphadde exclaimed that at yonder bend of the road we should see Kiloam, and when I saw the guards toss their spears and shout, my heart began to beat as it never beat but once before " ; and the princess gave me a look that I at once interpreted to mean, on the evening of the attack upon the caravan among the sand-hills of the desert.

" No, Kaloolah," I replied, " it is not foolish to feel as you do. Nothing can be more natural. Were I in your situation, man as I am, I 'm afraid I should not be able to control my emotion as well as you. Even as it is, Enphadde's announcement made my pulses throb like a frightened child's."

"Come, come," exclaimed Enphadde, after a pause, "lean upon our arms, and let us move up to this view that seems to frighten you so."

"Are you sure that it is there ?" said Kaloolah. "It seems to me as though the whole might be a dream. Here, pinch my fingers," said she, naïvely, throwing out her hands, "and see if I am awake."

I took one hand, and was giving it a gentle squeeze, when she suddenly pulled it away, and the color came into her face. "No, no," she exclaimed, "I don't wish to know ; if it 's a dream, it 's a pleasant one, and I wont be waked from it ; come, let us go " ; and putting her arms within ours, we slowly advanced to the crown of the hill.

Despite her assumed vivacity and calmness, I could feel her frame tremble, and could perceive the increasing pallor of her cheek. With a sudden effort she hurried us forward, mounted the projecting ledge of rock, and gazed at the vast ocean of earth that lay beneath and before us.

" *Loo, loo, bil sa Wollosab, bah loo, loo bil sa mahrah Kiloam !* " exclaimed Enphadde.

Kaloolah raised her hands to her eyes, as if the sight was too much for her, and turning away, fell sobbing into her brother's arms. I felt that this was a situation in which even the most sympathizing lover would be *de trop*. There were thronging associations which I could not share—vibrating memories to which my voice was not attuned—bonds of affection, which all-powerful love might transcend, and even disrupt, but whose precise nature it could not assume.

There are some lovers who are jealous of such things—fellows who like to wholly monopolize a woman—and who are constantly on the watch, seizing and appropriating her every look, thought, and feeling, with somewhat of the same notion of an exclusive right as that with which they pocket a tooth-pick ;—I am not of that turn. The female heart is as curiously and as variously stocked as a country dry-goods store. A man may be, perhaps, allowed to select out for his own exclusive use some of the heavier articles, such as sheetings, shirtings, flannels, trace-chains, hobby-horses, and goose-yokes, but that is no reason why the neighbors should be at once cut off from their accustomed supply of small wares.

I withdrew a few yards, to a higher and more projecting crag, not to obtain a more extensive view, for the character of the scene by no means excited that desire to see farther and still farther beyond what at first breaks upon the sight, which is so often felt in viewing a landscape, or any object which depends for its effect upon extent or size. The beautiful or the sublime emotion arising from form, color, motion or any combination of these qualities, may be complete, entire, mind-filling and soul-satisfying, because the causes may be perfect, and incapable of improvement or augmentation. Their power cannot be increased by adding a little more form, a little more color, or a little more motion. But, when extension is the only or the predominant element of the view, the mind is at once dissatisfied, and demands more and more, bounding its desires not even by the limits of human reason.

Now, in the view before me there was wonderful extension—an almost limitless expansion ; but it was subordinate to the magnificent combination of form, color, and motion.

Sheer down went the precipice a thousand feet, and from its base the country descended, by gentle slopes and wide terraces, a thousand feet farther, to the banks of the Wollosab, a distance of about fifteen miles. Far up to the left was the great Lake of Wollo, forty miles long and ten broad, with numerous islands—all of them in sight. From the lower end of this lake, and nearly opposite to us, on the farther side, opened two immense valleys far up, in which could be caught the glitter of smaller bodies of water. The mountain dividing the valleys ran boldly down to the lake, bearing upon its crest a stream, that, descending by two successive leaps, five hundred feet each, ran for a quarter of a mile, a broad sheet of milky foam, and again bounding over a lofty ledge, whitened, for a league, the surface of the Wollo. Ten miles below this and in front of us, where the river issued from the lake, was the great city of Kiloam, and more than fifty other cities could be seen at a glance.

Beyond the Wollosab, there stretched a plain fifty miles broad, traversed by numerous streams, and bordered by a sea of purple-bodied, white-headed mountains, that seemed as if in the very act of tossing themselves, in proud defiance, against the sky. Far away to the right this plain extended, to where the hazy cones closed in and left barely a passage for the majestic river.

Back of us the scene was equally gorgeous. There lay the rich rolling country that we had passed, bordered by hills, which, in the northeast and east, grew into mountains, among which, proudly conspicuous, stood the ever-flaming Kebbi.

The small chain of hills upon which we stood was thus the centre of a vast amphitheatre. The chain was not more than thirty miles in length, and was deeply serrated. We might have taken a more level road, through the deep passes, or escaped the hills altogether by a slight detour; but Enphadde had chosen the path over the highest peak, in order to give us a more striking and comprehensive view of his country.

There was a wonderful clearness and transparency of the air, that more than doubled the limits of ordinary vision. Cities, palaces, aqueducts, bridges, monuments, stood forth, at a distance of leagues, with telescopic distinctness. I gazed as one entranced.

My revery was broken by the voice of the princess, who called to me to come and take a seat by her side.

Together we gazed, lost to all sense of time, in the deep emotions of the scene, until suddenly, far below us, the spear-points of our escort gleamed from the overarching trees—" Come ! " exclaimed the prince, jumping to his feet ; " the sun is going down, and we must follow his example, or we shall have to find our way by starlight."

Our attendants bringing up our horses, we mounted, and descended a steep, winding road, running through dense arbors of flowering trees, and crossing several times, by light wooden bridges, a tangled silvery thread of water. We overtook our escort when in sight of a large town, where we were to stop for the night.

As usual, crowds of people were awaiting our arrival at some distance from the gates. Every one bore a bouquet in one hand, and a torch or paper lantern in the other. As darkness came on, the flambeaux were lighted, and from the walls, towers, and houses streamed the light of innumerable lamps.

From the gateway to the house appointed for our reception, a distance of full half a mile, we rode along under a continuous canopy of flowers. A netting of rope work had been stretched across from the tops of the houses, and into this the flowers had been interwoven, leaving, at intervals, dependent garlands and wreaths. The balconies and porticos were also wreathed with flowers, and filled with beautiful women. Thousands of lamps, torches, and lanterns diffused as intense a light as the full brightness of day. In front of us danced a dozen girls, in picturesque costume, with musical instruments, like tambourines, with which they accompanied their voices ; and on each side moved a dense throng, from whose throats every few minutes came a wild chorus, that fairly lifted the canopy of flowers, and that thrilled through me like ten thousand bowie-knives.

The good people of Jellalob had taken us quite by surprise. Orders having been issued that our journey should be conducted with all privacy, we were not prepared for such a display. Enphadde, however, was the only one of the party displeased; and he signified as much to the dagash and the authorities of the town. Kaloolah, however, interposed, and averted the storm of princely wrath; and Enphadde was fain to receive the excuses of the frightened officials, who represented that ever since the announcement that the princess was on the road, the people had been in the greatest ferment, and that it would have been impossible to prevent them from making some demonstration of their joy.

Upon reaching the palace we alighted, and were conducted across an open courtyard paved in mosaic--in the centre of which played an illuminated fountain—to a flight of low broad marble steps; ascending these, we were conducted through a wide hall to a lofty saloon, hung in blue and gold, and furnished with curiously sculptured alabaster pedestals, containing lamps, and wreathed on the outside with flowers. In a few minutes we were shown to our sleeping rooms. Mine led from the farther end of a long marble saloon, and opened out into a balcony that overlooked a small court, where played a lively jet of sparkling water. A flight of narrow stone steps led to the court, and thence to a bathing room, where a bathing tub of fragrant cedar, studded with silver, and filled with warm rose-water, awaited me.

I was preparing to enjoy the refreshing luxury, when a servant announced that Enphadde wished to see me. Upon repairing to the saloon I found him and his sister still in their travelling dresses, and apparently ready to resume their journey. They announced that word had just been received from the court that their father had gone to a royal chateau upon the banks of the Wollo, about ten hours' ride from us, and that he expected his daughter to come on at once, while I was to remain for a day or two at Jellalob, and to have a presentation to his majesty at Kiloam. I had no right to object to this arrangement, but I could not refrain from expressing my regrets at parting.

" 'T is only for a day," whispered Kaloolah, as I assisted her into a curtained palanquin.

" True, 't is only for a day." said I, smiling, and waving my hand as the bearers lifted their lovely burden from the ground, but at heart I felt as forlorn as if it had been for a year, or a lifetime.

" Pshaw ! " I mentally ejaculated, " this is too ridiculous, to let a little Congo slave-girl get the upper hand of my heart in this way ! "

Upon entering my saloon I found my lords-in-waiting, Jack, Hugh, and Hassan, engaged with a host of servants in arranging and displaying several complete suits of dress.   There were garments of fine linen, shawls like those of cashmere, figured muslins, and robes and surcoats of feather-cloth of the most gorgeous colors.

After my bath I selected a cashmere for a turban, and throwing a feather robe over my shoulders, I descended, with my companions, all dressed in a similar style, to the banquet hall, where the dagash, and forty or fifty officers were waiting to receive me.

After the feast came music, dancing, and a variety of juggling feats. The dancing girls were beautiful and very graceful in their movements, and their conjuring tricks were novel and performed with great skill. Some of them were truly wonderful, as, for instance, turning a man into a tree bearing fruit, and with monkeys skipping about in the branches; and another case, where the chief juggler, apparently swallowed five men, ten boys, and a jackass, threw them all up again, turned himself inside out, blew himself up like a balloon, and, exploding with a loud report, disappeared in a puff of luminous vapor.   My companions declared that we had got into a country of enchanters, and I could not but admire the skill with which the tricks were performed, although I was too much of a Yankee to be much astonished at any thing in the *hey ! presto !* line.

CHAPTER XL.

E set out, the next day, with an immense escort, and were followed by large crowds of people from Jellalob and the neighboring cities. Buffaloes, richly caparisoned, were provided for us, and for most of the accompanying dignitaries; but we preferred our horses; and, in compliment to us, the dagash and several high officers from the court also took their seats in the saddle.

On either side of us were footmen, who supported over our heads, by long slender poles, awnings of pure linen. These were bedecked with streamers of variously colored muslin, and with wreaths of fresh flowers. A little in the rear came a hand-barrow, in which were conspicuously placed our muskets and pistols. These seemed to attract the largest share of public attention, and the barrow was frequently raised aloft to afford the people an opportunity of seeing the wonderful machines, which, in the hands of the Footas, were beginning to threaten their existence as a nation.

We passed several of the columns that I have mentioned, surmounted with the usual cube of lava. A very lofty one having attracted my attention, *Seywad dal Gouk*, one of the lords of the court, who rode by my side, volunteered an explanation.

"You must know," said he, "that these columns are erected as mementos of the *Pholdefoos*, or the 'Seekers of Truth.'"

"True," I replied, "the young prince, Enphadde, told me as much, but I do not understand, precisely, who these 'seekers of truth' are."

"They are," said the Seywad, "a class of pure, holy, and wise enthusiasts, who withdraw from their fellow-men and the common concerns of life, and devote themselves solely to the search for the germs of moral, religious, and political truth, and to the inevitable fate that awaits them at the end of their search."

"An exclusive caste or order?" I demanded.

"No, any one can become a seeker, provided he gives evidence of the proper intellectual and moral qualities, and of those spiritual promptings which are necessary to carry him in triumph to the end. Such a one is permitted to take the vows of his order on his thirtieth birthday. From that time he devotes himself to meditation and study. A small stipend from the government barely supplies him with the necessaries of life. Part of the time he wanders about the country, studying human nature, investigating the laws of social organization, inquiring into the history, antiquities, and jurisprudence of past generations, and collecting from the monuments of departed 'seekers' the germs of truth for which they had sacrificed their lives. The rest of the time he devotes to meditation in some retired spot, afar from the bustle and turmoil of the world. Here he prepares himself for his fate, and eliminates the apothegm upon which his reputation for wisdom and virtue is to depend.

"A few days before his fortieth birthday, the announcement is made throughout the country, of the approaching sacrifice of a 'seeker.' People collect from all parts—the seeker, attended by the proper officers, appears, arrayed in white linen. Alone he mounts upon a lofty staging, erected over an immense pile of fagots. A chaplet of roses adorns his head—flowers bedeck the funeral pile beneath. A hundred virgins chant, to the music of sweet-toned instruments, the praises of Truth and her heroic 'seekers.' He now proclaims aloud the one single short apothegm or maxim, to the discovery or enforcement of which he has resolved to devote his life. The phrase is taken up and repeated by thousands of voices. Shouts of applause and admiration rend the air, the pile is lighted—the volleying smoke and flames ascend, and envelop the 'seeker,' who, waving his arms, triumphantly leaps into the glowing furnace below.

"A monument is at once erected to his memory, and ornamented, as you see, by a cube of lava—typical, in its shape, of the perfectly symmetrical form of a fundamental truth, viewed in whatever aspects; and in its composition, of the refining fiery influences under which the truth has been sought and obtained."

"How is it?" I demanded, "that while most of these monuments are of the same size, there are a few that tower far above the usual height?"

"Those," replied my informant, "are erected in memory of some great truth that has withstood the test of ages. It is permitted to the people at the end of five hundred years after the death of the 'seeker' to tear down his monument, if time has demonstrated the fallacy of his dogma, or to enlarge it, if public opinion so decrees. This high monument was erected thousands of years ago; since then it has received many additions, and more than a hundred other monuments have been erected in enforcement and elucidation of its *truth-speech.*"

" And what is its truth-speech?"

" Simply this: ' He loves himself the best who loves God the most; and he loves God the most who loves with his whole heart his fellow-men.' Yonder you see a modern monument, with a similar sentiment in different words. It says: ' The earth would be God's flower-garden, did not human selfishness choke the paths so that the Devil only can walk therein.'"

" And do not these apothegms," I demanded, "furnish texts for disputation; are all admitted, at once, as truth?"

" Certainly not," replied Dal Gouk, " some are of questionable truthfulness under any interpretation, and others give rise to sects. For instance, there is one expressing a moral correlative of the axiom I have mentioned. Its motto is, ' The love of their kind is a ladder by which men can climb to heaven.' This was considered plain enough, until, long after the ' seeker ' was dead, the question arose, ' whether a man, who, by cultivating a love of his kind to the complete uprooting of self-love, had attained the top of the ladder, would have reached heaven actually, or would have reached a height to ensure heaven after death.' At once two parties arose—the actualists and the super-actualists,—and the dispute between them is now at its height."

" And how will it be decided?"

" Why, as is usual in such cases, the people and authorities will have to tear down the monument, thus referring the truth to future seekers, who will develop it in a new form. But it is not alone moral and theological truths that furnish grounds for dispute—political and social maxims are equally prolific. Fortunately, the expounders and commentators and disputers are held in the greatest contempt, and although some few may for awhile be led astray, the people ultimately put the polemics with their dogmas, and half truths, and false facts wholly aside, and steadily adhere to the stately, strong, slow current of national opinion."

" And whither is this current tending?"

" Onward, ever onward, if not always directly towards the true and the beautiful, at least away from the ugly and the false."

" We shall have Dal Gouk turning pholdefoo one of these days," interposed a young noble, shrugging his shoulders at the Seywad's rising enthusiasm.

Dal Gouk shook his head, but made no reply, and for some time we rode on in silence. When conversation was resumed it took a wide range, and embraced a variety of subjects, which would be, perhaps, of interest to the reader, but which the extended space my manuscript has already reached warns me must be left for a separate work.

As we advanced, the glittering towers and domes, and lofty battle-ments of the great city grew more distinct. A three hours' ride brought us to a long stone bridge of twenty arches, leading across the Wollosab. Crossing this, we wheeled along the river for a few rods to the left, and then traversing a small promontory, came to a broad, straight road, bounded by lofty walls, which put me in mind of the *μακρα τειχη* by which Themistocles connected his famous city with its Piræus. Enter-ing this road through a wide-arched gateway, we again turned to the left, and, riding along for about a mile, debouched into a large place, sur-rounded by massive stone buildings, and ornamented with marble columns and fountains. The square was crowded with people, who received us with shouts and a universal waving of bouquets.

Several streets led off from the sides. Our escort took its course across the square and up a broad straight street, the pavement of which struck me as being considerably superior to the barbarous rubble work of Broadway. It was composed of large stones four and five feet square, and six or eight inches thick. Across the surface of each ran grooves half an inch in depth and width, and four inches apart, affording a foot-hold for horses, donkeys, and buffaloes. It costs but little time or trouble to lay this pavement, the blocks of stone being simply placed so as to break joints upon a foundation made by levelling the ground, and then driving wooden pegs a foot or more long, or rather of a length and size proportioned to the nature of the ground. These little piles are driven at intervals of ten or twelve inches apart, and being completely covered by the earth, they never decay and never give way—thus forming a foundation cheap, efficient, and durable.

This road runs directly with a slight ascent for a distance of two miles, up to the face of a precipice of rock three hundred feet high. Then di-viding, it turns at right angles, and runs, on either hand, entirely around this stately acropolis. The stone has been accurately scarped, and two deep stairways cut in it. Up these the people rushed, completely filling them from top to bottom, with a crowd which, slowly winding its way upwards, looked like two huge snakes of brilliant hues creeping along the face of the rock.

A lofty archway opened before us into a tunnel, fifty feet wide, and eight hundred feet in length, cut out of the solid rock. We entered this, and at the end of it came to a circular shaft, or well, that extended to the top of the acropolis, a height of more than three hundred feet. Upon looking up, the clear sky could be seen resting like a dome upon the mouth of the shaft. A broad, gently sloping road, making one of the most magnificent spiral staircases in the world, afforded an easy ascent to men and beasts.

On emerging from the shaft we found ourselves in the centre of a large square, shaded with majestic trees, divided into walks, ornamented with fountains, columns, and flower-stands, and surrounded on three sides with a parapet, from which one could look down on the city and its beautiful environs, and upon the vast expanse of country beyond. The fourth side was bounded by a range of buildings connected by terraces and balconies, the whole presenting one of those confused, irregular architectural masses, of not much pretension or promise externally, but which at once suggests the idea of long winding corridors, interminable halls, countless courts, private staircases and secret passages, and excites a longing to explore the presumed labyrinthian mysteries.

Passing from the gaze of the countless multitudes crowding the square, we were ushered through a low arched gateway into a small court, where, upon dismounting, I was met by Enphadde. He at once conducted us through several long passages to a fine suite of apartments overlooking the eastern side of the acropolis.

My first inquiry, as the reader may suppose, was after Kaloolah.

" She is well," replied the prince, " although still suffering from the agitation of meeting her father. Joy almost killed the great Shounsé. He has recovered now, but he still holds my sister to his heart. But see, she has not forgotten you—she sends you this," and Enphadde produced a tiny bouquet, not much larger than a rose-bud, and yet containing a dozen different flowers, each one of which conveyed some message, but which, as I was no adept in the language of flowers, I concluded it best not to puzzle my head by attempting to read. " No! no matter," I replied to Enphadde, who offered to explain ; " tell Kaloolah that the heart is an apt scholar in such cases, and that mine shall read her message for me."

" I must leave you now," said Enphadde ; " and when the sun has descended half-way the western arch of heaven I will come and conduct you to my father."

It was about three hours before Enphadde's return, and, in the meanwhile we had time for a delicious bath and an elaborate toilet, in which we were assisted by numerous attendants, between whom and my three personal followers there was a good deal of discussion in relation to the esthetics of dress. Jack was much the most difficult to please, rejecting each garment offered him, and making his comments upon the " monkey-fied, sodger-looking " dresses with an expression of the highest disgust. At last I had to interfere, and actually order him into a picturesque-looking costume.

" Well, if I must, I must ! " said Jack ; " but I 'm blessed if it aint a disappointment ! I 've navigated under all kinds of outlandish rigs, and it seems kind of natural to do so among the Bedouins and Blackamoors, and other savages ; but you have always said that we were coming among a civilized people. Well, here we are, and devil the thing that looks like a pea-jacket, or a pair of duck trowsers, have these fellows got in all this finifine toggery ! Civilized ! They don't know the rudiments ! I 'm blessed if I believe they could tell a piece of black ribbon a yard long, if they should see it. And as for a tarpaulin !—just think of a fellow's haul-ing out the weather-earing in a sou'wester with one of these feather things on his head ! "

We were all ready when Enphadde returned, and descending a broad flight of marble steps, we entered a paved hall a hundred feet in length, which conducted us to a large circular room, lighted by a dome, which was supported upon eight pillars of verd antique. The shafts of these pillars were fluted in spirals, and the capitals were elaborate imitations of bunches of flowers. The bases and entablature were nearly pure Corin-thian, and the general effect was very much the same as of that order.

The room was filled with officials, in rich dresses, who received us in silence, with a series of profound genuflexions. We paused for a moment in the centre of the room, where a slender fountain was throwing a jet of perfumed water. Enphadde raised his hand, and a pair of folding-doors, of panelled boxwood, inlaid with silver and ivory, drew noiselessly aside. A burst of delicious music, from a hundred soft-toned instruments, greeted us as we stepped into the great hall of the fountains.

As we stood at one end, the *coup-d'œil* was magnificent. As far up almost as the eye could reach extended two rows of tall columns ; each column represented two convoluted serpents, their intertwined tails coiled up for a base, from which their huge helicoidal bodies sprang to a height of twenty-five feet. At this point the necks of the serpents separated, and each one, curving outwards and upwards, longitudinally, again ap-proached the other, describing a heart-shaped curve, and, bending down-wards, took a single twist, from which the heads diverged in every variety of action and expression. These columns were of carved cedar, inlaid, or covered with the skins of serpents. Their surfaces had thus been made to gleam and glow, in the most natural manner, with all the rich and deep colors of the intertropical reptalia. A light entablature rested upon the curved necks of the serpents. Along the frieze ran a bas-relief of vines, with fruits and flowers of burnished gold, silver, and precious stones ; and in the mouths of many of the serpents were branches of gilded fruit.

The whole length of the hall was about four hundred feet ; its width between the rows of pillars, about fifty feet. Between the pillars and the walls, on either side, was a space of about fifteen feet, the floor of which was raised a foot or two above that of the centre, and strung the whole length with cushions, upon which were seated a double row of guards, habited in the most gorgeous uniforms. The floor of the centre, between the colonnades, was of the most elaborate mosaic, representing five large vines, with spreading tendrils and branches, among whose leaves played monkeys of every shape and size, some of them with wings ; and birds, rivalling in brilliancy of plumage their animate prototypes of the wood ; and all kinds of snakes and lizards, with glittering skins, and eyes of ruby, diamond, and opal.

But where were the fountains from which the hall took its name ? Above, directly overhead, on either side from the galleries, supported by the pillars, arose a thousand jets, each one arching itself, in a parabolic curve, across the hall, and falling into the opposite gallery. These jets, arranged alternately, were so adjusted that the spread of the water in one, as it fell, would just fill the space between the concentrated fluid issuing from the opposite pipes ; and in this way, by the accurate interposition of corresponding streams, there was supported a continuous canopy of water the whole length of the hall.

A flood of light was poured from myriads of unseen lamps upon the upper surface of this sparkling roof, while below, numberless hidden tapers were so arranged in tubes as to throw their rays against the under surface of the watery arch, from which they were returned, after countless refractions and reflections, to the delighted eye. A wonderful variety of effects were produced by the continually changing color of the water : for a minute or two it would be of a pure white, and then, slowly assuming a prismatic tint, run on through all the colors of the rainbow.

The low, hollow, rushing noise of the falling water filled the lofty hall, and floated in massive but most musical waves of sound upon the perfumed air. The glowing pillars seemed animated, as the bright and flickering light played upon their burnished surfaces. The vines of the mosaic pavement, and the fruits and flowers of the frieze, waved as if in obedience to the breeze; while the green, yellow, and scarlet monkeys gambolled among the branches, and diamond-eyed snakes and birds glided amid the quivering leaves.

Enphadde paused at the foot of the hall, and, for ten minutes, we stood silently gazing up the interminable vista. Hugh, Jack, and Hassan stood a few feet behind us, but so close that I could occasionally hear their remarks. Hugh was the first to find his tongue.

" Jack, dear!" he exclaimed, " do you think, those sarpents are alive ?"

" To be sure! Don't you see how they twist and wriggle about ?"

" I do; but I don't see how they can be made to stand so straight, and hould such a big weight on their necks."

" Why, it 's their edication! What makes a soldier so straight? What takes the kinks out of the back of a corporal of marines? Is n't it edication? These sarpents have been devilish well trained! Why, I 've seen, in the East Indies, a snake dance a hornpipe! Now, if a snake can dance a hornpipe, I argues that a snake can be edicated to do any thing; unless it may be, perhaps, to preach a sarmon, or cat and fish a frigate's best bower."

" What does the nigger say?" demanded Jack of Hugh, as Hassan interposed some observations in mingled Tuaric and Arabic.

" He wants to know," replied Hugh, " if we sha'n't be aten up by these creatures! Never you mind, honey! it 's just follow the captain, that 's all. When he 's swallowed you may begin to look out for Jonah's lodgings for yourself; but—whist!—whist!—Holy Mary!"

A roar, louder than the united voices of a million whirlwinds, arose throughout the hall, that drowned all sounds, and seemed to shake the solid pavement beneath our feet. For a moment I thought that it was an earthquake, but Enphadde and the Framazug nobles behind us were perfectly composed. The next instant I perceived my mistake, and discovered the cause of the sounds. The double row of guards behind the pillars, upon some signal, had sprung simultaneously from their cushioned seats, each one with an enormous gong in his hand, upon which he proceeded to drum as energetically as if announcing dinner to the hungry boarders of a New York hotel. Five hundred large gongs sounding together! Can any one conceive of a more horrible tympanum-stretching, soul-benumbing concord? Yes! there is one thing, and one thing only, that can surpass it—a concert of a thousand gongs! but who could survive to describe the effect?

The drum of my ear was just giving way, when the noise began to subside—it fell to the gentlest rumbling of distant thunder, and then rose, loud, fierce, furious, as the very "crack of doom." Again it subsided, and again it rose—three times—a royal salute, and an announcement that the great Shoumsé had taken his seat upon the throne.

Slowly we moved up the gorgeous hall, which now seemed, by contrast, as silent as death. The guards on either side presented their gongs, which proved to be shields, and stood with their heads bowed low, immovable as statues. We reached the upper end, and, emerging through an arched doorway, hung with heavily embroidered curtains, entered a large circular room of at least a hundred feet diameter. The roof was curiously arched and groined, and appeared to be of white marble, and from it depended several large chandeliers of alabaster, rock crystal, and gold, which diffused a brilliant but mellow light around. A large carved and gilded ring ran round the room for a cornice, and from this depended curtains or hangings of crimson and gold, which, at equal distances were pulled aside and looped up, disclosing the walls, empannelled in blue and silver. Two thirds of the floor was a rich arabesque mosaic, representing a variety of nondescript and fanciful vines, leaves, and fruits. This portion of the room was ornamented with vases of flowers, and was occupied by several groups of dignitaries, habited in flowing robes of gorgeous feather cloth, worked with gold and gems, and in crimson and blue head-dresses, from which waved the inimitable plumage of the froulbell.

The other third of the room was elevated to the height of two broad steps, and covered with a richly figured carpet of asphaltum, with tufts of cotton and wool of the kind that I have before described. In the middle of this portion of the room was a small carved ivory platform about eight feet square, and approached on three sides by three low steps, running the whole length. From this platform arose a curiously-constructed wide cushioned chair. The legs and arms were made out of solid tusks of ivory, inlaid with gold and silver. The back was formed of an immense gold shield, which was held in the claws of two large silver lions rampant, at the sides of the chair. One broad step upon which, at either end, had been placed two cushions, led up to the throne, over the arms of which, somewhat like a shawl thrown carelessly across a chair, was a purple cloth sparkling with gems. This drapery hung negligently in flowing folds—on one side, half hiding the lion supporting the shield, —and falling away to the right and left, in graceful amplitude, rested far out upon a carpet to which it was firmly anchored by tags of solid gold, about the size and shape of a six-pound shot.

From the ceiling depended a lustrous canopy, formed by eight winged serpents. They were represented as twisting their tails around a golden ring at the roof, and after uniting their bodies, descending, until, at a proper distance over the chair, they diverged like the radiating serpents in a sky-rocket, and spreading their wings, formed a large spherical dome. The necks of the serpents continued off beyond the circumference of the canopy, and, twisted in all directions, served to support long pendent necklets of precious stones. In the mouth of each serpent was a small bunch of natural flowers.

It must not be supposed that I observed all these minute facts during this, my first interview with the majesty of Framazugda. I have since had repeated opportunities of informing myself in relation to any circumstances about which my curiosity has chosen to make an inquiry. At the time I am describing, I was too much excited to note distinctly such little architectural details. There was a general sense of splendor and wealth, and this perhaps would have been quite overwhelming, had it not been that amid so much that was grand and gorgeous, I could perceive some evidences of a barbaric taste. This quite reassured me. I braced myself at once with the pride of superior civilization; and, although wholly unused to the glare of royalty, I felt my responsibilities as a representative of Christendom in general, and of the "greatest nation in all creation" in particular; and my deportment, I can assure the anxious reader, was characterized by the requisite dignity and composure.

As we entered the room the groups of dignitaries I have mentioned as occupying the paved portion of the floor, made way for us. Silently, and in obedience to the signals of an old fellow with a long white wand, they arranged themselves in three parallel rows on each side, between the arch by which we were entering and the steps leading to the elevated portion of the room. Another wave of the wand, and each noble put his hands to the floor, and with a very dexterous and graceful jerk, kicked his heels up in the air, and stood perfectly straight and motionless upon his hands, with his head downwards. As we passed on they successively resumed an upright position. I could not but admire this new mode of salutation —it was so graceful, such a pleasing exemplification of the line of beauty, such a combination of natural litheness with acquired dexterity, and so profoundly respectful!

Arrived at the steps that divided the room, I directed my three followers to halt, while Enphadde and myself ascended and crossed the tufted carpet to the foot of the throne. On this was seated a venerable man, with a long white beard, and a peculiarly benign countenance. He was attired, with striking plainness, in a loose flowing robe of white. His

"Esplandie and myself ascended and crossed the tufted carpet to the foot of the throne."

head was covered only by a few straggling locks, as colorless as snow, but his eyebrows were remarkably heavy and black. He was of middle size —his figure rather full,—his features large, but regular, and his whole face square and massive, with an expression that reminded me at once of the portraits of Washington.

We reached the ivory steps where, pausing, Enphadde addressed the monarch, but in a voice so clear and distinct as to be heard by the listening courtiers in every part of the room. He mentioned my name and the name of my country; alluded to the hardships to be endured and the dangers to be encountered in coming from so distant a region: spoke of the important services I had rendered to him and his sister; and ended with a glowing eulogy of my transcendent wisdom, generosity, and valor. The prince was really eloquent, and had not my modesty been fully equal to my other qualities, I should almost have believed that I merited his concluding laudation, he expressed himself with such a graceful warmth.

As he finished, the great Shounsé rose from his throne and stepped down upon the ivory platform. " The savior of my children is welcome ! " he exclaimed, stretching forth his hand, as I thought, for me to kiss. Instinctively I took a step upwards and forwards, and bowing my head, just touched his hand with my lips. Before I could recover myself, he threw his arms around my neck, and gave me a hearty embrace. " Welcome, *my son* ! " he exclaimed ; " I lost two children, and lo ! three have been returned to me. Who may dare question the wisdom and goodness of God ! Nobles, and wise men of Framazugéa, behold in this stranger the son of your king."

At these words the whole assembly flung their feet into the air, and the infernal noise of the gongs rolled adown the hall of the fountains. The king turned and ascended his throne, making the prince and myself take a seat upon the cushions at either side of the step by his feet. He now commenced asking questions about my country and the other nations of the world, and my own personal history, avoiding, as I could perceive, any allusion to the agitating subject of his daughter's adventures.

A slight noise inducing me to look up, I saw behind the throne a long strip of gilt lattice work, through which came, occasionally, the bright sparkle of diamonds, or the still brighter flashes of female eyes. Was Kaloolah there? I judged that she was, or else why did my heart give a leap, as if it was coming out of my mouth ?

After a conversation of half an hour the monarch rose from the throne, and my followers were called up and allowed to kiss hands, which they

did in rather a bungling manner, although I had taken the precaution to
school them as to almost every possible case of etiquette that could
arise. Descending the ivory steps, the old man supported himself upon
my arm, and followed by Enphadde, and a dozen dignitaries who were
standing behind the throne, we left the room. We traversed a long cor-
ridor that looked out from latticed arches into a tessellated court, and
entered a saloon, where, amid the richest display of flowers, were spread
the choicest viands of a royal feast. Not a lamp could be seen, but a
flood of sparkling light was poured from the ceiling, which consisted of a
sheet of rock crystal, set in burnished copper, and supported upon pilas-
ters of carved ebony and cedar. There were music, and incense, and wine,
and crowds of menials, and all and more than all of the conventional
accompaniments and accessories of an ostentatious Oriental entertainment, but which I have not now space to describe.

The monarch arose, and affectionately embracing me, bade me good
night. Enphadde assisted his trembling steps. At this moment an officer of the court presented me a little bouquet, which, in an instant, I saw
was an exact counterpart of the one I had received from Kaloolah. He
motioned towards a door at the lower end of the hall, and I at once
sprang to my feet and followed him through a succession of passages and
courts—a perfect labyrinth, to which, although I have since traversed it
a thousand times, I have hardly yet learned the clew.

CHAPTER XLI.

THERE was a low, large irregular room, divided into several portions by groups of slender columns. It was carpeted with the softest stuffs, hung with rich crimson drapery, surrounded by a row of ottomans and sofas, and perfumed with the scent-laden breeze that came through the arches on one side, from a garden of flowers. A few lamps of alabaster illuminated the apartment, and lighted up several clusters of gayly dressed and beautiful damsels, who were reclining in all manner of easy and graceful attitudes upon the cushioned seats.

As I entered, the officer who had conducted me threw his feet up into the air, and then stepping backwards, withdrew behind the drapery of the door. My appearance created quite a sensation among the beautiful occupants of the room. Several of them started to their feet, and for a moment I was apprehensive that I was about to be edified with a specimen of feminine litheness and agility, after the fashion of the nobles in the throne room. It was, however, only the start of surprise.

Rapidly running my eye over the charming groups, I saw that the princess was not among them. This compelled me to pause—for a moment I knew not what to say or do, and no one seemed disposed to come to my relief. My position was becoming awkward and embarrassing, when I was happily reassured by the glimpse of a female figure through a curtained window in the farther end of the room ; with noiseless steps I crossed the tufted carpet, and passed into a balcony that on one side looked down into a little parterre of flowers, and on the other almost overhung the perpendicular side of the acropolis. Far down below was stretched out, for miles, a populous section of the great city. It was illuminated by a number of light towers, each two hundred feet high, and each, surmounted by a large conical cap-like reflector, beneath which burned huge lamps, fed with prepared naphtha. The yellow light streamed down in heavy masses upon the flat-roofed houses, or poured in full radiance into the numerous open squares, or struggled from side to side of the balconied walls to the smooth pavements of the narrow streets. There was a breadth, and a strength of light and shade, a wonderfulness of chiaroscuro—a deep juicy jelliness of tone, that would have, probably, suggested the peculiar style of Rembrandt, had I ever had the pleasure of seeing the oft be-similied *chefs-d'œuvre* of that great master, and had I not had my attention mainly engrossed by the female figure that, habited in a robe of white, was leaning upon the marble balustrade of the balcony.

Kaloolah was lost in revery, and did not perceive my approach until I stood by her side. Without a word, I gently passed my arm around her, and drew her towards me. It was my first full, free, unmistakable lover's caress. Often had my arm been in the same place, but always with some reference to protection or support. My face was so close to hers that, although in the deep shade of the curtain, and with no light but that of the stars, I could see a liquid diamond trembling between the long black lashes of her eye.

" How is this?" I demanded. " I thought we had done with tears? What troubles you? What were you thinking of?"

" I was thinking," replied Kaloolah, " while looking down upon the scene below us, with its dark and bright spots, its illuminated roofs and walls, and its hidden chambers; its lighted parks, and its numerous shaded and crooked avenues, how like it is to our hearts. In these we find bright spots and dark, open places, and secret passages, and half-shaded, half-illuminated avenues and hidden chambers, where lurk thoughts and feelings unknown to ourselves. I was thinking, too, that, as in that scene below, it is no easy thing to acquire a knowledge of the heart's secret ways, no, not even when that heart is our own. And that led me to think, Jon'than, that—that—after all, we might both be mistaken in believing that you loved me."

" You mean that the last thought came first, and that it led you to your comparison. But come, tell me, what first put the thought into your head?"

" I do not know, but it seems to me now, when I look back upon our long intercourse, that you have ever treated me with a degree of coldness inconsistent with love. True, you have been kind, oh! how kind, but when I have felt that I could throw myself upon your bosom, weep and die—when I have felt that for an assurance from you of a love like mine, I would have sacrificed even the hope of home, you have treated me, I will not say coolly, distantly, but at least calmly, carelessly."

"And can you think that I acted thus without design? Can you think of no reason for restraining my communications to you within the bounds of the strictest decorum. Recollect all the peculiar circumstances of our relative positions."

"Yes, Jon'than, I know what you would say: think not that I do not understand your kindness, your generosity; you were afraid that with the smallest encouragement I would forget myself, my sex, my birth, all, every thing, but you, as I did once beneath the palm grove on the banks of the Sierra Leone; say, was it not so?"

"As I entered, the officer who had conducted me threw his feet up into the air."

"I confess it, but, believe me, that which is sometimes a reproach to unbridled passion is ofttimes the highest compliment that man can pay to female simplicity and innocence. I was afraid for you, but not you alone. There was one for whom I had much more fear."

"Indeed! whom?"

"Myself!"

"You? Jon'than."

"Yes, me! Oh, believe me, Kaloolah, I have loved you with a love too passionate, yet too pure, to permit its expression in the circumstances in which we were placed. I could not trust myself, and I did not like to run the risk of sullying the lustre of that sentiment, of which you were the object. Do you understand me, Kaloolah?"

"I do," whispered Kaloolah, "and oh!—how foolish not to have understood you before : but I am so weak and ignorant, while you are so wise and good!"

"I wish," I exclaimed, with a gentle tightening of my grasp upon her slender, but well rounded figure, "that I were a thousandth part as wise or as good as you are lovely."

"And you really love me?" murmured Kaloolah, as soon as her lips were at liberty to speak, "with your whole heart, Jon'than?"

"With my whole heart," I replied, and I spoke the truth ; and yet, at the instant, there came rolling in upon my heart, like a dark surf on a shining sea-beach, a flood of other feeling, and love was almost buried amid the mist and foam of memory. I thought of home, and all its associations came thronging to my mind. Could I give them all up, and that, too, for ever? Could I link myself to Framazugda for life? Could I curb, always, the strong yearnings for country and kind by affection even for the peerless being by my side? Could I live for love? Alas, I knew that only woman's heart is capable of that : men can merely die for the object of their affections –they cannot live on through all circumstances solely for love. Man's vigorous, coarse, sensual, and selfish nature requires more solid and varied food. Love has been said to be an episode in the life of man, but to be woman's whole existence. I prefer to carry out my metaphor, and say that to men love is always a condiment—an *entremet*—a kind of anti-prandial lemon and oysters; but to woman it is, sometimes, the first, second, third course, and dessert.

I felt and thought thus, although, perhaps, not precisely in these words. For a few moments I stood silent, abstracted, and irresolute. Kaloolah's heart, as she hung upon my arm, felt sympathetically the doubtful feeling of my own, and she looked up in my face with an anxious and inquiring look. And now what I am about to relate I hope no incredulous readers will pronounce to be a pure invention, however much they think it the mere fiction of my fancy.

There was a slight rustling sound, as of female garments trailed along the garden walk into which the balcony opened. Kaloolah started and listened. A white, misty, ill-defined figure swept past and around us, and in fact, for a moment, seemed to envelop us like a wreath of thin vapor. I felt myself gently compressed, as if in the embrace of some spiritual

being, and at the same time forced closer to Kaloolah by some power,
which, although almost imperceptible, was clearly external to us, and independent of our own muscular volition. At this moment there was a
voice—a low, sweet, and to my ear, familiar voice, and the words that it
whispered were: " My son! my son!" The last sounds came from above.
I looked up, and could see something white, quivering and gently waving
to and fro, and ascending. A dimness came across my vision, and when
it cleared away I found myself steadily gazing at a speck of shining cloud
far up in the starry sky.

Enough for me, that whether fancy or reality, fiction or fact, that
vision and voice drove all doubts from my heart. It was my mother's
sanction to my feelings for Kaloolah! And if she could thus visit me in
the heart of central Africa, why should not Framazugda become my
country and my home? It should! and my best energies and talents
should be devoted to the service of my adopted land. True, I would
have no chance to play the part of a Menes, a Moses, or a Manco Capac.
I could add nothing to the old and well-polished political, judicial, and
social systems of a highly cultivated nation; and it was questionable
whether, in relation to the arts of peace, I should not find much more to
learn than to teach; but I could, at least, show the Framazugs something in the way of war. I could give them discipline, and a system
of tactics that would enable them to meet the formidable barbarians who
were pressing upon them. I could give them a knowledge of that great
and happy discovery of the old alchemist—the art of manufacturing gunpowder: an art which has been often anathematized, but which may
justly be pronounced the best boon of science to a combative world, the
greatest blessing to humanity, the supporter and protector of civilization,
the spreader of true religion; an art, by the aid of which ignorance,
superstition, and idolatry have been in some countries utterly extirpated
—by the aid of which the bloody rites of Huitzilopotchli have been
swept from the plains of Anahuac—the Manito worship almost driven
out of my own enlightened country—the barbarous darkness of Atlas
pierced by the brilliant beams of French faith and politeness—the ferocious Mohammedanism of the Caucasus compelled to give way to the
blessing of the Greek Patriarch and the benign growls of the black bear
of Russia; and last, though not least, a flood of Christianity rolled in
upon the plains of heathen India, which, daily increasing, shall roll on
until the British Lion, with his paw upon every inch of ground between
the Euphrates and the Blue Sea, between the Indian Ocean and the peaks
of the Altai, shall drown with his roar the groans of Gooroo, Brahma, and

Fo, and wagging his tail in pious exultation, exclaim to the vanquished nations of Asia, " in the name of the Blessed Jesus, peace ! " I could give my new country this glorious art, and with it security from attack, and even the means of conquest. Dim ideas of civilizing barbarous tribes, reclaiming from rude nature a large and fertile portion of the globe, suppressing the vile traffic in human flesh, and extending the domain of Framazugda from the Indian Ocean to the Bight of Benin, floated through my mind. In a glow of love and ambition I pressed the princess to my heart, and anxiously inquired whether her father would have any objections to our union? " None! none whatever! " Kaloolah was positive that it would be the very wish of his heart.

At this moment Enphadde joined us, and he, too, expressed a like opinion, avowing, at the same time, his own satisfaction at the state of affairs between his sister and myself.

After a few minutes' conversation in the balcony, Kaloolah proposed that we should descend the marble steps, and take a turn or two in the garden. I at once complied, and leaning upon her arms, she led us to a large marble tank of water, in which were swimming a number of lightning-fish. They were of the shape and about the size of salmon-trout, and had the faculty of emitting, at intervals of a few seconds, a vivid flash of light from the surface of their bodies.

As we stood gazing down into the illuminated depths of the tank, we were started by the cries of a domestic, who, flinging open a gate, rushed into the garden, calling, in a coaxing tone, to some animal which had scrambled over the trellised wall, and appeared to be escaping from its keeper. We had hardly time to turn around when the little creature bounded down the path, and, springing upon the marble curb of the tank, jumped thence into Kaloolah's arms. It was Gogo—yellow-haired Gogo —a diminutive specimen of the ourang-outang. He was, when standing perfectly erect, about six inches high, and covered with a long silky fur, of a bright golden hue, except about the shoulders and arms, where there was a delicate shade of purple. We took him to the light that streamed through an open window, and examined him. It would be difficult to find a more lovely creature, or one better calculated for a lady's pet. Nestling in Kaloolah's arms, he grinned and chattered his delight ; and when Enphadde endeavored to take him away and hand him to his keeper, he screamed and clung to his mistress with the most affectionate tenacity ; but when Kaloolah told him that it was time for him to go to bed, and that, if he would kiss her hand, say good-night, and go without making any noise, she would see him in the morning, he at once obeyed, and with an expression of human intelligence and sympathy, that would have gone far to convince the sternest opponent of Lord Monboddo, that, if men are not monkeys with their tails cut off, monkeys may be, perhaps, degenerate caudalized specimens of humanity.

We entered the saloon by way of the balcony, and took our seats upon a low sofa, the ends of which, curving upwards, supported a graceful canopy of feathers and artificial flowers. Small stands, bearing golden trays, were placed before us, and were served with confectionery, sweetmeats, and a variety of liqueurs and cordials. Of the liqueurs, one, in particular, tickled my palate with an exquisite galvanic force, equal to the voltaic power of a dozen pewter pint-pots of porter. I was not, however, surprised at its thrilling flavor, when informed that it was made by digesting the pollen of numerous aromatic herbs with the dew of violets, and a minute proportion of venom, expressed from the stings of the honey-bee.

Upon a sign from the princess, a heavy curtain, concealing a deep alcove, was drawn aside, displaying a musical instrument resembling a church-organ. It had a keyboard, and within contained, in place of strings, a series of drums, running from C in altissimo down to D, two and a half octaves in pitch below the G string of the violincello. A piece of mechanism, like the pedals of a pianoforte, enabled the composer to change the whole, or any number of the drums, from stringed to muffled, at pleasure. A performer now stepped from a side door, and placed himself at the instrument. His first notes were electric, and fairly startled me from my seat in delight and surprise, at the astonishing fulness and richness of tone. No stringed instrument every produced any thing like the effect. A few preliminary flourishes were followed by a grand piece, composed in honor of Kaloolah's return. The musical reader will, perhaps, regret that my ignorance of the technicalities of the art prevents me from attempting to convey any very accurate idea of the qualities or merits of the composition. Suffice it to say, that it was spirited and expressive, and that the execution, in some passages, was truly wonderful; particularly in a number of brilliant runs, and in an occasional powerful and prolonged shake upon the big bass-drum, which was positively awful. It may, perhaps, be wondered how a performer can evolve, with his fingers merely, sufficient power. The explanation is easy: the keys do not communicate with the drums directly, but are used as a means simply of geering and ungeering, at the will of the player, a row of heavy drumsticks to a series of ratchet-wheels, which are kept in motion by a band running to a shaft, turned by a donkey in the court below; so that it is the donkey that makes the music. Of course there is nothing very novel about this instrument, it being simply the application of well-known principles ; but I mention it because of its striking effects.

At the conclusion of the piece the prince inquired whether I should not like to witness a performance upon the perfume-machine, which had often been the subject of conversation between us. I at once assented, and rising, we all repaired, by a short passage, to a low, narrow, but very long hall. It was destitute of furniture, except a couch in the centre, upon which we seated ourselves. At one end of the hall there were two large circular apertures, the open ends of pipes leading to a centrifugal blower, precisely like those in use in the Hudson River steamboats. Opening in at the centre of motion, around the axis of the revolving fan, the action of the blower was, of course, to suck the air out of the hall, through the pipe, in a steady current. The upper end wall of the hall was studded with the open mouths of very small tubes, the other ends of which communicated with reservoirs of perfume without the room. Below these projected from the wall a carved shelf, or rather box, supporting a row of keys, the extreme ends of which were attached by wires to valves in the tubes. Upon pressing the keys, corresponding valves were opened, and jets of scented air thus allowed to enter the hall. These odors, borne on the steady current, passed down the room, and out through the pipes leading to the blower.

There were more than fifty distinct perfumes, that stood in the same relation to each other that tones and semi-tones do to the different parts of the scale in music. The harmonic combinations of these were infinite. There are also several fundamental and controlling odors, by which the whole scale can be modified at pleasure. The three principals of these are garlic, musk, and sulphuretted hydrogen. The garlic, which corresponds to the minor key in music, is exceedingly plaintive and affecting. Compositions in this key almost invariably excite the smeller to tears. Compositions in the musk key are very varied in their expression ; sometimes grave and solemn, like church music ; at other times gay, lively, and redolent of chalked floors and gaslights. Compositions in the sulphuretted-hydrogen key have invariably a spirit-stirring and martial expression. It is the proper key for odorate marches, battle-pieces, and storm-rondos.

The Christian reader, with an uneducated sense of smell, may, perhaps, turn up his nose (in profound ignorance of his nose's capacities) at the instrument I am describing : but if he should ever have an opportunity of snuffing the melodious streams and harmonic accords evolved by a good performer, upon a properly constructed instrument, he will be compelled to admit that his nasal organ was given to him for a higher purpose than to take snuff, support spectacles, or express contempt. True, at first he may not appreciate the more recondite combinations and delicate *aperfumes*, any more than a novice in music appreciates the scientific arrangement of notes in Italian or German opera, but he will at once be able to understand and admire the easy melodies—the natural succession of simple fragrances, and, in time, the cultivated sensibility of his nasal organ will enable him to comprehend the more elaborate harmonies—the most subtile and artificial odoriferous correspondences and modulations.

The name of this instrument is the *Ristum-Kitherum*, which, if my recollection of the Greek serves me, is very much like two words in that language signifying a nose and a harp. It was played upon the occasion of which I speak, by the same artist who had just performed upon the sheepskins, and, although hardly qualified to judge, I had no hesitation in setting him down as equally a master of both.

For some time I sat, the complete verification, notwithstanding the presence of the princess, of an observation, I think by Hazlit, that odors, better than the subjects of the other senses, serve as links in the chain of association. A series of staccato passages amid bergamot, lemon, orange, cinnamon, and other familiar perfumes, quite entranced me, while a succession of double shakes on the attar of rose made me fancy, for a moment, that the joyous breath of a bright spring morning was once more dashing the odors of that old sweet-brier bush into the open window of my chamber at O——.

The night was well advanced when the performance concluded, and bidding Kaloolah good-night, I was conducted by the prince to my own apartments, where Hugh and Jack were waiting for me. In no mood for talking, I despatched them to bed, and withdrew to my own chamber, where, revolving in my mind the question whether odors, instead of being material emanations, may not be, like light or sound, mere vibrations propagated in an elastic medium, I threw myself upon my couch, and was soon in a sound sleep, hardly dreaming even of Kaloolah.

In the morning I arose early and strolled out into the garden. Nothing could be more magnificent than the fountains and arbors and grottos and broad gravel walks, but my mind was too busy with its own thoughts to heed them very closely. I plucked a cluster of roses and seated myself upon a marble slab beneath an umbrella tree, and beside a fountain composed of a dozen bronze monkeys, that were dashing water at each other in every variety of attitude and expression. As I knew nothing of the language of flowers, and could not, therefore, construct a bouquet according to rule

I took out my writing materials, which, since my visit to the well-stocked markets of Sackatoo, I had always carried on my person, and composed a few verses, which, although in English, delighted Kaloolah very much. I give them here, because they really were expressive of my feelings for the princess, and because they indicate my notions of her style and character. Elaborate versified sentiment requires a higher inspiration than mere good looks. Many a man's fancy is taken with nothing but a pretty face, or a fine figure; but in all such cases the captive will, I take it, unless he is a professed poet, and running over with rhyme, do all his love-making in prose.

TO KALOOLAH WITH FLOWERS.

Musing in deep and unmixed pleasure,
O'er my heart's love—my prize—my treasure,
I paced in slow, abstracted measure
    A garden round.
I heeded not the flowerets springing,
Nor yet the odors they were flinging,
Nor yet the warblers that were singing,
    Nor sight, nor sound
Of Æolus, from the tree-tops crying,
Or Zephyr, through the fresh blooms sighing,
Or lights or shadows ever flying
    Along the ground.

'T was thus mechanically walking,
Quite heedless whither I was stalking,
That sudden a sound of voices talking
    Startled my ear—
Arousing me from my fond dreaming,
With tones like moonlight, fitful gleaming,
O'er ruffled waters, ever seeming
    Distant, yet near.
I turned me whence those tones were flowing,
And, turning, turned where roses growing
Their richest odors wild were throwing,
    And paused to hear:

I heard the roses softly telling
Of hopes and fears, their bosoms swelling.
Ah! me, to find such feelings dwelling
    In things so fair.
They told of the fickle south wind's sighing,
Of dewdrops false their bosoms flying,

Of drooping, fading, withering, dying
    Of chill despair.
And as with many a modest token
Their tales of hapless love were spoken,
It made me feel almost heart-broken,
    I do declare.

So piteous was their sighing, blushing,
I could not hold myself from rushing
And nearly in my hurry crushing
    Their tender weakness,
To catch the perfumes they were weeping,
To save the freshness their hearts' steeping,
To rescue them from the rough keeping
    Of morn's chill bleakness.
Come, come, cried I, ye beauteous creatures,
Ye heavenly ministers, ye angel preachers,
Ye man's most soft, persuasive teachers
    Of love and meekness—

Come, come with me, your sad eyes drying,
I'll take you where, in her smiles lying,
No more shall ye have cause for sighing,
    Or love-lorn tears.
Beneath her soft and kindly smiling
Ye'll bloom a time, pale memories wiling
With fondest hopes, and life beguiling
    Of doubts and fears—
And death! Ah! what more pleasant feeling
To die! when Death, his form revealing
'Mid floods of light from Her eyes stealing,
    All bright appears.

CHAPTER XLII.

EVER was the oft-quoted adage about the course of true love more fully falsified than in the case of Kaloolah and myself. Not a breath of opposition ruffled the deep, calm current of affection ; not a cloud lowered in the horizon of love. The old king readily gave his consent to our union ; the court approved, and the people were well pleased.

Three or four months glided by in a round of festivities and rejoicings. We visited the royal chateau. We made excursions into the country. We climbed the slopes of Toosh Gualabemba. We boated on the broad bosom of the Wollo. In this way I enjoyed not only opportunities of gratifying curiosity, but also of collecting materials for my proposed work upon the political and natural history of the country.

Several weeks of this time were given to sight-seeing alone, in the great city, to which it will be, perhaps, thought pardonable if I devote a page or two of my present manuscript.

Kiloam, according to the most accurate observations that I have been enabled to make, is situated in 32' north latitude, and somewhere between 25° and 30° east longitude. My longitude is, of course, not much better than guess-work, as it is arrived at only by a comparison of my rate of travel, and the bearings of my course from Sackatoo. My latitude, however, is nearly exact, and was obtained by a series of meridian altitudes of the sun. The instrument employed is one that, notwithstanding its rudeness, I have great confidence in. It consists of a large circle, six feet in diameter, made of a very hard, dense, highly polished wood. A steel axis, like the arms of a transit telescope, supports the instrument upon two pillars of stone. Through this axis, and at right angles to it, passes a tube of brass eight feet in length and one inch in diameter. This tube crosses the face of the circle, in the line of a diameter, and, as near as possible, like

343

the telescope of a mural circle. On either side a curved bracket projecting from the tube grasps the periphery of the wheel, and by turning a screw the tube and circle can be clamped or loosened at pleasure; another screw clamps the circle to one of the stone pillars.

To get this instrument into the meridian was a job that puzzled me a good deal. I had no practical knowledge of astronomy; no nautical almanac or catalogue of the stars; and, although happening to recollect the declination of two fixed stars, I had nothing like an accurate idea of the right ascensions of a single one, and I was too far south to avail myself of the upper and lower transits of the circumpolar stars. My only resource was in repeated observations upon the shadows of perpendiculars.

It may be asked how I got along without a table of declination. Fortunately I recollected, from frequently referring to the tables in Bowditch, and the nautical almanac, the sun's declination for most days in the year, and there were two points—the solstices—about which there could be no mistake. Besides which, as I have said, there were two fixed stars whose declination I had in mind, namely, Arcturus and Alpha Lyra. Upon them I have made many observations; sometimes for altitude, and sometimes, after adjusting my tube perpendicularly by a plumb line passing through it, for zenith distances.

I have been somewhat particular in the description of this instrument, in order that the reader may judge for himself as to the correctness of the data upon which I put down the latitude of the great city at 32′ 31″ north.

Great city I call it, and well does it deserve that title. Few capitals in Europe compare with it, either in extent or the architectural elegance of its public and private edifices, the beauty of its parks, or the number of its population. Situated on a peninsula, formed by a bend of the Wollosab, it is surrounded on three sides by water. The city proper, however, does not come down to the water's edge, but is separated by a wall and a wide open piece of ground, across which runs several roads enclosed by high walls, and terminating at little ports, or at the entrances of long stone bridges stretching to the opposite shore. In the centre rises the acropolis I have mentioned, on three sides perpendicular, and on the fourth communicating by a narrow ridge of rock with the country beyond the isthmus joining the peninsula to the mainland. The top of this acropolis is about a quarter of a mile in breadth by three quarters of a mile in length, and nearly one half of it is occupied by the royal buildings and courts. From the base of this hill the houses stretch far away in every direction until they reach the lofty battlemented walls, within which, according to the official registers of the census, is contained a population of six hundred and twenty-three thousand souls.

The houses are mostly built of a cream-colored freestone, although there are some of marble and granite, and even some of brick. They are invariably large quadrangular edifices, with massive walls, two stories high, and all of them have an open court in the centre, with a fountain. The roofs are flat, and formed of timbers of a species of cypress, which are almost proof against decay. They are placed close together, and covered with a plating of lead. Upon this is placed a layer of earth six or eight inches deep, which is laid out into walks and beds, and cultivated with flowers and fruits. High parapets of stone protect these aerial gardens on the outside, while inside a light iron railing serves to keep the careless lounger or romping children from falling into the court below. Nothing can be more magnificent than the view of this boundless contiguity of flower gardens from the palace on the rock.

Some of the public thoroughfares are very broad, but in general the streets are of a moderate width, paved, as I have mentioned, with large grooved stones, and kept scrupulously clean. Indeed, what would strike a visitor, from the Christian cities of Europe and America, and particularly if he should happen to be from New York, is the close attention paid to every thing relating to municipal hygiene. The general health of the city, the people of Kiloam consider to be the first great object of police regulations ; the protection of property and the facilitation of trade are of secondary importance. They look upon a great city, as something better than a mere collection of reckless money-getters, who, in the blind pursuit of wealth, are as willing to sacrifice their own and the general health, as they are to forego the pleasures of taste, the enjoyments of reason, the delights of the heart, and the hopes of heaven. They look upon the assemblage of men in cities as an admirable modification of social life ; but admirable only as it affords an opportunity of attaining many of the higher objects of humanity. The elevation and polish of intellect—the cultivation of taste—the refinement of manners—the development of the social sympathies and philanthropic emotions of the heart, are the great objects among the Framazugs of city life. To these they add, as lying at the foundation of mental and moral as well as physical activity and power, the preservation of health.

To secure this last great end, every means has been adopted. The streets are not only swept, but washed every day, a complete system of sewerage, serving to carry off the refuse water and materials. With regard to dust, the Framazugs are very particular. Never was the governor of Kiloam more astonished than when, in the course of conversation, one day, I told him that three or four hundred people were annually killed in New York by dust alone. He would not believe it possible. "It is a fact," said I, "at least that number of fatal consumptions are owing to that one cause, but that is not the worst of it ; several hundred thousand dollars' worth of property are also annually damaged or destroyed." He threw up his hands in astonishment and horror, and blessed his fate that he did not live in such a barbarous community. The sewers are large vaulted tunnels, in substantial masonry, into which leaden pipes lead from each house ; and they not only serve to drain the city, but for passages along which are laid the iron pipes that supply the city with water. There is room for workmen around these pipes ; so that in repairing or replacing them, it is not necessary to turn up the earth of the street, and if one happens to burst, as is sometimes the case, from the enormous pressure, the water runs off by the sewer, without overflowing the neighboring houses and saturating the soil for half a dozen blocks around.

Besides the tubes conveying water into and from each house, there is an air tube which runs from the sewer to the mouth of a small centrifugal blower ; from around the centre of motion of this blower go two tubes, which, dividing into many small ones, penetrate every room and nook in the house. A small wheel, turned by a jet of water, communicates motion by a band to the fan, which, in its revolutions, sucks into the blower all the foul air in the chambers, and forces it out through the main pipe into the sewer, leaving its place to be supplied by the pure air that draws down into the court from above. The whole apparatus occupies but a small space in the basement, and can be put in motion any moment by turning the faucet of a water-pipe. The openings to the sewer are air-tight, excepting at distant intervals, in the larger ones, where there are placed ventilating towers two hundred feet in height. These, with a liberal use of quick-lime in the tubes leading into the sewers, prevents the accumulation of foul air, so that when the stones stopping the ordinary street openings are removed, the eye and not the nose takes cognizance of the fact. The mode, too, of cooling apartments in hot weather, which is in general use, and which might unquestionably be advantageously adopted in all warm climates, contributes much to the purity of the air. By means of a condensing apparatus, air is forced into copper reservoirs, capable of resisting a great pressure : in this way it is compelled to give up a large portion of its caloric. When this condensed air is suddenly turned into a room, it enters with a wonderful capacity for caloric that enables it instantly to reduce the temperature of all the air in the apartment. Besides its caloric, the air is compelled to part with some portion of its moisture which condenses at the bottom of the reservoir. With the moisture are precipitated all impurities, and the compressed air issues cold, dry, and pure.

The streets are furnished with sidewalks, and shaded by rows of trees, the foliage of which is clipped in the French style. No manufactories of any kind are allowed except in certain streets, and those which are offensive to the senses or dangerous to health are wholly excluded from within the walls. The slaughter-houses, for instance, are confined to the other banks of the river; and thus, beside the unhealthy effluvium and the disgusting associations, the danger of driving herds of cattle through the streets is wholly obviated.

He is sentenced to a douche bath, and to be publicly scrubbed from head to foot."

The same care is exhibited in the construction and management of the markets. These are immense squares with roofs, supported upon columns of marble, and with smooth stone pavements, laid in asphaltum. The fish, meat, and even fruit-stands are all of marble or granite, and not a particle of wood is to be seen, except in the cedar of the roof. Every article is closely examined by competent officers before it is admitted; and unripe or decayed fruit and vegetables and unhealthy meats are rigidly excluded. Numerous fountains play in the broad lanes and passages, and several little rivers, running in marble beds, intersect each other, mingling the sounds of moving water with the busy hum of trade.

More than fifty free baths, for the poorer classes, attest the opinions

of the magistrates of Kiloam, that personal cleanliness is essential to
health. At these baths an artisan or laborer, after his day's work, can
obtain a cold bath without charge, or a warm bath by paying a small
copper coin—the estimated expense of heating the water. Besides these
municipal baths, there are great numbers of public and private baths that
invite to ablution, the practice of which is also rendered obligatory upon
every citizen by law. If any one is accused of neglecting to bathe for
one lunar month, he is brought up before the proper court, and, upon
conviction, he is sentenced to a douche bath, and to be publicly scrubbed
from head to foot by men appointed for that purpose. The penalty is,
in reality, much more severe than might at first be supposed, inasmuch
as the sufferer, however hard he may have been scrubbed, invariably
comes out from his forced ablution with the reputation of a dirty fellow
for life.

The law may seem arbitrary, but it is founded upon the justifiable assumption, that personal cleanliness is a duty that every citizen owes to
the community, as well as to himself—that no man has a right to clothe
himself in filth—to encrust his carcass in its own vitiated and putrefying
secretions—to turn his body into a generator of the miasms of typhus
fever, plague, scrofula, and a host of cutaneous diseases—to perambulate
the streets, a spreader of pestilence, an offence to the eyes and noses of
all good citizens.

Acting upon the same principle, the municipal authorities will not
allow the over-crowding of houses by poor tenants; and when there is
more than one family in a house, the owner is made responsible for the
cleanliness of the premises. In cases where there is a suspicion of dirt or
bad ventilation, the police make sudden and unexpected domiciliary
visits, and immediately order the necessary alterations, repairs, and ablutions, charging the owner with the expense.

More than a hundred public squares and parks, of which at least half
a dozen are of vast extent, each of several hundred acres, contribute an
important part to the ventilation of the city. And, still more, they afford
those opportunities and incentives to exercise, so essential to the health
of metropolitan society. At the same time, they serve, with the statues,
columns, fountains, and trees that adorn them, to cultivate the taste, to
develop and elevate the sense of the beautiful, to soften rudeness, polish
coarseness, reform vulgarity, and to administer to the proper and patriotic
pride that a citizen ought to take in his country and his city.

The success that attends this attention to municipal hygiene amply
repays the labor and care. Formerly, before it was deemed a matter of

so much importance, the city of Kiloam was hardly more healthy than many Christian cities—the deaths being annually one in forty-five, or about the same proportion as in London, the healthiest city in Europe. Now the proportion has been reduced to one in seventy-six, and each year shows a gradual improvement. There can be no doubt that similar means would produce like results in the cities of America, and it is in the hope of stirring up some of the New York readers to the importance of the subject, that I dwell upon it to the exclusion of more interesting details.

In the number and splendor of its public edifices Kiloam probably surpasses any city in the world. Full fifty ventilating columns of the great sewers, and as many more lofty towers supporting fires lighting the city, and the monuments of distinguished Pholdefoos, are a peculiar and striking feature. Besides these, there are the royal buildings upon the acropolis; the numerous public edifices for the accommodation of the officers of the city; the fifty large baths; the markets, and innumerable temples.

These temples are large mounds of earth, terraced on the outside, and planted with flowers. The interior is excavated into intricate winding passages, leading to a central hall, in which is a slight tottering bridge spanning a deep pit. A solitary lamp throws its feeble light but a short distance into the black obscurity of the hall, faintly illuminating a few jutting points on the sides of the pit below, or of the lofty dark domes above. It is in vain that the eye is strained to discern either the top or the bottom of the vast vacuity in which the trembling bridge is hung. At one moment a misty, lurid light, like the vapory recollection of a dream, rolls far below, and the next instant all is blackness. At one moment a flickering beam glances athwart the gloom above, and the next, sight is lost in the thick darkness, and the devout gazer is conscious only of the narrow bridge upon which he stands, the single dim lamp, and the silent priest—his guide.

But few worshippers visit the central hall. Most are content to stop in a large vaulted room near the portal, where they listen to discourses upon morality, and occasionally to an exposition of religious doctrine. They are taught that there is but one God, the creator of all things; that in making man he implanted in him certain religious instincts, which he intended should be developed in a variety of ways, and that thus every religious system, including the idolatry of the Kyptiles, the Mohammedanism of the Footas, or the antiquated faiths of their ancestors, is from God. They are taught to believe in a future state, or rather states, there being an infinite ascending series of conditions, or modes of life, in each of which our happiness or misery depends upon our conduct in the one just preceding. That, in the state next beyond death, the mind, freed from the trammels of a material body, will recall every thought, feeling, and emotion by which it was ever agitated; and that the slightest of our actions, the least hidden of our motives, the most trivial of our passing sentiments, will stand forth clear as day, in all their moral beauty or deformity, and that there will be no diverting the mind from the sight.

At the end of one hundred thousand years the soul will be refurnished with a body, and again make its appearance upon the earth, where it will remain in the enjoyment of the highest happiness until the final destruction and annihilation of all mundane things, both spiritual and material. The new body will be endowed with senses infinitely more acute, so as to bring the purified soul into relation with the mysterious worlds of life, and sound and motion, by which we are even now immediately surrounded, but from which we are cut off by the narrow limits bounding our hearing, reason, and feeling. As to the final destruction of the world, the Framazug divines do not, like some Christian theologians, attempt to settle the exact day and hour in which it is to take place—although they have quite definite ideas upon the subject. They believe that as human life has a fixed average duration, so has the life of races, of nations, and of worlds, and as the average life of the individual is measured by years, that of the nation is by generations; or, what amounts to the same thing, by social and political revolutions; and that of the world by the astronomical cycles that are marked out by a complete retrocession of the equinoxes—making periods of twenty-five thousand years each. They believe that, as the duration of a generation is about forty years, the average existence of large and healthy nations is about forty generations; that the duration of the race of man, as at present situated, is intended to be about forty times the lifetime of a nation, and that man is now in the twentieth term. As to the world itself, its course, it is estimated, will endure for one hundred complete retrocessions of the equinox, forty-six of which cycles have already been finished. As this puts off the final destruction of the world for more than a million of years, it is, perhaps, unnecessary to inquire minutely into the accuracy of the calculation.

The enlightened Christian may, perhaps, say that in some particulars these views are unscriptural; and that they are wholly insufficient to salvation, but he can hardly deny that if the doctrines of the Framazugs wont ensure them salvation in the next world, they offer strong incentives to virtue in this.

The government of the city of Kiloam is administered by a dagash appointed by the king, and ten assistants selected by himself, from among the literary men of the city. Only those who have written a book, or perpetrated something in the literary way, are considered eligible to the office, for two reasons. The first is, that an opportunity is thus afforded the people of judging of the general capacity, the mental and moral tone of their rulers; and the second is, that contrary to the opinion that obtains in some countries, literary men, particularly the poets, are considered to be the best qualified for almost any kind of public business.

The general government of the country is equally opposed to the received notions and definitions of Christian nations. It may be said to be an hereditary, elective, democratic, despotic monarchy. The king inherits the throne, but at the end of every five years the votes of the people are taken upon the question whether he has properly performed the duties of his office. If two thirds vote in the negative, he is compelled to resign, and his heir takes his place. In every thing, except in relation to this one constitutional provision, the king has unlimited power, with the understanding, however, that it is derived solely from the consent of the people, and that the great object of its exercise is the comfort and happiness of the great masses of his subjects. There is no hereditary aristocracy—the honors and dignities granted by the king being only for life.

Such dignities, however, are merely political, and confer no social distinction. The principle upon which all rank in society is founded, is the comparative degrees of refinement of manner and mind. All questions in relation to rank are settled by a capital institution, which may be called the Board of Commissioners of Position, and also by the suffrages of society as in Christian countries, only here the votes are actually taken by ballot. For instance, when a lady wishes to assume a certain position, the question is submitted to her friends, it being understood that if they will vote for her, her enemies will make no objection. If the vote is favorable, the commissioners examine the candidate as to her social experience and qualifications, and issue a patent of position, accompanied with a medal, made of the tanned hide of the hippopotamus, colored to correspond to the rank assigned. In case her social ambition prompts to a higher flight, she wears for some time a parti-colored medal, and again undergoes the ordeal. The advantages of this custom are apparent. The position of every one is, for the time, fixed, and there is consequently none of that jealous fear, lest it should be compromised, which obtains in some countries. It allows much greater liberty of social intercourse, inasmuch as a red medal can be seen talking to a green medal, or even smelling at the same bouquet, without any apprehension of losing caste. It strikes me that this custom might be advantageously transferred to America, where in the absence of an hereditary aristocracy, birth and family go for but little—and where money, the great rank-giver, is so frequently unaccompanied by the social essentials, refinement and agreeability. The adoption of the medal would certainly give great relief to the muscles of many, who, although well up in the world, feel that their social pyramid is resting on its little end, and that it is necessary to stand bolt upright to preserve their equilibrium. There is one obstacle, however, in the way of introducing the use of the medal, and that is the difficulty, or, perhaps, impossibility of procuring, in sufficient quantities, the skins of the hippopotami. But American enterprise is proverbial, and it would be well worth while to make the attempt.

There are some things in the political system of the Framazugs as well as in their manners and customs, and their knowledge of the arts, that would lead to the idea of their being of Chinese descent. Moreover, tradition ascribes their origin to a country due-east, and across a great water. But there are so many points of difference that, upon fuller investigation, the notion has to be given up. They have nothing of the Chinese physiognomy, nothing of the angular eyes and high cheek-bones of the Tartar races. Their style of dress, the general use of feather cloth, their knowledge of some arts that the Chinese have not, and their ignorance of others which the Chinese have, and their peculiar style of architecture, looking like a light and elegant modification, or rather development, of the Egyptian, prove them to be of a different race.

Some circumstances would lead one to infer that they were a colony of Hindoos, who had migrated before the division of people into castes ; but their light complexions and vigorous frames, to say nothing of other points, belie the idea.

Their aquiline features and fine Egyptian heads would indicate an origin from the banks of the Nile, did not tradition point so strongly to the east.

The same circumstance militates still more strongly against the idea that they are a colony of Carthaginians ; and the conclusion that I have come to is, that they are from Yeman, or the coast of Hadramaut. The chief ground for the opinion is in certain grammatical affinities between the Framazug and the Arabic languages ; but I am reminded, by having reached the customary longitude of a chapter, that such speculations are forbidden at present, even had I the philological and ethnographical erudition and acumen necessary to make such speculations interesting or useful, and that I must confine myself, in the coming chapters, to the more pertinent details of personal adventure.

CHAPTER XLIII.

A Marriage—Public Curiosity—The Hall of Doubt—A Chorus—An Idle Ceremony—Queer
Notions of Marriage—The Princess' Toilet—A Curious Veil—A Marriage Procession—
Sculptured Nondescripts—The Mound Temple—The Marriage Ceremony—Buried Alive.

IX months passed, when one day all Kiloam was in a fever
of excitement.   There was to be a marriage—a marriage
in high life—a royal marriage.   One of the sovereigns of
the great Yankee nation was about to espouse a princess
of Framazugda. If marriage in the upper circles of American society
can create so much of a sensation, as they frequently do—if the question
of three or four hundred dollars, more or less, in the cost of the
bride's lace veil and dress can agitate a cultivated community for a
week—if bridal presents, consisting of a few pieces of plate, a solitary cashmere at five hundred dollars, or a set of glazier's diamonds at a
thousand or two, can be considered fit subjects for ostentatious display,
and of the most profound admiration of the wealthy community generally,—it cannot be considered strange that the elegant and refined but
still barbarous quidnuncs of Kiloam found themselves in a perfect
flutter of delighted curiosity over the magnificent "doings" and superb
"fixings" of Kaloolah's wedding.

For three days, according to custom, the princess had taken her seat
in the Hall of Doubt—a dismal-looking chamber, hung with gray.   Her
sisters—not the children of the great Shounsé, but a band of maidens,
who, having been born on the same day, had been selected, when infants,
as her companions—were around her.   In mournful garb, and with sad-
dened faces, ever and anon they sang, with plaintive voices, a melancholy
chorus, portions of which ran thus:

Stay, sister, stay !
Why shouldst thou go away ?
Why withdraw thy maiden hand
From the warm claspings of thy sister
    band ?
Stay, sister, stay !

Think, maiden, think !
While thy foot is on the brink ;
Think, ere thou tak'st the final leap,
Little thou know'st whither the swift waters
    sweep.
Think, maiden, think !

353

Take heed, ah ! take heed !
Thy step is in the flowery mead ;
Why ? oh ! why should the happy maid
Seek the unknown paths amid the forest's shade ?
Take heed, ah ! take heed !

Doubt, sister, doubt !
Oft the fire of love goeth out ;
Flames it now ? erewhile thou 'lt find
Nothing but cinders and ashes are left behind,
Doubt, sister, doubt !

But despite all that could be said or sung, Kaloolah persisted in her determination of becoming my wife. " It is an idle ceremony," said the princess.

" Not so," said her father, " the custom comes from the olden time, and it has ever been considered a good ceremonial enforcement of caution and dubitation."

" True," replied Kaloolah, " the intention of the custom is well enough, but it fails in its effect from the peculiar qualities of the female heart. A woman who is thoroughly in love never doubts about the propriety of marrying the object of her affections ; if she is not in love she needs no solicitations to do so."

" Ah !" said I, " that sentiment would hardly go down in my country, particularly the latter part of it ; with us it is no uncommon thing for a woman to rush as unhesitatingly into a marriage, in which her heart is not interested, as if she were desperately in love."

" A strange idea your people must have of marriage," replied the king.

" Not so, your majesty," said I ; " their ideas are very simple, and very natural. They look upon marriage as an alliance offensive and defensive between two naturally antagonistic powers—a contract between two co-equal sovereignties—a limited partnership for the common carrying on of some of the duties of life, in which special provisions are necessary to guard the respective independent rights of the parties—a convenient mode of assuring the paternity of children—a respectable mode of obtaining a livelihood."

" And is that all," interrupted the king.

" All !" said I, " what more would your majesty have ?"

" Ah !" replied the king, " our notions are very different. We believe that marriage is not a common contract, and that there can be no real marriage unless the parties are firmly drawn together by the cords of love. We believe that there are two great changes for the soul, marriage and death, and that the first is by far the more important. At marriage, two single souls become one soul. This one soul is no longer like a single soul, but its component elements, united by the power of love, become a very different kind of spiritual entity ; and this union is so intimate as to admit between its parts only the relations of duty and privilege, not of right. No marriage is valid— no marriage is a marriage, without this fusion of the duality into unity."

It was evident that the great Shounsé was growing a little transcendental; luckily he stopped short, and I turned to the princess.

" And you, Kaloolah, in view of such an idea of marriage, have you no doubts ? "

" Not of the heart," said her father, putting his hand familiarly on my shoulder, " but of the head ; or, rather, I have for her."

" And in what respect does your majesty doubt ? " I demanded.

" Your age," replied the king. " You are either too young or too old ; younger, you would more easily forget your country and early associations, and more readily absorb the life and spirit of Framazugda ; older, you would have proved many things in your own country, against which your imagination will now chafe itself into restlessness and discontent. I foresee that you will long to revisit your native land ! "

" But not more than I shall," replied the princess. " When Jon'than wishes to return to his country I shall wish to go too—I long, even now, to visit his great city of New York."

" You forget the savages and wild beasts you would have to encounter in going," said one of her attendants.

" And the bad smells," whispered another.

" Yes, and the bad smells after you had arrived there," thought I to myself, but, it being no very pleasant subject, I said nothing, and the conversation was turned to the preparations for the wedding, which was to take place the coming day.

The reader need not be afraid that I am going into a minute detail of all the circumstances and ceremonies, but I must dwell on Kaloolah's appearance for a moment. Her full rounded figure was habited in a tight-fitting spencer of the richest feather-cloth, to which there was attached a flowing skirt of the finest lace, worked in gold and silver filigree. Her bare arms were wreathed from shoulder to hand with spiral, serpent-like bracelets of rubies, emeralds, and opals—a gorget of amethysts encircled her throat. Her rich dark hair hung naturally in thick clusters down her neck. On her head she wore a golden crest, like a cock's-comb, or very much like the crest of the old Roman helmet. It ran along the centre of the head from the front backward, was in height about two inches, and was thickly encrusted with diamonds—the end over the forehead terminating in a slender crescent of gems, encircling a sun, the centre of which was a large brilliant yellow diamond. From the top of this crest arose a golden staff, or standard, three inches high, surmounted by a plume of froulbell. Around this staff was twisted the middle of a long veil of spider's web that fell down on either side to her feet. Nothing in the fabrics of Valenciennes or Brussels ever approached, in delicate legerity and exquisite workmanship, to this veil, which was made, not as has been frequently done in Christian countries by twisting the fibres of spider's web into thread, and then weaving them into tissue, but by making the spiders actually spin out the veil complete. The spider employed for this purpose is of a peculiar species—being very docile and easily governed by its master by means of a small twig of bamboo, so as to be made to work out any figure designed. The only difficulty is, that in working large articles, the spider is apt to spin himself out before his work is finished, and it is impossible to get another spider to carry out the same design. This enhances the cost enormously—I am sorry that I cannot give the exact expense of Kaloolah's veil in dollars and cents, but a rough estimate will, perhaps, do something towards satisfying the enlightened curiosity generally felt on such subjects. Taking the average price of wheat in New York at ninety cents a bushel, and estimating the bushel in Kiloam to be worth as much as the bushel in New York, the veil must have cost, say at fifteen thousand bushels, thirteen thousand five hundred dollars! My estimate may be wrong as to the price of wheat, but if so, some of my female readers, whose fathers are in the flour trade, can easily correct the mistake.

The morning dawned brightly, as all the mornings in Framazugda do, not even excepting those of the two short rainy seasons. After an elaborate toilet, of which shawls, feather-cloth, and fine linen were the principal materials, but which I shall not stop to describe, I descended with my suite to the vestibule of the great central pavilion, where, in a short time, I was joined by the princess. After some little delay, Kaloolah and myself took our seats beneath a canopy of flowers, supported upon an immense gilt machine, like an ancient triumphal chariot. To this car were harnessed eight pairs of buffaloes by strips of burnished snake-skin. These buffaloes were of a spotless white; their horns were wreathed with flowers, and each one bore on his back two trumpeters, who blew their instruments with almost as much vigor and perseverance as they could have done had they been educated in the American school of trumpeting. Behind us came a train of buffaloes, bearing howdahs containing Kaloolah's companions; and on either side of our car paced a stately escort of young nobles, mounted upon giraffes. Farther in the rear came another magnificent chariot, bearing the great Shounsé.

A tremendous salvo of gongs, and a flourish of trumpets, drums, and cymbals, mingled with the shouts of the vast multitude, announced our arrival at the great Mound Temple. Parallel rows of colossal stone figures formed a long avenue leading to the portico. Each figure represented the body of an elephant, with a human head and face having a remarkably sagacious expression. The trunk of the elephant represented the head and superior portion of a large serpent; the hind legs were formed by two crouching figures of men in chains, and the forelegs were precisely like those of the domestic cat. A long tail like a monkey, but terminating in a hard horny sting like a scorpion, completed the form of these stone nondescripts. I have seen nothing in all Framazugda more curious, and nothing that I should like better to send to America than one of these figures. If mounted upon a proper pedestal in front of the City Hall, or in Wall Street, before the Exchange, New York could boast a sculptured curiosity that would throw entirely into the shade the horses of St. Mark, the obelisk of the Place de la Concord, or the marbles of the British Museum—one that would have more beauty, more meaning, and more antiquity than the Memnon, the Sphynx, the bas-reliefs of Persepolis, or the grotesque carvings of Elephanta.

Through this avenue we were conducted on foot by a company of yellow-robed priests into the great central hall—a vast gloomy apartment lighted by colorless flames, like those from burning alcohol. The contrast between the light, noisy joyousness that we had just left, and the dismal stillness of the temple was almost appalling. No one, with the exception of the king and his privy council, Kaloolah's sisters, and my immediate attendants, had entered with us; and upon them and the long trains of priests fell the dubious light with a most ghostly effect.

Led by two aged priests, whose tottering forms trembled beneath the weight of a hundred years, we advanced to the great altar. A deep pit, into which there was a descent by a few stone steps, yawned at our feet. A heavy marble slab rested by its side. Slowly, a long train of priests, looking more like spectres than living beings, wound round and round us and the altar, from which some burning material threw up its flickering and lugubrious light, and solemnly rolled the deep strains of a monotonous chant among the heavy stone columns and along the lofty arches.

It was intimated that the princess and I were to descend into the tomb before us. Instinctively, and without thinking, so completely was my reason and imagination mastered by the dismal mummery going on around, I led Kaloolah down the steps. We seated ourselves upon a projecting ledge of rock, and in an instant the heavy marble slab was lowered upon the mouth of the pit, and we were shut in from the least ray of light. There were sounds as if of earth or mortar being filled in upon the marble covering—fainter and fainter came the choral wailing, and then all was still. We were buried alive.

Buried alive! And might it not be? might it not be that we were the victims of some political or social jealousy, or of some priestly superstition? Might it not be that, despite the kindness with which I had been entertained, and the love which her family unquestionably bore to Kaloolah, that we were to be sacrificed to some supposed necessity; to avert some omen, perhaps, or to fulfil some prediction? I started at the thought—a thousand little circumstances flashed conviction to my mind —there could be no doubt of it. The perspiration stood upon my forehead—my blood froze in my veins—a thrill of horror ran through my frame. I dashed Kaloolah from my side and rushed up the steps. Madly, in tones of mingled rage and fear, I shrieked, "Off! off with the stone! Let me out! Priests! villains! dogs! I'll throttle the whole of ye! Let me out!" Madly I struggled to raise the stone. Ah! confirmation strong! I could have thrown off a slab of twice its weight; but, horror of horrors! it was fastened down. Madly I exerted myself— madly I dashed my head against the immovable marble until, completely exhausted, I fell back to the floor. Kaloolah's arms were around me— she raised my head and pressed me to her bosom, and her soothing tones fell upon the ear—a revulsion of feeling took place—"At least," said I, throwing my arms around her, "we will die together."

At this moment there came to our ears sounds, as if of blows struck by a heavy hammer, and, suddenly, the top and sides of the tomb flew apart in the most mysterious manner, leaving us exposed in the full glare of day, upon an elevated platform, outside the temple, to the eyes of the shouting multitudes crowding the vast court below.

If attitude is graceful in proportion as it is unstudied, ours must have been the impersonation of Hogarth's spiral. The princess was seated on the floor supporting my head, which was still throbbing with its wild excitement, while I was stretched at length with my arms around her waist. For a moment I was somewhat stupefied by the glare, the crowd, and the noise—the next, a feeling of indignation at the barbarous ceremony and the ridiculous exposure to the eyes of the crowd, so strangely in contrast to the quiet privacy, the refined delicacy, the reserved dignity with which marriages are always conducted in Christian countries, nerved me for the finishing performance, which consisted simply of a procession to the garden of the Wollo, outside of the city, accompanied by the whole population of Kiloam; and a grand feast, of which all partook, amid its shady avenues and around its gleaming fountains.

CHAPTER XLIV.

The Honeymoon—News from the Borders—Ravages of the Jalla—Alkafuz—A Night's Reconnoissance—Riding a Boa—A Battle—Marching into the Jalla Country—A Novel Battering-Ram—Jebha—A Strong Position—Enphadde's Plans—Capitulation of Jebha—The Grand Shocco—The Source of the Nile—Origin of the Jalla—Queer People—Gourd Huts—A Country of Snakes—Return to Kiloam.

T was three or four days after our marriage, that the princess was seated upon a bank of turf in the great garden of the Wollo, engaged in the interesting employment of twisting my long hair and beard with the flowers that Gogo industriously gathered. The deep sounds of the great cataract were borne upon the scent-laden breeze, mingling, in luscious harmony, with the rustling of the leaves, the melodious strains of innumerable birds, the dreamy hum of bees, the tinkling plash of a tiny fountain, the chattering of Gogo, and the delicious notes of Kaloolah's laugh and voice. I looked up into the clear depths of the blue sky. I looked up into the still clearer depths of her large dark eyes, and a feeling of exquisite happiness came over me, marred, however, by the reflection that such foretastes of heaven are liable to many interruptions, and are, necessarily, of short duration in this mortal world. At the instant, as if in confirmation of the reflection, Enphadde made his appearance, with a command for my immediate attendance upon the king.

We found his majesty, with his countenance troubled by news just brought from the eastern border of his domains, of an irruption of the fierce Jalla, who were desolating with fire and sword a fertile and populous tract, not more than two hundred miles from Kiloam. We had hardly entered the council-room when another messenger was announced, with news from the northwest, of an expedition of Footas into the country of the Kyptiles. The foreign relations of Framazugda were evidently getting into a bad way.

In a short speech, I proposed a plan of operations which met with instant and unanimous approval. I explained that, as far as regards the Footas, we must meet them with their own weapons, and that some time

359

would be required to make the necessary preparations, but that the Jalla required our immediate attention, and that we had ample means at hand to repress their ravages, and to compel them to observe, in future, a respectful distance from our borders. I therefore suggested that messengers should be despatched to the cave, near Garazha, to collect the saltpetre that I had observed incrusting the sides and floor of the entrance, and also to the slopes of the great volcano for sulphur, and that in the meantime Enphadde and myself should set out, and, making a rapid march to Alkafuz, put ourselves at the head of what few troops we could find at that frontier town, and proceed to chastise the Jalla. Upon our return I would commence the necessary preparations for carrying fire and sword into the heart of the Foota country.

Early the next morning we left Kiloam, and took the road for Alkafuz, which city we entered on the fourth day, with a body of eight hundred Framazugs and two hundred Kyptiles, whom we had picked up in our rapid march.

We found Alkafuz a pleasant little town, of five or six thousand inhabitants, but containing for the time being, double that number of people, who had been compelled to take refuge within the walls, from the attacks of the Jalla. Situated at the edge of a lofty plateau, it looked off upon a beautiful rolling country towards the northeast, which, falling away to a much lower level until it reached a hilly district, made a kind of neutral ground between the Jalla and the Framazugs.

According to the best information we could get from the frightened people of the country, there were two bodies of these savages, numbering twelve or fifteen hundred men each, at no great distance from the city. The next day we got news of another small party of three or four hundred, and the day after, word was brought that one of the large parties, laden with spoil, had commenced a retreat, while the other was still advancing up the country, and was at the moment attacking a small town to the south of Alkafuz, which, however, being well defended by high walls, would probably be able to withstand a long siege.

Leaving the besieged town for the time to defend itself as it best might, I drew out my forces from Alkafuz, on the morning of the third day after our arrival, and commenced a pursuit of the retreating party. Our army, amounting to about twelve hundred horse and a thousand foot, well armed with spears and bows, was in capital spirits, and animated with the highest confidence in the invincibility of its Christian allies, and in the gallantry of its youthful prince.

At the close of the first day word was brought, by the scouting parties

I had sent out, that three or four hundred of the enemy were close at hand in a small valley not more than five or six miles from our camp. The valley was a hollow way about two miles long, and a quarter of a mile broad, between two low but precipitous ledges of rock, and just the spot to trap the whole party, if we moved with sufficient celerity.

Giving orders to Enphadde to march the main body of our forces, after they should have had a few hours' rest, to the mouth of the pass, and to take up such a position by early dawn as to prevent the escape of the Jalla, I selected six hundred of our best-mounted men, and set out at once for the head of the ravine.

It was midnight when we entered it, and moving slowly down the grassy slope, in about two hours we came in sight of the smouldering fires of the unsuspicious Jalla. Halting my weary troop I made the men dismount, and each one, with the bridle of his horse in his hand, stretched himself on the thick herbage. Leaving them, with the strictest orders to Hugh and the officers in command of the battalion not to allow a man to move a foot, I went forward with our guide to employ the short hour until daylight, when Enphadde would be in his position, in a closer examination of the Jalla camp.

It was a clear, starlight night, and as there were no obstructions, we made our way without difficulty to within twenty rods of their fires. I could see the tall forms of the savages flitting about among the crowds of crouching captives, and the long lines of horses, picketed by ropes to pegs driven into the ground. Occasionally the guards would stir up the embers, and throw on an armful of dry grass to warm their nearly naked skins in the cool air of the morning, or to give light by which to reduce to quiet a restive and pugnacious steed, or drive back to the captive flocks and herds some fugitive sheep or cow.

Anxious to obtain a more accurate idea of the number of horses, I whispered to my companion to remain in his position, while I crept a little closer to a small knoll, whence could be obtained a better view of the encampment.

I had gone but a few yards when I fancied that there was a slight rustling, as if of some wild animal in the grass before me. I paused, and listened intently. My gun had been left behind, in charge of Hugh, but I had in my belt my doubled-barrelled pistols, one of which I drew, and carefully cocking both locks, held it in my left hand, while in my right was a short but heavy and serviceable sword, that by daylight would have been a very dangerous weapon for any animal, not even excepting a lion, to run upon.

After waiting awhile, and finding that all was still, I concluded that my ears had deceived me, and although a perceptible tinge of light in the eastern sky warned me that it was time to hurry back and lead on my troops to the attack, I thought that I would venture a few yards farther, and finish my reconnoissance from the knoll.

I had advanced, perhaps, a dozen steps, when I encountered what seemed to be a large log lying across my path. Without pausing to think of the improbability of the object being a log, when there was not a tree larger than a man's arm within ten miles, I jumped upon it, and stretched myself up for a good look. It gave a little to my weight, like many an old half-rotten trunk that my feet have pressed in the forests of the St. Lawrence. It seemed so much decayed as hardly to be able to bear me—as if it were about to break asunder and let me down into its spongy interior. My foot slipped upon the yielding surface—I recovered my balance, and on the instant felt myself elevated two or three feet. The whole log was alive beneath me, and—good heavens! I knew the boa!

My feet went out from under me—and I fell with my back across the writhing monster. For the fraction of a second there might have been some question as to which way my body was going, but a twist of the animal soon settled the point by letting me down upon my head and shoulders, and leaving my feet elevated on his back in the air.

I fell partly on my right side; my sword flew from my hand, but I still kept hold of the pistol. I glanced upwards—a huge, black object was hovering over and rapidly descending upon me. It was the monster's enormous head with jaws outstretched wide enough to engulph an elephant! Instinctively I stretched out my left hand. The pistol barrels rattled against some hard bony substance, and at the instant my fingers contracting upon the triggers, both charges exploded simultaneously with a loud report, and with a recoil that wrenched the weapon from my grasp.

There was a snort of agony and instantly a flouncing as if, to use a common Yankeeism, "heaven and earth had come together," amid which my feet were thrown into the air, and sent flying over my head, my neck twisted almost to dislocation, and my body projected through an indeterminate series of ground tumblings to the foot of the knoll.

Jumping to my feet, and recalling my scattered senses, the first inquiry was whether the creature was pursuing me, and the second as to the state of my bones. A tremendous floundering about a hundred yards off, on my right, that made the ground tremble like the shocks of an earthquake, relieved me of all fear of the first, and a slight examination showed that no material damage had been done to the second.

The Jalla camp was all alive, and our hopes of taking the enemy by surprise at an end ; so, following the example of my companion, I commenced a retreat in double-quick time.

My men had heard the alarm, and were all ready to mount. They sprang into their saddles just as a score of Apollo's outriders leaped the barrier of the horizon into the eastern sky.

" Charge !" was now the word, and away we rattled, as fast as our jaded steeds could get through the tall grass, down upon the foe. About half the distance was passed, when a party of three or four hundred Jalla drew out from the main body, and advanced towards us. It was evident that they were not so easily frightened, and that they were determined to fight, if necessary, to cover the retreat of the guards in charge of the captives and spoils.

Seeing them so well prepared and resolute, and knowing that they could not escape, prudence dictated that we should follow without attacking them, until we should hear something from Enphadde. It was apparent that the numbers of the enemy had been greatly underrated. Their whole force considerably exceeded mine, and they were all fresh and vigorous, while my men and their beasts were somewhat exhausted from fatigue and want of sleep.

The enemy, on their side, had apparently no stomachs for any unnecessary fighting ; and finding that we were not about to charge them, they drew back, and followed slowly their main body. Occasionally they would face about when we closed up a little too near to them, and ride towards us, and, upon our halting or moving more slowly, they would wheel and retreat.

Backing and filling in this way, we followed them for nearly an hour, until the sun was up, and pouring the full light of day into the lovely little valley. Suddenly there was a tremendous commotion in their ranks, their van recoiled upon their plunder-laden centre, and all was confusion. At this moment there came the report of a musket, and the next instant another which I knew must be from the guns of Hassan and Jack, who were with Enphadde. Soon the fierce sounds of strife came rolling towards us, and finding that Enphadde was fully engaged, and that a panic was extending through the ranks of our enemy, I led forward my men to the charge.

It is needless to go into a minute detail of the battle, which lasted about an hour. The Jalla fought bravely, although the occasional discharge of our fire-arms deprived them of their usual confidence. About two hundred and fifty were left dead upon the field, two hundred were made prisoners, and two or three hundred, deserting their horses, clambered up the sides of the hollow, and made their escape across the level country. On our side we lost a hundred and fifty men, some of whom were killed by being ridden over by the charging squadrons, or knocked down and trampled to death by the herds of frightened cattle, who, hemmed into the narrow battle-ground, were soon mingled with the combatants in inextricable confusion. In this way a score of the women and children, captives of the Jalla, were killed.

As soon as the fight was at an end, our prisoners secured, and order in some degree restored, my surgical skill was put in requisition, and for two or three hours I was employed in dressing wounds. It struck me at the time that were princes, prime-ministers, generals, and demagogues compelled to dress all the wounds that they caused, there would be but little fighting in the world.

I was just finishing with a flesh wound in the shoulder of the prince, which he had refused to have touched until all the men were cared for, when Hugh came running up with the news that the dead body of a huge serpent had been found among the rocks at a little distance. We went to see it, and found that it was the very fellow who, resenting my familiarity, had compelled me to my involuntary somersault. My pistol had been fired into his open mouth, and the balls, penetrating diagonally upwards and backwards, had passed through the palatal bones, and lodged in the brain. He was truly a monster, measuring fully one hundred feet in length, five feet in circumference, and with a head as large as a wine-cask. Great as was the veneration for our fire-arms, they rose to a still higher point in public estimations when it was understood that such a monster owed his death to one of our smallest weapons.

It was not until next morning that our army was in a condition to resume its march, and in the meantime word had been brought that the large detachment of the enemy which we had set out to pursue had got so far the start of us that it would be useless to follow them with an expectation of coming up with them before they reached the friendly shelter of their hills. Our plan, therefore, was to turn back and intercept the party, who, ignorant that there were Framazugs near them in such force, were still busy in attacking and sacking villages, and plundering and desolating the country. This done, I was determined to attempt inspiring the Jalla with wholesome terror by a vigorous, offensive war, carried into their strongholds in the hills.

It made it very inconvenient to us that they would not keep together in one body and allow us to defeat them in a lump. Enphadde and Thompson, however, succeeded in intercepting a party of five or six hundred, when a desperate fight ensued, in which we lost two hundred men, and Thompson was so severely wounded that we had to send him into Alkafuz. More than half of the enemy were killed or captured, and the rest were glad to leave their plunder and escape with their lives.

It was now our turn to assume the offensive. A week's rest recruited our forces and enabled us to assemble an army of five thousand men, with a train of buffaloes for our baggage and provisions. Unfortunately, Thompson's wound, much to his chagrin, compelled us to leave him at Alkafuz; but his gun was entrusted to the charge of an officer of distinguished bravery, so that its moral influence was not lost to the army.

A march of three days to the northeast took us obliquely across a fine rolling country, which descended by a series of gentle inclinations from the plateau of Alkafuz to a level plain at the foot of the Jalla hills. We encountered several rivers; but as it was the dry season there was no difficulty in fording them, except in one place where the creek expanding into a marsh made the clay soil so soft that our animals in attempting the passage sunk up to their knees at every step. Here we should have been compelled to stop had it not been for an ingenious expedient of the Kyptiles Collecting a species of tough dry grass, they twisted it into ropes of about an inch diameter. With these they wrapped the feet of their horses and cattle until they were encased in bundles of hay as large as was consistent with motion. The whole was firmly secured with an outside lacing of stout thongs of untanned skin. Equipped in mud shoes our animals skimmed the surface without any difficulty.

Shortly after crossing the marsh we encountered, in succession, several untenanted villages, the Jalla having had notice of our approach; but we found great stores of wheat, barley, rice, honey, and oil in caves in the ground.

Burning the villages, which were composed of reed houses, plastered with mud and thatched with straw, and destroying such stores as we did not want, we moved on until we came to a large town at the foot of a mountain pass, which was defended by a stone wall and a ditch. The wall was very slight and the ditch narrow; but there was a formidable force within the defences of nearly a thousand men. Upon our appearance the enemy mounted the walls, and evinced, by words and gestures, their determination to make a vigorous resistance.

It would not answer to penetrate into the mountains, leaving such a post in our rear, and yet, how to take it? We had nothing but a few light scaling ladders, and there was not a piece of timber large enough for a battering-ram within ten miles. The thought occurred to me of collecting some small trees, and making a catapult; but there were two strong objections: the first was, that it would take too much time; and the second, that I knew nothing about the construction of the machine. The last objection may seem to some insuperable, but it would be dishonoring my Yankee blood to allow that it alone prevented a catapult from being made. A thoroughbred Yankee, I take it, can make any thing, upon a pinch, that he has ever heard the name and use of, even if he has never seen it, and has no idea of its form and structure.

The enemy, confident in the strength of their position, were loud in their insulting bravadoes, refusing to listen to any terms, shooting at the heralds we sent to parley with them, and even exhibiting the heads of Framazug captives, stuck on pikes, upon the wall. Oh, for one single field-piece, of even the smallest calibre!

Something must be done, and that quickly, if we wished to press matters home to the Jalla in the hills. At last a plan occurred to me, which we at once proceeded to carry into execution.

The town was of an elliptical shape, and covered an area of about one hundred acres. Two gates, opposite to each other, were the only means of entrance or egress. These were evidently old, and very weak, and in front of them the ditch, instead of continuing on, stopped short, on either side, leaving a broad, level path leading up to them. Our forces were divided into four divisions; two of these were stationed opposite the walls, at an equal distance from either gate. Each of these divisions was furnished with three or four ladders, and every man was armed with a large fascine of bushes, which, upon a given signal, he was to rush forward and throw into the muddy ditch, or with a bundle of dry grass, which was to be set on fire, and thrust over the wall, on long spars, to disorder the enemy while the assailants were planting their ladders.

Had we had a few more ladders there could have been no doubt of carrying the place by escalade. As it was, I expected merely that they would answer for a powerful diversion in favor of the other two divisions that were destined to attack the gates. One of these divisions was under the immediate command of Enphadde, the other I took charge of myself. Each division was drawn up under cover of their bucklers, as close to the walls as the bows and slings of the enemy would permit.

Our battering machines, two in number, were now prepared and levelled for the charge. They consisted of three horses each. The animals being first blindfolded, were harnessed together abreast, and laden with a heavy weight of stones in panniers. On either side rode a horseman, who was stuffed and padded with skins, until he was arrow-proof. Halters attached to the heads of the three doomed horses enabled the outriders to direct their course so as to strike at full speed the feeble gates.

When my preparations were all finished, I rode round to the other gate, and found Enphadde, with his three-horse battering-ram, ready for the charge. The enemy had suddenly become very quiet; they were beginning to feel a little dubious as to our intended movements. Returning by a circuit of the walls to my post at the northern gate, I gave a sign to Hugh, who fired his musket. It was answered by Hassan, from the other gate, and at the report the drums beat, the trumpets sounded, and all hands rushed to the walls.

The three blind horses, guided by the riders at their side, and goaded by bunches of thorns, attached to thongs that flapped against their flanks, rushed at full speed upon the gates. When within thirty or forty feet, the two guides checked their horses, leaving the others to pursue their way. The feeble barrier yielded to the shock as if it had been made of paper, and the animals moving with irresistible momentum, dashed through the splintered bars as easily as a reckless steed through the painted canvas walls of the Corso in a Roman horse-race, and were precipitated dead or dying into the town.

Charging at a full run, we reached the gates before the astonished Jalla had time to take any measures for defending the breach. On his side Enphadde was equally successful, and the panic created, allowed the other assailants, on either side, to plant their ladders and climb over the walls.

The town was now carried in all quarters, and our four divisions came pouring in, driving the enemy before them, and slaughtering them without mercy. I rode forward and met the prince in the market-place, and together we tried to draw off our troops, and give the enemy an opportunity to ask and receive quarter. With much difficulty we succeeded in saving about two hundred warriors, and a great number of women and children, who had taken refuge in a small enclosure of reeds surrounding the Shocco, or chief. All the rest were killed with the exception of about fifty, who in the confusion of the *mêlée* had jumped the walls, and eluding our outposts, made their way to the hills.

There remained now no obstacle to our march into the mountains, and it was decided to set out at once, and move rapidly upon Jebha, the chief town of the Shelwhuck tribe of Jalla, and take it, if possible, before assistance could be collected from the more distant tribes. If we could not succeed in taking it, we could at least desolate the environs, and perhaps frighten the Grand Shocco into a treaty of peace.

At the first view of this stronghold of the Grand Shocco, I gave up all hopes of taking it by storm. Situated in the midst of a small slope about half a mile in length, and less than a quarter in breadth, upon the side of a steep rocky hill, that rose nearly perpendicular from the plain, it was approachable only by a narrow pathway that led directly up the face of the cliff. Ten men could easily defend this road against ten thousand. The elevation of the village was about one hundred and fifty feet. There were no walls or other artificial defences, except a mound of large stones, that were ready to be rolled down the steep and narrow path. Where the road commenced to ascend, there was a conical hill about fifty feet high, and some three or four hundred yards distant from the face of the cliff. It would have made a beautiful spot for a mortar battery. From the upper part of the town rose a steep hollow way, which, at the end of five or six hundred yards was crowned with a beetling ledge of rocks. A mountain howitzer, had we had one, and could we have got it up there, would soon have rendered the town untenable.

The first thing to do was to take possession of the small hill that commanded the commencement of the path—certain, that if we could not get up, the enemy could not get down. We were now in a position to starve them into submission; the only difficulty was that we could not afford the time. The enemy seemed to think that was our only plan, for they appeared capering upon the edge of the cliff, with loaves of bread on the points of their swords and spears, to indicate that they had an abundant supply of provision for a siege.

For several days we remained inactive. No plan of operations presented itself. I had examined the whole circumference of the mountain without being able to find any point at which it could be climbed, and was about giving up in despair, when the prince rode into camp from a reconnoissance, and stated that he thought he had discovered a crag, from which, if it could be reached, the ascent would not be impossible to the top of the cliffs commanding the town. He proposed to take the ladders and splice them together, and, with a body of two hundred men, make the attempt. If he succeeded, he would detach some of the masses of rock that were, apparently, trembling to a fall. From the nature of the ground these would necessarily take their way down through the midst of the town. Or, if it was found impossible to loosen the rocks, he would guard the passage by which he had ascended, until I led up our men in full force, when we could descend the ravine to a proper distance, take up a position, and open our batteries of slings, arrows, and fire-arms from a commanding height.

I gave my assent to this proposition. Taking with him the ladders and a large quantity of stout cords, made of braided skin, Enphadde set out at night-fall for the spot that he had noted, about four miles from our camp. There was not much danger that he would meet with any opposition from the enemy; but in order to make a diversion in his favor and to occupy their attention, I ordered large fires to be built, and made some of the soldiers busy themselves around them, as if constructing monstrous machines. Others were employed in digging, under a full blaze of light, in a trench that had been commenced across the foot of the road to the town, while others amused themselves and the enemy, who crowded the ledges of their plateau, blowing horns, beating drums, and dancing, leaping, and yelling.

As morning dawned all eyes were strained in the direction of the peak. A light cap of vapor for a time obscured the view; but as the sun rose it suddenly lifted, disclosing, not more to my delight than surprise, a group of figures upon the highest rock. One of them came forward and waved a banner. The Framazugs knew their prince, and a loud shout went up from the camp in reply.

Enphadde lost no time; one half of his men were distributed out upon the jutting points, so as to command the approaches from the town, the others, divided into three parties, commenced their attacks upon as many masses of overhanging rock. Some plied the pickaxes at the crumbling bases, others adjusted levers and ropes to the crevices above. When all was ready, according to agreement, the prince made a signal by waving a flag.

In the meantime the enemy had been invited to parley, but they would receive no proposition. We waved a white flag to them; they answered with yells of defiance. Anxious to save bloodshed, I sent a single man to attempt the ascent; he was repelled with stones and arrows. Although somewhat confounded by the appearance of our men on the peak, it was evident that they had no idea of the intended plan of attack. With a feeling, compounded of anger at their stupidity and obstinacy and sorrow for their impending fate, I was compelled to give the signal to Enphadde to let fall.

Instantly his men threw their full strength upon the levers beneath the tottering masses, which, slowly yielding to the force, hung for a moment as if trembling at the fearful leap, and the next, like the stone of

Sisyphus "resulting with a bound," thundered impetuously down the
precipitous ravine directly into the town. One of these masses in leap
ing from a projecting ledge was broken into a thousand pieces. A second was diverted somewhat from its course by the inequalities of the
ground, so as to strike only a couple of houses at the side. But the third,
a huge rock of ten tons, rolled straight through the town, carrying every
thing before it ; prostrating twenty houses, killing and wounding more
than fifty people, among the latter of whom was the Grand Shocco himself ;
and leaping from the edge of the inclined plain with a force that projected it a distance of forty yards on the ground below.

The prince and his men sprang at once to work, preparing for another
discharge, while from the town went up a chorus of sounds that almost
sensibly aided in loosening the trembling rocks.

"*Oie hco lu ! Oie hi hco lu !*" yelled the frightened Jalla. "*Zi-le—li-
e—li-ee !*" screamed the women and children at the top of their shrill
voices. The men leaped about like so many monkeys, gesticulating furi-
ously, throwing themselves upon the ground and tearing their long hair,
which, frizzled and stiffened with a composition of beeswax and mutton
tallow, had very much the appearance of a grenadier's cap saturated with
soap fat. The women ran about with their children in their arms or
clinging to their garments ; while any number of dogs, partaking of the
general panic, scampered through the town, with their voices elevated in
long-drawn howls (they were incapable of barking) to concert pitch.

Making a signal to Enphadde to suspend his operations, I again expressed to the enemy our desire to offer them terms. The sense of security
in which they had hitherto contemned our proffers, was now gone, and
they signified their disposition to treat for a surrender. Our messengers
were despatched into the town, and in a few minutes they returned
with a deputation from the Grand Shocco. As there were no complicated diplomatic forms to be gone through with, the business was soon
settled. My ultimatum was stated without circumlocution. Immediate
surrender, the Grand Shocco and twelve principal men to put themselves
into my hands without conditions, and the lives and property (except
provisions necessary for our army) of all the other inhabitants to be
saved, were the terms to which they at first demurred, but which, as
there was no alternative, they were compelled to accept.

A great many people from the surrounding country had flocked into
Jebha for security ; as soon as these had evacuated the narrow plateau
we marched up and took possession of the place. We found it to consist of about three hundred dwelling-houses, and a dozen large stores

filled with grain, honey, oil, wool, woollen cloths, dates, and weapons of war—the whole belonging to the Shocco, who ruled with despotic power this particular tribe, the Shelwhuck Jalla, who, far more than the other tribes of the same people, had molested the borders of Framazugda.

Understanding that the chief was lying badly wounded, having been buried beneath the walls of his house, which unluckily stood in the way of Enphadde's irresistible messenger, I went to see him, and found him with a dislocated shoulder and two or three fractured ribs. He could not conceal his astonishment, when he suddenly found himself treated as a patient—his broken bones bandaged up, and his luxation reduced. It was equally a matter of surprise, the attention that I paid to the wounds of his people.

" I cannot understand," he exclaimed, " why you should take so much pains to cure what you have come so far to make ! "

We explained to him that we had not come merely for revenge, but to recover the captives that he had sent his people to steal, and to compel him to keep the peace. We told him that the Great Shounsé bore him no ill-will, and wished him no harm ; but that he was determined that his people should no longer suffer from the predatory excursions of the Jalla, even if he had to quarter a permanent army in their country, desolate it with fire from one end to the other, and slay all who should be caught—men, women, and children. I told him that, for my part, I felt very friendly towards him, but that I had undertaken the command of all the forces of the great king, and that, if I was compelled to return into his country, I should bring with me great guns, fifty times larger than our muskets, which would reach him, even if he built his town upon the apex of the peak, and that I should then have to exterminate him and all his people.

Reinforcements of both Framazugs and Kyptiles, among which was my old friend Sooloo Phar, arriving, our force was swelled to ten thousand men. Leaving, therefore, a strong garrison at Jebha, we set out on an expedition to some other tribes. As we advanced, the chiefs came forward, and submitted without opposition, pledging themselves to peace with both the Framazugs and Kyptiles.

For ten days we continued our march, penetrating the country for more than a hundred miles. At last we came to a small stream, which we should hardly have noticed, had not the inhabitants called our attention to it, asserting that it was the beginning of the greatest river in the world. That after running an immense distance, receiving streams from every direction, it joined itself to a great river farther to the east, and that both together ran on for several moons' journey, and emptied into a salt lake. Could it be that I stood at the sources of the *Bahr el Abiad?* that my feet pressed the spot which Bruce so longed to tread, and which, when standing by the fountains of the Blue River, he vainly fancied he had found? It was possible, in fact probable. I stooped, and kissed the water where it rilled from the ground. Perhaps, thought I, the very drops, touched by my lips, may course on their winding way, for thousands of miles, until, leaping the cataracts of Syene, and passing the palaces of Luxor and the pyramids of Geeza, they reach the Mediterranean, and lave the keel of some one of the many ships, bearing the stripes and stars, that proudly part its clear blue waters.

I asked our guides if it would be possible to follow the stream to its mouth ; they held up their hands in amazement at the idea.

" Why not ? " I demanded.

" Oh ! because of the savage countries through which it runs. In some places through barren deserts, and dense forests, in others, through countries inhabited by wild men and cannibals."

" How do you know, then, that this stream is the head of a great river, if no one has ever traced its course ? "

" Our ancestors have told us so. They knew, because thirty thousand moons ago they lived upon its banks, where it was a broad stream. But they were compelled by their enemies to fly up into this high country; and on their journey, which lasted a hundred moons, they were forced to fight their way through nations so fierce, that no Jalla have ever since attempted to return."

" What kind of people are these that you speak of—white or black ? "

" Oh ! of all colors," replied my informant, the Shocco of a Jalla town ; " white, black, red, blue, and green."

Upon expressing some surprise at this statement, the Shocco appealed to several of his nobles for its truth, and even offered, if I would go with him, to lead me against a people who had their faces, arms, and breasts, all covered with blue lines, or, if we pleased, he would make an expedition with us to the east, where lived a nation of a little people, covered with green hair, who lived in holes that they dug in the ground with their hands, " or among the branches of the trees."

" In other words," I interrupted, " a nation of monkeys."

" Not at all," replied the Shocco, " they are human beings, speak a language that sounds like the whistling of arrows, are governed by chiefs, and when caught, as they sometimes are by the D'jhas'r'hue Jalla, they make good slaves. But why should I talk when I can show you one of them. Here Syedge! Galloom! Miefrah!" shouted the Shocco, calling to his slaves, "run up the mountain to the goats' valley, and tell Jicric that I want him!"

In a few minutes Jicric stood before us, and a comical-looking little fellow he was. In height he was about four feet to the top of his shoulders, which were elevated to a level with the crown of his head. He had no neck, and his head was half buried in his chest, so that his mouth came just above the upper edge of his sternum. His arms were long, terminating in hands resembling claws. His body was thick and short,

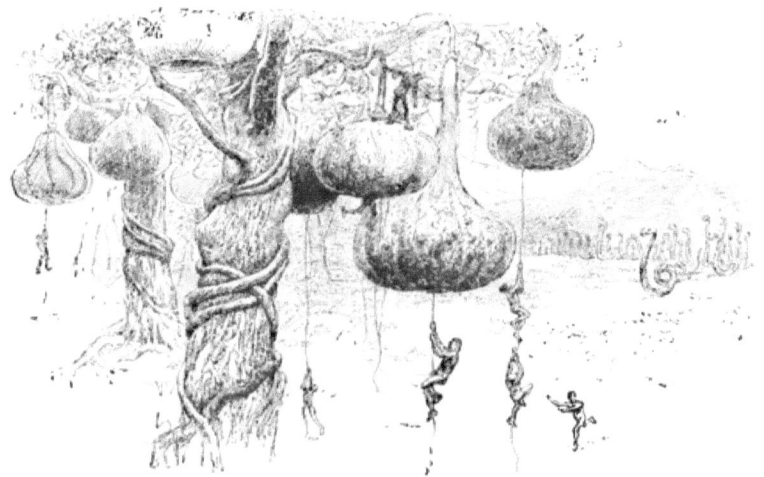

" You will sometimes see twenty of these houses hanging from one tree."

with a protuberant abdomen, and his lower limbs slender, but strong and sinewy. He had no clothing, but instead was covered with a thick coating of long, coarse hair, of a light pea-green tint. What was my surprise to find such an animal speaking Jally fluently, and answering, through an interpreter, my questions with spirit and intelligence.

He said that his people were divided into many tribes; and that they inhabited a great marshy country intersected by rivers running to the east. That they lived upon the spontaneous productions of the soil; such as nuts, wild fruits, and edible roots; and also upon insects, locusts, and serpents. That their chief enemies were a white people on the east, with long hair, who annually made an incursion into their country for slaves ; and on the north, a nation of red men, who painted their faces, and lived in gourds.

Not understanding what Jicric meant by a people living in gourds, I demanded an explanation.

" You must know," said he, " that these red men live in a country that produces a vine that bears a gourd as large as a Jalla hut. The stalk of this vine is frequently more than two hands'-breadth in diameter, and the fruit that hangs from it is sometimes more than five paces through. These vines the red people train upon large trees ; and when the yellow hard-shelled gourds have attained their growth, they excavate them, and convert them into pendent dwellings, where they are secure from the attacks of the numerous serpents that infest their country. You will sometimes see twenty of these houses hanging from one tree."

" How do the inhabitants get in and out ? "

" Why, by a hole in the bottom, to which they draw themselves up by ropes, or which they can reach by climbing the trunk of the tree and stepping down round the outside of the gourd."

" Capital houses they must be for the rainy season ! "

" Oh beautiful ! beautiful ! " exclaimed Jicric ; " and for snakes ! wonderful for snakes ! "

" Why, are the snakes so numerous ? "

" Numerous ? why, there is a country not twenty days' from here, where they are so thick that even the people who live in squashes are compelled to desert it. The snakes, in the morning, when they come out of their holes, erect themselves as high and as thick as trees. Sometimes, when you look over this snake country you would think that you saw a leafless forest waving in a storm ! "

Jicric's tones were beginning to assume an air of exaggeration, but they were abundantly corroborated by the loud assertions of the Shocco and his friends.

I asked Jicric if he would accompany me ; and, upon his assenting, made a bargain for him with his master. The little fellow has been with me ever since, and has grown to be a great favorite with Kaloolah, although at first she could hardly bear him in her sight.

Having now ventured as far from home as prudence would permit, with so small an army, we set out on our return to Jebha. Here we picked up the Grand Shocco, with his twelve principal men, and started for Alkafuz.

At Alkafuz we left him to come on by litter, and the prince and myself, mounting the fleetest horses, set out for the capital. In four days

we reached the city, and such a time as we had in making our way
through the crowds in the streets, and into the great square into the palace! There was nothing like a regular procession, and no parade of captives or spoils: but our reception was a complete impromptu popular
triumph. I thought of Bacchus on his return from his Indian expedition; but Bacchus, if I recollect aright, was accompanied by all his
women folks, and he could afford to dance and fiddle his way along
leisurely, whereas mine I had not seen in some time, and I knew that she
was waiting for me; so, jumping from my horse, I dashed through the
crowds on foot, leaving the prince to do the honors of the occasion, and
crossing the court of monkeys, entered a room hung with feather-cloth
and filled with flowers. A female, draped in flowing robes of white, was
waiting to receive me, but she was so tall, so dignified, and had such an
air of social and regal *aplomb* that, although she was my own wife, a decided sentiment of the reverential qualified the embrace with which I
received her, as she threw herself into my arms.

CHAPTER XLV.

EVERAL months elapsed from the time of our triumphant return before all our preparations were completed for my proposed system of operations against the Footas. In the meantime, however, there had been a number of skirmishes and small battles, in which the Framazugs, and a few Kyptiles, under the command of Enphadde, and assisted by Hugh, Hassan, and Thompson, had conducted themselves with a good deal of spirit. In general, however, they were indisposed to attack an enemy armed as the Footas, and no affair of any moment, in consequence, took place. The enemy made continual incursions into the Kyptile and Kimboo countries, and, although they met with more opposition, and had to fight a little harder, they succeeded in making many slaves, and in some places in driving the Kyptiles quite into the Framazug lines.

My preparations were pushed, under my own personal superintendence, with the utmost vigor. Every means in the kingdom was placed at my disposal, and the most stringent orders issued by the Great Shounsé, to the effect that the most implicit obedience was to be rendered to any directions that I might give.

The first thing I set about was the manufacture of gunpowder. Fortunately, I recollected the proportionate numbers of the ingredients, but I knew not to which article each number applied. That is, I knew that there must be about seventy-five parts of one of the constituents of gunpowder to fifteen of the second, and ten of the third, but whether the seventy-five parts were to be of charcoal, sulphur, or saltpetre, was a point which had wholly escaped my memory. It did not, however, require a long course of experiment to determine the matter; the powder was at last produced, and that, too, of a very excellent quality. A large manufactory was now established, and a hundred hands set to work at the several processes; some pulverized the materials, others mixed the paste in large wooden bowls, and others granulated it by passing it through sieves of copper.

The next thing was to make the machines in which the powder was to be used. As for casting solid cylinders of metal, and then boring them out into cannon—it was out of the question. The most that we could do was to cast a hollow piece, and then work the bore as smooth and as straight as possible. We tried this, but with many difficulties and accidents. The artists in my employ were unused to casting in such large masses, their bronze work, of even their largest statue, being all done in small pieces. We could not undertake, therefore, any thing larger than a four-pounder. In the course of our experiments we met with many accidents; several times our moulds broke down while in the act of running the metal. At other times the guns came out crooked, full of flaws, and incapable of standing the most moderate proof. And once the liquid metal was poured into a damp mould; the moisture was instantly converted into steam of a high expansive power. An explosion took place that threw the hot bronze in every direction; killing two of the workmen, and severely wounding several others.

After a great deal of trouble in this way, and having succeeded in making only three small pieces that were good for any thing, I concluded to adopt an entirely different plan, and to go back to first principles, or rather to first practices. It occurred to me that I had read somewhere of wooden guns being used in the infancy of artillery science, and even cannon made of leather. Acting upon this idea, I caused the trunk of a peculiar species of palm to be sawed into proper lengths; the soft pith or heart of one of these was easily rem ved, leaving a smooth bore of about five inches and a half in diameter, surrounded by a shell three inches thick, of wood surpassing in hardness lignum vitæ, or the still harder fibre of the cabbage tree. An iron breech, through which was bored a vent, was now adjusted into one end; next a number of wrought-iron rings, each two inches thick and four inches wide, and a very little smaller in diameter than the external circumference of the wooden tube, was prepared. These were heated so as to expand them, and passed on in succession, until the whole length of the tube, from breech to muzzle, was encased. Each ring was so fashioned as to dovetail, or interlock, with the ones above and below it. The whole length of the gun was about four feet, and the bore, as I have said, a little more than five inches and a half, making it, as near as I have been able to form any notion on the subject, about the size of a twenty-four-pound howitzer.

Great was our delight upon trying this piece to find that it fully answered our purposes. More than forty rounds of leaden grape-shot were fired from it before it was materially injured, and even then it was serviceable for thirty or forty charges more. The action of the powder upon the wood hardened it almost to the density of iron. Another piece stood more than thirty discharges of round shot, and we found that by taking the precaution of wrapping the ball in greased cloth more than a hundred rounds could be fired, and still leave the gun capable of service.

Encouraged by this success, it was resolved to prepare twenty-five pieces, and five hundred of the best artisans were at once employed in preparing the palm trunks, making the ironwork, casting balls, making up stands of grape and canister, and constructing the carriages. These last were composed of a wooden shoe, into which the gun was fastened, and which was placed upon a stout, heavy plank, with grooves in it that allowed the shoe to slide back and forth about eighteen inches. The recoil, when it had reached its greatest limit, was checked by stout iron springs. Three wooden rollers of different sizes served to elevate to any required angle the forward end of the plank, and ropes attached to the other end served to give a horizontal motion. To rings in the plank were fastened two spars, each thirty-five feet in length, and by means of lanyards to these spars, forty men could lay hold of them, and carry off the guns with ease. When the gun was to be placed in battery these spars could be at once unlimbered and drawn to the rear.

The organization of the *personnel* of my army was conducted *pari passu* with the preparation of the *materiel*. A hundred thousand men were anxious to serve; but I was determined not to embarrass myself with a horde that it would be impossible to reduce to discipline, or to find any use for. I resolutely insisted on limiting the whole number to twenty-four thousand men. These I divided into eight brigades, each brigade into three regiments, and each regiment into ten companies of one hundred men each. They were all armed with bows and arrows; the bows were carried at the back; each man was also furnished with a large sling to use in case his arrows gave out and stones could be got. Besides these, he carried a short strong spear or pike, about six feet and a half in length, and with a stout double-edged iron point. This shortening of the spears from twelve feet to six was the only thing in all my innovations that excited any question as to its propriety; but my orders had to be obeyed, and twenty-four thousand broad-bladed, sharp-pointed weapons, having the well-balanced and agreeable hang of a ship's boarding pike, were made.

It was fortunate, perhaps, that I knew nothing of military tactics beyond what any Yankee youngster obtains from reading of battles and seeing "general trainings." I might otherwise have been perplexed with knowledge, and anxious to communicate too much of it to my troops. As it was, I felt no inducement to indulge in any of the superfluities of drill. In the school of the soldier a simple system of manual exercise was the first thing that demanded my attention. The nature of it will be best understood, perhaps, from the words of command. These were: "shoulder spears," "charge spears," "ground spears," which meant sticking the spears upright into the ground in front of the soldier; "unsling bows," "notch arrows," "draw arrows," "fire." Hugh, who undertook the entire superintendence of the manual exercise, wished to introduce several other commands, such as "carry arms," "present arms," etc.; and had the men had any thing about them that could have been twisted by any effort of fancy into a resemblance to ramrods and cartridges, he would have insisted upon their drawing the one and handling the other. As it was, I had to compromise matters with him, and, in consideration of their utility in relieving the men upon a march, permit the use of "slope spears" and "trail spears."

In the school of the company there were no very difficult or important points necessary for our purposes to be attended to. Marching by whole front or platoons, wheeling, changing face, and halting were all that we attempted, and these were not performed, as Hugh loudly protested, *secundem artem ;* but as he could not demonstrate that the practice of the royal marines was any better, he was compelled to swallow his professional pride and follow the army regulations, as by myself and my respectable old father-in-law established.

The school of the battalion was more difficult to arrange, and tasked my invention the most severely, inasmuch as neither Hugh nor myself knew any thing of battalion or regimental manœuvres. But, although ignorant of the means, or rather the *modus operandi*, the indications to be fulfilled were evident enough. Of these, the two most important were, deploying from column, and forming squares. The latter, in particular, was of the highest consequence, inasmuch as upon it depended the entire success of our operations against an enemy whose whole force consisted in cavalry.

After much consideration, I succeeded in arranging a series of evolutions, by which each regiment could be thrown into square, solid or hollow, according to the exigencies of the case and the extent of the ground, at a moment's notice, either from column or line, and when marching or stationary. It would take too long to give all the details of the manœuvres, and, besides, I have no wish to shock the professional sensibilities of any of the accomplished tacticians and martinets of the New York militia. Suffice it therefore to say that, upon my system, squares to resist a charge of cavalry can now be formed with all necessary rapidity and precision.

A system of tactics having been matured, it became necessary to apply it in practice, and to discipline twenty-four thousand men, to train them to new uses of their weapons, to new combinations of movement—to teach them the more effective Christian mode of fighting. This was accomplished in a wonderful short space of time, by collecting all the officers of the army into a battalion about eight hundred strong, and drilling them first. They were then dismissed to their respective corps, when each regimental staff exerted itself in emulation to communicate its knowledge to the men. To favor this emulation, the regiments were encamped apart, and for three months the drills were conducted without any one but the members of the corps being present. Every day the battalion line of officers was formed, and either Hugh or myself put them through their evolutions, but I carefully abstained from visiting the quarters of the different regiments when they were at their exercises. At the end of three months it was announced that the king and myself would make a tour of inspection, and that those regiments that best performed their exercises would receive marks of the royal bounty. It must be understood that the army was composed of picked men, men chosen for their intelligence and activity, and that the spirit of emulation had been carried to the highest pitch in order to comprehend the wonderful progress that they had made. The emperor was in raptures, and ordered that every man should receive a month's pay as a present, and that the officers should be rewarded with an increase of salary and with decorations and orders. Captains of companies were allowed to add a green parrot's feather to their caps, and the field officers were each presented with a stuffed monkey's paw, to be worn suspended from the neck by a blue ribbon.

The army was now collected in one camp on the outskirts of the city, and the drilling went on under my own personal inspection. Particular pains were taken in the formation of the squares. The officers, when in the centre were taught to use a number of encouraging expressions to their men, and the firmness of the kneeling ranks was assured by the repeated charges of squadrons of cavalry up to the very spear-heads. No military manœuvre, when well performed, can be more beautiful. Upon the word, each regiment rapidly closes into a solid mass; the men, with their polished spears and their light-red uniforms, and the officers in the centre with their dancing, many-colored plumes and rich uniforms of brilliant feather-cloth. A second order, and the flashing spear-points are levelled and inclined outward, the front ranks drop to their knees with a movement that, to a spectator at a little distance, looks not unlike the bursting from bud to flower of a gigantic rose, or rather like the blowing of a large red thistle.

At length all was ready, and early one beautiful morning in the beginning of the dry season the army commenced its march for the Queal—which river was reached without any difficulty, the roads being good, and every thing having been prepared to facilitate our progress. It was my plan to cross the stream, and, pushing on down to the lake, lay siege to Goolah. Here it was thought that the Footas would make a vigorous defence, but it was not expected that they would meet us in full force in the field. We were, therefore, somewhat astonished, though far from displeased, to find the enemy in considerable numbers, occupying the opposite bank of the river. I at once decided, instead of depending upon our skin boats, to throw a bridge across the river, and to fortify it so as to secure a means of retreat, if necessary. For this purpose Enphadde was despatched across with a detachment to seize a position, which he did without opposition, the attention of the enemy being diverted by the main body of the army, and in a few hours had it strongly entrenched.

In three days we had a fine wide bridge, consisting of a strong framework, covered with planks, floated by means of boats and inflated skins, and defended at either end by a stone tower. We crossed, and took up our line of march through a wild, open country—the Foota horsemen appearing in great numbers, but retreating as we advanced.

It is unnecessary to detain the reader with all the details of marching, bivouacking, and skirmishing. Suffice it to say we at length reached the banks of the lake, and within sight of the walls of Goolah. We found the enemy in full force, occupying a wide level piece of ground that stretched from the town along the lake, up to the mouth of the Queal. On the other side, this plain was bounded by a ridge of wooded hills. At one place these hills came down to within half a mile of the water, so as almost to cut the plain in two, and then fell away again, with a bold sweep around the town. A thorough reconnoissance satisfied us that the hills were uninhabited, and that it was possible, although difficult, to pass along through them, and reach the narrowest part of the plain; thus cutting the Footas off from their town, and compelling them to a general engagement at once.

Leaving Dal Gouk at the head of half my disposable force of twenty thousand, in an entrenched camp, to occupy the Footas and to cover our detour, I set out, accompanied by the prince and my companions, with the remaining ten thousand, and three complete batteries of artillery. Luckily, our batteries were not composed of Christian cannon, or we should have found the way perfectly impracticable. As it was, it was very heavy work carrying our light guns up and down precipices, and over jagged rocks; but perseverance conquered all obstacles; and at nightfall, after a terrible day's march, we reached a point still covered by the hills, but whence we could at once debouch upon the narrow portion of plain before mentioned. Little did the Footas, who were assembled some thirty thousand strong, at the upper part of the small prairie in front of Dal Gouk's lines—little did they dream that their flanks had been turned, and that their enemy, with a divided force, it is true, but still a sufficient one, had reached their rear. And just as little did they dream of the death-dealing properties of the formidable machines that they were soon about to encounter.

Putting the army in motion at daybreak, in a few minutes we reached the level ground. A small rocky islet stood out a little distance in the plain; upon this I placed three pieces of artillery in care of Jack, with orders not to fire a gun until the enemy's charge had been repulsed. When fully in position, our right flank, under Enphadde, rested upon the bank of the river, and was supported by three pieces in charge of Hugh. The remaining artillery, consisting of twelve pieces, I drew up under my own personal superintendence, upon our left flank, at the base of the hills, and three or four hundred yards in rear of Jack's masked demi-battery.

It was the middle of the forenoon when all our positions were taken, and by that time the enemy were fully informed of our movements. In fact, our operations had been conducted after daylight, directly under the supervision of bodies of horsemen, who, however, had offered no opposition. Large masses of cavalry began to accumulate in front of us; until about noon the enemy's full force had moved down from Dal Gouk's camp to the barrier so suddenly raised in their rear. They were not long in coming to the conclusion to ride over us, a feat which they had no doubt about being able to perform on level ground. As soon as it was evident, from their motions, that there was to be a general charge, I threw my troops into squares, and passed up and down the whole length of the line, addressing to each battalion a few words of encouragement, which were received with the utmost enthusiasm.

Grandly the whole mass moved down upon us. There was no effort at order, but for spirit, rapidity of pace, and numbers, there was never a cavalry charge of the French more magnificent. On they came, the ground trembling and groaning beneath the tramp of twenty thousand horses, twirling their muskets and spears high above their heads, and beating with might and main on their shields of buffalo hide. On they came, with their white teeth flashing, their scimitars gleaming, and their ornamented trappings rattling like pebbles amid the thundering of a heavy surf. On they came with trumpets sounding, cymbals clashing, and each voice shouting the famous battle-cry of the Saracens that battle-cry which, however Christians may boast of their achievements, has been heard on more fields and has heralded more bloodshed than any Christian battle-cry ever uttered, not excepting the exciting oaths of the English soldiery, the blasphemies of the French, the obscene anathemas of the Spanish, or the elegant and encouraging " give 'em hell " of my own countrymen. On they came, but still my men stood as firm as did the English squares at Waterloo. Suddenly the roar of the batteries on our left was added to the tumult. It was answered by Hugh's three pieces, and by a general discharge of slings, arrows, and small-arms from our lines. The enemy immediately in front of the batteries were completely demolished by our first discharge, when, changing front to the right, I opened a tremendous flanking fire upon the dense masses, very much to the relief of the hard-pressed squares. As the enemy recoiled, Jack's gun came into play, and the rapid discharges of grape and canister, from eighteen pieces, carried death into every portion of their disordered ranks.

At this moment a body of a thousand horse came creeping down on our left, under the shadow of the hills. They proved to be our Kyptiles and Kimboos, under Sooloo Phar, from Dal Gouk's camp. At a word they threw themselves upon the struggling and reeling masses, and the rout was complete. Five thousand were left dead on the field—while several hundreds were forced over the steep banks into the river, and many more were destroyed by the Seywad as they fled by his camp.

The next day the whole army made a regular investment of the town, which had refused all offers for a capitulation. Our batteries were at once placed in position, but after a hard day's firing, we found that they were utterly inadequate to making any impression upon the massive walls. In addition to their want of size, our guns began to show signs of weakness, and it was evident that another day's cannonade would use them up entirely.

For three weeks we lay before Goolah, suffering many inconveniences, especially from want of provisions, the remnants of the defeated Foota army occupying our rear, and cutting off our communications. And there we might have stayed until the present day, had I not thought of a plan for taking the town, which, if not as ingenious as that adopted by Cyrus for the capture of Babylon, was at least as novel and as successful.

On the east side of the town, the wall, crossing between two elevations of ground, had been carried the same height as upon the eminences; the consequence was, that at this point it was more than sixty feet from top to bottom, and that this very height rendered it unlikely to be attempted by escalade, led to its being less vigilantly guarded than the more accessible portions. A close and continued watch satisfied us that at night the enemy wholly neglected it, while at the gates and walls generally they kept themselves pretty wide awake.

My plan once formed, I instantly set about preparing the machinery for carrying it into execution. Two large strong concave disks of copper, about the size of soup plates, were first made. Around the edge of each was fixed a rim of leather, and into the back, or convex side, was firmly inserted, perpendicularly, a pistol barrel. A piston adapted to the barrel converted it into a pump, by which the air within, when the disk was pressed against a flat surface, could be exhausted. The pistol barrel projecting horizontally when the disk was placed against a perpendicular surface, served as a projection for the hand to grasp, while from each depended a loop or stirrup for the feet. The method of using this apparatus is simple enough: all that is necessary is to place one disk against a smooth wall, as high as the arm can reach; the piston is worked for a few seconds by means of the thumb forcing it in, and a spring driving it out—a partial vacuum, produced when the disk is held firmly against the wall, by the pressure of the external air. Upon standing up in the stirrup, the other disk is applied higher up, and fastened in the same manner, and so on alternately. In this way a person can creep along a smooth wall to any height or distance.

Upon trying this apparatus, one dark night, on the lofty portion of wall that I have mentioned, I found it to answer my expectations perfectly. Reaching the top without any difficulty, and without exciting any alarm, I drew up, by means of a cord, a ladder of ropes. Up this quietly crept a body of two hundred men, headed by Jack. When all were assembled, and dawn sufficiently advanced to see our way, we passed swiftly along to one of the gates, and descending, took possession of it almost without opposition. The alarm had spread, but before the enemy could recover from their surprise, the gate was thrown open, and the prince, at the head of a battalion, with two or three guns, came rushing in. The other gates were soon secured, and the town was ours.

CHAPTER XLVI.

Return from the Wars—Hammed Benshoolo—Message from Kaloolah—Mysterious Indications
—Gogo in Chains—An Infant Phenomenon—Conclusion.

IT was about three weeks after the capture of the city that, accompanied by Hammed Benshoolo, a Moorish trader from Morocco, whom we had found in Goolah, and a small escort, I started on my return to Kiloam. The main body of the army, under the command of the prince, was to remain for a while on the further banks of the Queal to enforce the terms of the treaty, the principal items of which were the suppression of all slave-hunting expeditions, the demolition of the walls of Goolah, and the payment of a tribute to the Great Shounsé.

The lofty acropolis of Kiloam was in sight. I pointed it out to Hammed. "You little expected to find such a country as this, and such a city as that yonder," said I.

"Not so populous and so large," replied the Moor; "but still I have often heard rumors at Jennee and Timbuctoo of a very rich white nation beyond the Djébel el Kumri. In truth, I should not have journeyed to Goolah, so much farther than any Moorish trader ever came before, if it had not been in hopes of seeing something of the great unknown land."

"You are determined to return?" I demanded.

"With your permission," replied Hammed. "It will be a long and difficult journey, but, with the blessing of God, I shall get back as I came, in safety."

A capital opportunity, thought I, of sending some news to my Christian friends of my whereabouts and prospects. At this moment my attention was taken by the flutter of a royal banner from the turret of a chateau we were approaching, and in a few moments we encountered messengers, who had been despatched to inform me that the princess had come thus far to meet me.

For more than a month I had heard no news from the court, and the anxiety with which I questioned the messages may be imagined; but they had nothing to tell, except that the princess had been ill, but was own much better, and that she was awaiting me at the neighboring chateau. There was an air of constraint in their manner and answers that I thought a little singular, but which I suffered to pass without further question, hurrying my pace only, and riding down any bodements before they had time to form.

We entered the gates of the chateau. Throwing the reins of my horse to an attendant, I strode across the court-yard to the great hall, at the entrance to which stood Clefenha, making all kinds of grimaces and gestures. She rolled her eyes, showed her white teeth, threw her arms about in all manner of ways, and, dancing up and down, muttered a string of unintelligible exclamations—" Oh, Wollo! Wollo! how big! how fat! how beautiful!" At the same time, seizing my hand, she half devoured it with kisses.

" The girl must be crazy," said I to the surrounding groups, who, however, made no reply.

At this moment I noticed Gogo—yellow-haired Gogo—poor fellow!— he was seated in a corner in a very desponding attitude ; but what was most singular, he was firmly secured by a stout wire chain around his neck.

" And what can this mean?" I exclaimed, advancing towards him, " Gogo in disgrace!"

But the negress intercepted me, sputtering out in broken sentences of Framazug her indignation at some offence Gogo had been committing. As she spluttered and shook her hand at him, he chattered and rattled his chain, until, at last, excited beyond all bounds, the negress flew at him and gave him a smart box on the ear. The explosion of rage on both sides was exceedingly comical, and wholly incomprehensible, except on the supposition that Gogo had become mad, and that Clefenha had been bitten by him.

" I must ask Kaloolah what all this means," said I, as I ascended the stairs, followed by the negress, who, amid her objurgations of Gogo, contrived to intersperse her indefinite admiratory exclamations of something that was " Wollo! Wollo! how beautiful! and how fat!"

Kaloolah stood beneath a curtained archway to receive me. The passage was in shadow, but I could perceive that she was pale, and that she was holding on by the golden fringe of the drapery to support herself. I rushed forward to her, and she fell, sobbing, into my arms.

" Kaloolah! *Lolo Yarra! Lolo Semah!* My life! my heart! What is this? What has happened? Are you ill? Has any accident befallen the Great Shounsé? And, Clefenha, what is the matter with her—has she gone crazy?"

The princess looked up, with a smile, in my eyes.

"And Gogo—what is the matter with Gogo, that he is banished from your presence in chains?"

"Oh, the naughty little wretch!" said Kaloolah, shuddering. "And yet, I ought not to say so. Poor fellow, I pity him."

"Why so? What is the matter with him?"

"He is jealous."

"Jealous! of what?"

"I'll show you," said Kaloolah, looking up in my face with an expression of mingled pride and affection, and with a cunning smile, that, flashing through my memory, instantaneously lighted up each little spot and dot that marked the train of reminiscence from the princess of Framazugda, back to the little slave girl on the banks of the Congo.

"I'll show you," said Kaloolah, and leading me along the passage, she pulled aside the curtain, and we entered a room in the centre of which stood a couch formed of ivory, pannelled with the beautifully polished hide of the rhinoceros. On one side of the couch sat Jicric with a palm-leaf fan in his hand, and so busily engaged in the investigation of some mystery hidden in the drapery, that he did not perceive my approach; while on the other stood Clefenha, still dancing, and wriggling, and rolling her eyes, and muttering "Wollo! Wollo! so big—so fat—so beautiful!"

We advanced to the couch. Kaloolah drew down the light covering, and there was exposed—what shall I say?—what shall I call it?———It is to be hoped that the reader is fond of fat babies—for this was a perfect little monster—a regular little Daniel Lambert of a baby; and then such red cheeks, and such big black eyes!

Baby was awake, and, of course, had to be taken up and receive his first paternal kiss—a performance which he took quietly enough, but which nearly threw Clefenha in convulsions. "Wollo! Wollo!" she shouted, dancing about the room—"so big—so fat—so beautiful!"

There was a scratch upon one of its round red cheeks. "Ah! that is Gogo's villainy," said Kaloolah—"when he first saw his rival in my arms he flew at him like a little fiend, and before Jicric could come to my assistance, inflicted the wound you see."

After sufficiently condoling with Kaloolah upon Gogo's rascality, admiring the points of little Jon'than, and amusing myself with the odd sound of my own voice in English baby-talk, the infant phenomenon was handed back to his couch, and Jicric, squatting by his side, resumed his intense search for any straggling fly.

And there he lay, cooing and looking with his great eyes at nothing, and doubling up his fat fists, and blowing bubbles with his round pouting mouth, just like any Christian-born baby; there he lay, a glorious lump of human possibilities—a tiny candidate for the world's prizes—a new entry for the race to eternity. There he lay, an offshoot of American institutions—a seedling of Christianity and republicanism—of the first, yes, for I will indoctrinate him; of the latter, as circumstance may determine,—republicans are born, not made. There he lay, the seal of my fate—the estopple upon any vague longings or designs of returning to my own country, at least for the present.

"Yes." said I, aloud, "the thing is settled; my destiny is fixed; the chain of matrimony merely might be carried around the world, but not when loaded with a baby—where is Hammed Benshoolo?"

Hammed was soon in attendance.

"How soon do you wish to set out on your journey?" I demanded.

"As soon as your highness pleases," replied Hammed; "after I have feasted my eyes, with your permission, upon the glories of the great city."

"And you intend to journey by the way of Timbuctoo and Tafilet to Morocco."

"I intend to return, God willing, to my native town of Alkassar, near the city of Fez."

"From thence to some of the seaports of Morocco will be but two or three days' journey."

"A mere step, your highness, to one who has visited the Djébel Kumri, traversed the Soudan, and crossed the desert."

"And will you undertake to deliver a parcel of manuscripts into the hands of the American consul at Mogadore, Mazagan, or Tangiers?"

"I will do it," replied Hammed, "if it should cost me the little profit that, with God's blessing, I hope to reap from my long journeying."

"No fear of that; it will cost you nothing; and, besides, I will fill your hollow staff with more gold dust than you could collect in ten trading trips across the desert; will you promise to carry what I entrust to you, with care, and to deliver it faithfully?"

"I swear it," exclaimed Benshoolo, solemnly, "by Allah and Mohammed!"

And now, dear reader—permit me to call you so, especially as I know that, most probably, you have an existence only in my own imagination; that you are but a bare possibility of animate intelligence—dearest reader, the preceding pages are the manuscript so intrusted to the Moor, in the not very confident hope that it will reach the eye of some one, who, considering the circumstances under which it has been written, may think it worthy of being given to the world. It was at first my intention to rewrite it, but I content myself with cutting it down a little, and with throwing out some portions that personal delicacy would permit only in a journal that by no possibility could ever meet the public eye. Still, there are some things for which I owe an apology—some expressions of sentiment and feeling—some confidences in relation to the sacred secrets of the heart, fit only for the pages of a sentimental poet, or of some gentleman all soul and but little delicacy ; and the apology that I have to offer, is the uncertainty whether my manuscript will ever meet a civilized eye ; and the vast distance that separates me from all Christian curiosity and sympathy—a distance which, like death, will, I hope, magnify into objects of some interest my otherwise unimportant adventures, and mellow down any impertinences of egotism.

Kaloolah is looking over my shoulder as I write. She wishes me to express to you, reader, her profound wishes for your health and happiness ; in fact, to say to you, and to every man, woman, and child in America, that she loves the whole of you—that to such of my fair countrywomen as may take any interest in this tale of my journeyings, she sends a thousand kisses each. As there is such uncertainty of their reaching their destination in this way, it will be best, perhaps, for me to receive Kaloolah's kisses on deposit ; and should I ever succeed in my plans for reaching the Bight of Benin, and opening a communication between Framazugda and the Christian world, under liberal reciprocity treaties, which I am in hopes of being able to do in four or five years, or sometime about 1849 or '50, I shall hold myself ready to deliver them most faithfully to all claimants, in the promptest manner, and upon the slightest demand.

THE END.